Riverwalk
Chameleon

Also by Joanna Foreman

The Know-It-All Girl

(Hydra Publications)

Ghostly Hauntings of Interstate 65

Visit the author at

http://joannaforeman.com

Riverwalk Chameleon

Joanna Foreman

Per Bastet

Riverwalk Chameleon

Published by Per Bastet Publications LLC, P.O. Box 3023 Corydon, IN 47112

Cover photo by Joanna Foreman
Cover design T. Lee Harris

ISBN 978-1-942166-26-9

For Gretchen

Riverwalk Chameleon

Acknowledgments

I must express my gratitude to Per Bastet Publications. Their editorial staff's attention to detail significantly enhanced the subtle flow of *Riverwalk Chameleon's* timeline. My heartfelt thanks to T. Lee Harris for her artistic vision; the scenic book cover layout is precisely what I'd pictured as the story took shape. The Southern Indiana Writers' Group was by my side while I experimented with various tense and point-of-view changes; I appreciate their determination to ensure my successful quest to create this story exactly the way I'd envisioned it. Early readers offered many useful suggestions and gave me their finest feedback: Michele Hubler, Linda Herzler, and Jacqui Cook.

I am incredibly fortunate to have a family that appreciates and accommodates my dreams. First and foremost, I dedicated this novel to Gretchen, my mother, because she *told* me I could write this story when I didn't believe I could. My cousin Tracey Foreman was my first cheerleader at the onset of my writing career and I love her for that. My husband Craig has been my constant companion and most tireless cheerleader of all time. My three grown sons and my grandchildren are on my team, too, and their steadfast belief in my goals moved me forward.

Thank you, K. T. Edwards for introducing me to the San Antonio Riverwalk, and thanks must go, as well, to that very Riverwalk itself for the inspiration it offers to those of us who are dreamers, artists, and writers, and for the hospitality it extends to inquisitive sightseers from all over the world.

*Suggested reading: *RIVER WALK, THE EPIC STORY OF SAN ANTONIO'S RIVER,* by Lewis F. Fisher, copyright @ 2007 by Maverick Publishing Company, San Antonio, Texas; *A DREAM COME TRUE, ROBERT HUGMAN AND SAN ANTONIO'S RIVER WALK,* revised edition, copyright @ 1994 by Vernon G. Zunker.

**The character, Josh Katzen who keeps secrets for a living: Josh Katzen is a fictional spy created by T. Lee Harris. Katzen moves around in the shadows of short stories such as Hanukkah Gelt, The Pecan Pie Affair, and the novel, The Case of the Moche Rolex. For more information see: www.tleeharris.com

The Clifford Building

THE CLIFFORD BUILDING is a low-rise, Romanesque Revival beauty on the San Antonio Riverwalk. Without a doubt, the building was my muse for this novel, and because of its very existence *Riverwalk Chameleon* took shape.

In late December of 1995, The Clifford Building called my name. I'd spent most of the day with my family in the energizing subterranean dreamland one level beneath the real world: the San Antonio Riverwalk. Arched stone bridges, low-slung across the narrow Paseo del Rio, allowed river tour barges to float underneath while people leisurely criss-crossed, accessing either side of the river with its sidewalk cafes, boutiques, art galleries and live music drifting from a wealth of eateries. Dusk settled in and I was saddened to leave that magical place. As we climbed a winding stairway to the street level and shuffled toward the parking garage, I turned to take one last look at the river's reflective surface. That's when I *really* saw it—The Clifford Building! A handful of windows on the third floor were outlined with medium-sized clear holiday lights; I presumed it was a tenant's residence. From that moment, I wanted to *live* in The Clifford Building on the San Antonio Riverwalk.

I set this story inside of The Clifford, employing it as a main character. But I wondered how I could effectively pay tribute to the elegant riverside structural design. How would I acknowledge the contribution of the building itself?

As the plot for the novel unfolded, I lived vicariously with Julia Tyler in The Clifford. When I traveled to San Antonio, I often had the urge to walk into the building as though I belonged inside. Alas, residents use a code to enter. Finally, I mustered the courage to ask for an invitation. William F. (Rick) Grinnan, Jr. cheerfully accommodated me. As I entered his unique oval office on the second floor overlooking the Riverwalk, he introduced himself as the owner of The Clifford Building and the river-level restaurant. Rick takes considerable pride in the well-designed building and its tenants, both past and present. I was pleased to see his enthusiasm for my project. He presented me with written records of the building's design and he arranged a walk-through of an unoccupied apartment. The interior of The Clifford Building bore no significant resemblance to the one described in the novel, *Riverwalk Chameleon*. I smiled inwardly because I'd already answered my earlier question: How would I acknowledge the building's contribution? I'd already done so by making it much larger in many ways than it actually was; I'd created attention-grabbing fictional inhabitants that lived and worked in it; other folks came and went via an art-deco express elevator that did not really exist, yet one that lived and breathed life into the core of the setting.

There are five floors in the building, but I added a sixth for the purpose of fiction. On that sixth floor is where I envisioned the wealthy, male-only Roosevelt Club of the 1930's, with its grand smoking lounge, massage rooms, and what some might consider typical shenanigans of the downtown members of the club. Eventually the sixth floor became Julia Tyler's place of residence and the business location for Tyler Professional Services. In other words, what happens on the imaginary sixth floor stays on that non-existent floor.

~Joanna Foreman

Chapter One

Retrospection

I took aim, but it didn't seem real to me. Before that day, the trigger of an air-soft BB gun was the only one I'd ever pulled.

Yet, here I sit — a hero. Fame and fortune are mine, just like that. And to think I'd never once dreamed of such a scheme. Never. I mean really, it's not like one *plans* to be a hero, unless they're, oh, maybe in the rescue business, which I'm not. I've come to realize (now that it's over and done with) that the entire thing had been out of my hands from that first phone call. By all reports, reputable journalists and sleazy tabloids included, I had no choice.

I was 39 when this all happened last year. But I didn't feel my age, however *that* was supposed to feel. No, I'd say I was quite perky, like on our wedding day when Richard Andrew Tyler, five years my senior, made me his pregnant 17-year-old bride. But would Richard believe it? No way. If he could see me now, I know as sure as I'm stretched out on the sun deck of the most elegant cruise ship in the Mediterranean Sea, Richard would insist I'd made it all up. I confess, I am a daydreamer, but I never imagined a scenario like this.

~*~

At this very moment, I am sipping afternoon tea, on the second day out of port on a two-week Western European voyage, a passenger by invitation of the Queen herself, and not just *any* passenger either: "The guest of honor," she'd insisted. I accepted, figuring it was the very least she could do, considering the circumstances.

I sense quick random glances aimed in my direction. Am I paranoid? I consider . . . but then, no, I'm *recognizable*. Everyone on this ship knows who I am, what I did. Of *course* they're looking at me. Why, back home in San Antonio, the Riverwalk still crawls with paparazzi. That's what happens when you become famous overnight. What bugs me the most are the insufferable tourists loitering on the sidewalks, gawking in awe at my notorious residence as though they're on a Tour of the Stars' homes, like I'm a sideshow circus performer, not a clown so much, more like a trapeze artist. While it's true I performed a kind of tightrope act, they have no real idea what I'm all about.

~*~

Towering over me is a dark man with gorgeous, deep brown eyes and a smile that's genuine if one ever was. "More tea, madam, and a pastry perhaps? The éclairs are particularly divine." He offers a carafe, and with the sun located where it is at this instant, a halo effect permeates his dreadlocks, creating an image of a divine pastry offered to me from above — I dare not refuse. I offer my teacup for a refill of the Queen's favorite, Earl Grey, although I favor a mellow English Breakfast blend.

His nametag reads Miguel. Fitted trousers, white tailored jacket with brass buttons, white gloves. Nice touch, the gloves.

I sip tea, extending my right pinkie just so, to satisfy the curious watchers. Fact of the matter, I prefer steaming coffee from an earthenware mug, both hands wrapped around it. Alas, dainty teacups seem to be the vessel of choice on this ship. A Canadian travel writer lounging next to me tells me the Queen personally selected this china, a translucent cream color, with pale blue dots around the edges. Very nice. I politely nod my approval, select a pastry from Miguel's tray, and he positions it gently with silver tongs onto a dessert plate next to a stylish silver fork.

The fork — now there's a buggy thing about Richard. He ate pastries sissy-style with a knife and fork, the same way you'd eat meat or vegetables, and it always irked me to no end. Even fried chicken was a gastronomical disaster for him. I nearly gagged the first time I saw him dissect a chicken leg at a KFC joint in Louisville. I mean, come on, just hold it to your mouth and chomp on the damn thing!

I pick up the éclair with my fingers, take a dainty bite, and wouldn't you know crème filling plops out the other end onto my lap. I pray no one notices. *Fat chance.* I'm certain the travel writer sees, but pretends not to. In a normal situation I'd bend over and suck the crème right off my bare leg. State of affairs as it is, I use my cloth napkin to wipe it off. Such a waste of a perfectly good napkin, not to mention the crème. Maybe Richard had a good thing going with that fork, after all.

Due to my daydream tendencies, Richard had often accused me of living in a fantasy world. In fact, not long after we married, he declared we no longer lived in the same galaxy. "Julia," he would say with a condescending look on his face, "you *live* in a daydream, whereas I live in the real world." He'd enunciate the "I live in the real world" as though his world was the only suitable place to reside. Which, of course, to Richard it was.

Our courtship — now that was another story. He had me way up on a pedestal. Couldn't tell me often enough how perfect I was. Too bad our courtship didn't last longer. I loved that pedestal. Sadly, within a handful of days after the wedding, my elevated position was usurped because he expected me to be more like him — *exactly* like him, to be specific.

Take it from me — the awesome view spoils you when you're at high altitude. The bathos, however, the descent from my sublime perch to the commonplace, can only be described as an anticlimax. Descending so abruptly into reality was quite the humbling experience. That's the way it goes. Richard didn't show me his *superior* self until after the honeymoon. From that time forward, he rarely passed up an opportunity to point out the error of my ways.

I visit his grave now and then and talk for hours. Of course he can't answer and I'll bet it drives him crazy, wherever he is.

~*~

How did I end up here? "An opportunity," Lady Sophia Vanderhawk had said, "to find your peace and privacy." She knows how it is, having experienced just as much anxiety as I with the abduction of her son, but Lady Sophia is one tough broad who has lived with, possibly even thrived upon, mega negative publicity since the day her mother, the Duchess of Stratford, was photographed in the doorway of St. Mary's Hospital in Paddington, Sophia all rosy and sweet, swaddled in pink baby bunting.

I was leery at first about taking a long vacation. My trips in the past had been short, the four-day weekend type. I had a business to run and people depended upon me. Now, those very same people insist I allow myself this luxury. In fact, it's a *necessity* for me to find peace of mind. But what if I'm unable to unwind? God forbid. Back home, Doc Emmett, my loyal friend and oldest client, had urged me to accept the Queen's invitation. "Go on and do it, Julia. Get some rest." So, I did, but still haven't experienced the required relaxation. It's like a dream, deep in the dark night, where you toss and turn and wish you could wake up, but don't. Or maybe you do, and wish you hadn't. You know the kind. This has been going on day and night, and I don't feel rested at all. Maybe it's jet lag.

Now here's the kick — three days from now I'll be interviewed by a well-known fiction writer in the port of Bordeaux, France on the Garonne River. He plans to write a novel about me — fact into fiction — and claims I can have final approval before it goes to press. While I have my doubts, he's going to publish it whether I participate or not; if I don't put my finger in, who knows what a mess he might make of it? There's also talk of a screenplay. My control issues aren't nearly the problem they used to be, but I still want a voice.

Before I explain it to him, I have to understand it all myself. He said facts and details make up the centerpiece of a good novel, and he wants all the particulars I can come up with, the essentials, the *whole story*. "Julia dear, the devil is in the details," he'd said. I always thought the phrase was "*God* is in the details," but who knows? Before this happened, I didn't believe in either one of them. I'm currently in a re-thinking process about the so-called divine, along with the fork situation.

I had decided to journal everything that went down, try to make sense of how it started and why it happened to *me*. Doc Emmett gave me the journal idea, but I would have thought of it myself, sooner or later, probably later, considering my state of mind. So, with my favorite pen and pink writing paper, here I sit with the Queen's teacup, still unable to think straight, my mind in a fog. If only I can get this story on paper where it belongs, perhaps it will quit rolling around in my head. I need to get on with my life.

Would I go back if I could and change the outcome? What about Bill Murray in Punxsutawney, suffering Groundhog Day over and over, until he finally got it right? No, I wouldn't change a thing — the adventure of it all was worth more than I can explain. When you walk the tightrope, you simply step over the knots. Besides — get real — who ever has the chance to go back and untie them? You know, besides Bill Murray.

Miguel collects the teacups, and as I watch his fitted trousers walk away, I think of the old adage: what doesn't kill you makes you stronger. At least I appreciate the male physique, in spite of what some men have put me through. I glance at other passengers. Maybe I'm the only one who has flown in from the States, because these people don't appear jet-lagged. They all seem relaxed; they read, they chat, they catnap. I must be the only guest whose brains are scrambled. The travel writer has obviously developed a system to stay on task throughout his travels. He's dictating into a small voice recorder. I wonder if he's writing about me.

The recordings – of course! My heart pounds at high speed as I remember Marten's recordings. No sooner had I developed a romantic relationship with Marten than all hell broke loose. I picture his boyish smile and tears well up. *Enough! I can't write and cry at the same time.* Perhaps if I listen to his recordings, his voice, I might achieve a breakthrough. I dig through my bag for the little high-tech mobile phone he had specially designed with a chip to record conversations with no one the wiser. I hold his phone in the palm of my hand and recall the last time he used it. That in itself makes me sad, but I suppose it's necessary if I am to work backwards to the beginning. I remove the battery to expose a tiny chip and I insert it into a separate electronic device. I put both ear-buds in place. *Is it smart to do this now?* These are Marten's private telephone conversations; I'm not sure I can bear to hear his sweet voice. My mother always told me to trust my gut and right now it tells me not to listen.

I press PLAY.

Chapter Two

The Luxury Bath
. . . Last Year

I throw lavish parties in my bathroom. Indeed, with a grand bathing lounge like mine, it would be a crime not to exploit it. However, on the night of my Open House, a *real* crime was set into action. It began in my private elevator down in the lobby and traveled uninterrupted to the penthouse. I was oblivious until it was much too late.

After four years of renovation, I was eager to showcase my new place to the public and they couldn't wait to take a peek.

A Romanesque Revival architectural delight, The Clifford Building sits strategically at an angle and parallel with the San Antonio River, offering breathtaking views on all sides of the narrow, winding Paseo del Rio.

The Italian marble tub commanded center stage in the great washroom, once an integral part of The Roosevelt Club, a distinguished male-only, rich-only, select membership society, long before the San Antonio Riverwalk was a prime tourist draw. The Roosevelt Club had occupied the entire sixth floor of The Clifford Building.

Most of my guests would be my business clients, each a highly respected member of the local community. They would step through the leaded-glass doors of my art-deco elevator, to be transported into times gone by — right in the middle of my condo! While the revelry wouldn't start in the historical bathing lounge, those with coveted invitations would ultimately be drawn into it, and once in, they would hover like steam rising from the infamous hot tub, where rumor has it a prostitute was found floating, lifeless as an upside-down Texas lizard, back when the top floor of The Clifford Building was in its heyday.

~*~

The event was the largest I'd hosted, and I was edgy from the moment I woke up. While quick showers were ordinarily my daily routine, I'd set my alarm an hour earlier than usual to allow myself a relaxing spa bath.

As I tilted my head back onto the marble ledge, submerged in a whirlpool of citrus scents, I surveyed the space once reserved for those with both ancestry and affluence. I'd claimed that spot as my self-nurturing center. Across the room, the clear glass walls of the steam bath sparkled. Light from the early morning sun cast a glow on an old primitive cupboard in the corner. I'd rescued it from an antique shop in New Braunfels and covered it with seven coats of black paint and lacquer for protection from steam. It was positioned with the top doors wide open to expose shelves stocked with aromatherapy spa supplies: loofa sponges, lavender creams, minty foot lotions, citrus bath oils.

My grandmother's small Majolica dish sat tub-side, filled with fresh orange slices and heavily buttered toast strips. *Breakfast in the bath.* Pleased with my self-indulgence, I took a bite of toast.

By noon, the florist would have the lounge transformed into a tropical rain forest: areca palms, banana trees, lily pads and orchids. I wondered if I'd gone overboard with the party décor. Should I have hired a professional party planner? I repeatedly told myself there was no point in worrying about it. Just the day before, my friend Nina Emmett assured me as much over lunch at Boudro's. "How could a party with *Islands* as its theme be overdone with tropical plants, Julia? Everything will be fine, dear. Don't worry your pretty little head about it at all." She'd patted my hand for support.

I closed my eyes . . . and breathed deeply. I barely heard an annoying buzz over the sound of churning water. *Damn the phone!* I considered letting it go to voice mail, but it was *the double ring, my business line. Who in the name of Saint Anthony?* I needed my glasses to read Caller ID but they were steamed up. I was pretty sure I knew who was calling, anyway. I stepped up and out of the tub, paused the humming jets, and, in my best early morning voice, I answered: "Good morning, Tyler Professional Services."

"Julia? Doc Emmett here. Sorry if I'm a bother."

Who else but Doc? I planted a smile on my face, a noble attempt to mask my irritation, suspecting my voice would reflect a frown if I wore one, which I so felt like doing. "Of course not, Doc, what can I do for you?"

"I know what a busy day it's going to be for you, but my transcriptionist . . . you know Judy? Well, her water just broke and she's left me with an entire weekend's worth of dictation to be transcribed. I'm at my wits end."

"Oh, no! It's terribly early, don't you think?" If I remembered correctly, Judy wasn't due until late next month.

"Nonsense. I've seen babies delivered much earlier than this; it's past six a.m., you know?"

"Oh . . . well." Was he joking or confused? He was past retirement age: a good excuse to be confused if he wanted one, but his sense of humor was rather funny in a *pun-ny* sort of way. I was in no mood for humor that early in the morning. I hadn't had my coffee yet. Standing, dripping wet in my birthday suit, I imagined if I had one of those newfangled television phones Doc would get to the point in a hurry.

He continued. "I have three tapes I need typed up: hospital rounds, office visits, reports and the like. Nothing complicated. Can Andie help me out for a few days? Or perhaps I should get a temp . . . or should I just ask Nina to do it?"

"No temps for you," I said, "and leave your wife alone! She has enough to do to get ready for my big night; you know we've been working for *weeks* on the greenery design. Just a second; I'll check Andie's schedule."

I put Doc on hold, grabbed my white Egyptian cotton towel and wrapped it loosely around myself. I hurried down the hallway, leaving a slight trail of water on the hardwood floor which glistened from its most recent waxing. I padded through the kitchen passageway, flipped on the coffee maker and continued to my left toward the corridor of six small rooms. According to Doc, they were used for private massages in the days of the old health club. I entered the room with a brass number one on the door and checked my master schedule; my daughter would be free after lunch. I decided not to pick up the call there in my office because Doc liked to talk and I wanted to bathe.

Back in the bathing lounge, Doc and I reconnected. "Andie will have your paperwork all wrapped up for you by three o'clock." I grabbed another slice of toast and slid into the tub. Out of respect for the loquacious Doc, I left the jets off.

"I knew I could count on you," Doc was saying. "My girl may be out six weeks."

I winced at Doc's "my girl." *Old school.*

"By the way," Doc said, "an Englishman, Dr. Marten Wells, has contacted me about doing some business here. He's bringing a children's health clinic to San Antonio, apparently funding it with grants and contributions. I don't know the details yet, but I've an appointment with him to discuss it."

"Sounds intriguing," I said, but the thought of water swirling once again across my flesh was much more interesting.

Doc cleared his throat. "Julia, are you eating?"

"Toast."

"Smothered with butter, I presume?"

"Busted."

"Julia . . . dear Julia." (I visualized him shaking his head in displeasure.) "Anyway, yes, Dr. Marten Wells. He's recently arrived from London and is looking for a downtown location for his clinic. He's currently working out of the Hilton."

"On the Riverwalk? A little extravagant, wouldn't you say?"

"Perhaps. But, it's temporary. He asked me to recommend an accounting service. Of course I gave him your number. He should be calling soon."

"Sure, I'll be glad to take a look. And thanks."

I minded everyone else's business and got paid for it. At Tyler Professional Services, we did a little bit of everything — accounting, secretarial, property management — you name it. Andie worked with me along with three other employees. I used four of the six old massage rooms as offices, much like other businesses have cubicles. An express elevator opened in the center of the entire top floor — My Home Sweet Home.

Doc still wasn't done. "Oh, yes, one more thing. I do hope you don't mind, but I told him about your Open House party tonight, and . . . well . . . um, I actually invited him to attend. Was that terribly bold of me?"

I laughed out loud. "Don't worry about it. It is an *Open House* after all. I sent invitations, but I'm also making a list of potential walk-ins for the lobby security. I'll put him on the list." He sounded like a perfect fit. My cash flow needed a boost and I trusted the party would bring in a few new clients.

"Good idea. Dr. Wells specifically insisted I call to authenticate I hadn't committed a *faux pas* by inviting him."

Well, now wasn't that just like a prim and proper Englishman to request an invitation to an Open House? I pictured him stepping off the elevator and heading straight over to the bar. "A Bloody Mary, if you please my good lad, and make it a bloody double," he'd say.

"Did you give him directions?"

"Certainly. It's just a hop, skip and a jump from the Hilton to your place."

Doc and his clichés. He always amused me with them, even when I was in no mood to be amused.

"Oh, Julia what a *grand* entrance you have, complete with the old accordion-style gate. You rarely see those anymore. Why it seems like only yesterday Alonzo would kindly say, 'Good afternoon, Doc,' and shuffle me right on up for a relaxing bath or much-needed massage. You know, my dear, you should invite a specialty magazine of some sort to do a piece on your unique place up in the sky. What you've done with the old club shouldn't be kept a secret."

"One does need a secret or two, Doc," I reminded him. We'd had this conversation umpteen times. "This secret is all mine. Only a chosen few can share it, and you happen to be one of the lucky ones. Besides, after tonight the mystery will be revealed, don't you think? See you around six, and thanks again for the referral."

"You're quite welcome. And Julia dear, well . . . he's wonderfully British, quite charming, and, frankly . . . *unattached*." Both Doc and Nina had made it perfectly clear they thought it was high time I begin dating again. Nina went so far as to set me up on a blind date three weeks ago. A total waste of my time, but I suffered through it, told Nina I appreciated her thoughtfulness and begged her to never do it again.

"Okay, Doc, warning heeded." I used my best British accent. "How British and charming is he?"

"Bloody fantastically charming!"

We shared a hearty laugh as we disconnected.

I set the whirlpool timer for 10 more minutes to bask in the delightful aroma of sandalwood and orange bath oil, Andie's latest concoction.

I knew I was lucky to have a father figure like Doc in my life. I selected another slice of toast, cold by now, followed by an orange portion, and literally shivered when I thought what life would've been like without him. Richard had succumbed to cancer nearly five years ago, leaving me with our very pregnant teenager to care for. Doc and Nina had been the major crux of my support system. Doc had answered many a phone call from me at times when I awakened, terrified to find myself alone in the middle of the night. He could call me anytime — I owed him that.

The bubbles subsided, leaving the bathing lounge peacefully serene. When the aroma of freshly brewed chocolate-almond coffee reached the bathing lounge, I drained the tub and slipped into my pink chenille bathrobe. I towel-dried my hair, went for the kitchen and poured the steaming java into an artsy pottery mug, topped it off with cream, and sat at the kitchen bar to savor my quiet, early morning routine of sipping coffee from an earthy vessel, elbows planted just-so upon the countertop. The sleeves of my robe were two inches too long; I bought it because it reminded me of Meg Ryan in a movie I'd seen, years ago. Her fingertips had barely peeked from the edges of a sweater's sleeves to grasp a mug of hot cocoa.

I wondered if the catering preparations were already underway. My cousin, Dana Cavanaugh, who owned The Stock Market, a restaurant on the river level of The Clifford Building, was to cater the party. I checked the clock on the stove. No, it was way too early for anyone to be in the restaurant's kitchen. I anxiously pulled a small prescription bottle out of my robe pocket, broke a tiny white Xanax in half, placed it under my tongue and dropped the other half back into the container. It was going to be one of those days.

I retrieved my mug and parked myself at the oversized window in the turret section of the grand living room. I gazed down on the Riverwalk to contemplate my fantasy of being a movie star. There they were, the camera crew, the gaffers, key grips, director, script supervisor, and Dana and me, arm in arm, cast as best friends in a movie with *Riverwalk* in the title. I'd toyed with the idea of writing a screenplay. But when would I ever find the time? I had a business to run, and (I checked the clock again — 6:59 a.m.) a grandson to get off to Montessori. Not that life wasn't good. It was! But I secretly longed for an adventure. I suspected I was on the cusp of a mid-life crisis, but it was too ominous to think about, especially on that day. Anyway, my future was still in the planning stages. If I didn't write a screen-play soon, Dana and I would be too old and feeble to walk along the river. *Riverwalk on Wheels*, they'd call it.

Here I am. Julia Madison Tyler — 39-year-old mother, grandmother, and successful businesswoman. By all outward appearances I have it all, but is there something lacking — something more? I rinsed my coffee cup and took one last glance out the window. *At least this spring I'll be able to personally meet Lady Sophia Louise Vanderhawk of London; not every woman can boast of that kind of excitement!*

Chapter Three

The Penthouse

It's been said there are two cities in San Antonio: Alamo City — historic site of eighteenth-century missions and famous battles, and River City — personified by the Riverwalk, meticulously designed by Robert Hugman, an architect and long-time resident, who, in the early 1920s, envisioned a romantic and historic park on both sides of the narrow Paseo del Rio, a meandering, looped diversion of the San Antonio River, smack dab in the middle of downtown. Thousands of tourists whose only intention is to *Remember the Alamo!* find themselves seduced by curving stairways, arched bridges, lavish fountains and rich foliage one level beneath the bustling city streets. San Antonio Riverwalk: a cool and refreshing subterranean world of sidewalk cafes, boutiques, art galleries, and live music drifting from an abundance of nightclubs.

At precisely nine o'clock, a river barge loaded with sightseers will navigate the narrow channel-like river. A clean-cut young man in tan Bermuda shorts, blue cotton shirt and a straw hat will recite his shtick into a microphone: "And now, ladies and gentlemen," he will drone in a sing-song fashion, "look up ahead to your left, my right, where you will see the Hilton Palacio del Rio. In 1968, HemisFair, the World's Fair, celebrated the 250th anniversary of San Antonio's founding. With millions predicted to attend, suddenly the race was on to accommodate the anticipated guests; the fair spurred on the city's first major new hotel in years, The Hilton Palacio del Rio. In timely preparation for HemisFair, modules were stacked, room-by-room, each already wired, plumbed, and furnished with a bed, linens and even a Gideon Bible! Now, folks, you've seen modular homes being pulled single file along the highway, but these Hilton units were brought in on flatbed trucks and stacked in place by *crane!* It was quite the spectacle, and hundreds of people lined these very sidewalks to catch a glimpse of a world record being set for major hotel construction. It's a fact, folks — this entire hotel was constructed in 202 working days!"

Texans own a genetic pride — they perceive their ancestors' accomplishments as their own. The young tour guide will stand tall and proud as though he himself had conceived the crane/module idea. The boat people will *ooh and aah*. Many of them will photograph the famous hotel; some will capture the penthouse balcony, but not a single one would realize a conspiracy of great magnitude was in progress in the penthouse on that very day.

~*~

Perry Roberts stood in a suite atop the Hilton Palacio del Rio, tapped his foot and glared at his watch while an antiquated fax machine laboriously yielded a document.

"Rubbish — still nothing!" Roberts crumpled the paper and hurled it across the room. "Why is this taking so long? I'd thought our precious Sophia's visit would have been meticulously scheduled and public knowledge by now," Roberts said. "It's common knowledge she's touring the globe with her beloved Chesley, so why no announcement regarding a stopover in San Antonio? My preparation has been tedious — it *must* come to fruition!"

Leonardo Newman gestured emphatically outside, through the glass of the large balcony doorway. "Don't fret. My London friends assure me *this very river city* is to be the last leg of Lady Sophia's itinerary." Leonardo, a man well known in London circles as a tittle-tattle, was one who made a profitable business out of knowing everything about everyone, and was the common denominator in a complicated abduction set-up. He was a man the ladies described as tall, dark and handsome, with mesmerizing light blue eyes, although ladies weren't of interest to him.

Perry Roberts wasn't involved personally with Leonardo's sources, nor did he want to be, but he had no doubt the information he received from him was right on the mark . . . so far. Roberts pounded his fist on the desk. "But we need dates, specific arrival and departure times!"

Leonardo nodded. "I agree. And you shall have them soon. Trust me." Hitching the strap of his leather satchel over his shoulder, he added, "I'll make inquiries. Ring me if you don't hear anything useful within the hour." The door closed quietly behind him.

~*~

Perry Roberts always had a deal going; this one would set him up for the remainder of his life. He already had the perfect place in mind, which out of necessity would be far from the reach of the law, a concession he willingly made. He was tired of rubbing shoulders with people anyway. Hadn't met a person he liked in years — didn't plan on meeting one at this stage. There was just something terminally wrong with humans.

He carried a handful of shelled pistachios out to his penthouse perch and observed a black vulture circling high above the Riverwalk, its trained eye on the lookout for carnage. *How curious. I am precisely like the vulture. My eye is on the lookout for something from which I can benefit — not to kill it — only to gain from its demise.* Then again, his associates were naïve to believe Roberts' promises. He knew he would kill, if necessary.

From his vantage point he had studied each twist and turn of the Riverwalk — months of watchful schemes and scenarios ran through his mind. The Vanderhawk aristocrats had ruined his career — they would finally pay. He couldn't believe his luck; he had the inside track — a fixed race, this time in his favor. How could he lose?

He steadied his telescope, adjusted the focus and zoomed in on the sixth floor of The Clifford Building. *My, my, what a busy woman. Tonight will belong to Ms. Tyler, and yet she makes time for coffee and daydreaming. This present moment is as close to peaceful as her life will be from now on.*

Roberts headed back into the suite and removed the white paper lid from a Hilton bar glass. He tossed it toward the waste bin but it was a rim shot — landed on the carpet. He smiled as he imagined a well-endowed Hispanic maid bending over to pick it up. The short one with elbow dimples was his favorite. He scooped four ice cubes into the glass and unscrewed the top from a half-empty bottle of Glenlivet, admiring his image in the mirrored closet door as he poured. Swishing liquid over the ice reminded him of the surf pounding the beach at high tide, one of his favorite sounds. The one he longed to hear every day once this job was done. Commotion from the Riverwalk drifted upward occasionally: music, laughter, horns honking and sirens blaring all up and down the city streets. He was tired of hearing the incessant racket. Tourists are people, and he hated them more than most. *Gawkers. Just like London. Changing of the Guard — Buckingham Palace — damn Americans can't get enough of royalty.* He leaned into his reflection and worked the remainder of pistachios from between his teeth with a toothpick.

The click of an electronic key inserted into the door lock distracted Roberts from his image. Marten Wells, good looking and impeccably dressed, entered. "This is lunacy!" Marten hissed. "What are you doing in broad daylight with the telescope out on the balcony? Get it back in here. Housekeeping is probably already suspicious. You *idiot*! Are you mad?"

"The maids are paid quite well to look the other direction, and yes, I'm mad. Madder than hell."

"Not *angry* mad, you fool . . . crazy . . . that is what you are. You have gone round the bend." Marten stared at Roberts' whiskey glass, the desperate way he held onto it like a lifeline. "We have complex business to conduct here on the Riverwalk. You must be more discreet with your petty annoyances."

"Poorly chosen words, my young nephew. Neither petty nor annoyed come halfway close to describing the situation into which we've been put." Perry Roberts had never been one to back down. Wasn't that why they were here?

"Granted," Marten said, "but for now, let's put emotions aside and get down to business." He walked out onto the balcony and took a deep breath of the morning air. Even from the top floor he detected the river's musky odor combined with intermittent traces of hot croissants and Eggs Benedict from the hotel's sidewalk café. Much to his surprise, he'd found the Riverwalk a great deal more pleasing than the travel brochures had described it. He folded the telescope into an upright position and called back inside to Roberts, "Any reports from London?"

"Bugger all."

"Well, there is *some* good news," Marten said. "Leonardo Newman has located two possibilities, and I believe the ideal place for our so-called clinic is the one only three blocks away, good size, rather pricey, but worth every pound. Come. You can see it from here."

Roberts strolled over and slouched against the door jamb. "You can see *everything* from here — that's why we chose this place." He downed his drink and poured another. "*This* bottle has seen its better day," he said as he held it up to the light. "I'll make a note to myself to get more. Can't be without tonight."

Marten's dark eyes narrowed. His uncle knew how to push his buttons. He'd easily guilt-tripped him into this caper, had even gone so far as to tell Marten he had no choice. However, Marten knew he could have refused. But why had he not? He'd only recently pondered that question.

He turned to look down on the river city. "It's an old warehouse, thus will need very little in the way of reconditioning to make it workable for our purpose." Marten stepped back into the suite and carefully leaned the telescope against a wall. "The only drawback will be the large windows on the Navarro Street side and the exterior wall facing Charles Court. I suggest we cover those during construction, away from prying eyes. Perhaps something appropriate would be artwork or murals painted by local youngsters to match the theme of our children's clinic."

"You can handle it. I want nothing to do with bratty ankle-biters. Besides, I'll be keeping myself invisible after we've left the Hilton."

"Good idea. Perhaps as an opener, once I've met the woman, I might suggest her grandson's Montessori class donate some drawings for the windows."

"No! Don't go daft on me now. If she gets *that* involved, she'll be loitering over there all the time, dragging her girlfriends along to show off the kid's artwork."

Marten stroked his chin. "True . . . if she's a *typical* grandmother, which I assume she will prove to be, although have you noticed how good-looking she is?"

"Don't be a nutter — I warn you," Roberts said sternly. "It's a job, Marten — that's all it is."

Marten snorted and waved him off. "Not to worry. But I did get a good look at her last night. She reminds me of that actress, you know the one?"

Perry Roberts shook his head with disinterest.

"The redhead with freckles. You know, the gal who played the lead in Zero Dark Thirty."

Perry Roberts' expression remained vacant.

"Dammit! The movie about Bin Laden, *you* know."

"No, I do *not*. I don't go to movies."

"Well, maybe you should. Get out of this stuffy room and breathe the fresh Texas air. Anyway, it surely won't be a chore, now will it? Seducing Julia Tyler, I mean. In any case, I want you to see the inside of the building. It has a large loft for your use, both as an office and residence for a few weeks. I'd like your approval before we move over."

"That's *your* end of the business, Marten, the first half; I trust you know exactly what we need. I mustn't bother myself with business details. I am more concerned with *my* end of the job, the last half." Roberts' wide gesture caused golden liquid to leap from his glass.

Marten jumped back. "Blast! Watch the drink. It's not even *close* to noon yet! My attire could have been soiled. I had it custom designed and I don't have a replacement."

Perry Roberts tossed a hand towel onto the carpet and pressed on it with his leather morning-slipper. He faced Marten. "I'm on London time, as a matter of fact, my lad . . . a fine garment indeed . . . what's the occasion?"

"Ms. Tyler's Open House. What? You forgot?"

With a Texas drawl, Roberts answered, "Aw shucks. That fancy-dancy affair's not till tonight. You gonna wear these silly overpriced threads for the next 12 hours?"

"Of course not. I merely wanted your opinion on my appearance. After all, this *is* a crucial night for both of us. Once I plant the Trojan in her system, we're ready for business." He looked into the closet door mirror and smoothed the sleeves of his jacket, one at a time. "In any case, let's not change the subject. Cut down on the alcohol, or it may ruin our plans. It's already affecting your memory."

"There's absolutely nothing wrong with my memory," countered Roberts. "That is why I'm here. Have you forgotten your poor mum?"

"I have not. Damn the Queen to bloody hell!" Marten picked up the white paper lid Roberts had left lying on the floor. "Everything we've got is riding on this. Our futures are at stake. Protect them!" He tossed the lid into the bin and slammed out of the room, spewing profanities all the way down the hall into the next suite.

Roberts chuckled, waited a few minutes, then cracked open the door and whispered into the empty hallway, "Why'd ya always want to go and ruin me fun, laddie?" He closed the door, retrieved the paper lid from the waste bin and placed it strategically back on the carpet. "Oh, and Marten," he murmured, "have no fear, you look flawless, as usual." He set his highball glass down temporarily to carry the telescope back out onto the balcony. Leaning slightly over the railing to view the sidewalk café, he thought of his glory days on the Vanderhawk Estate. He'd spent countless hours hiding in the enormous stable loft, watching the comings and goings below. Amazing what you could see and hear when you lay still, up in the rafters a few feet above everyone else. Somewhat like God, he had imagined.

He adjusted the scope, eyeing a morbidly obese couple seated at the café. He snorted. *They're shoveling huevos rancheros into their pie holes like there's no tomorrow.* He tossed down a few pistachios to annoy them. The man squinted upward toward an oak tree, as though they'd fallen from it.

Perry Roberts adjusted the lens and read her lips: "Teenagers," the man's wife said. Roberts sniffed. *At least she has enough sense to know pistachios don't grow on oak trees.*

Chapter Four

Marten's Dreams

Marten Wells saw himself trapped on the silver screen of old, a character in animation form, as he shuffled in slow motion on the thickly carpeted hallway to his hotel room. It seemed to him his entire life had been held captive in black and white, a voiceless film from an age-old script, manipulated by the projectionist — his mother's brother. The siblings had been raised by mute parents acting in a silent movie of their own.

In his suite, Marten selected a glass from the shelf above the wet bar and drew water from its ornate arched faucet. He shook out three capsules. The headache had started just before sunrise, typical for nights when he dreamed. He glanced longingly at the balcony — Texas morning air would clear his head, but knowing his uncle, Marten assumed the telescope had gone back in plain sight within minutes after he left. He chose not to deal with reality.

Changing into casual attire, he placed his evening garment on a wooden hanger. He ordered breakfast from room service — sausage patties on English muffins, soft-boiled eggs, and blueberries in cream.

He focused on the details of his recurring dream — a complex puzzle based on childhood memories he'd secreted away into the black depths of his subconscious. Was the puzzle about to be solved? Earlier, upon awakening, he'd hurriedly jotted notes in his journal: "*Wallpaper more vivid than before, a floral in muted tones. Massive, winding stairs covered in thick, burgundy plush carpet softly indented with a leaf pattern.*"

His stomach muscles tightened. What *is* it? He wondered. Jealousy? *Yes that's it, for I was merely a child . . . it would have been normal for me to envy Basil — the new kid who stole Father's attention.*

He returned to the scribble in his journal: *"I grabbed my favourite little pillow out of mid-air. Incessant crying of a child below. Looking down from the upper landing, I saw white-clothed figures hiding behind columns. Crying stopped. White figures disappeared."*

Why couldn't he remember more detail? He longed for an end to this lifetime of sadness — caused by an act as a child, *an accident* (he kept reminding himself, for it *had* to be) which led to the death of Basil and the ruination of his mother's career.

Just days before she passed away, she had given him details of the event. Finally — closure to his wretched childhood memories. He'd been unable to understand his melancholy before — assumed he'd never been a happy child, but, oh yes, he *had been*, she'd insisted. Now, though, he was aware of only one thing — his misery caused his mother's death.

Our lives . . . so intertwined, circular and tangled.

Looking back to fleeting events of childhood, he felt emptiness. Loss, *grief, sadness*. Occasionally, there was a flash, a tidbit of joy, a moment with his father holding him, playfully tossing him up into the air. (Or was he remembering it from the photograph?) He was daddy's little boy — on top of the world — loved. But it had all changed so quickly. They'd been spirited away from the palatial manor to a cottage in a small village in Wales; young Marten had intuitively known he would never again be Daddy's little boy. On the rare occasions when his father came to visit, his eyes reflected only the darkness hidden inside his son.

Perry Roberts returned to his suite for a scotch refill, leaving the telescope outside. He glanced once again in the mirror and squinted. His thin, brown hair had receded measurably in the two years since he'd turned fifty-five. He stood a mere five feet tall and weighed 7 stone, or 104 American pounds, the perfect size for a jockey, although those days of glory were long gone. Turning to view his profile, he laughed. A distinctive point at the end of his nose, along with his tiny, beady eyes gave him pause; he considered how much he resembled the circling vulture outside. *We look so much alike that vulture could be my pet!* His laugh was piercing, wickedly mimicking the Phantom of the Opera. He'd seen the play in London three nights in a row and had adopted the legendary cry.

Surprisingly, he was generally considered to be attractive by women. "It's me small size," Roberts would explain to anyone who would listen. "There are women out there who have a soft spot for a small-framed man ... oh Laddie, they only want to mother me, but then, I never turn down a little mother's milk." Due to his extensive travels, he found himself easily able to imitate the accents of people around him, and while a taller man would have seemed offensive with such behavior, Roberts knew short guys could get by with murder. Exactly what he was counting on — no one saw him as a threat, if they saw him at all.

A knock at the door, with the accompanying "Housekeeping" call, aroused him. He went for the bathroom, saying nothing. As he watched through the slightly opened door, a maid emptied trash containers throughout the suite. When she bent over to pick up the white Hilton lid, Roberts quietly crossed the threshold and stood closely behind her.

"Oh! How's my little man today?" the housekeeper said, without actually looking up at him.

"He isn't so little at the moment, my lovely," Roberts whispered.

The housekeeper glanced up and did a double take, her eyes drawn to his midsection. She turned swiftly toward the door, hung the Do Not Disturb sign on the outside knob and double-locked the latch. She winked at Roberts.

Chapter Five

Popsickle Sticks

Had it not been for the strong brass bolts inserted through the center of its old hinges, the massive oak door would have gone into orbit when Boone thrust it open. Like a torpedo tracking a target, he bounded from his bedroom, through the kitchen, and halted only slightly to hug my leg.

"Mornin', Gran." The boy continued his flight into the living room and grabbed the television remote. *Mr. Rogers' Neighborhood* appeared on the large screen. Boone had a fondness for *Mr. Rogers* reruns. He especially loved the Land of Make Believe with King Friday and his loyal subjects.

I watched my grandson's maneuvers with amusement. Carefully, so as not to spill my coffee, I took a seat next to him on the pink leather sofa.

"Gran, look!" He pointed the remote toward the screen. "King Friday and Prince Tuesday are building a ship with Popsicle sticks for Lady Elaine's craft carnival. I need to do that. Could we go to the store and buy some Popsicles?"

My nose wrinkled automatically. "You know, Sweetie, they make craft sticks for projects such as this. See? I believe that's what Prince Tuesday is using." Smart King Friday — his little prince won't have orange lips, purple teeth, nor a tummy ache, not to mention an assortment of multi-colored Popsicle sticks tucked away in a royal armoire somewhere deep in his castle, forgotten and unused, with a trail of ants a mile long.

"Like those things Doc sticks in my mouth when I have a sore throat?"

"Tongue depressors," I said. "Well, sort of like those, but smaller. They sell them by the boxful."

"Cool. So can we get some? I *need* craft sticks."

Boone's tendency to say I *need*, rather than I *want*, was adorable. But, Andie had told him he had his needs and wants mixed up. One time I'd chimed in, "If you ask me, I think he needs whatever it is he wants." Andie replied, "Yeah, but I didn't ask you, now did I, *Grandmother*?" Later, she confessed she'd secretly wished her own Grandmother Tyler would've been so indulgent, the way grannies are supposed to be, even the very young ones. Like me.

"So can we buy craft sticks after school? *Please*?"

"Okay, Boone," I said, "but not tonight, maybe tomorrow, because tonight is our big party, remember? Oh . . . well . . . and you'd better check with Mommy first. Let's ask her when she wakes up. If it's okay with her, then we'll do it."

"You forgot, didn't you? I did, too."

Boone and I had, once again, nearly left Andie out of the parenting loop. In theory, Boone understood the difference in authority but, for the first three years of his life, I took care of him with very little help from his mother. Andie gave birth on her sixteenth birthday, only two weeks after the death of her father, and I threw myself into mothering them both for two reasons: one, because they needed it, and two, it kept my mind off being a widow. So, I supported the household and exercised my right to run it on my own terms.

Initially, we lived comfortably together, but then Andie laid new ground rules. She and I had watched Joan Rivers' coverage of an award show. I hadn't actually been in the mood to watch the red carpet glamor with Joan's hoot owl screech and Halloween appearance, God rest her soul, but Andie had insisted. I was more appreciative of the old days, back when Rivers had her God-given face. Joan's talk show had been one of my favorites, with her famous slogan, "Can We Talk?" The episode where Pee Wee Herman came out on stage with a large heart-shaped box of chocolates, and Rivers opened the box only to discover most of the candy was already sampled by Pee Wee, was my favorite. It can still be found on YouTube.

So, early the next morning, Andie had waltzed into my bedroom all made up: fake eyelashes, hair teased and sprayed sky high — the works, with those big red wax lips you see in gag gift shops. She removed the wax lips and announced: "Can we talk?" She slid in next to me under the covers (I warned her not to get any awful make-up on my clean sheets) and informed me of her wish to change our family structure. She said she wanted it to be healthy, more like *normal* families. She wanted to be Boone's sole parent, along with the responsibilities that went along with it, to have the right to discipline her son as only *she* saw fit. I had suspiciously eyed my daughter, a trick-or-treat freak talking about motherhood, over-dramatizing as usual, but in reality I was all for it, the family structure change. I'd yearned for the freedom to lighten up and spoil my grandson as frivolously as most other grandmothers do. For example, giving him what he said he needed, just because. Rather indulgent? That's exactly what I wanted. What *I* needed. Whether or not that was Andie's idea of 'healthy and normal', I didn't know.

I soon discovered giving up control was harder than I thought it would be. Andie continued to pamper herself, sleeping late, expecting me to take care of Boone every morning. "He wakes up way too early for my taste," Andie complained, "and you're always up at the butt-crack of dawn, anyhow. You have no social life to speak of, so what's the harm?" I felt a searing pain as though Andie had forced a dull knife through my stomach, but I hadn't said a word because I was afraid of saying the *wrong* thing. Besides, it was true about my non-existent social life. I'd allowed it to dwindle since the death of Richard and I liked it that way. And so it was: our family life resembled the inner workings of a dangerously chaotic airport control tower where no one was in charge, airplanes landing and taking off at will, narrowly missing one another by an inch or two.

We'd consulted a family counselor who suggested we make the switch much like in a business environment — keep emotions at a minimum. Ideally, an employee trains her replacement and assumes the new person can handle the position. Once she's gone, she doesn't helicopter the situation, coming in to make sure everything was done correctly. For the most part, it worked well for Andie and me, but Boone continued to test us.

"Don't stress over it," the counselor had said. "Kids do the same thing with their biological parents, so why not with a mom and grandmother? Give it some time, and someday, when Andie and Boone move to a place of their own, it will feel natural."

Move? To a place of their own? I hadn't even considered such a thing! Oh sure, Andie had mumbled once in a while about moving out, but I hoped it wouldn't be any time soon. Just the thought of not having Boone in my daily life made my heart ache.

I'd also tried individual therapy to deal with the loss of Richard, but quickly gave up, much to the dismay of the therapist. "You will have to grieve sooner or later," she'd insisted. I opted for later. I had a dark secret about the actual cause of Richard's demise and feared it would inevitably come out. I planned to take that secret to my own grave. If Andie ever found out the truth she would be overwhelmed with guilt. I convinced myself I didn't need a therapist to tell me what to do, so I stopped going.

I didn't visit Richard's grave the first year after his death. The responsibility of having an infant in the house had been overwhelming. I hadn't the interest or the time to grieve. Andie had expected me to do most of the work and I'd allowed her to get by with it. Caring for a newborn took more energy than I'd remembered. It had been much easier when I was 18 with my own baby. What a difference a few years made!

Mr. Rogers ended. Boone grabbed the remote and absorbed himself in a commercial. I saw it coming: next he'd ask me to buy him whatever it was they were hyping. *He's not a newborn anymore — he's a self-sufficient little boy. He doesn't keep me so busy. So what's my excuse now for putting the grief work off?*

I'd accepted Richard's death without much effort — he'd been terminally ill for over two years. The funeral director had loaded me up with brochures about the stages of grief, informing me that the boundaries for those left behind could be vague compared to those experienced by the person who is dying. Anger, for example. Some people never feel angry because the death delivered their loved one relief from pain and suffering, or perhaps the passing on brought along with it a celebration of the long and happy life of the deceased.

Oh, but was I angry? You bet your life I was, even after five years. If there was an avoidance period, I'd been in it for months. Had I put grieving on hold? There were unresolved communication issues, things left unsaid between the two of us. Yes, I *would* visit the grave more often, maybe even that afternoon, if I could make time for it.

Chapter Six

Why Do Models Walk the Way They Do?

Whenever Andie entered a room, I wondered why models walk the way they do. Although she was not a model, Andie knew how to walk the walk: one step purposefully in front of the other, Versace-style, as if to say "Here I am, world!" She wore black spandex pants and a white DK sweatshirt, her long, blonde hair was pulled back at the nape of her neck with a single red ribbon. Her lean 5'7" frame moved smoothly, as though in two sections; her hips and legs aimed in one direction while her head glanced to the right, then the left, as her dark eyes surveyed the entire living area.

"Good morning, family dear," Andie said, tossing Boone's jeans and striped shirt toward the sofa.

Boone caught the clothes in midair. "G'morning, Mommy."

Andie ruffled her son's blond curls and gave him a kiss on his cheek, which he promptly wiped off. She floated into the kitchen, selected an orange from the fruit bowl and squeezed it with an upscale deco juicer, her first eBay win.

The auction had ended three weeks ago, just before midnight on Christmas Eve. She'd burst into my bedroom and flipped on the overhead light. "Mom, you're not asleep are you? Guess what! You know that juicer on eBay I told you about? I won it!"

I'd moaned and blinked, disoriented. Did Andie equate *winning* with *free*? She'd bid it up a little more every day and it had taken every ounce of self-control I could muster to keep my mouth shut.

My first reaction was to lecture: "You woke me up to tell me this? Don't you realize you may have won an auction but you still have to pay for the goods, not to mention the shipping?"

What I really said was nothing like it: "How exciting . . . and Merry Christmas to you! Now, turn off the light and get to bed before Santa sees you in that skimpy nightie!" I pulled the covers over my head and went back to sleep. A few days after the juicer arrived, I saw an identical one at the River Center Mall for half the price. I didn't mention it. What would have been the point?

The hardest thing was for me to stand by while my daughter made mistakes with her personal money, but if I didn't I'd be cleaning up Andie's messes for eternity.

I watched Andie's satisfied expression as she forced the juicer's elaborate chrome handle downward. "We're both going to be busy today, you know?" I said.

"Oh, for sure. What've you lined out for me? Anything new?" Andie's bare feet danced softly in circular patterns, caressing the clean, polished oak floor of the 18-foot long corridor kitchen.

We reviewed Andie's assignments, including the transcription she would do for Judy during maternity leave.

Andie downed her orange juice and made some for Boone. "Okay, no problem. I can handle it. Boone and I are going to have an egg and cheese bagel down on the Riverwalk on our way to Montessori. I'll check on Judy at the hospital, too. What are you wearing tonight? Pink, I assume."

"I've laid out two outfits but I can't make a decision. One is that backless black cocktail dress with the see-through ruffled fabric at the hemline."

"Bor-ing," Andie sang. "Seems to me everyone wears black to these affairs. You *live* here for heaven's sake; wear clothes that celebrate, Mom. Geez — tonight of all nights!" She rinsed her glass and placed it upside down in the dish drainer.

"Well, then," I said, "that leaves pink — flared silk pants and lace camisole topped off with a hot pink bolero jacket, the layered look you love so much."

"Yummy. Now we're talking. It's the one we found in the Junior Department at Dillard's, isn't it? By the way, I want to borrow it next week."

"Hmm." I tilted my head slightly to study my daughter's profile. "It would look even better on you. Perhaps I shouldn't wear the layered look at my age."

"*Your* age? Oh please . . . you don't look even close to your age. I mean, everyone thinks you're my sister. Wear it. Trust me. Plus, those crimson heels are killer."

"Try standing up in those suckers; they'll be the death of me, no doubt."

"Ah, but Mom, they're so sexy, don't you get it?" She delivered Boone's juice to him and stared at my mug of caffeine. She pointed with disgust at the coffee, as though she were in the witness stand during a murder trial, identifying the defendant as a criminal. "The additives in that chocolate coffee you're drinking will cause your early death, not those spiked heels in your closet. If you *must* be addicted to a liquid, why not make it fruit juice?"

Now who's the parent? I saw myself mirrored in my daughter's attitude toward fitness. Andie had been a strict vegetarian since she was in junior high; I had assumed it to be a phase, but she refused to outgrow it. Oh, sure, I knew I should pay more attention to my own health, but couldn't commit to a routine. I was way too busy — maybe later on.

I made a weak attempt at rationalization. "Coffee and chocolate are my only real vices. It could be worse, after all. I blame your dad's cancer on his intimate relationship with cigarettes in his teens. I have never smoked a cigarette, not even one. And," I added, "if it makes you feel any better, I had toast and an orange already. You just want an excuse to use that new-fangled contraption of yours, little girl."

Andie did her best to stare back at me, eyes narrowed and cold. "Oh, yeah? So, tell me your toast wasn't slathered with that fat yellow stuff you seem determined to overindulge in."

"Okay . . . okay. Squeeze me a glass of the orange and make it snappy."

Andie grinned as she proudly prepared my juice. She handed me the beverage and turned off the television. She removed Boone's Sponge Bob pajamas and pulled his tee shirt over his head, fitting his arms one by one into the armholes. "There goes Mr. Left Hand, and here comes Mr. Right Hand," she said, as it emerged from the sleeve. Boone thought they were playing, but he has known his left from his right since he was two. Andie helped her son with his socks and shoes. She double-knotted his laces.

"We're off," Andie said. "I'll check on the flower arrangements, too." As they headed through the kitchen to the elevator, the boy remembered his excitement over Prince Tuesday's ship project. He popped up and down, requesting his mother's permission to build one of his own.

"Sure, Sweetie, that'd be fun. I'll help you if you like. When we're sick of Popsicles we can buy boxes of sticks at the craft shop, did you know?"

Boone nodded proudly. "Gran told me."

"Oh yeah," Andie said. "You'll love the craft shop. You can get all kinds of ideas for things to make. We'll go tomorrow after school, okay?" They entered the elevator and pulled the accordion gate shut, waving and blowing kisses to me as they slowly disappeared from view.

I listened as they descended to the lobby, wishing I could share the news with them of Lady Sophia and her son's upcoming visit, but it was still top secret. Boone would be so excited about seeing a member of British nobility his own age, he'd want to tell his schoolmates right away. I couldn't risk even hinting at it since security was involved.

The assignment I'd received to help plan the event with one of my clients, River Protocol, Inc. was big — really big. To be among the very few who knew about it gave me a rush. Of course, I was merely one of several cogs in the wheel, but an important cog.

I reached into the pocket of my robe and washed down the second half of the Xanax with orange juice.

Chapter Seven

The Romantic Riverwalk

I had an early appointment with Frederick, my friend who was known as the hair color specialist extraordinaire, but I needed only a cut, or *design*, as he called it. I surveyed the condo to make sure nothing was out of place. Damn, wouldn't you know, Andie left Boone's pajamas on the floor. I took them into Andie's room, tossed them onto her unmade bed and started to close the door behind me. That's when I saw it — a well-worn paperback romance on her nightstand.

I gave up reading love stories long ago. The characters were nothing like anyone I knew. Brawny, ruddy-complexioned, retro-sexual men with chiseled jaws. And the women, shrewd and savvy hourglass types whose closets bulged with designer shoes, their long, golden hair braided down to their butts, or up in a chignon, whatever in the world a chignon was. I flipped through a few pages, speculating that the total saturation of this type of crap into Andie's adolescent brain undoubtedly contributed to her pregnancy at 15. The sperm donor had been a blond-haired, blue-eyed foreign exchange student from Norway. At the end of their sophomore year, he flew gaily across the ocean to his homeland, none the wiser. I didn't know anything about him other than the blond curls and blue eyes which he'd given to Boone. I'd overheard one of Andie's phone conversations, or I wouldn't have known that much. I never knew his name, although I assumed she did. Probably Sven, or Erik, or something equally Nordic. He was a subject Andie wouldn't discuss with me, her mother, the one parent who truly cared. Her father's only emotion back then was embarrassment. Richard's mother and her religious rules always seemed to dominate his decisions, and he pretended the pregnancy wasn't real until it was too late for denial.

I sat on the edge of the bed and turned another page or two to find the first sex scene. Would the descriptive writing be any better than years before when, rather than coffee, my addiction was romance novels? I recalled it was usually somewhere before page 80, those carefully-plotted love/sex scenes, usually repeated in each cookie cutter novel (if what you're doing works, why change it?). I found the words — three raw pages of them — and thrust myself into the experience. Oh, my. The images I conjured sent shivers up my spine and down again, and here I was *39! I* vaguely remembered being 15 with raging hormones.

I skimmed a few more pages. The book appeared to be no different than any other, same words — different characters — and I tossed it aside. I didn't mind the shivers going up, but when they came down, they had no place to go. I hadn't had (or wanted) sex in the five years since Richard died. I wondered if I'd forgotten the right moves, in the event I ever had the opportunity again. Most people say it's like riding a bicycle, but those same people were convinced I had grieved long enough. Personally, I thought I still had a way to go. I just wasn't that into it, anyway. At least, I hadn't thought so until last night. I'd been thinking about it ever since. I would tell Frederick about last night if he was alone in the salon. If anyone could help me understand what was going on with me, it would be Frederick.

~*~

In the kitchen, I checked to make sure the coffeepot was turned off. My keys hung just above the coffee maker, but, because of the elevator's unique pass code system, I ordinarily left them at home. I dropped them into my purse in case I was able to manage a quick drive to the cemetery.

Aromas from The Stock Market soothed me when I reached the lobby — early preparations for the party tonight: grilled rare, filet of beef on French bread slices, bourbon-soaked shrimp, Parmesan toast crescents, to mention a few items from the menu. I'd decided on butler-carried appetizers — Dana said it would add class — although the bourbon-soaked shrimp would occupy its own table.

I stepped outside and inhaled the fresh morning air. The sounds of the day were alive, as though someone in charge had pushed the button for everything pure and natural to begin anew. Barges, empty save for their drivers, revved their engines as they maneuvered the narrow channel in preparation for tour boat rides. Crisp and breezy air offered the background and set the scene: Young men in clean white aprons hosed off the eatery sidewalks, and scores of birds pranced around in tall trees. A harmonic concert — soprano, alto and bass. Mornings on the Riverwalk were much better than any other time. It was somewhat like being in an aviary.

Foot traffic was light early in the day, making it easier to get around than at mid-day, or God forbid, in the evening. Forget evenings, unless, of course, you actually *want* to be *on* the Riverwalk for dinner or revelry. At least half of the folks out at night were tourists, and they walked very, very slowly.

The Paseo del Rio was the life of the city and a prestigious address to have. I absorbed energy from the Riverwalk. Maybe that's what I needed, I thought — to be a sightseer myself for a few days.

I made a mental note to clear my schedule after the Open House and plan one of my four-day weekends to Sedona. First, I would add a piece or two to my Native American pottery collection, and then I'd fill my backpack with supplies and enjoy a day-hike on Bell Rock Path. I never tired of the beauty of Sedona's red rock canyons, especially the well-known vortex sites where the earth was alive with energy swirls, drawing everything surrounding them to their center. Juniper trees reacted to the vortex energy in tangible ways that revealed where energy was strongest. The stronger the energy, the more of a "twist" the trees had in their branches. The growth lines followed a leisurely spiral along the length of the branch. I'd visited all four of the main sites and had seen juniper trees that had developed these twisted, swirling trunks due to the powerful vortex energy at the core of the area. The spiraling effect had sometimes even bent the branches. Merely thinking about Sedona and the sweet, balsamic aroma of juniper made me eager to return soon.

Pausing at the doorway of the florist shop, I was drawn inside by the scent of lilacs and damp earth. Cramped aisles full of lush tropical plants and the hint of a breeze from the overhead ceiling fan put me on a beach. For a moment, I was on an island far away — far away from Texas.

The florist peered over the top rim of her eyeglasses as she arranged pots. "Good morning, Ms. Tyler. Andie just left. She gave us the go-ahead to deliver and set up for your party."

"Ah, good. I knew I could count on her. I just couldn't resist stopping in myself. Wanted a little eye candy, you know what I mean?"

"Oh, yes . . . these tropicals came in yesterday afternoon, and they will unquestionably have the effect you're going for." She brushed a lock of silver away from her eyes with her forearm. "We'll get set up in about an hour."

"Terrific! Nina will be there to show you where we want everything placed."

"Yes, ma'am." The florist nodded. "Mrs. Emmett has been wonderful to work with."

My inner spring unwound with the florist's reassurance; I could always count on Nina.

Chapter Eight

Window Reflections

I sprinted up the creek-stone steps, layered precisely to reach a second-floor balcony with a row of specialty shops overlooking the Riverwalk. These businesses were situated so as to be accessed from the Riverwalk on one end and Presa Street on the other. There was a Christmas shop, a candy store, a Taxco Mexican silver shop and Frederick's salon. I stopped before going in, admiring his "Before and After" photographs. They were featured in popular beauty magazines, touting his extensive training and expertise in hair color. The positive response inspired Frederick to mount the photos and display them in his shop window. Tourists see the photos, then walk in and demand a makeover, when five minutes previously they'd had no idea they could use improvement.

Slipping quietly into the cozy waiting area, I chose a soft, red leather club chair. Frederick was as crazy about red as I was about pink. The salon resembled a Tuscan villa: cobblestone floors, bricked walls smeared partially with authentic Venetian plaster, and, at the windows, dark oiled wooden shutters with matching window boxes brimming with red geraniums. Italian music played softly in the background. Close your eyes and you picture yourself, if not in Italy, at least in a classy Italian restaurant. Frederick's ancestors hailed from a little village in Northern Italy. Every summer his entire clan flew in for a visit, and Frederick always said after they'd gone back home that he might move to Italy someday. But I knew he never would. Italy was his daydream, whereas he *lives* his real dream every day in his salon.

Frederick was wearing his usual work uniform: pleated black trousers and a silk shirt, long sleeves rolled up to just above his wrists. His brown hair was long and curly and pulled into a ponytail, framing a face rather thin, although not disproportionate with the rest of him. Around his neck, loosely knotted below the collar, a purple necktie sprinkled with red smashes dissected his dark chocolate shirt. Deep purple socks and mahogany leather moccasins completed the look. Around his waist he wore a hairdresser's belt with an assortment of styling gadgets.

He was weaving solutions of three separate colors into the tresses of a middle-aged woman who was going on about her son-in-law and how she had told her daughter not to marry the loser. She wasn't one of his regular customers — just another tourist lured in by "Before and After" shots. Makeovers were the rage.

With a few minutes to kill, I picked up a beauty magazine and contemplated a makeover for myself, perhaps an entirely new hairstyle. I found one, rather choppy, which caught my attention, but I wasn't sure the timing was right to change my appearance so drastically. Yet, I was tempted.

Frederick's customer was still talking, barely taking a breath between sentences. Frederick made eye contact with me in the mirror, and I smiled back at him and made a chatterbox hand gesture. He silently moved his lips, "Yak, yak, yak." I stuck out my tongue; he reciprocated. Back and forth we communicated in the mirror, but the lady (still obsessed with her daughter's idiot husband) didn't notice. The more I overheard, the more I had to concur — the guy was definitely a moron. I felt like I was watching a bad movie and I wondered why on earth *did* the lady's daughter marry the jerk? He was probably good in bed.

A lot of people make that mistake. Take my cousin Dana, for example. She married husband number two for the very same reason. That, and he was a musician — Dana's major weakness. I wondered what my weakness would be if I started dating again. I got married the first time at seventeen because I was pregnant. I hadn't a clue what to look for in a man the second time around.

Frederick's hands worked quickly over his lady's evolving coiffure. He moved his lithe body in smooth wave-like motions around the woman, delicately weaving an invisible cocoon from which a new and beautiful creature would emerge. He made each customer feel like she was the only important person in the world while she sat in his chair. It was his personal goal in life to be a day-maker, and he was quite successful at it.

He took his time with the lady and I glanced at my watch, eager to tell Frederick about last night. I flicked my fingernails on the arm of the chair, unaware of what I was doing until Frederick glanced at me with one eyebrow raised, an expression that said, "What?"

I shrugged.

From my handbag, I removed a to-do list; all but three items had been checked off. I scratched out *Select Outfit for Tonight*. Underneath, I wrote *The Pink, definitely The Pink*. I ran a line through *Beauty Shop*. Only one thing left on the list now. I folded the paper and shoved it into my purse. Wouldn't Frederick be pissed to know I'd written *Beauty Shop*, and not *Salon*? I suppressed a wicked smile. Well, he didn't have to know everything. I walked over to peruse his new display of Italian hair products and selected a travel-sized shampoo and conditioner set for the trip to Sedona. I'd start planning it tomorrow.

~*~

Eventually, Frederick situated his customer under a color enhancer and set the timer. Then he looked longingly at me. "Come here, you simmering vixen of wild abandon."

It was my turn to have my day made.

"Frederick, I'm dying to tell you about a man I saw last night."

"Ooh, for me?"

"No, not for you. For me — well not really for me. But . . . oh, just *listen!*"

"Come. I'm all ears." He escorted me to the shampoo area.

"It all happened at the Little Rhein Steak House where I went for dinner and to watch the festival on the stage across the river."

"Oh yes, at the Arneson River Theatre. Was it *that* good?" Frederick offered a coy smile.

As he tilted my head back into the red enamel sink, he sprayed warm water over my scalp. "I have no idea. I don't know. I think so."

"Well, make up your mind, silly!"

"The thing is, I could barely pay attention to the performance. Shortly after I was seated, a man was ushered to a table fairly close by and I lost all interest in anything else. I haven't been so befuddled in years!"

"He was handsome?"

"Fine-looking, double-whistle quality, no doubt about it. Tall, with black hair and dark eyes, in a black tee, black leather jacket, and jeans."

"Uh-oh. I know how you like that look, the black shirt thing," he said as he generated lather with his palms.

"Oh, yeah. I couldn't take my eyes off him."

"Who is he?"

"I don't know. I doubt he's from around here; he wasn't wearing boots or a gigantic Texas belt buckle. He was *sans* wedding ring, not that it means anything."

"It does have meaning though: Your hormones are back on the job and it's about time. I knew it could happen!" He rinsed, then applied a generous amount of lavender-scented conditioner with his palms.

Frederick has this thing he does, only when he's in the mood and if I'm lucky. It's a scalp massage, but not just any. The way he does it triggers those little synapses in my brain something fierce. The first time he gave me one, I swore I had an out-of-body experience. I call it BTS (better than sex) massage.

I continued my story. "Right after he was seated . . . ah, feels good . . . where was I? Oh, yeah, so I noticed he was staring at me, smiling. I thought maybe it was my imagination and I looked away."

"You didn't even return his smile?" Frederick scolded, as he gave me a final rinse.

"No . . . I thought . . . you know . . . I resembled someone he knew."

"A movie star, no doubt."

"Maybe . . . you never know."

Frederick scowled and accompanied me to his stylist chair, shaking his head the entire way. He secured a towel under a cape. "How do we want it designed?"

I handed him the magazine, opened to the page with the choppy style.

"Oh my Lord, she's come *alive*!" For as long as he'd known me, I'd worn it all one length. Before I had a chance to change my mind, Frederick worked his magic with comb and scissors. I watched the reflection of my widening eyes in the mirror.

"Relax, girlfriend. I'm giving you an entirely new look, the *shattered* look. But I warn you, because of the way it will emphasize your eyes, you'll look even younger now!"

My mind wasn't on my hair, or my eyes. "Whatever . . . what's worse, I couldn't even taste my steak, because each time I glanced over, the guy was watching me, sometimes out of the corner of his eye, but he was looking, all right. Oh, I don't know . . . maybe I'm wrong. Surely he was watching the festival across the river, because he tapped his foot to the music like he was genuinely into the presentation. He's probably attending a conference, because I've never seen him before, and I'll almost certainly never see him again."

"Don't bet on it."

I gave him an eye roll. Frederick was always so dramatic, so *karmic*. "Just beholding that specimen in black was enough for me. It jump-started my battery all the way. I even thought of him early, while in the hot tub this morning. Let me tell you, what he did for me last night won't soon be forgotten."

One eyebrow raised again, and Frederick's thinking face was reflected in the mirror. "Girlfriend! Why didn't you make a move?"

"A move? Me? I'm not a move maker. Besides, we weren't in a bar; it was an open-air restaurant. Anyway, I think he was much too young for me."

"How young is 'much too young'?"

"Umm . . . It's hard to tell sometimes."

The front door opened and a man entered. He nodded, said he was early, sat down and picked up a magazine. "Moreover," I whispered, "if he was a convention person, all he'd have been after was a one-night stand, and there's no way I'm up for that." I paused for a moment of thought. Speaking in a voice even lower than before, I said, "What move do you think I could have made that wouldn't have given me the appearance of being, you know, *easy*?"

"There's any number of things you could've done. You should have thought of *something*. Now you're down in the mouth because you'll never see him again."

"You know what? I don't care about seeing *him* again. What's important is I finally noticed a *man*. It's a sign the old Julia is coming back. A real, live ticking time bomb, that's what I am, and I can't wait to tell Richard."

"He'll probably roll over in his grave, but that's what he needs to do."

"No need for sarcasm."

"It's not sarcasm, Julia. I'm serious. You really should let go. Send him off to where spirits belong. Leave him be."

I ignored his unsolicited advice. How could I let Richard go when I had unfinished business with him?

"I haven't told you the best part," I sing-songed.

"There's *more*?" Frederick squealed, exasperated, seeing as I was dragging the story on so, but that's what I liked to do to get each and every juicy reaction out of him. Once I'd learned how to push his buttons, it was like playing with one of Boone's old baby toys, the one where you push the cow button and it moos, the chicken clucks, the sheep baas.

"When the guy got up to leave, he walked by me and placed a single rosebud from his table next to my evening bag. I thought I would just give it up right then and there."

Frederick let out a wolf whistle. "First class," he said. "Apparently *he* didn't think you were too old for him! Odd, though, he arrived *after* you did, but left *before*."

"It's a mystery all right." I cast a sarcastic smile into the mirror.

Frederick ignored it. "So, what did you do when he gave you the rose?"

"I searched for something clever, but truly, Frederick, my mind was numb. He walked right on by . . . I mean . . . I didn't get the impression he *wanted* me to say anything at all, so I let the moment go."

"I would have pinched his ass as he passed, at least," Frederick said at the top of his voice.

The waiting customer looked up from his magazine and winked at us.

I felt myself blush. "Well, spontaneity is your calling card. You'd better watch out; someday it might get you into trouble."

Frederick offered a mock insulted look. "Someday is a long way off, Sweetie. And, you have to admit, I do lead a colorful life."

"Colorful, that's only the beginning. Anyway, my server saw it all. She brought me a damp napkin and a small plastic bag. I gave her a huge tip, wrapped up the rose stem and took it home."

"Put it on Richard's grave next time you go. Show him you haven't lost your sense of humor."

Now he was being sarcastic. He made no secret that he found it bizarre for me to sit in a desolate graveyard and talk to the dead. And just maybe it *was* weird, but it accomplished a purpose for me. Although Richard couldn't reply, I got answers to my questions whenever I was there.

"I won't waste my flower on Richard. It's in a little vase in my office for now. I'll dry it as a memento of the night Julia came back to life."

A moment passed and I chuckled. "By that time, my stomach was tied in knots. I was on and off the commode for an hour after I got home last night."

"Hah!" Frederick slapped his thigh and let out that rowdy laugh of his. I loved to make him laugh just to hear it — a laugh-out-loud kind of hoot. Whenever I saw LOL online, I thought of Frederick. He applied a touch of hairspray on the finished product and gave me a hand-mirror, swirled my chair around and I evaluated my new look, front and back. "What a great style! I'll be a hit at my party tonight for sure."

"I couldn't have done it without you," Frederick said. "I was the architect and you were the landscape."

"You say that to everyone, Frederick."

"And I mean it every time."

~*~

The old buildings on both sides of the river were built with their backs to it, as if to ignore it. The front doors faced the streets, but after the Riverwalk became a reality, artistic riverside facades were erected which eventually proved to be their busiest entrances, where the main dining and drinking areas were located. Many of the adjoining buildings housed a variety of shops, such as jewelry, clothing and colorful folk art.

I made my exit onto Presa. On impulse, I peeked into the doorway of a new nail salon I'd been meaning to try. They worked me into their schedule for a pedicure. I selected the shade of *Criminal Crimson*, handed it to the nail technician and eased my feet into the swirling water-bath.

It was going on noon as I headed for the parking garage, when I noticed a briskness to my step that hadn't been there before. I observed an attractive woman walking next to me, and as I turned toward her, I found my own reflection in the window.

Damn, I do look fine!

Chapter Nine

A Visit With the Dead

Realistically, I hadn't the time for it, but practicality blew in the wind along with my new hairstyle after I slid onto the leather seat of my white Grand Cherokee, lowered the windows and headed straight out of town. I scanned the highway, hungry for signs of beauty, but saw only scraggly trees and dried-up shrubs scattered on either side of the endless road. Humdrum Texas highways — the one and only part of south Texas I had never warmed up to. I longed for spring and Interstate highways cloaked with wildflowers: vibrant corals of Indian Paintbrush, rich blues of Texas Bluebonnets, soft pinks of Evening Primrose. *Thank you, Lady Bird Johnson.*

The cemetery was located on a dreary, sparse half-acre of soil, tucked away from civilization on a dirt road. Its only saving grace was an ancient pine in the center. Otherwise, typical Texas landscape: cactus, sand and weeds. Sagebrush here and there.

My tires churned desert dust at the primitive side-road entrance. Its arched sign, EVERGREEN CEMETERY, rickety and rusted, emitted eerie screeching sounds as it swayed overhead in the breeze. What a joke. There was very little *green* about this place. Richard's family had used the graveyard for generations. Such practical people, they designated two plots for him on the day of his birth. *Welcome to the world, little guy, and when you die here's where we'll plant you. Two plots, for surely you'll have a wife someday, won't you, and of course she will want to be buried next to you, won't she, and just look how we've saved her the trouble of making a decision as to her final resting place.* They gifted me long before they realized Richard would be stuck with a mate painfully dissimilar to anyone else in the Tyler family.

~*~

On the first anniversary of Richard's death, I'd finally gathered the courage to visit his grave. I'd been quite anxious about it and had gone early in the day, hoping I wouldn't have to share the cemetery with anyone. I stood still, admiring the lone pine tree, when I saw a chilling new addition to the landscape. I let out one of those horrified, blood curdling screams, as though I'd seen a ghost. And, in a way, I had — my own. My mother-in-law had had the audacity to place a large tombstone without my knowledge, and *my* name was to the right of Richard's on a double granite monument. Madelynne Tyler got away with it because it was her family's plot, thus she was the owner — always in control.

Under Richard's name were the exact dates of his birth and death, but my birth date was nonexistent. Apparently I'd merely floated in and out of existence. Rather than plant me *next* to Richard some day in the future, Madelynne surely fantasized she'd already buried me *with* him. Did she even *know* the year of my birth, let alone the month and day? I tried to recall if she'd ever sent me a birthday card. She always mailed one to her son, usually with money inside.

I'd stared at the monument and wondered how the woman could be so thoughtless, so cruel. I couldn't imagine any young widow feeling good about seeing such a sight — her own name engraved in a tombstone! What if I wanted to get married again someday? What about that, Madelynne? I'd kicked off my shoes and climbed up on top of the tombstone. Standing straight and tall, arms outstretched to the heavens above, I made an announcement: "Newsflash for the ancestors: Forever will there be a blank space under my name. My ashes will be strewn over Siberia before I allow the Tylers to lay me to rest in *this* desolate space!"

Well.

That's when I knew — the cemetery was my very own spiritual vortex. A peaceful feeling had settled over me, like when I was seventeen with Richard's arm around me and I was protected from all harm. For several months after that day I made sporadic trips, talking to Richard about anything at all. He helped me find resolution, not essentially in person, of course. On my way home, for example, I would hear the lyrics of a song on the radio or I'd overhear a conversation on the

Riverwalk and find clarity. It happened much too often for me to label it a coincidence. No, there was no such thing.

I nicknamed it my *answer chip,* down deep inside, and solutions emerged only when I asked a precise question, pushed the right button, so to speak. Oh, those glorious moments of illumination when my light bulb glowed and enlightenment was achieved. I'd explained it to Dana and Frederick, the answer chip, how it worked only when a person had done her own work. No one else could do it for them. Not their mothers (they would if they could), not their preachers (although they insist otherwise), nor dead husbands. I didn't believe Richard himself handed me answers, although he surely thought he had them all when he was alive. But, since we're all connected, I gave him some of the credit.

~*~

On the day of my Open House, I was convinced it *was* Richard himself who sent me a message of clarity. I wiped the dust and pine needles off a concrete slab bench and sat down. The scent of sage wafted on a delicate breeze.

"Richard, something is coming my way which I have no control over. Last night, I dreamed I crawled outside of my body. Can you imagine? I slithered out of it much like a snake and observed my surroundings. I felt lost, or possibly in search of something. I shivered and awakened to find all the bedding on the other side of the mattress. Boone is such a cover hog, and we had fallen asleep watching television last night. Now, I know how you feel about adults sharing their bed with children, but Richard, if you only knew him and how he loves to cuddle, I just know he'd have you sharing your covers with him in a heartbeat. Anyway, I carried him into his room and tucked him in, but I never did get back to sleep."

After a few moments, I said, "I guess it's no surprise that I'm still mad at you. You could've hung around for a while longer, couldn't you? Yes, I'm sure of it. I've worked through most of my anger, and I understand your guilt about Andie. I've felt it, too. You were wrong, though, about keeping up appearances. Lots of people have illegitimate grandkids and no one thinks any less of them.

"Nowadays, I feel more alone than ever. There's not nearly the weight on my shoulders as before, and the spare time makes me anxious. Oh . . . and you'll love this." I laughed out loud at a memory. "Remember those nights when you set the sleep timer on the television in our bedroom and it drove me nuts? Well, guess what! I do it now, mainly so I won't have to think when I lie down in the dark. Ironic, isn't it?

"Sometimes I dream of being, oh, you know . . . held . . . loved . . . cared for, the way you used to do. Yeah, I know I complained that you smothered me, but it sure was nice to have someone to lean on. Since you've been gone, I've come to appreciate you more. I could always rely on you for support. I just want you to know that. But, then, I guess you probably already do."

I walked to the Jeep for a bottle of water. I grabbed an old rag, doused it and ran the cloth over the surface of the tombstone. "There, that looks better, now doesn't it? Geez, it sure is dusty out here." I drank a swig of water and lay down on the bench, flat on my back. Overhead, a mockingbird squealed the sound of someone hailing a cab. The branches of the pine tree fluttered as a male sparrow chased a female. At least that's the way I had it figured. Maybe it could've been the other way around. Even the birds had partners. My eyes filled with tears.

A puffy cloud had formed the curious shape of a chameleon. I watched, amazed, as it slowly transformed into the form of a shrimp, reminding me of my upcoming party. I needed to end my visit, but I had a confession to make.

I sat up straight and stretched, leaning closer to the monument and whispered (other corpses might be listening), "I actually took a second look at a man at dinner last night, and that's not anything I've ever done since the day I met you. I think I'm ready to care for someone else, to share the intimacies of my world, parts I don't share with our daughter and grandson. Even parts of me that I never dared share with you, if you want to know the truth." Why had I thought Richard would want to know the truth? He was always in denial when he was alive.

I slowly shook my head and allowed an overwhelming sadness to wash through me. "What happened to the three of us — you, me and

Andie? We had a happy family, didn't we? Now, there still are three of us, but little Boone is the third . . . and you're gone. The math is the same, but the numbers look different. Oh, Rich, I took you for granted, I see that now."

I wept as I watched two squirrels dance seductively overhead. I hadn't felt compelled to cry at the grave before then and I welcomed the relief it brought. I wiped my eyes with the back of my hands, and it occurred to me that I was, in reality, much further along in my grief-work than I'd thought. But how was I going to deal with the *secret*? Could I ignore it?

A slight breeze rustled again, easing the unseasonable heat and humidity of mid-day. I followed my ordinary graveyard routine and gathered three pine cones from the sandy soil. I laid them on top of the elaborate granite rock. One for me. One for Andie. One for Boone. I brushed my fingers with a kiss and pressed my hand against the monument, then I softly ran one finger over the engraved letters. R.I.C.H.A.R.D.

At the funeral, I did not say goodbye, nor had I ever brought myself to say it at the grave. Someday I would, but not yet. "Gotta run. Tonight's my big party, you know." I turned toward the Jeep. A pine cone abruptly fell from its branch high above and crash-landed directly in front of me. I picked it up and held it to my nose. It smelled like the Christmas tree Boone and I had taken down a couple of weeks before. The cone was perfectly shaped and much larger than the other three. I retraced my steps to place it on the headstone with the others. When I stood back to admire the display, there was no doubt of the meaning. There were four of us, after all. Richard's strength was forever mine. I'd always known, but it was nice to receive a sign.

Chapter Ten

Open House

Cucumber-Mint Lassi
1/2 cup peeled, seeded cucumber chunks
1 cup buttermilk
1/8 tsp. salt
1 tsp. sugar
1 scallion, chopped
10 mint leaves

In a blender, combine all ingredients and puree until smooth. Serve cold, garnished with a stem of fresh mint leaves.

Makes two servings.

5:00 pm — I darted from the elevator straight to my kitchen. I'd had a craving for shrimp ever since the clouds at the cemetery. Add to that two facts: I skipped lunch and the aroma in the elevator triggered a significant rumble in my stomach.

Dana had expertly converted the kitchen into a chef station with trays of hors d'oeuvres efficiently stacked on a tall cart on wheels, and the wait staff — costumed in Hawaiian shirts and leis — stood at attention, pending Dana's signal to carry silver platters throughout the anticipated crowd. The Clifford Building's dumbwaiter made continuous runs to convey the delicacies for which The Stock Market's catering service was well-known.

"Step away from the shrimp and exit my domain immediately," ordered Dana in a robotic voice.

"Okay, okay." I surrendered with both palms up. "Just a little teensy taste?"

"One, just one, then you skedaddle, little girl."

Skedaddle, now there's a word I hadn't heard in ages. Uncle Ned used to say it when we would sneak into his tool shed to watch him build inventions that never went anywhere, even though he was always sure they would. "What a loser," Dana had whined on numerous occasions when we were teenagers. Uncle Ned was the ultimate futilitarian.

I hurried into Andie's bedroom to make sure she had straightened the place before leaving with Boone for the babysitter's. The narrow French doors to the bedrooms were to be left open with a soft ribbon draped at the doorways — the curious could take a peek without venturing inside. Obviously, the bed had been hastily made — no big surprise there. I smoothed the comforter and fluffed the pillows. Jesus! The damn paperback was still on the nightstand! I threw it into a drawer and slammed it shut.

In my room, I stepped into *The Pink, definitely The Pink*. I sprayed Ralph Lauren Blue on my wrists, rubbed them together and ran a hairbrush through my new *shattered* design. I bent over from the waist to shake it out. Long, silver earrings and a triple strand of miniature pink and silver beads added the perfect bling. I evaluated the finished product in my full-length mirror. "Oh yeah . . . you're a *hottie*." Now where on earth had *that* come from? My oh-so-sexy crimson heels clicked on the hardwood floor as I pranced around the room to get adjusted to being three inches taller than normal. I didn't want my room to emit a stale odor as older buildings sometimes do, so I squirted a few mists of Blue into the air, toward the ceiling fan.

~*~

The elevator brought the first guests promptly at 6:00 p.m. — Nina and Doc Emmett. Nina bubbled over the lavish floral decorations and bustled from one plant to another. She tenderly caressed an orange and purple Bird of Paradise and moved on to inhale the pungent scent of an ivory-colored orchid with vibrant yellow at its center, a *Chysis bractescens Lindl,* according to Nina. Personally, I wouldn't know, but Nina was a botanical aficionado.

She was the perfect Spanish-Caucasian mix. Her chestnut brown shoulder-length hair was silky and sleek and her dark eyes intense with perfectly shaped brows — no need to wax or tweeze. Nina's ivory cocktail dress complimented her velvety complexion, the color of coffee with extra cream.

"Your florist has outdone herself!" Nina exclaimed.

"Nina, you know you have a blueprint in that little Prada handbag of yours showing where each and every pot was to have been placed. *You're* the one who did it and I thank you so much for that."

"No, really, it was nothing. Besides, spending someone else's money is such fun. So thank *you* for the generous floral budget. Oh Doc, would you look at these huge elephant ear palms? I've never seen them so large!"

"Yes, they're elegant!" Doc stood proudly by his wife's side.

"Julia, what are you going to do with these beauties? Keep them?" Nina asked.

I've had no success with indoor plants. I never remembered which needed misting and which ones didn't tolerate it. But I couldn't blame Nina for falling in love with them — she simply touches a green plant and it flourishes forever. "I'd planned to donate most of them," I said. "You want some?"

Nina's eyes brightened. "The kids would love these elephant ears in Doc's waiting room."

"Consider it done. I'll send some of them down to the second floor tomorrow. Oh, and Nina, check out the bath. It's overdone to a fault." I paused for effect. "And I wouldn't have it any other way."

Nina and I made our way toward the bathing lounge. Her enthusiasm assured me that I'd worried unnecessarily over the party décor; Nina was right on task with positive feedback. I felt myself relax, and until that moment had been unaware of holding my breath.

"That's it," said Doc, watching over me as usual. "Just breathe, Julia, in and out. You look marvelous tonight, so pretty in pink." He gazed downward. "Lovely shoes."

Nina had told me all about Doc's foot fetish. Any man in his late sixties who still finds enjoyment over a woman's nicely pedicured toes in a strappy pair of heels is my kind of man. Most ladies know one thing for sure: A redneck ogles cleavage — the classy fellow gazes discreetly at a lady's feet.

In the grand living room, a quartet from the San Antonio Orchestra had positioned itself beside the piano. Doc offered his arm and we walked across the room to watch. The white baby-grand was encircled by potted banana, orange and palm trees, with small strings of twinkling lights intertwined around the fronds. The musicians tuned their instruments and introduced a pulsating interpretation of echoes from distant islands.

Open House was my way of thanking my clients. Many of my regulars had expressed a desire to tour the condo once it was finished. It had taken me so long to get everything the way I wanted it, and that night was *the* night. I hoped to be rewarded with some new assignments, which would be good for my part-time employee, Britt Waterman, a 23-year-old grad student. Each employee was an invited guest, but Britt wanted to tend the bar, as well. He had a double major going on, chemistry and business, and he was eager to mingle with the business community and earn extra money at the same time. I admired his enthusiasm. He was such an ambitious young man, though not unattractively so, and I wondered if he and Andie had been spending a little more time together than usual. Of course, it could've been my overactive imagination, or even wishful thinking.

The elevator signaled Andie's return from the babysitter, and all heads turned. Her tight-fitting Calvin Klein jeans sported side-slits at the bottom edges, revealing black sandals decorated with leather fringe. A white, Western-style blouse was topped off with a cherry blazer, and her hair was held back in one long braid, allowing her slinky earrings to dangle freely. She wore silver neck chains in assorted lengths and an intricate turquoise cuff bracelet. (I bought it for myself last week, noticing only yesterday that it had apparently walked off.) Andie stepped off the elevator, so refined and sophisticated. She smiled coyly, as though she had rehearsed her entrance and was rewarded with precisely the reaction she'd anticipated.

With each new arrival, Andie and I alternated giving tours of the professional office environment, and I handed out brochures to newcomers detailing our business capabilities, including the actual design of the brochure. The route originated in the sizable lobby, which doubled as the conference room, then down the hallway to the six massage rooms-turned-offices, and ended in the bathing lounge where the real party was going on.

My client base was located primarily within one square mile of the Riverwalk, and I used the services of several of them that night. Riverwalk Land-S-Cape transformed the bathing lounge into a rain forest. The tub was filled with aqua-tinted water; lily pads and various water-plants skimmed its surface. White orchids rested on the outer edges, interlaced in vines of miniature ivy. A sculpted fountain of smooth rocks, courtesy of Monte Wade Art Gallery in La Villita, dispatched small streams that trickled down into the tub, generating an ever-so-slight movement — the lily pads floated effortlessly. A steam machine, secreted away behind a troupe of greenery, emitted just enough vapor to create a haze. Muzic-Walk provided jungle sounds — birds, breezes and ocean waves — to complete the effect. Enchanted party-goers, tropical drinks in hand, soaked up the ambiance. The bathroom closely rivaled the size of the grand living room, and it was magnificent.

The corridor kitchen was off limits to the tour because Dana and her staff were moving at the speed of light. The cucumber Lassi was going to be a hit, I just knew it. I'd taste-tested it a few days before. "That's a big ten-four on the cucumber," I'd told my cousin. Each person was served a small sample of it when they arrived, and I figured it would be a favorite in Dana's restaurant from now on. A cold cucumber drink on a hot day was hard to beat, and San Antonio had more than its share of heat.

Dana laughed when asked for the recipe. "Wait for the cookbook," she exclaimed. She scribbled names and e-mail addresses on a spiral notebook, taking advance orders for her forthcoming work. Her publisher promised it would be on bookshelves everywhere by the end of June. The florist (of *course* I invited my florist) asked Dana how on earth she accomplished so much in a 24-hour day. "Well, honey, first off, I finally memorized the spelling of *hors d'oeuvres;* that was the hard part. Imagine trying to invoice a customer and having to look it up every time. So, that right there was a big time saver!"

Dana has a squared jaw line and straight hair with bangs. This week, her hair was the shade of Hershey dark. Frederick designed her style, cut short right below her ear lobes, as a picture frame to capture Dana's signature mischievous grin and dazzling violet eyes. Ebony nail polish and dark russet lipstick accentuated her Goth look.

A willowy woman with red hair down to her thighs was overheard saying how she just *loved* Dana's hair, *Daahling*. Frederick appeared, took full credit and quickly offered his calling card. The redhead gazed dreamily at him, wedged the card into her bosom and promised to call tomorrow for an appointment. She pronounced it all Texan-like, *ta-mar-ra*. I recognized the lady's voice from somewhere. She seemed like she'd be a fun person to hang with and I made a mental note to get acquainted.

The conversations ranged from cholesterol levels — good and bad — to cell phone preferences, to investments. It's interesting that even though my clients had their chance to escape the world of business that night, business was the main topic of conversation for nearly everyone.

Doc stood, alone, behind the piano. I made my way over to join him.

"Julia, these musicians are excellent."

"They are, aren't they? I'm lucky they were available."

Dana laid a plate, piled high with goodies, on the piano bench. What was she up to now? Had she taken on the task of single-handedly supplying the entire ensemble with food, or just the pianist?

"That's my special snack offering you're nibbling on," Dana told the pianist, with a sly wink. When she noticed me and Doc, she winked at us, too.

I smirked and rolled my eyes. "Dana's keeping the piano man happy," I whispered to Doc.

Doc leaned toward me. "And have you noticed he can't take his eyes off her?"

"He's a musician. They have a built-in homing device."

Doc chuckled. "Evidently," he said. "How do you like the Lassi?"

"It's good, isn't it? I overheard someone telling Britt to add a touch of vodka, though, so guzzle it at your own risk."

Doc finished off his drink and smacked his lips. "No, mine doesn't seem to have been contaminated, although I never could actually taste vodka in a cocktail." A waiter passed by with a beverage tray to collect Doc's empty glass.

"Another, sir?"

Doc looked at me and squinted. "Ah . . . better not, thank you."

"Don't worry," I said. "I doubt Britt would spike a drink in secret . . . unless he wants to lose his job."

"No, surely not." Doc laughed. "But, he *is* studying chemistry, so it could be an experiment." He looked back toward the elevator. "By the way, I haven't noticed a Doctor Wells yet, have you?"

"What? Oh . . . no, I haven't. He must have had a change of plans. No worries. If Mr. British and Charming shows up, I'll be sure to introduce him to you properly." I grinned and patted his arm and a comfortable silence ensued. Doc appraised the grand room, and I assumed that, rather than hearing snippets of dialogue going on at that moment, portions of conversations past — ones that took place in this, the old smoking lounge of the club, were running through Doc's mind. Was he remembering the very first massage he got here? He'd told me my office was used for couples, although since it was a male-only club it wouldn't have been what we think of as a romantic couples massage. More like two businessmen taking respite and conducting business at the same time. Somewhat like playing golf — business is won and lost on the golf course. Perhaps some were won and lost in that very same massage room. I always felt refreshed when I walked into my office, closed the door and sat at my desk. I thought of it as constructive energy left over from the past.

I closed my eyes to bask in this moment. I'd actually pulled it off — my grand living room was full of people in high spirits, enjoying my carefully selected cuisine, and all I had to do was stand back and take pleasure in my success. *Wouldn't Richard be proud of me?*

In the far corner, a handsome chiropractor explained the benefits of regular chiropractic care to two of Doc's "girls" from his office staff. If I heard correctly, he told them he uses the missionary position on his new patients, but surely he didn't actually say that. *They'll be getting their bones cracked next week.* I frowned, thankful I hadn't said *that* out loud. I examined my empty glass, suspecting it may have contained a touch of alcohol, after all.

Britt received compliments on his bartending skills while lawyers and other politically inclined persons huddled close to the bar, discussing last November's election. Britt was in the thick of it all.

Each time the elevator opened, everyone glanced to get a look at the new arrival. If the newcomer wasn't easily recognizable by anyone else, I made them welcome right away, then handed them off to Andie or Nina. I'd put them in charge of "breaking the ice," as Doc called it.

In Doc's day, uniform-wearing elevator operators broke the ice. They drew everyone together in most of the old buildings downtown. The passengers routinely spoke to one another no matter how small the lift was. Nowadays, people stand rigid, stare straight ahead — heaven forbid if the walls are lined with mirrors — one might have to actually make eye contact with another! I've heard plenty of stories about Alonzo Menendez. Ah, the old days — just ask Doc. Alonzo knew your floor number by heart, and you knew his name and all about his wife and kids. "Those were the good old days," Doc had said.

By 8:30, I'd forgotten about Marten Wells. Doc gave up on the man and wandered off for a Lassi refill. I chatted with Elise, the woman with the long red hair. It was her voice that had made her seem familiar to me. We'd spoken on the phone: *My pleasure, my pleasure,* Elise had repeated each time I said *thank you,* although it sounded more like *Ma playzure* when Elise said it. She was the new receptionist at River Protocol, Inc., a specialty business that planned and organized social functions on the Riverwalk. I had full charge of their accounting and had made bank deposits for several events that would accompany Lady Sophia's public appearances. No doubt Elise wasn't privy to that information yet, so I steered our conversation far away from the subject.

The elevator launched, summoned from the sixth floor down to the lobby. I prepared to greet its occupant. A minute went by, then two. I wondered why the delay. Finally, the familiar whirring and the ding of the bell. I glanced at the ornate doors as they opened to reveal an attractive man with jet-black hair and eyes to match; impeccably dressed, he was a package of European grace and elegance. My glance turned into a stare, and my heart raced. All conversation came to an abrupt halt; everyone seemed to have a sixth sense about this moment. It was monumental, indeed.

I blinked. Could this be? The mysterious man from last night was standing in my elevator! The phrase "Be careful what you wish for" suddenly took on new meaning.

Marten Wells, British and charming, and, according to Doc, *available*, made his entrance.

Chapter Eleven

Marten's Entrance

Thankful for the flute of champagne in my hand, I took a healthy swig. Eight words tumbled out of my mouth before it went completely dry: "Good evening. I'm Julia Tyler . . . and you are?"

"Dr. Marten Wells." He grinned a rather lopsided, Indiana Jones kind of smirk, and he grasped my extended hand with both of his. Soft and manicured, I noticed, like those of a surgeon, or could he be an anesthesiologist? The man continued. "I spoke to a Dr. Russell Emmett regarding a business service such as yours. He suggested I attend your gathering tonight. I do hope you don't mind." He spoke as though he selected each word from a smorgasbord, meticulously, with precision, certainly not in any hurry whatsoever.

"Mind? Oh, no. I was expecting you, in fact." I took a deep breath and pushed my shoulders back in an attempt to appear composed. "Allow me to show you around. Shall we visit the buffet first?" I prayed my knees wouldn't buckle on the way toward the kitchen bar.

It appeared he might have skipped lunch, as I had. He heaped a mountain of shrimp onto a plate. Without apology, he turned to me, his lips forming the most amazing, boyish smile I'd ever seen on a grown man, well maybe with the exception of Harrison Ford, of course. *If he'd smiled at me like that last night, I would've done just like Frederick said, "pinched his ass as he passed, at least."* His dark eyes were enchanting, and when they locked with mine, I felt as though I'd known him forever. Was he a character straight out of Andie's romance novel? *Should I say "Aren't you the guy I was drooling over last night?" Should I mention last night at all?*

Dana stood, waiting, her hands on her hips and a question mark in her eyes, watching us parade toward her.

I offered an introduction. "Dana Cavanaugh, owner of The Stock Market down on the river, meet Dr. Marten Wells — from London, correct?"

"Ah, yes . . . London. But please, just call me Marten. Actually, I've been in the States for several months now." He took a step back and cocked his head. "So *you're* Dana Cavanaugh! You own The Stock Market? I've dined there often, here of late." He dipped into the cocktail sauce. "Also, I plan to purchase your cookbook, once it's available." Another shrimp. "What have you marinated these in, bourbon?"

"Right on," Dana said, "and the sauce is my secret recipe." (She buys the cheapest stuff she can find, adds raw horseradish and a touch of organic cane sugar.) "I'm selling advance copies of the cookbook tonight at a discount, if you're interested."

"Then I just got lucky, now didn't I? It's such a pleasure to meet you." His lips began to form that lopsided smile but, as though on second thought, he added, "My work brings me here. I'm opening a health clinic in San Antonio and I've immensely enjoyed making Texas my home."

I recalled a bumper sticker: I WASN'T BORN IN TEXAS BUT I GOT HERE AS FAST AS I COULD. I'd proudly stuck that clever statement on my BMW right after we moved here, shortly before Andie was born. Richard was furious and demanded I remove it, but I was too pregnant to mess with it, so he spent an hour scraping my bumper. I wondered if "Just-call-me-Marten" had one on his vehicle. Probably not. I pictured him in a small European coupé with a funny-looking license plate on the front. If he had a rear bumper sticker at all, it would be a circle decal with a solitary letter. I'd never understood what those letters meant.

"Your accent is marvelous," Dana was saying. "You'll unquestionably add a touch of class to this city. Is your family with you?" Oh my God! She was actually *gawking* at his left hand.

The boyish smile reappeared, slowly — pleasure, that's what it was — he was comfortable in his own skin. I wished I could be more that way.

Marten leaned in toward Dana, one elbow on the kitchen bar. "I'm a bachelor, age thirty-four, 5'11", right-handed. I play the piano, attend concerts of all kinds, and especially enjoy dining alfresco — waterside, if possible. Those are my stats, and yours?" He knocked back another shrimp as he observed Dana's reaction with amusement. He hadn't missed her checking out his marital status. Dana was so busted she was blushing. That didn't happen often.

I took note of the fact that, while he was a younger man, five years didn't seem scandalous. I felt as though I was in a bar, watching Dana reel in yet another romance victim. Whether I was rescuing Dana, Marten Wells, or maybe myself, I wasn't sure, but I didn't like being the fifth wheel at my own party, so I handed the gentleman a brochure. "Let's get your tour underway, what do you say?"

I beckoned him around the corner into the reception area. "The condo here on the sixth floor has a fascinating history. Originally a health club, its membership was male only, with the majority of its associates being downtown businessmen seeking a place to relax and smoke in the middle or at the end of their hectic day. These rooms were quite elaborately decorated at that time with plush carpet, flocked wallpaper and soft leather club chairs and sofas. This space has been used since then for various restaurants and, at one time, a banquet hall, but eventually legal complications from someone's estate got it all tied up and it sat empty in foreclosure. I bought it four years ago and moved my business here."

"Just-call-me-Marten" stroked the ornate woodwork and remarked about the floor, how rich and warm it looked. He said it reminded him of old structures in London, and in Wales, where he grew up. He asked about the six little rooms down the hallway.

"They're our work cubicles. These have the original brass numbers on the doors, back from when the rooms were used for massages. Each room has its own computer but we're all networked. We use a color coding system for confidentiality purposes. In other words, each client is known by a code in the file, not a name. It's a security measure to prevent computer geeks from hacking in. Even if they were to get in, they wouldn't know anything. It's a highly protected structure, and of course I keep separate back-ups off-location in case of fire or theft."

I watched to see, and, yes, he did a double-take when he saw the yellow rose in the crystal vase on my desk, but would he guess it was his?

Texas was famous for its yellow rose, after all. In retrospect, if I'd imagined the guy from last night would be standing here in my office . . . well, I wished I'd stored the flower in the laundry room.

"It seems you've thought of everything," Marten said. "I'm impressed!"

I humbly shook my head. "I had tons of legal advice, and my clients participate by telling me exactly what they want out of my service. I create basically around the needs of each individual, making it rather unique, customized."

"It must have been a large start-up investment for you," Marten said.

Well now, that wasn't any of his business, but perhaps he was simply making conversation.

"I wasn't even the least bit concerned about the profit margin," I said, "which would make many a financial analyst cringe, but I knew if I did it right it would all come together. I'm proud of it, and it is a family business. My daughter, Andie, works with me, along with a few employees who are like family. I feel strongly that if you want to run a business you should do it right, from the very beginning."

Marten listened intently. "I have a confession to make," he said. "Dr. Emmett assured me that you are a conscientious businesswoman, and it's true that I am looking for a personalized service such as yours. I'd prefer to discuss it with you further at a later date, though, because I don't want to keep you from your other guests."

What kind of a confession was that? I wondered. But he'd only just begun. He took a step closer. "Please forgive my aggressiveness, but I noticed you last night at the restaurant, and I kicked myself later for not saying something to you, but I hadn't wanted to appear forward. I walked up and down the Riverwalk hoping to see you again."

I nodded but said nothing. My mouth had gone dry again.

"So," Marten continued, "you can imagine both my surprise and my delight to see you here. I realize this is terribly inappropriate, but I find I cannot stop myself from saying it. I was thinking only that, if you make it a rule not to date your clients, I might have to take my business elsewhere."

Oh. And there was that smile again. Damn! Did this man just undress me with his eyes? His intensity nearly panicked me. He was supposed to be merely a fantasy. I wasn't prepared for reality.

I lavishly waved one hand in the air, as if to blow it off. "I haven't seen anything lately about that subject in the employee manual, but I *would* highly value having your business, Dr. Wells."

"Marten," he interjected.

"Yes, okay. Marten, then. Suppose we make an appointment for later in the week, any time that's acceptable with you?"

He does remember me from last night! I told myself to act unruffled. I could pretend he never said the four-letter D word, D-A-T-E, and wouldn't acknowledge that I'd ever seen him before, but if he was into face reading, he'd just read my first chapter and maybe half of the second one.

We made a tentative appointment for Friday afternoon. Without delay, I guided him down the hallway toward the bathing lounge where several others mingled in the sultry mist with their Rum Runners and Pina Coladas. Andie, in contrast, was drinking a Cosmopolitan, which she boisterously proclaimed was made especially for her by Britt Waterman. Heavy on the vodka.

I introduced Andie to Marten and, rather than shaking his hand, Andie toasted him with her drink. She didn't seem to notice Marten did not have a drink in his hand.

"So, have you been to Julia's bedroom yet?" Andie asked.

I sharply inhaled and shot my daughter an anguished look. When Marten answered "No, I haven't, but I'd like to see it," I thought I heard someone, concealed by the haze in the opposite corner of the room, say "We'd *all* like to see Julia's bedroom."

Once again, I felt like I was in a bar. This wasn't exactly following my party's theme.

Marten turned to me. "Your bedroom . . . you live here as well?" he inquired. "Julia? Ms. Tyler?"

Marten's face was inches from mine, and I brought my thoughts back to reality. I took a step back. "Oh, well, yes. I live here with my family. Our bedrooms were part of the club at one time, overnight quarters for traveling dignitaries. Anyone can see them, including you; they're on the corridor on the opposite side. Follow me . . . I'll show you."

On our way to the private living quarters, Marten ordered a Bloody Mary from Britt at the bar. I thought back to my early-morning bath where I imagined he would do just that. I wondered if I'd suddenly become psychic.

"I'm afraid if my sleeping quarters were on a public tour," Marten said, "it would take a week or two to prepare. As a matter of fact, I currently don't even have a room to call my own, just a suite at the Hilton, which the housekeeper takes care of — lucky me."

"Ah, well, don't forget, I've been working on this place for nearly four years," I said. "And my bedroom is notorious for two reasons: the first of which is that, supposedly, some serious gambling took place in it at one time, although I can't imagine why anyone cares; it's not like they practiced slave-trading or something more horrible."

"People live vicariously through the rich. They imagine themselves there and it gives them a thrill of some sort." Marten explained as though he knew from personal experience. "What's the second reason?"

"The second? Oh, yes . . . well, it may have been overdramatic to describe it as notorious, but I've done up the room like a jungle. You'll see . . . take a peek into it."

Bamboo covered the walls and ceilings. Green and black rugs, embedded with bamboo designs, blanketed the hardwood floor. The furniture consisted of a tasteful mix of cane and rattan. A boatload of silk palm trees surrounded the king-sized bed, which was canopied with mosquito netting.

I offered an explanation, "My mother was an interior designer; she would either cringe or be proud, I don't know which."

"I think it's fabulous," Marten said. "It looks like a luscious tropical forest."

"Tropical forest . . . I like that description. It's my answer to living downtown in a concrete world, except for the river, of course. It's my own little private garden."

Marten nodded agreement as he took in every last detail. "It's lovely. And the crocheted hammock over there in that little alcove says it all."

"Thanks. Boone, my grandson, loves it, too. He called dibs on the hammock early on. He occasionally watches television cocooned in it.

Now and then, I awaken to find he's fallen asleep and spent the entire night."

I immediately realized Marten Wells surely must have thought I had no social life at all, outside of my family. Well . . . it was true. For some reason I'd thought he needed to know. But, if my being a grandmother bothered him, too bad.

"Julia?" Doc stood at the far end of the hallway.

"Yes. Doc, I'm coming." I headed toward him with Marten in tow. "Here's that charming gentleman you wanted to meet. Dr. Marten Wells . . . Dr. Russell Emmett. I believe you've already spoken on the phone."

The two men embarked upon a discussion about the upcoming health clinic and the benefits it would bring to the inner city. Doc was always interested in new business ventures, especially those involving the health of children. He had been my biggest cheerleader when I started my business after Richard died. He'd alerted me to the availability of the condo when it went on the market. He walked me through the paperwork and financials, and signed up as my first client in the building. He referred to The Clifford as being "up in the sky", because it was one of the tallest buildings downtown when it was built. But that was over a half century ago. Now, San Antonio has them just as tall as any other large city, but The Clifford Building is the one with history.

I eased away from the two doctors, got a champagne refill and went back into the bathing lounge. Wasn't it fantastic to see so many happy people in here? *I throw parties in my bathroom!* Not a bad idea, I thought. I wondered if there might be a way I could further capitalize on the ambiance. I had an idea that people might actually pay good money to privately bathe in this lounge. I'd tell Andie about it later.

I recalled the day an overzealous realtor showed me the dusty old place. He'd insisted someone else was about to make an offer, so I'd better move fast. I knew it was a hustle technique, but I loved the bathing lounge so much I bought it on the spot. Black and white art deco porcelain bathroom fixtures blended with the white ceramic floor. I admired the floor insets (black, diamond-shaped tiles) and the sleek and shiny brass faucets — accoutrements that could never be duplicated in today's market. What a perfect place to live, and to work, I thought. I couldn't imagine ever regretting my decision to relocate here.

~*~

By midnight, all of the guests had filtered out, and the elevator made its final run with the remainder of Dana's wait staff aboard. The whirring stopped and the sound of nothingness filled the air.

Britt assisted Andie as she tottered into her bedroom and he quietly closed the door. The click of the lock echoed through the great room when it fit into place. *Well, what do you know?* I'd figured it would happen eventually. Boone was to spend the night at the babysitter's.

I took a deep breath, pleased that my responsibilities for the day were over. Dana was boxing up leftovers and I shuffled into the kitchen to offer assistance. She wouldn't hear of it, though, and ordered me to go away and relax somewhere else. "By the way," Dana said, "what kind of medicine does that Marten guy practice? Gynecology, I hope."

"Forget about it," I said. "I overheard him tell someone that his degree is a Ph.D. and not a medical doctorate."

Dana's face fell. "Oh, rats! And here I'd envisioned him in a white medical jacket."

"Stiffly starched," I added.

"With his name embroidered on the pocket in navy blue thread."

"Umm . . . a stethoscope hanging around his neck." I grabbed one last shrimp before skipping down the hallway toward the bathing lounge. The tub was drained of its aqua water and lily pads, with only the ivy and orchids lying on the edges. I refilled it, added a drop of perfumed oil and turned the jets to low speed. I allowed my layered-look pink outfit to fall onto the floor, slipped out of my crimson shoes and stepped cautiously down into the water. I rested my head back against the cool marble ledge and positioned my feet precisely up against the jets of warm water, kneading my extremely sore arches.

My day ended exactly like it began. *If only I could live in this tub.*

Chapter Twelve

The Spy

His Grace, Ludwig Wellson Vanderhawk, Duke of Stratford was a wealthy man with interests spread over scores of endeavors, the most well-known being his talent for breeding superior thoroughbreds. His enterprise had sent second and third generation mounts to America, capturing the winner's circle at races such as The Kentucky Derby and the Breeder's Cup at Santa Anita Park. The Royal Family stabled their thoroughbreds on the Vanderhawk Estate.

Perry Roberts had spent his early childhood with his deaf parents on a thoroughbred horse farm in Lancashire. Lady Luck beckoned at 13, when his older sister Adelina, at that time a maid for the Vanderhawk family of Stratford, referred her brother. He was hired as a stable boy and quickly became a member of the stable staff where he looked after the racehorses and exercised them every day. He worked closely with the trainer who ran the business of the racing yard. Duke Vanderhawk found it advantageous to send him to the British Racing School for advanced jockey training, all the while keeping a close eye on his progress.

At 18, Roberts became a household name as *the* jockey to watch after he created a stir at The Kentucky Oaks. Leaving the gate as the long shot at 50-1, hugging the inside rail, he burst forth with only two lengths to go and crossed the finish line first by a neck. Two years later, he was the winning jockey on one of Queen Elizabeth's fillies at Newmarket and from then on was a celebrity among horse people worldwide.

A two-year-old filly, Bella's Whistle, had been presented to Sophia Louise Vanderhawk, the Duke's only daughter, on her 10th birthday.

Roberts victoriously crossed the finish line on Bella's Whistle the following year at The Epsom Oaks. The Duke and Duchess were charmed by Roberts and they hired him as their exclusive jockey.

Outside of racing season, he spent most of his days in the stable, chumming up to the horses and gathering secrets. Roberts would arrive before dawn and slither up high into the loft rafters. As others arrived, he watched and listened. Conversations carried upward, and the information he obtained often proved invaluable to his employer.

Since the curious death of her younger brother Basil when she was six, Sophia Vanderhawk hadn't much noticeable interest in anything — until Bella's Whistle came along. As a teenager, she developed a habit of riding daily. It was no secret how thrilled the Duchess was that her daughter shared her love of the equine. Roberts didn't have the heart, nor was it his place, to inform his employers that it wasn't only the love of a horse that brought their coquettish offspring into the barn each day. The stables were brimming with sturdy young boys who were happy to practice in empty stalls whatever techniques the rich girl requested. More than once, Roberts saw her seductively lure a groom into a stall, with no one but Roberts the wiser. After all, he had the ringside seat. He kept a log of the dates and the young men involved, but he never shared those valuable morsels of data with Vanderhawk. He waited for a day when it would be most profitable to reveal them.

There were times in racing when he'd honestly considered himself lucky to cross the finish line first; one morning in the barn took the prize as the *luckiest day* of his decade. While it had nothing to do with horse racing, he most definitely crossed a line, but not the *finish* line. More like the starting gate, Roberts figured later. Sophia had crept into the stable just before daybreak, checking each nook and cranny to guarantee no one else was there. She located herself in an empty stall, pulled out a leather-bound journal and started writing in it. While this in itself was nothing new — she routinely chose the barn for solitude as she wrote — that day proved to be a pivotal one for Roberts.

Teenage girls and their diaries, Perry Roberts thought at first, and he placed his attention elsewhere. However, he took notice both times she stood up to look around, making sure, once again, of her privacy. His curiosity was piqued; what could be so secret that she didn't just jot stuff down in her bedroom like his sister used to do? His first thought was that she'd got herself knocked up. He wondered who'd fathered it? Hard telling — there had been a few contenders lately.

Through the loft window, Roberts caught sight of Duke Vanderhawk's farm truck heading across the field from their manor house. The Duke stepped out of his vehicle, shut the door and called his daughter's name. Sophia visibly flinched and threw her journal onto the floor of the stall, covering it quickly with straw. She ran to the door, telling her father she'd wanted to visit with Bella's Whistle for a while. He insisted she ride immediately back to the manor house with him for breakfast.

Roberts acted as soon as they left. He jumped directly from the loft into the stall and sifted through the hay. He put the journal in his locker, planning to read it when he had more time. Some of the staff had arrived and they'd already set fire to a heap of refuse outside. They would soon come into the barn.

Later that morning, Sophia's maid showed up to retrieve the diary, but, of course, it was nowhere to be found. The servant was agitated with her inability to meet Lady Sophia's demands. "I'm going to be sacked; I just know it!" Roberts put his arm around her in a comforting gesture. "My lovely, what is causing your distress? May I be of assistance?" She crumbled in the jockey's arms, and, through copious tears, she confessed Lady Sophia's fear: Had someone read it?

Roberts promised to do all he could to locate and return it unscathed. "Explain to milady the stalls were already shoveled out and piled onto that heap of rubbish outside that's burning now. I'll get the boys started on rummaging through, just in case." He took the girl outside and called to the men, instructing them to search and do whatever it took to find it. She carefully described it so they would know what they were looking for — something they would never find — but so what?

Roberts suspected the journal contained information he could use. *What a coup*, he thought. He returned to the barn and slipped the journal into his jacket, then he drove into town; it was too risky to use the copy machine in the Racing Secretary's office.

He'd skimmed each page until he reached an entry about poor little Basil. Roberts' sister Adelina had been promoted from maid to nanny when Sophia was born; she'd been nanny for both children when Basil died. No logical explanation had ever been given as to the actual cause of the toddler's death, but suspicion was cast on the nanny who'd insisted he was alive and well at bedtime. She found him dead in his crib the next morning, and on that day her career in British service came to an abrupt halt. Duke Vanderhawk moved Adelina and her son, Marten, age four, to an obscure location, taking extreme measures to keep them out of the public eye.

When Basil died, little Sophia was repeatedly questioned by the authorities. Her story never wavered. She'd insisted she saw Marten push the toddler down a flight of stairs. Her journal entry on *this* day, however, *if it were true*, would be a game-changer. On that very day, Roberts' rage took root and he vowed revenge for his sister's disgrace.

After copying the entire book, Roberts returned to the stable and went about inspecting the smoldering fire pit. Certain no one was looking, he dropped the journal at one edge, made one loop around, and came back to find it in exactly the condition he'd hoped for. Singed edges, pages curled and darkened, but not destroyed. He sent a message to the maid. When he presented it to her, she was so relieved that she broke down in tears once again. Roberts assured her that one of the stable boys had found it earlier but he had been too busy to notify her until now. He knew Sophia would be skeptical, but there was nothing she could do about it.

When Lady Sophia came into her own wealth at 18, Roberts blackmailed her by showing her his records of her trysts, the dates and young men involved. He had no photos, but claimed he did. Sophia gave in, supplementing his income with cash payments, suspecting he knew more about her than he claimed to have seen or heard.

For a while, life had been more than comfortable for Roberts until Sophia turned the tables on him. The rumors she cleverly leaked caused him to forfeit his career and the grand reputation that had gone along with it. Rumors, mind you! She had no proof of anything; nothing but her word against his. Nobility vs. a horse jockey — a previous hired hand. He couldn't blame her, but he hadn't figured her for being so slick.

He reached out to his sister, who insisted he come to Wales and stay with her and Marten for a while. During that time, a plastic surgeon readjusted Roberts' nose, producing the beak-shaped tip of which Roberts was so proud. In further efforts to become unrecognizable, he listened to foreign language tapes, picking up accents, slang, and nuances of speaking in diverse ways. Before long, his British accent disappeared. He left his beloved homeland and traveled the world, attempting to escape his past. He'd spent years scheming revenge. This game was fun . . . he had the next move.

~*~

Duke Vanderhawk, though respected as a gentleman and successful businessman, had a reputation as a womanizer. His wife turned her head and ignored all signs of his wanderings. After all, some of her friends in high places had husbands just like him, even getting housemaids pregnant. The Duchess felt superior in that her husband had not bothered with any of their staff. At least he had higher ethics than the others, she'd thought. The fact that the Duke had impregnated Adelina shortly after Sophia's birth was known only to Adelina and to the Duke. The house servants surmised her pregnancy was caused by rape, perhaps by a houseguest, a passing aristocrat, or even a commoner from the local tavern on one of Adelina's nights off. Several of them eventually suspected the Duke because of the excessive amount of time he spent with the baby boy. One of them spread a juicy gossip tidbit within moments after she overheard him call Marten "son." They nodded among themselves but never talked about it openly for fear of losing their jobs. Two of the housemaids smugly thought, "There but for the grace of God, go I."

Even Roberts did not realize that Vanderhawk had fathered Marten until he stayed with Adelina in Wales after being ordered to leave the Vanderhawk estate. His sister called it a mutual love affair, but Roberts put the blame on the Duke, a man of nobility who should have known better. Roberts had shared several man-to-man chats with Vanderhawk, who'd made it clear that he desired many sons to carry on the family name. Yet, up until that time, the Duchess had produced only one child — a daughter, Sophia. Adelina had described how Vanderhawk recklessly showed a preference for little Marten over Sophia, but when Basil came along, the man seemed to ignore both Marten and his daughter. Roberts figured that lack of attention caused Sophia to be promiscuous as a teenager. What a tangled mess at the manor house!

~*~

Perry Roberts, at the helm of the telescope, observed Marten Wells sauntering beside the river, his shoulders sagging and the soles of his shoes clinging to the sidewalk. Something was nagging at him, sure enough. The Riverwalk, well-lit at night, made him easy to spot. Roberts was eager for a play-by-play of the party, but there was his nephew, lollygagging, as though he had things of monumental importance to sort out. Roberts' worst fear was that his cover may have been blown somehow. But, no, it was probably something utterly ridiculous, perhaps Marten's conscience, which seemed to get in the way more often than not.

Planning versus the unfolding of the event were poles apart. Yes, the close proximity of reality, Roberts guessed, was probably the culprit. He could tell Marten a thing or two about reality, if Marten ever cared to listen, which he usually didn't. But he knew his nephew well; Marten would be strong and rise above it. They had been planning this job together for a very long time. Nothing must go wrong. No — nothing *would* go wrong. Marten owed it to his mother, after all. And Roberts owed it to himself, not to mention the woman who triggered the entire predicament. *That bitch*, Roberts thought. *She's had it coming for a long time. Time's up, Sophia.*

~*~

Marten entered the darkened penthouse suite and removed an orange diskette, labeled A-12, from the room safe. He inserted it into the computer, just as Roberts expected. Roberts sat in the corner, motionless. The files on A-12 were schematics and blueprints from the original Clifford Building's design. Another file contained Julia's client list. Leonardo Newman had obtained them and the information was used to determine if the Clifford Building would be of use in their plan to abduct the Duke's grandson. The client list indicated that Riverwalk Protocol, Inc. was in charge of Lady Sophia's detailed schedule while in San Antonio. Marten recalled Julia's boast about the security of her clientele, how it was color coded and hack-proof. He now felt more respect for Leonardo Newman's network of covert agents and their skill in obtaining that list. Must have cost extra, but well worth it.

Marten mumbled to himself. "Hmm . . . the blueprints are outdated somewhat, but then who doesn't do remodeling on old buildings? Yet, she's made no major changes to the sixth floor since the days of the health club." He chuckled. "She must be a sentimentalist, keeping the old brass numbers on those doors." He switched on the desk lamp, removed a small digital camera from his pocket and popped its memory chip into the computer. He reclined slightly and chewed on a toothpick as he downloaded the photos he'd taken.

Perry Roberts chose that precise moment to jiggle the ice cubes in his glass.

Marten nearly fell backward out of his chair. "Damn you! What's wrong with you, the way you spy on people?"

"I'm testing your powers of observation." He shook his head. "You get an F."

Marten glared at Roberts, sitting cubby-holed in the dark with a smirk on his face. "I've got an F for you, too."

Roberts snorted. "And what have we discovered at our party?"

Marten took a labored breath and opened his mouth as if to protest further, but appeared to think better of it. He let an entire minute pass before he replied. "It went as planned," he said flatly. "I set up the trackers in the elevator and lobby. The wiring and telephone systems I will investigate once I've spent more time with her."

He didn't seem nearly as excited about that prospect as he had before, Roberts noted, detecting a rather distressed look on Marten's face. *He's turning to mush, the little sissy.* "Buck up, buddy. You'll get to where you dig using people, once you've tried it. Spending time with the Tyler woman *is* a major part of the plan, you know."

Marten studied Roberts' face like he would a jig-saw puzzle. "What? Now you're a mind reader, too? Stick to the spy trade, you and your beady bird eyes." He tossed his toothpick into a waste bin.

Roberts sanctimoniously waved both hands in the air. "Sorry."

The photos downloaded, Marten set them up in a slide-show fashion on the monitor. Roberts stood behind his nephew, intrigued with the screen's display. "So . . . fill me in . . . what's she like?"

"How about I do that tomorrow, chum? I have a headache and you're drunk."

"You've always got a headache," Roberts snipped.

"And . . . you are always drunk."

"Careful, the people in the next room will think we're married." Roberts exaggerated a stagger toward his room. He'd waited up for this?

The door closed, but didn't latch, leaving a crack through which Roberts watched Marten as he studied old blueprints, comparing them with digital photos he'd taken in the elevator.

That's a good lad, Roberts thought. You get that elevator password from the Tyler woman. And anything else, while you're at it. Women deserve to be used — they are our greatest teachers.

Chapter Thirteen

Marten's Musings

Marten Wells gathered his briefcase and went for his suite down the hall. He propped three pillows against the padded headboard and reclined on his bed, reviewing the evening's events. The party had been a success, at least for him, and probably for Ms. Tyler, as well.

After the gate opened, Marten had confidently stepped off Julia Tyler's elevator. There she stood, right in front of him, appearing more shocked than he'd anticipated. For one fleeting second, he wanted to turn around, ride back down to the lobby, return to the Hilton and fly back to England. He'd wavered to think he must deceive *this woman*. A voice in his head buzzed as he stood close to her. *"This is serious business,"* it said. However, if he performed well, she would never have to know. That was his goal. Finish the job and leave no traces.

It had taken only two minutes in the lobby to install a password override device in the elevator. Its purpose was a precautionary one; if he couldn't establish a friendly relationship with Julia Tyler and gain access to her computer, he would enter the condo when no one was there. That would be the tricky part. Seducing her would be much more enjoyable.

There was no way to turn back now. Marten suspected his uncle's telescope had him located right there in the party — every move he made recorded — if only in Perry Roberts' warped brain.

So, Marten had cleared his head of all negative thought as he made his way around the crowd with Julia as his guide. He enjoyed the appetizing food and drink and the company of other guests, *normal people,* he thought. He savored each moment, not visualizing the possible outcome. If he could accomplish that, everything would turn out just fine.

In the grand scheme of things, that party could most assuredly prove to be just as successful for him as for Ms. Tyler.

Chapter Fourteen

The Day After

As I awakened, I had that new bride feeling — it's over? Is this all there is? Last night's party was history. Then, I thought of Marten Wells, my very own mystery man and his magical appearance in my elevator. I pulled the covers up to my chin, stretched my legs and curled my toes. Through the mosquito netting surrounding my bed, the sun shone brighter than ever before. Even the palm fronds were more vivid and green. I flipped a switch on the universal remote and the ceiling fan began a slow cycle, stirring up the lingering hint of Blue fragrance from last night.

After my shower, I chose coral Capri pants and a white blouse for my workday. No shoes, of course. I wore them only when I absolutely had to.

A delivery came from Doc Emmett — a fruit basket with a note: "Thank you for transporting us . . . once again."

I made coffee, peeled a blood orange and wandered into my little office, standing barefooted in front of the monitor while retrieving my e-mail. Twenty-three jovial *"thank you for the superb party"* messages, each one praising Dana's lavish dishes. Her restaurant traffic was sure to pick up now!

I sat down and wrote checks to the vendors, along with notes of appreciation for those who worked so hard. After all, just because you pay someone to do a job doesn't mean they don't deserve a customized thank-you note for doing it well. I embellished each envelope with red sealing wax on the back flap and planned to hand-deliver them that afternoon.

Shortly after 10:00 a.m. my cell phone rang. It was Elise, asking me to hold for Noah Forrester, the CEO of River Protocol, Inc. I attached my Bluetooth and headed for the kitchen to refresh my coffee while I waited. When the call came through, Forrester asked me to write a blog post regarding Lady Sophia's visit to San Antonio. Forrester ordinarily released River Protocol, Inc.'s news with an innovative flair: He'd write a blog and post links on social media sites. The news channels immediately picked up most of them, and, in some cases, local newspapers would print the news the following day.

"I'd write it myself, but I want it to be a touchy-feely piece, and you do that much better than I do, plus it will be posted online the day before Valentine's Day, so you're elected, kid."

I was pleased that he'd chosen me. "All right. Anything you want me to leave out, or especially put in it?"

"Yeah, you have all the dates: arrivals, school visits, speeches, etc., but we'll release those later on. Just the date of their arrival for now, I guess. Note that San Antonio will be the last stop on her world tour. Make sure you mention that she's traveling with her only child, Chesley Regan Vanderhawk.

"Of course," I said.

Forrester cleared his throat. "Anyway, the purpose of the tour is to promote world peace through *Our Children, Our World*, a program designed by Lady Sophia Louise Vanderhawk herself. Submit your write-up to me in a sealed envelope marked *Confidential*. We'll work out any edits together between now and then. Oh and get this — I'm going to attach that photo of her that's on the front cover of the book I saw on your coffee table at your party."

"Do you have the rights to that?" I asked.

"Not yet, but I'll have it by then. What an attention-grabber that will be! And remember, it's still hush-hush for now."

And there was even more exciting news. Chesley had e-mailed other children in the previous cities he visited. He was allowed to choose with whom he wanted to communicate. Noah Forrester submitted Boone's name as a candidate. The boy might chat personally with Boone! *Won't Boone be proud?* There was also a chance that he would meet Chesley in person upon his arrival in San Antonio.

Lady Sophia would arrive in two months! *Haven't I been dreaming of more excitement in my life? What could be more thrilling than this? Marten Wells, perhaps.* I could hardly concentrate after the phone call. Lady Sophia was greatly admired by everyone for her humanitarian work, and, to top it off, she was utterly beautiful. The book Forrester referred to was one I'd splurged on, an over-sized coffee table book with nothing but photographs of her, getting out of carriages and limousines, giving speeches, and caring for the sick and elderly in remote places all around the globe. Sophia graced the front cover, naturally, seated side-saddle on a black stallion. She was elegantly dressed for her photo-shoot with Balmoral Castle in the background. English organdy beaded lace cascaded from underneath the hem of her flowing emerald-green velvet skirt, as well as from the cuffs of her English-style tweed jacket. The steed stood at attention, head tilted to the left, ears pricked. His neck arched proudly as if he intuitively recognized the importance of his passenger.

The blog would emphasize that San Antonio was selected as a venue because of its diverse ethnic population. According to Forrester, the Convention Office was using local businesses to organize the events surrounding Sophia's' appearances, but my office was the only one on the Riverwalk. I had the view, the ambiance and the location. How lucky was that?

My professional life had gained a new dimension with British clientele, and I wondered if Marten Wells had ever met Lady Sophia. Did he know she would be here soon? Would he be impressed, or would he even care?

Chapter Fifteen

The New Client

During the next few days the office was swamped with new assignments. Britt Waterman and Andie worked overtime and I called in two temps to handle the transcription. By Friday morning, the week's activity had smoothed out, and I phoned Marten Wells to confirm our appointment.

"I'll be there promptly at 3:30," he said. He'd gathered most of the data required to give me an idea of what he would need, and he mentioned something about software but didn't know if it would be compatible. Said he'd bring his laptop to convert anything that wasn't. "Of course, I don't expect you to do it all today. I merely want to show you what my business is about so you can take the paperwork off my hands."

"That's exactly what we do here."

"And exactly what I need . . . and not a moment too soon, I might add. I have so many other matters requiring my urgent attention. My associates are handling most of it, but rather poorly. Of course, I'm a perfectionist, so I suppose none of them can please me. At least, that's what I've overheard."

He laughed, and I pictured his deliciously crooked smile. I couldn't picture him as a slave-driver, but everyone has at least two sides. *He may keep his dark side well hidden.*

"It never hurts to hear your employees' views," I said, "especially the ones they wouldn't dare tell you to your face. A little eavesdropping now and again might be the best way to sort the truth."

Andie had gone to fetch Boone from school. When the elevator delivered Marten, I automatically gave him the once-over — khakis and a black tee shirt. I hoped he didn't think my scrutiny forward or flirtatious. Perhaps he didn't notice.

We exchanged pleasantries and his gaze wandered into the living room. "What a huge apartment! I didn't get the full impact of its size with so many people here the other evening." He followed the ceiling line all the way around the semi-circular living room. "Such magnificent views! If this were my place, I would be tempted to stare out the windows night and day and accomplish nothing else. How *do* you get any work done?"

"Oh, I can easily dream an entire day away if I'm not careful. In fact, I've been known to do just that."

"The kitchen was off-duty for tours the other night, you know." He cupped my elbow and steered me there. Distracted by his touch, I had no idea what he was talking about for a few moments, although I thought he said the words *vintage cabinetry* and *marble*. Were customs between European and American men different? I was uncertain and didn't know what to think of being *handled*. I rattled on about the kitchen.

"This room was the Roosevelt Club's bar and was circular," I said, using the word *circular* as an excuse to gesture widely and remove my elbow from his grasp. "Members could access it from both the smoking lounge and the foyer, which also opened into the bathing area and massage rooms." I took a few steps toward the counter where the brochures remained in a stack left over from the party. I handed him one, showing the photo of the old smoking room. "You probably saw this Monday night."

"Yes, it's now your spectacular lounge," Marten said. He turned around, and as he walked past, I caught a scent of his cologne, one I couldn't place. "Look, it's 1950 and a group of businessmen are lounging in here, drinks in one hand, cigars in the other — thick, smoke-filled air. I can hear them now . . . planning a future city full of skyscrapers perhaps?" He looked at me. "Don't you see it too?

"Sure I do, and I hear them all the time, especially when Doc's here, reminiscing. Doc joined the club when he was fresh out of med school. Actually, I like to think the Riverwalk itself was developed in this room, which is possible, you know. Its architect had an office downstairs where The Stock Market is."

"Really? How very interesting!"

"But, it's my club now. I make the rules. Drinks are allowed, business is encouraged, but smoking is definitely taboo. Anyone who wants to smoke uses the rooftop through that alcove." I pointed to a small recess through which one could access either the roof or the bathing lounge.

"Yes, I noticed that at your party, but I didn't go out. I'd like to see it, though; now, if you have the time."

"You're my last appointment of the day. Follow me."

I'd designed the rooftop area as a Japanese garden, a quiet meditation hideaway. The dry, southwestern climate perfectly complemented my collection of cactus and bonsai plants. An ornamental feed-tube hung under the cupola roof; underneath, two dozen red plastic BB pellets were scattered on the decking.

Marten reached down and picked one up. "What are these? Some type of exotic bird seed?"

"Oh, those. They're my defense system against the squirrels. They insist on stealing the bird food. I use my BB pistol to scare them away."

Marten let the pellet fall to the floor, took a step back and stared at me.

I laughed. "Oh, don't worry; it's an air-soft gun. It doesn't hurt them — within minutes, they're back. But I get lots of practice — I come up here with my coffee on Sunday mornings and scare the nasty long-tailed rodents away long enough to enjoy a few redbirds. They take me back to childhood."

"Where was that?" He was still staring.

"Southern Indiana. A quaint little river town called Madison. My mother loved it so much she used Madison as my middle name. She always kept sunflower and safflower seeds out to attract cardinals, she so loved their early-morning song. And so do I. They prefer to feed on the ground, but a few have grown to count on me, and they come back every year. They might not be real cardinals — I think they're the Northern Cardinal's kissing cousin here in the Southwest. But whatever they are, I don't want the squirrels to eat all their food. Surely you can't blame me for that."

"I suppose not. Remind me not to make you mad — you must be a good aim, with all that target practice!"

We went back inside, and Marten continued to scan the living room. "I've never seen such an unusual . . . what do you call that . . . divan?

"Oh, that's my Julia sofa. It's an S-shaped sectional, but if you take the foot-rests away, it becomes J-shaped, so I named it after myself."

"The clever lady who named her sofa. Damn . . . that's *pink*!"

I was delighted that he noticed the sectional. It was, after all, the centerpiece of my living area. "Much like being on the inside of a conch shell, don't you think? I spied it late one night a few years ago through the window of an old-world shop on Royal Street in the French Quarter. The display was of a room done entirely in pink and white, and that sofa was definitely calling my name."

"Incredible! So you bought it then?"

"No . . . the shop was closed and I was scheduled to fly home the next morning. However, that night I dreamed, not of pink elephants, but pink furniture, so I changed my flight, and was waiting at the shop when they opened the next morning." I shrugged and grinned sheepishly. "Just like that."

"I suddenly feel the urge to ask you how much it cost," Marten said.

I snorted. "Well . . . you might want to rethink *that* one."

Marten clasped his hands together. "Okay! A woman who knows what she wants," he said as he observed my pink outfit. "And she wears clothes to match!"

I'd been going through my pink phase ever since I found the Julia sofa, which my therapist said dated back to when I was little (not the couch — my pink fetish). "No, Julia, you cannot have the pink blouse, darling. Little girls with red hair like yours do not wear pink or red," my mother had said. "It just isn't done." Period. In elementary school, I admired my schoolmates' pink angora sweaters, but could only dream about wearing one myself. (Sometimes I tried one on when I spent the night at a friend's house.) "And you *never* mix pink with red," my mother had clucked. "Such a shameful designer *faux pas*!" A couple more clucks, the shake of her head — her point was made. She worked at a fabric/wallpaper store and fancied herself an interior designer, though she never had formal training. She did have a good eye for color, but she favored matching over mixing; she played it safe. I, on the other hand, mixed: rose, soft bubblegum, magenta, fuchsia.

"Yes, well, once the furniture was delivered I began seeing pink everywhere, and soon I found myself buying clothes . . . shoes . . . handbags. Pink is in, and truly, any woman can have a wardrobe to match her furnishings if she wants." I raised one eyebrow. "If you're clever, you can take a nap on the sofa and no one will know you're there."

"Camouflage, eh? I know women whose outfits *and* personality coordinate with their furniture — beige or black. That is to say, I've never met anyone as colorful as you, and that, Ms. Tyler, is not an overused pick-up line . . . it's the truth. By the way, you looked very pretty adorned in the pink number at your Open House."

Although I was rarely at a loss for words, I said nothing. I felt myself blush and worried that Marten would think I wore make-up to match my sofa.

Marten checked his wristwatch and reached into his portfolio to remove a small container of old-fashioned orange diskettes. "These don't match anything in here. Let's get them into a cubicle before the color police come and take me away."

I laughed. "People still use those things? I hope you have a contraption for me to install them," I said as we headed down the hallway to my office. I'd taken his rose out of the vase and dried it.

He showed me the blueprints for his new office to be located in what was currently an empty building on the edge of a smart downtown area, Charles Court, three blocks over with its main entrance on Presa Street. I'd watched firsthand the development of the stylish Charles Court and was surprised he'd found anything available there. It was *the* place to be. Marten explained he'd been made aware of the location a few days ago when another business lost its funding. A complete remodel was planned and the clinic would open in three months. There would be little for me to do until then. I was disappointed because I'd expected instant gratification — thought I'd be working with him right away.

"When the time comes, what we would like from Tyler Services," Marten said, "is to have our vendor invoices entered and paid in a timely manner, payroll figured . . . and, oh yes, see that appropriate taxes are paid, quarterly and year-end, W-2's or whatever tax forms are required. I want to make sure all is on the up and up with everything handled legally."

"I can assure you, payroll will be legal as long as your employees are."

"Yes. Interviewing will begin shortly. We'll be hiring all sorts of medical positions, and I may ask you to help me place classified advertisements."

"Certainly." Maybe I *would* be involved with his business sooner rather than later.

"Now," Marten continued, "the receivables will be entered online from our home office. You needn't worry yourself over the deposits, nor will we need income statements. We will keep that information separate."

"Oh. Well. I usually keep a paper trail of all transactions, even when my clients make their own deposits — for accuracy in profit and loss statements. But if you say it's not necessary, that's fine."

"No. They have me on a long leash. London is taking care of it."

London? Who in London would want to fund a health clinic in San Antonio? I didn't question him further on this, although I thought it unusual. This was, after all, his business, and exactly how it would be funded was of no real concern to me unless he wanted me to figure his income taxes. That would require more detailed information. I quoted the job and he signed a contract.

I offered Marten a cup of coffee. "Or would you prefer tea?" I cautiously asked.

"I *would* enjoy a cup of tea, if it's not too much trouble."

I went for the kitchen and he followed. I turned the burner on underneath my teakettle and handed him a basket containing an assortment of tea bags. He rummaged through, settling on Earl Grey. "The Queen's favorite," he said. I filled my teapot just as the water reached a boil. I hoped I was making it correctly; Marten seemed to be scrutinizing my technique, but it was probably just my imagination. How would I know, really? Coffee was my hot beverage of choice, but I recalled reading somewhere that boiling water shouldn't be used for most types of tea leaves. Should I serve with a cup and saucer? Ultimately, I poured the steaming, finished product into two sturdy mugs — after all, this wasn't a tea party — we had work to do. We returned to my office and completed the installation of software to enable our computers to network.

Marten looked at his watch again and excused himself to the restroom. I was loading his data into my accounting system when a call came in — an inquiry from a potential customer with several questions. His accent was difficult to understand and I paused the download. Marten returned and stood idle for a while. Next, he touched my shoulder and made a hand gesture, kindly motioned me out of my chair. He said could finish loading the records. I resumed the call in an adjacent room, and, after I finally satisfied the caller, I returned to my office and found Marten waiting — he'd already completed the task. I thanked him, pulled up a chair beside him, and we reviewed the information together.

I was intrigued by this clinic he planned to bring to the inner city. It would service children of poor families at no cost. The physicians would be paid for their time, usually one-half day per doctor, and there would be one full-time physician assistant on duty. I was even more curious about how it would be funded. Doc Emmett had said he had an appointment to discuss it with Marten, and I wondered if he had any clarification. But it might be unethical of me to inquire of Doc. I'd have to think about that before bringing it up with him.

We headed back to the kitchen for a tea warm-up. Marten held his mug with both hands while he looked at the Riverwalk view from the window. "Are all your clients located downtown?"

"The majority are," I said. "I prefer downtown businesses, but I occasionally work in other areas of the city." I joined him at the window, careful not to stand too close. I hoped he wouldn't attempt physical contact again. It didn't feel right, somehow. "I love to walk to my clients' offices periodically. The smell of the river, the tourists, the sun, it all keeps my mood cheerful."

He placed his empty mug on the counter. "Did you open your business after you moved in here?"

"No, it was a couple of years before that. I leased office space on Commerce Street, which was the perfect location for collecting clients along the Riverwalk. Back then, I lived in the suburbs about 15 miles out of town and rush hour traffic was a drag. When this condo became available, I recognized it as the solution."

"You must have been very determined — that's a quantum leap you took."

"I suppose you could say that. The remodeling was a tricky project, since we lived here during most of the construction."

"If we're playing 20 Questions, I have one more!" He laughed and I liked the way his voice put me at ease. Marten asked his last question, "How do you like working out of your home?"

"Definitely the best thing I've ever done for myself. Some of my friends who work at home get bored — lack of human contact, I suppose. But, for me it's great. No more daily commute, and I get out several times a week with deliveries of hard copies to those who prefer a personal touch. Sometimes I take the extra time to stroll along the Riverwalk, rather than street side, just so I can get a whiff of the delicious aromas coming out of the various restaurants. I'm fortunate to be doing the kind of work I love, especially in this setting."

"I agree," Marten said. "The Riverwalk is magical. And as far as the smells from the restaurants, sometimes I've found myself eating lunch twice in one day before I realize what I've done." He laughed.

It had been a long time since I'd had such an attentive male audience. Oh sure, there's Frederick, and Doc, and of course Boone. But this was different — like being a stand-up comedian in front of a new crowd that applauds and shouts Encore! I was encouraged to continue. "One day, an elderly man shuffled past me over on Losoya Street, and I caught the distinct aromas of cilantro, cumin and corn tortillas. I wondered if he worked in a Mexican restaurant."

"You have some of the finest right here on the Riverwalk!"

"No doubt. In any case, I could think of nothing but tacos the rest of the day, so I made them for dinner that night."

Marten chuckled again. "You have such a positive way of looking at life." He studied me as though he'd never known a woman quite like me. A comfortable silence developed between us.

The elevator bell rang, announcing Britt Waterman's arrival. Right on time, as usual; I entered the password on the security box, bringing the elevator up. Britt said his hellos, shook hands with Marten, and headed toward his office, Massage Room #3.

I called to him, "Oh, Britt. Use my work station tonight. I've got a temp working in yours for the time being."

"Yes ma'am."

"That fellow makes killer drinks," Marten said. "But I wasn't aware he worked in your office."

"Britt Waterman. Yes, he never stops. College during the day, work in the evenings, and on weekend nights he tends bar at Zinc. You've probably seen the place, over on Presa Street, at the entrance to Charles Court."

Marten had turned his attention to the elevator. I assumed he was preparing to leave, and I hoped he was, because the time I'd spent with him had emotionally drained me.

"This is unlike any lift I've seen," he said. "You surely have a high-end security system in force, I presume."

Of course, safety precautions would be a concern to him since his company's sensitive financial records would be kept here. I explained, to put him at ease, "In the old days, there was an operator who knew who to let up into the club and who didn't belong. You had to get past him — you'll have to ask Doc Emmett about Alonzo — he loves to reminisce. But, yes, I've had a top-notch protection system installed. Very few people know the pass code; otherwise, just anyone could come and go. I change the code at my whim. It's particularly handy, not having to lug a set of keys around with me all the time."

"Yes, well . . . I did so enjoy your party Monday evening. I hope I wasn't too abrupt, or put you off, but I was happy to meet you in person — the pretty lady from the Little Rhein."

I felt myself blush again. "I'm happy to have your business."

"Uh, oh," Marten said. "I've thought of one last question."

"Oh, all right then. Have at it!"

"Was the yellow rose in your cubicle Monday night the one I left on your table?"

"On my table?" I blinked and cut my eyes back and forth, feigning an effort to remember what had been on my desk that night. "Oh, that. I believe the waitress put it back into the vase on your table. I get yellow roses all the time. After all, this *is* Texas, you know."

"I see . . . I think," said Marten, although I could tell he didn't actually comprehend my meaning.

"It's an old song," I explained. "*The Yellow Rose of Texas*."

"Okay. Now I truly do see. Hmm. Well, then." Marten shifted from one foot to the other; he seemed to be searching for a way to make this encounter last. "I suppose my next project will be to locate an apartment for myself downtown."

"I've noticed some very nice ones at Charles Court on the second and third floors, but I'd imagine they're pricey."

"Yes, but it would be convenient, wouldn't it? I'll have to make an appointment to look at them." A vague look swept Marten's face. He inserted his hand into his coat pocket and pulled out his cell phone. "I'm being vibrated. I'd better get back to work and wrap things up for the evening." He looked at his watch again and smiled at me.

"With both of us in residence on the Riverwalk, we'll probably be crossing paths as we come and go from now on," I said.

"Of that, Ms. Tyler, I have no doubt."

~*~

I watched the elevator disappear. *Oh sure, people send me yellow roses all the time. What on earth has come over me?* Usually I was calm and confident after establishing a new client, but I was apprehensive, like my first day of middle-school in a strange, new place. It was the Tuesday after Labor Day, the summer I'd lost my parents and moved to Louisville to live with Dana. As I walked through the large doors of the old brick building, I'd been overcome with foreboding. Nothing was familiar at all about the smell of that school, nor its massive size; I had come from a much smaller town, *cozier*. What if I got lost? That was the first time I experienced an anxiety attack. Fortunately, Dana had been right by my side. I longed for that same support again, so I picked up the phone and pushed the speed button.

"Stock Market," Dana answered.

"I have a chilled bottle of champagne."

"And I, dear cousin, have two flutes with our names on them."

"Haven't heard as much as a peep from you all week," I said. "I assume your business is booming, just like mine."

"You nailed it. Get on down here and we'll toast to success!"

I retrieved my favorite jacket, the one I'd bought in Sedona two years before, a soft, loose-fitting pied garment made from old Indian blankets with multi shades of red, purple and blue on an earth-tone background. On my way out, I noticed an orange disk labeled A-12. Marten must have neglected to return it to his portfolio. I didn't know whether it had been overlooked, or if it was even of value. While my mouth watered for the liquid celebration, my sense of responsibility told me to do *something* — but what? Andie had just returned and was supervising both of the temps, in a frenzy, I figured, so she could finish her tasks and go out with Britt. Since all computer stations were in use, I quickly copied the disk onto my infrequently-used old Dell and laid it back on the J Sofa where I'd found it. If the information on it was important, I'd transfer it to my office computer later, and if not — no harm done.

Chapter Sixteen

The Deception Begins

Marten let himself into the penthouse suite and situated his laptop on the desk. The telescope sat just inside the balcony doorway, angled downward, focused specifically on the roof of the Arneson River Theater. Leonardo Newman and Perry Roberts looked like giddy school boys. *At least it isn't out in plain sight,* Marten thought.

"Here it is, the Arneson!" Leonardo said, all puffed up like a self-important bull-frog.

"You've narrowed it down, the scene of our exploit?" Marten asked. He walked to the doorway and joined the two men, who parted to make room for him. Marten looked into the viewfinder. The theater stage was bare, unlike last Sunday evening, when it vibrated with costumed dancers and musicians. *The night I caught Julia's attention.* He smirked and shook his head at the serendipity of it all. He returned to the desk and waited for his computer to make the online connection with Julia's business service, and he thought about The Arneson — such a twist of fate. Oh, she'd tried to sound convincing that the little yellow rosebud wasn't the very same one he'd given her. She was rather cute, he had to admit. No, he'd caught her attention all right, that he knew for sure. He'd stood in the background — watched her wrap the flower in a napkin and tuck it into her handbag.

"This is definitely our venue," Leonardo said. "I'm 99 percent certain."

"Damn it!" Roberts snapped. "There's no room for even one percent of doubt!"

Marten wondered what they were paying Leonardo Newman for. His fee was exorbitant, in Marten's opinion. The man was an imbecile, to suggest this location to them without being absolutely positive. Leonardo had bragged of his connections, how precise and loyal they were, yet Marten wasn't convinced he could be trusted. Then again, his uncle had put the man through a rigorous screening process and had no doubts about him at all, up until this moment.

Leonardo was supposedly licensed to lease and sell commercial real estate in Texas, although Marten doubted the authenticity of the certificate; nonetheless, they were using him as their broker for the new office space. His eyes held a distinctively greedy look, and, even worse, he had a somewhat campy air about him. Marten figured him for a homosexual, and, while he had nothing against them, he preferred not to work this closely with one, coming and going from the hotel room . . . and at all hours. Marten certainly did not travel down *that* street, and he was pretty sure his uncle didn't, either. No, Roberts had an obvious taste for the ladies, albeit short fat ones. Why such a preference? Marten could understand the *short*, but the *fat*? He would never ask; he didn't want to be told not to knock it till he'd tried it. Marten wasn't about to travel down that street, either. He liked the feel of his arms wrapped entirely around a woman's waist, and his arms reached only so far, after all.

His uncle had accused him of being bigoted and narrow-minded. But Marten scoffed at labels. He'd simply been raised among very wealthy people as a child, and then moved to a small village without the benefit of associating with others who were different from himself. If being uncomfortable with certain others made him a bad person, then so be it. Marten was careful not to voice his dislikes anymore, but he had opinions and feelings, just like everyone else, he thought. There was a thin line between tolerance and acceptance. He merely tolerated people whose behavior or lifestyle he did not fully grasp. If he identified with them, he easily accepted them.

Marten had returned to his laptop, and he summoned the two men. "Gentlemen, allow me to introduce our new accounting service — Tyler Professional Services. I can stop wasting my time with the mundane aspects of our faux clinic and devote myself to *real* details, that is, why we're actually here in San Antonio."

Roberts glanced toward the desk and nodded, acknowledging Marten's computer. "Making yourself useful now, eh, nephew? Good boy.

When will you have the two systems linked? We can make no further progress until then, you realize?"

"Perfectly aware of that, little buddy," Marten said.

Roberts cringed. Marten had meant it as an insult; Roberts hated it when he was referred to as tiny. Marten had to admit, though, it was due almost entirely to his uncle's small size that this scheme at the famous theater would be pulled off the way they'd hoped.

"Watch this," Marten instructed. He clicked the mouse and motioned toward the display.

"By God!" Roberts said. "He's inserted a Trojan Horse into that woman's system right under her nose!"

"While she was conducting business on the phone — you — using one of your clever nonsensical accents," Marten said.

A wry smile brushed Roberts' face. He wiped his brow with a bar towel and heaved a sigh of relief. "Phase One is complete . . . let's celebrate!" He went for his briefcase and ceremoniously selected a narrow, mahogany box. As he fingered a brass latch, the lid opened revealing a red velvet lining inset with four handmade Russian crystal shot glasses. He filled three of them with fine liquor. Marten examined the bottle: The Glenlivet 12 Year Old Single Malt Scotch Whiskey. They raised their glasses in triumph and Marten savored the liquid as it slid down his throat like a gleam of sunshine.

Roberts explained the details to Leonardo, who understood already, but who, having a healthy respect for his employer, listened attentively. "We are now privy to every bit of data we need, details that even you have had no access to, as of yet — your *99 percent* — if you will. Coupled with what you have given us so far, we are on task." He pointed at the computer. "This link, here, to our lovely and naïve Julia Tyler and her network, along with our technology, will allow us to eavesdrop on all of Ms. Tyler's clients. Every move Lady Sophia makes, we will know about in advance. A brilliant and fail-proof system, if I do say so myself."

"Correct," Marten said. "Going in the back door this way will never raise suspicion. And now we can be 100 percent sure. Check this out, will you?"

Roberts examined a document Marten had pulled up: detailed information on Ms. Tyler's client schedule from River Protocol, Inc. for Sophia's visit. "Bingo! It *is* the Arneson, just as we'd hoped."

"*Just as I told you,*" Leonardo whined, "the final appearance of our dear Lady Sophia is scheduled at the historic river theater!"

"Good job," Roberts said to Leonardo. "Good job, indeed!"

"Just as I thought," Leonardo boasted, "the Arneson Theater is the perfect venue, not only because of its architectural design, but for its close proximity to Charles Court."

Roberts nodded. "Both of you must figure a way for me to swiftly abduct the boy and transport him to the clinic for safekeeping while we await the transfer of funds from the Vanderhawks."

"I'm developing a plan already. How about you, Marten?"

Marten tapped his fingernails repeatedly on the desk. "Yes, I'm with you on it. But, look at this . . . the timing of it." He winced. "It's nine weeks away! I don't know . . . can we complete a partial mock-up of the roof by then?"

Leonardo checked the calendar, counted off the days until Sophia's visit. He re-checked the telescopic view. "Hell yes, we can! What's got you all rattled? Roberts will easily fit in between the flat roof and the partial fake one we'll build. It looks exactly the same as in the photographs, the perfect space for hiding the night before."

"A good thing," said Roberts. "Change would be hazardous to the mission. Don't forget I'll have tools with me. We'll have to keep those hidden, as well."

Marten poured another shot of scotch. He'd earned it and his nerves needed soothing. "We could do with two or three more grunts on the double!"

"No worries — I'm already on it," Roberts said. With the noisy construction going on over there, no one will question that it is, in fact, a clinic being built inside. He took the opportunity for a scotch refill of his own. No one offered Leonardo another.

Leonardo dramatically cleared his throat and removed a stack of papers from his briefcase. "Can I assume, now, gentlemen, that we're prepared to sign the lease?"

Marten wondered if he was the only one with reservations. "Is anyone having second thoughts?" he asked.

His uncle cut loose with a sinister laugh, the kind you'd hear in a horror movie. "Sorry, it's way too late for that now," Roberts said. "Jesus! Cut the fussbudget dance and just sign the damn paperwork. Let's move this operation over to Charles Court tomorrow!" He scribbled illegibly on the signature line, then picked up Marten's portfolio, dumped it upside down on the king-sized mattress and sifted through the orange disks. "Where is A-12?"

"In the hotel safe where it belongs," said Marten, quickly. Too quickly.

Roberts glared at him suspiciously. "Be a good pup. Run down and fetch it, spot on. And hurry right back."

Chapter Seventeen

Marten's Fatal Mistake

Marten feared he'd lost his focus. He fidgeted in line at the hotel front desk for a good 15 minutes. The lobby was a madhouse with a large Japanese group checking in. A-12 had to be in the main safe. He'd studied it right after Julia's party, then tucked it into his portfolio. That much he knew for sure. He'd intended to replace it, but could not remember. Thoughts of Ms. Tyler had preoccupied his mind.

After a fair measure of attempted communication with the Hispanic girl across the counter, Marten was allowed access to the safe. The one and only file that Julia Tyler should never see, A-12, did not appear. Marten carefully replaced the other contents and tried to imagine where he'd left the file. How would he ever explain it? Responsible to a fault, she most certainly would be curious and examine it right away. Marten called but reached her voice mail. He hung up, feeling panicky. Maybe he could get in and out of her office with no one knowing, if he used the password bypass device he'd installed.

He ran to The Clifford, pushed the elevator call button and hoped no one would answer. No such luck: Britt's voice came over the intercom. Marten asked for Julia. "She left right after you did," Britt said. "But you're welcome to look around. I'll call you on up."

Marten hurried into Julia's office with Britt in tow. "Maybe it fell underneath her desk," Marten said as he searched her desk top and the floor while Britt stood close by, but the disk was not there. What if she'd already discovered the contents and had gone to the police? Marten was petrified to think of the consequences.

"Where did you first remove the disk from your briefcase? Maybe it dropped out before you went into her office," Britt suggested.

Marten nodded and rushed into the living room. The disk was lying on the sofa. Marten offered a hefty sigh of relief. "Oh, good! You were right. It must have fallen from my case when I removed the other disks. But, now I'm mortified that Ms. Tyler will think me scatterbrained if she finds out I allowed a file to go missing. It's not valuable in any way, but still, she might not want me as her client after all!"

Britt smiled. "I assure you, your error will be kept between the two of us. Everyone makes mistakes. Evidently this one won't hurt anyone."

Back at the Hilton, Marten rushed into the penthouse, using the earlier congestion in the lobby as his excuse as to why it took so long to retrieve the disk. The other two conspirators didn't seem to realize how long Marten had been gone. When Marten gave A-12 to his uncle, he thought he'd dodged a bullet. But, a disaster had only been delayed — not diverted.

Chapter Eighteen

The Stock Market

I punched six keypad numbers, sending me directly to The Stock Market. I loved that clever lift! Marten's fragrance remained — mint with a subtle hint of lime. *Add rum and a stick of sugar cane and I'd have a Mojito.* Opening into the restaurant's kitchen, the elevator was taken over by the aroma of green peppers and onions simmering in a tomato base, one of Dana's southwestern seafood experiments.

Dana held a spoon to her lips. "Too much pepper."

Aunt Betty claimed Dana had been born with a tasting spoon in her mouth. I maneuvered around chopping blocks, copper pot racks and fast-moving servers in the kitchen. Pulling the bottle from its tote, I offered it to Dana. "Chilled to perfection."

Dana's eyes brightened. "Umm . . . bubbly." She looked at the label — Moët & Chandon. "I see you've spared no expense." She untied her apron and wiped her hands with it. "Go on and help yourself to some dinner. I'll be right in," she said, waving toward the dining room.

The evening was warm and breezy and several diners were already seated outside at water's edge. I located a small table inside, near a window, and threw my jacket over a chair. I made my way to the buffet line, standing back to examine the flashing menu on a marquee-style, ticker-tape display. **TODAY'S STOCK PRICES: CHICKEN — BEEF — VEGETABLE**

Under each category, gumbos, bisques and chowders were described with computer-style lettering. The special of the day was described as *Today's Stock to Watch* on a sign similar to one on Wall Street in New York City.

Three years earlier, critics had predicted the restaurant wouldn't last long with its cold city-style interior of chrome and glass, when what San

Antonio tourists wanted, they'd insisted, was a warm, earthy atmosphere to achieve respite from a day of shopping and sightseeing. But Dana's business plan hadn't counted on tourism for her success; she was going after the locals. Hers was the only cafeteria downtown — a quick in and out. Hundreds of people worked and lived on the Riverwalk, and they liked The Stock Market at lunchtime precisely because of the business atmosphere — it set an energetic mood, propelled their momentum well into the afternoon.

The custom-made tables boasted shiny pedestals shaped like dollar signs and tops of thick Plexiglas, inlaid with coins from all over the world. The floors were covered with matte black tiles embracing small triangular glossy insets of red and blue, smartly inlaid with thick, red grout. Along one wall was a bar with all organic salad ingredients. It cornered at the buffet line with daily soup selections, two cold and four hot.

I prepared a small plate of baby spinach leaves topped with red onions, Greek olives and feta cheese, and a cup of *Today's Stock to Watch* — Southwestern Seafood Stew. At the end of the buffet line, I sliced a chunk of warm French bread and selected two coin-shaped butter pats. I noticed a little basket containing a printed invitation, "Take One." Dana had not taken my advice: *If you give away your recipes, people won't buy the new cookbook.* Dana's philosophy was simple: "If you give them just one recipe they'll want to purchase more. Besides, the cover alone will be reason enough to buy it." I couldn't argue with that; I had two cookbooks I bought simply because of their covers. They looked ideal displayed on my kitchen countertop.

The evening crowd was growing quickly, although it was early, but The Stock Market had become increasingly popular for dinner as well as lunchtime. Dana worked her way around the tables, carrying the chilled bottle, a bucket on a stand and two crystal flutes. She popped the cork like the pro she was. "Okay, tell me."

"Tell you what?"

"You have a silly grin that can't be wiped off your face, it seems."

"Well . . . for one . . . this soup is fantastic!"

"It's not *that* good. What's up? Tell me."

"Well, let's see, that must leave only one thing — my newest client, Marten Wells. He left the office not 15 minutes ago." I shuddered involuntarily. "My skin tingles when he's around. Isn't he awesome?"

"I'll say! Which one of us is going after him?" Dana poured bubbles into both flutes.

"Which one is *he* going after?"

"Darlink," Dana said, definitively holding her glass up high, "it's the woman who chooses."

"In that case, I saw him first, so I get dibs." We clinked our glasses and sipped our celebratory beverage.

"Actually, I got the impression that he was already interested in *you*," Dana said. "So tell me more."

"Okay. It was Sunday night at the Little Rhein Steak House. Let me tell you, he definitely caught my attention. I sat a few feet away from his table and couldn't take my eyes off him. Which is why, I might add, I was in shell shock when he arrived in my elevator at the party."

"Ah ha! So *that's* why you turned 10 shades of pale," Dana said. "And now you're glowing. Am I seeing the old Julia come out to play?"

"Maybe. But what if I've forgotten how?"

Dana snorted. "They say it's like riding a bicycle — I don't know, I've never gone without as long as you have, but it's about time you tried it. You've been away from your old self too long." She leaned on both elbows toward me and her purple eyes twinkled. "Does this Marten guy have a brother?"

I laughed and said, "You sound like Frederick. He asked me the same thing."

"Frederick and I think alike. That's why my hair always looks so good. By the way, I love your new style."

"Frederick at his best," I said, running my fingers through my hair. "Oh, Dana, you outdid yourself on the Open House. Thank you so much. So . . . how's business since then?"

"See for yourself." Dana held her arms out, palm side up, and cut her eyes to the right and left. "It's overwhelming so far. *Incredible.*

I've been busier than ever and Emilio practically sleeps in the kitchen. As sous-chefs go, he's the best. I gave him a $300 bonus. Now he acts like I'm a goddess."

"I'm sure he needed it with another baby on the way. How many will this make for them?"

"Four, I think, but the first boy. He took off yesterday after lunch for their sonogram. It's an Emilio Junior, he says, no doubt about it. Anyway, thanks for the opportunity to cater the party. I had a fine time, too." Dana's eyes twinkled again. "The music was great."

My phone vibrated and I checked the number — my office. Someone had left a voice message on my business line. I called to retrieve it.

A regular customer stopped by the table to tell Dana what he thought of the seafood stew and to ask about the cookbook. "Soon," she promised him, "very soon." She turned her attention back to me. "What's up?"

I shrugged. "A hang up," I said, "with a blocked number. Probably a telemarketer." I tossed the phone into my purse. "Now, where were we?" I said with a hint of sarcasm. "Oh yes, you said something about the music at the party. You had time to notice the *music*?"

Dana sank down into her seat. She knew what was coming.

"I thought you had sworn off musicians after that last guy!"

"No — truck drivers — I gave up on truck drivers. Ha. Ha. No, wait!" She cocked her head slightly. "I've never even dated a trucker, come to think of it! Oh sure, I wrote off musicians after *whatshisname*, but Julia, this Nathan is one classy guy."

"Nathan, huh?"

"Yeah, well. He's a pianist, for Pete's sake, so maybe he'll be safer than the others; you know . . . the drummers, guitarists, bass players. Pianists are more, oh, cultured, I'd say. We're going out to Boudro's tomorrow night."

Boudro's was a long-time favorite of mine. At least one afternoon each week after my deliveries I took a riverside seat at Boudro's, famous for its potato chip-shaped umbrellas, and I ordered a Prickly Pear margarita and guacamole for two, prepared tableside. I usually would share the leftover guacamole and chips at home with Boone while we watched a Sponge Bob video.

"Hmm. The pianist," I said slowly, drumming my fingertips on the tabletop, mulling over the new information from my cousin. "I could see he was dying to join your fan club the other night, but he didn't impress me as being your type."

"My type — who knows — who cares? I haven't had much luck with my type anyway. It's time I moved up a notch. This guy, Nathan, he's a dancer and I haven't been dancing in decades. Lyle Lovett is playing at the dance hall in Gruene tomorrow night, so we're going there after dinner."

"Oh yeah, I read about that. I'd love to see Lyle myself, but surely he's sold out by now."

"Oh, but Nathan knows somebody. I'll get extra tickets; why don't you join us?"

"You're sweet, but I'll leave you to your own devices, thanks. I've seen the kind of work you do in a tree house, remember?"

Dana groaned. "Don't remind me of the old days, girl. They went by much too quickly."

When Dana was nine, she had asked her father for a yellow playhouse with white shutters. But Ned Cavanaugh had always wanted a son, so he built a rustic two-room cabin with tiny windows up in a tree. It was a sight to behold. Dana had always grumbled when she had to climb the ladder to reach it, like a weary soldier assigned to lookout duty at night.

During our pre-teen years, my parents allowed me to take the bus from Madison, Indiana to Louisville to spend the month of July with Dana. One year older, my cousin was further in development, and one day in the tree house she told me everything I hadn't yet thought to ask about sex. Dana kept her collection of Barbie dolls in the little fort, and she'd scribbled on them in precise locations with felt-tipped pens, making the entire Ken and Barbie assortment anatomically correct. When I saw the dolls, I immediately gasped, but Dana scolded, "Oh don't be a prude. We're all naked under our clothes."

It was nearing 100 degrees that day, and the atmosphere in the tree house was stifling. "This place is a hothouse; let's take off our shirts," Dana had said as she pulled her t-shirt over her head. I slipped out of mine, as well, but then I couldn't believe my eyes. "You've got boobs already?" I winced as I looked down at my own flat chest. Dana had laughed at me and said, "You'll get yours soon enough, Jules." I'd made a point to never again remove my clothing in front of my cousin that summer, but Dana had no sense of modesty. She still doesn't.

"You're right," I said. "Time went by much too fast. We grew up, I guess."

"Now, those were the days," Dana said, refilling our glasses.

"Hear, hear!" I raised my flute. "To your date with Nathan the pianist. And to Lyle Lovett. There's just something incredibly sexy about him."

We toasted to childhood, to romances past and present, and to success. Before long, the champagne bottle was empty.

When I entered the elevator for my return trip home, a trace of Marten's lime-mint was still there, even stronger than I had remembered, but how would that be possible? *My imagination is in overdrive.* I closed my eyes and inhaled his fragrance. *If he were a Mojito, he'd be my choice of a tall, cool drink on a hot Texas day.*

Chapter Nineteen

The Irish Pub

Perry Roberts warmed a bar stool at The Leapin' Lizard. He was on a mission and needed a head start on the booze. In the rear, an Irish band featured ballads between 4 and 6 p.m. Roberts liked that — easier on the ears than the old jukebox scene. In jeans and a pair of well-worn boots he'd found at a consignment store, he'd tucked his plaid flannel shirt under a hand-tooled leather belt, the one with a buckle half the size of Texas. He fit right in, although the hard part was finding a western hat that didn't slip down over his ears. The pub was crowded with Mexicans, which suited Roberts just fine. He admired men who knew the meaning of hard work and weren't afraid of it. The topic of conversation focused on one thing — new construction on the San Antonio Water Works building. The project engineer had hired too many laborers and none were getting the promised overtime. Happy Hour wasn't all that happy.

A wiry, bow-legged Mexican man, about the same height as Roberts, swaggered in.

"Hey, Gonzalez!" the bartender greeted him. "Any luck?"

"No way, man." He hopped onto the stool adjacent to Roberts.

Perry Roberts believed short guys should stick together. He ordered two Dos Equis and slid one of them over toward Gonzalez. "*Hola*," Roberts said.

The man grasped the bottle by its neck, angled it slightly toward Roberts and nodded as if to say *gracias*. He took a long swig of the cold liquid and slammed the bottle down so hard the brew spurted out onto the bar. He used the long sleeve of his shirt to soak it up. "Son of a bitch didn't hire me — never gave me a chance."

Roberts used his Texas accent. "A strappin' feller like you? Looks to me like you'd be a plus on a buildin' crew."

Gonzalez grimaced. "*No documento*."

Roberts nodded with understanding . . . *exactly* what he was looking for.

"If that high-falutin' old lady of mine would get a real job, I wouldn't be in this mess," Gonzalez groused.

"What's she do, *amigo*?"

"Nada. She sits around all the live-long day with a paintbrush stuck up her ass. Calls herself an *artiste*. I'll call her an artiste all right — a starving one."

Perry Roberts blinked. Didn't he have an immediate opening for a painter — one who needed fast money? "What does she do? Paint-by-number landscapes and shit?"

Gonzalez grunted. "No way. *When* she paints, it's murals she calls 'em. Insists someday them damn wall pictures will make her famous."

Roberts recognized a lucky day when he had one. He shrugged one shoulder in an attempt to appear disinterested in *amigo*'s woman, as Gonzalez chattered on about her. Turned out, she used to do what any respectable Mexican woman should do, Roberts gathered, housekeeping for wealthy Texans.

"She went off and got herself discovered by some far-distant relative of the Bush clan when she painted a desert on the walls of his fancy dining room."

"Impressive."

"Yeah. He even paid her in advance so she could stock up on good supplies." Gonzalez pulled a folded postcard from his wallet.

"She did this? It's good!" Roberts said. The walls appeared to be at least twenty feet tall and were decorated with whimsical Prickly Pear cacti, red succulent plants, quirky mesquite shrubs and tumbleweeds, bright yellow roadrunners and a fanciful pair of mining burros. The background was *faux*-finished with a realistic look of drifting desert sand. Roberts handed the photo back.

Gonzalez held it briefly to his lips. "My meal ticket," he said. He tapped his finger on the picture. "See here, the shelves of this old cabinet

— all layered with Mexican pottery and Cherokee art? She used to have to take each one out and dust it off every week. God help her if she dropped and broke anything. But no more. No sir."

"She doesn't clean for him now?"

"She don't even clean for me! No way. Shit . . . that man threw a high-society dinner party to show off his desert room, and some rich old woman stood up and nearly spoke in tongues, she was so damn excited." Gonzalez giggled like a little girl. "She said it was *novelty art* — hired my old lady to paint a Beatrix Potter wall for her granddaughter's nursery. You know . . . that Peter Rabbit cartoon character. Olga hasn't lifted so much as a feather duster ever since."

Olga. Roberts liked the sound of her name. "How much does she charge?"

"Five hundred for the last one, and it only took her two days!"

Perry Roberts whistled through his teeth. Way too cheap, he thought. "Big money," he said.

"She got another whole room comin' up — claims they gonna pay her $2,000. She thinks she's big-time now. She's too good to clean toilets, including her own. But referrals come slow and her English stinks. Rich people don't like that. If they could draw a picture of what they want, well hell, they could paint it themselves! Lucky for her, they have Hispanics working for 'em who can translate."

Roberts had plans for Olga Gonzalez, and if she dreamed of being famous without scrubbing toilets, maybe her dream was about to come true. She could hire her own maid if she wanted. "I might have some art work for her," he said.

Gonzalez sat up straight. "I can get her to meet with you," he said, "but I warn you, I think she quotes her prices too high for the *pequeño*, no offense, *hombre* — blue collar guy. It's like she works for high-class so she can act high-class. She turns *into* the people she works for. If somebody's common, then she thinks *she* is common. You see what I mean?"

Roberts nodded slowly as he peeled the top edge of the label off his bottle. He'd been drinking beer so he wouldn't appear uppity, but he was eager to get to the hard stuff. "I worked for a rich family a long time ago. When they fired me, I felt like shit. So, yeah, I get it."

"She thinks she's too good for the little jobs. I try to tell her those are the stepping-stones from the pond to the lake." Gonzales made his fingers walk across the bar, hopping from one invisible stone to another. "She don't listen to me." Gonzalez shook his head. "She never listen."

"She should take an English class, eh?"

"No. Don't tell her that! You remember after 9/11? Some self-righteous American, probably a damn Texan, no offense, passed around a chain letter on the Internet warning off immigrants, something like, 'Welcome to America. We speak English here and we're proud of it. You want to make your home here, FINE, but learn to speak ENGLISH. That's our language!!!'"

"I know the one," Roberts said. "That shitty piece of work made the rounds, over and over and over again."

"Well, since Texas was part of Mexico in the beginning, she thinks Texans should have learned Spanish, not the other way around. She's as stubborn as they come here in Texas. She come from a long line of stubborn, clear back to the Alamo days."

"No shit?"

"*Sí.*" Gonzalez nodded emphatically. "She claims her great-great-grandfather was at the Santa Anna siege in 1836, but she ain't got no proof. She's one proud Tex-Mex with a strong resentment toward Whitey — his oil *and* his money."

Roberts, laughing, ordered a bottle of Jose Quervo, two glasses and a lime. "She sounds like a ring-tail twister all right, *amigo*. You don't mind if I call you *amigo*, do you?"

Amigo rubbed a lime slice on the thumb and forefinger on the back of his right hand and sprinkled salt on the dampened area. He shook his head and waved his left hand, as if to say, *Call me whatever you want.* He licked the salt and leaned back, downing a tequila shot. "My old lady — she's way too big for her britches," he said, "and, trust me — I should know, they're pretty damn big!" He sucked the meat out of a lime slice and laughed loud and long at his own joke.

Roberts followed the same tequila routine without the annoying "he-he" at the end. This Olga person sought fame and fortune the quick and easy way. Roberts' kind of woman. Now he decided he liked Gonzalez's old lady even more. She sounded like the spirited type he needed to have around for the next few weeks. The fact she might be a plus-size would be an added benefit for him. She'd be fun to watch while she painted, and wouldn't he have the perfect perch for observing her in his new loft on Charles Court?

Roberts plied Gonzalez with a few more tequila shots and, in a lowered voice, suggested he might have work for him as well, on the side, *under the table* so to speak.

Amigo's eyes lit up. "I don't care what I do if the money is good."

"Good money," Roberts assured him, "but the hours, not so good — night work . . . very little time for sleep."

"*Sí,*" Gonzalez said with a toothy grin. "So that will make my old lady very happy. I will be out of our bed and out of her hair." His eyelids were half closed by now as he leaned toward Roberts. "Olga likes to sleep alone," he slurred. "She makes no secret 'bout that."

Roberts didn't respond. The bar vibrated with music and chatter; anyone watching would assume he hadn't heard Amigo's last statement. The little Mexican, too, may have made that supposition, but Roberts had carefully filed the information away with the other facts he knew about Olga Gonzalez.

Chapter Twenty

The Invitation

Early Saturday morning, Boone scampered into my room to watch cartoons, an apple in one hand and his craft-stick creation in the other. A pirate's hat floated on his blond curls. Britt and Andie had helped Boone finish his version of Prince Tuesday's cruise ship the night before, and it sailed upon waves of sea green sheets to the land of Nomnonica.

I snuggled up to my grandson. "Where, exactly, is Nomnonica?"

"In here, Gran. Nomnonica's in here," the child said, pointing to his temple. "And I'm the King."

"Oh, you cutie pie. Your imagination is the best. That's just one of the things I love about you." I reached for the little boat. "This is good . . . maybe you'll be a ship builder when you grow up." After all, he enjoyed watching the river floats on his walk to school.

I handed the boat back to Boone. He grinned and gave me a hug, then offered me a bite of his apple. I wished Andie had been as thoughtful as a child. Even now it seemed her first thought was always *how does this affect me*? I knew I'd enabled her, first when she was little, and secondly after Boone was born. Why, she'd never even had to make her own bed, I realized with a pang of guilt.

My thoughts were interrupted by the telephone — the business line.

"Good morning, Julia. It's Marten Wells. I hope I didn't awaken you."

"Oh no, my grandson took care of that already. What can I do for you?"

"I'm interested in exploring the German heritage around here. I've been told there is real, authentic Bavarian food in the vicinity. Do you know where I might find it, and, if so, perhaps you would be so kind as to accompany me?"

Marten was the type who got right to the point. No guessing where he was coming from. I liked that in a man — honest, sincere. "You're speaking to an expert," I said. "Of course, there's the delicatessen across the street, but I'm sure you've seen that. I presume you want to sit down and be served?"

"Actually, yes. It's a home-cooked meal I crave."

"Ah, well, German food *is* home-cooking. Let's see. New Braunfels and Gruene are old world towns about thirty miles north. I go there occasionally to browse the antique shops and boutiques, and, of course, for Bavarian cuisine. When do you have in mind?"

"Tonight."

So soon. "Tonight? Let me check . . . hold on a moment, please."

I flew into Andie's room and found her with a pillow over her head — her way of drowning out the morning's activity. After all, if she doesn't hear her son, how can she be responsible for him? I lifted the pillow and her eyes opened slowly, squinting from the bright sunlight.

"Sorry," I said, "but this is important. Are you planning on my watching Boone this evening while you go out?"

"Tonight?" Andie squeaked. "What day is it?"

"Saturday."

"Um, no. Why?"

"I'll tell you later. Go back to sleep."

"Right, like I can do that," Andie grouched. She yanked the pillow away from me and put it back in place.

I closed the door behind me, ran back into the bedroom and skated across the hardwood floor in my socks. I'd read in one of Andie's recent issues of *Cosmo* that a girl should never accept the first date right away. Always say something like, "I'm busy tonight, but I'm free the following week, blah, blah, blah." But this wasn't a date, was it? I picked up the phone. "Tonight would be fine. What time?" I wondered if I sounded breathless.

"You like to shop. Would you want to go early, maybe hit an antique store before dinner?"

"Umm, tempting. . . ." *Is there a red flag in here somewhere — a man invites me shopping?*

"How about 3:00?" he suggested.

"Okay, sure. Shall I meet you at the Hilton?"

"No need. I'll walk down to pick you up and we'll go from there."

I glanced at the clock — six hours before my first date since Richard's death, with the exception of that awful blind date a few weeks ago. Was it wise to go out with a client? Didn't matter — I wouldn't let it get physical.

What, I wondered as I surveyed my closet, do people wear these days? I decided on my skinny Levi jeans and red western boots. I laid out a denim shirt with embroidered red cactus on the yoke and silver hoop earrings. I purposefully did not go with pink; I didn't want Marten to think my obsession with it was over the top.

In the kitchen, I brought water to boil for a pot of English Breakfast tea. I pulled a box of blueberry muffin mix from the cabinet but couldn't read the directions without my glasses. They were nowhere to be found in the main living area. I finally located them right where I left them, in my bedroom on the nightstand next to the telephone. *Doggone if that phone call didn't set me on edge.*

The muffins tucked safely into the oven, tea pot under the cozy, I went back into my jungle bedroom, a.k.a. Boone's Saturday morning domain. Lifting Boone's pirate hat, I kissed his blond head. "Come to breakfast." He rolled out of the hammock and skipped into the kitchen. "Gran, I've decided; I *am* going to be a ship builder! I will build beautiful cruise ships so people can take their kids on trips."

"To Nomnonica?"

"Maybe," Boone said with a grin.

"Good choice, Boone. It's hard work, but fun, too."

"How do you know, Gran?"

"Well, long before your mom was born, at lunchtime I'd go to a little pizza place across the road from a ship yard and I watched them construct huge ocean liners."

"Where do people go to buy ships?" he asked. "Is there a ship store or something?"

"There are yacht and boating showrooms, sure. But the big, custom-made ones like you're talking of building would be ordered from you, the ship builder, and your customer could watch it being constructed, like I used to do. When it's finished, the craft floats upriver and out to sea to the new owner. At least that's the way I've always imagined it would be."

"How do they get it to the river?"

"Well . . . ship yards are usually right at the edge of large rivers, like Jeffboat on the Ohio River, near where I grew up. The captain and his team would go through a lot of training to learn all about the computer gadgets you would have put onboard. After that, he'd be involved with the last stage of construction, with inspections of the boat, and preparing it for the new guests and crew."

"Way cool! I could be a captain and navigate my ships to my customers."

"Navigate, now there's a big word," said Andie, who had stumbled into the living room, the aroma of blueberry muffins luring her out from underneath her quilt. "Ahoy, mate," she said as she lifted Boone's hat and ruffled his hair.

Boone frowned and pushed the hat down firmly on his head with both hands. That wouldn't stop the women in his family from trying to get our hands in his gorgeous hair. "Mommy, will you take me on a cruise someday?"

"Why yes, son. Someday I'll do that," Andie said. "Mom, what are you going to do tonight?"

"I have a date!"

"Good . . . who with?"

"Don't you think you should find out with whom *before* you say good?"

"Oh, I'm sure you're using your usual superior judgment," Andie said dryly.

Boone ran into the living room and jumped up and down on the sofa, singing, "Gran has a date! Gran has a date!"

I couldn't help but laugh. "With my new client, the charmingly British Marten Wells. You met him at the Open House."

"So, you're a cradle robber now?"

"He looks younger than he is — he's actually thirty-four."

"Humph." Andie shook her head. "I should have known. You've mentioned his name over 100 times this week already. He's a charmer, all right." Andie raised her voice, "Boone, stop jumping on the furniture!"

Andie didn't seem disapproving, just concerned . . . maybe a little curious. I wondered if she was thinking of her father and what he would think about this.

"I've said Marten's name only 100 times? I guess I like the way it sounds. My destiny is calling; I must answer."

Andie smirked. "My destiny is calling me, too." She was peeling navel oranges, methodically placing the slices in a serving bowl. "Britt is coming over tonight to help me develop a strategy to market my new fragrance. We're going to research the chemistry and marketing industries."

"If you ask me," I said, "there's chemistry between the two of you already."

She smiled, obviously pleased that I'd noticed.

"Marten and I will probably be out late," I added. "Dana and her date are going dancing in Gruene. I'll bet Marten hasn't seen the inside of a Texas dance hall yet; I may ask him if he'd like to join them." I hummed Lyle Lovett's song, *San Antonio Girl,* and danced with an invisible partner around the kitchen.

Andie seemed to be trying to suppress a grin as she watched me. "Mom," she whispered. "You're horny."

"Oh, my. I'm sorry." I didn't realize I was that transparent.

"It's okay . . . I mean, you're human and all. Just be careful. Geez, I can't believe you're dating a *client*!"

"Oh, it's not really a date, *per se*."

"Right. I know," Andie said. "I would say, 'Don't get your honey where you get your money,' but I guess that would be the pot calling the kettle black, huh?"

"And way too many clichés for my taste!"

Andie arranged three place settings on the breakfast table with the orange slices, muffins and the tea pot. Finally, she situated Boone's cruise ship in the middle as a centerpiece, and my family enjoyed what Boone called our *happy meal* together.

Chapter Twenty-One

The First Date

The German restaurant achieved its unique ambiance from a mixture of red hanging lanterns, lively Polka music and old Bavarian cupboards chockfull of antique beer steins. Apple turnovers, lemon sponge cakes, and luscious chocolate concoctions were displayed on a table near the entrance. My eyes lingered on the Black Forest Cherry Torte as soon as we walked in.

The hostess showed us to a table for two, adorned with a red and white checkered cloth. "Helga will be serving you shortly. Would you care for wine this evening? We're offering a Gewürztraminer, crisp and spicy."

Marten agreed to her suggestion without conferring with me. I relaxed, finding his assertiveness comforting. It was nice to have someone else take charge. We got down to a serious contemplation of the menu, and I decided on Sauerbraten. German fries were listed as the standard side but I wanted späetzle. However, the menu said "No Substitutions" in bold red letters at the bottom. The potatoes would suffice.

A waitress in a long flowered dress, a starched white apron tied around her sturdy waist, spoke directly to Marten. "Well, hello there, handsome," she sang. "I'm Helga . . . here to serve you."

She placed a glass of ice water in front of each of us. "Have we decided?"

Marten ordered: "The lady would like Sauerbraten and I'll have the Rohm Schnitzel."

I admired the distinct way Marten formed his words. It wasn't just the accent, although that was a big part of it. He spoke slowly with a deep voice. Obviously, Helga enjoyed listening to him, too. I took a deep breath and let it out, bit by bit.

"And, oh yes," Marten added, "for me, späetzle in place of the German fries, and a cucumber salad." He looked at me. "Ever since your party I can't get enough cucumber."

Undaunted, Helga noted his substitution selection, smiled brightly, and said, "My pleasure." She swished away in what I could only describe as a provocative manner.

My pleasure? Geez, everyone is saying that these days. I wondered if I could've gotten away with a substitution as easily as Marten did. Probably not. I promptly let go of that thought and asked him about his parents. He had mentioned his mother earlier in the day while we were antiquing in Gruene.

"They've passed, both Mummy and Poppa."

"Oh, I'm so sorry, Marten. Mine are gone, as well."

Helga reappeared and placed a small plate of rye bread with foil-wrapped butter squares next to Marten.

After I reached across the table for a slice, Marten rearranged the plate more toward the center of the table, next to a small vase of white gerbera daisies. "Were you young?" he asked.

"Thirteen years old." The cold butter ripped a hole in my bread as I attempted to spread it. "I was a bratty teen, but they loved me and took it in stride."

"Sounds like they were good people."

"They were the best parents. I appreciated them even more after I lost them . . . and after I became one myself. The only thing they did wrong — or, not wrong, but something I decided not to do with Andie — they boxed me in pretty tight with religion. Look at this! Why do they serve cold butter with soft bread?" I threw my shredded bread down in disgust. "Anyway, when they died, I went straight to my godparents, my aunt and uncle, who were of the same faith as my parents. So, in my box I stayed until my escape at 17, and then I kinda went crazy for a while."

Marten searched for the waitress, summoned her with a nod, and then inquired of me, "What do you mean, *boxed in*?" He seemed more interested in the subject of religion than in what I'd meant by going "crazy for a while." For that, I was grateful. I didn't even know why that had slipped from my mouth.

"Oh, you know, the usual cans and shoulds: what you *can* wear, what you *can't* say, how you *should* feel, whom you *should* marry. Typical rules of religion. Need I go on?"

Marten shook his head. "I get it. I was raised just the opposite. Mummy's cottage always emitted the scent of incense, and often you would hear chanting coming from the record box."

"New Age before there was such a thing." I wondered if Marten had been a mamma's boy, or rather . . . a *mummy's* boy.

The waitress materialized and Marten requested soft butter. She lightly touched his shoulder and hurried along to check on it.

"So, Julia, this interests me. How did your family's religion cycle start?"

"Let's see. My maternal grandparents were stalwarts in a cult." I made quotation marks in the air. "My word, cult, not theirs; Grandpa was highly offended when someone even suggested that. He preferred it be called a *sect*."

"Still . . . a four-letter word," Marten said.

I laughed. "How true. They raised their two daughters with rules for everything. The girls bought it — lock, stock and barrel. They knew no other way and were given no choice."

The waitress delivered a small bowl of butter pats and bragged that she had warmed them herself, especially for Marten. I imagined her nesting them in her cleavage, and I felt the corners of my mouth turn downward.

Marten spoke German to Helga who replied in kind. The only word I understood was "lieb" which I was pretty sure meant sweet.

"What did she say?"

"She says she loves me," Marten said with a smirk. "You're not jealous, are you?"

Yes, I was jealous; something strange had come over me, for sure, and once again words fell out of my mouth without my permission. "Me? Jealous? Heavens no. That cow of a waitress is the type of woman who jumps to attention whenever her husband snaps his fingers for another can of Heineken, *if* she even has a husband . . . which she probably doesn't." I took a deep breath.

Marten's eyes sparkled. "Oh boy! Julia's dark side is showing now. It's *you* I'm taking to dinner here; *she's* jealous of you, can't you see that?"

I flashed Marten a quick smile. That answered the question of whether or not he classified this as a date. I took another deep breath and, as I sipped my wine, I pulled myself together. "So, my mother and aunt — back to that subject — each obediently married men of their own faith, and, being such good followers, they mindlessly planned to continue the tradition. You know, keep stocking the pond, so to speak."

Marten grinned at me. "And you were their first little minnow?"

"Yep. Mom and Dad laid a good foundation on turning me into a droid . . . until their accident."

"Automobile?"

"Well, yes. And a train."

Marten raised one eyebrow and his face took on a curious *Tell me more look*.

"They were stopped at a railroad crossing when a drunk driver came from behind and shoved them right into the front of the locomotive. They died instantly . . . never had a chance."

"That's horrible! I'm so sorry."

My throat tightened. "The other guy didn't get a scratch on him, which is usually how it goes, isn't it?"

Marten nodded, cupped his chin in one hand and shook his head.

"At the funeral, people from the church told me God needed two more angels in heaven, so I lost faith in God right then and there. I thought, 'What? I didn't need them down here on earth, at least for a few more years?'" I looked down at the napkin in my lap, blinking back my tears. I should have saved that conversation for later, but Marten had asked, after all. Still, it was probably information overload.

Marten sat quietly, taking occasional bites of his cucumber salad, glancing my way from time to time.

I looked back up at him, finally, and continued "My mother's sister Betty married Ned Cavanaugh, a nice enough guy, but half-hearted about the religion. Probably went along with it to please his family, as many of them did, and he didn't give her much support in raising Dana according to the church's standards. Dana never did take to the religion either. Aunt Betty blamed Uncle Ned's laid-back attitude, but if you want to know the truth, Dana's personality is the type that would never have conformed anyway."

"Dana? *Stock Market* Dana is your *cousin?*"

"Sure is. I used to spend a few weeks with her every summer. We had the best of times growing up together. We were like sisters, and a good thing, too, because neither of us ever had siblings."

I smoothed out cleavage-warmed butter on another slice of rye. "What about you? Do you have any brothers? I hope so, for Dana's sake. She's smitten with your accent."

Marten chuckled and smiled knowingly. "No — only child." He cleared his throat, and his voice sounded more formal with his next sentence. "If I have extended family I know nothing about them." He quickly diverted his eyes and I knew in an instant it was a lie. Why, I didn't know, but I didn't care, either. We all have skeletons in our closets. Anyway, he was only a client, I reminded myself.

"Maybe we should start the Only Child Club," I said. "We've got three members already."

He twisted in his chair, ignoring my statement, looking at various memorabilia on the walls.

Thinking it best to change the subject, I said, "Well, Marten, that's enough about me. Let's talk about you. What do *you* think about me?"

He had just taken a sip of wine. Holding his napkin to his mouth, he laughed appreciatively at my joke. His eyes danced when he smiled. I thought I could study his smile for many weeks to come, if he'd let me. I didn't care where he'd been in his past, only that he was with me right then.

My vital signs could have caused a code when he stepped off the elevator earlier that afternoon. He'd loaded up on his Mojito scent and wore blue Levis, a black silk shirt with a lapis bolo, a hand-tooled leather belt with a silver tip and black boots. It was almost as though he'd dressed to match my outfit, but then, how could he have known?

At the antique shops in New Braunfels, Marten had handled several items to gain the sense of them, their surface texture and density. He didn't look at anything without touching it, and I liked that about him. He wasn't there just for the visual experience; he was making it a sensual thing, as though he could absorb history through his fingertips. Boone always wanted to touch everything, so it was like shopping with him except I didn't have to worry about Marten's breaking something. Of course, he could break my heart, but I wouldn't allow that, plus I was sure he had no such intention.

He'd shown particular interest in a large display of vintage quilts. "Mummy used to make and sell quilts," he said, as he unfolded a blue and white log cabin pattern to check the price tag. "Her collection is in storage at our cottage in Wales." He refolded the quilt and tucked it under his arm. "I'm a sucker for blue and white. I don't know why. I suppose Mum wrapped me up in one the day she brought me home."

I'd pictured a mummy wrapped up in an old quilt somewhere far away, and felt rather guilty for being so crude. He was, after all, speaking of his mother. I valued motherhood more than anything, even more than a lucrative career. I'd have to familiarize myself with the vocabulary of proper English if I were to hang with Marten, or for the visiting British dignitaries, for that matter, who would be in San Antonio for nearly a week.

After dinner, we ended up in the Dance Hall in nearby Gruene. Marten insisted he couldn't dance, but I showed him the Texas Two-Step and he picked it up like a pro. Dana was there with her piano man, and she waved across the crowded hall. I caught a glimpse of them a couple of times, but Lyle and his Large Band had the place so packed, there was barely room to move around. We two-stepped with the pulse of the crowd until we were both ready to call it a day.

We got back to my place well after three o'clock. We sipped cappuccino out on the roof as we gazed at the stars. *Just like they do in the movies on a first date.* But this was better than a movie because it was my life *happening . . .* finally. I wondered again if I should mix business with pleasure. I'd heard it could be disastrous. I made up my mind to manage somehow — if, that is, Marten asked me out again. And even if he didn't, I thanked the stars above for estrogen and progesterone, and whatever other hormones that made me feel like a vital woman again.

Chapter Twenty-Two

Cousins

At noon on Sunday, I heard the rumble of the dumbwaiter and found a note stuck halfway under a bowl of cold cucumber soup. *"J — Get down here ASAP. I have to hear all about last night! ~D"*

I'd been expecting the third-degree from Dana.

"What took you so long?" Dana said, her purple eyes flashing. She was standing right by the elevator, waiting. "Were you working or what?"

"I don't work on Sundays and you know it. Chill out, woman. You wanted me to try your soup, right?"

"Did you like it?"

I nodded emphatically.

"Good. We altered the recipe. The staff has everything under control; I'm just here for effect, really . . . not working much today, either."

"That might just well be a first."

"Emilio gave them all a pep talk last week. So, tell me. Do you like him?"

"Emilio?"

She leaned over close and squinted, pointing her finger at the tip of my nose. "You. Know. Who. I. Mean."

We trailed into Dana's cubby-hole of an office, where I gave her details of the night before. "There isn't anything particularly juicy to tell. The man was a perfect gentleman, engaging in conversation; he laughs easily and makes great eye contact."

"That's how you judge a person's character, right?"

"Yes. He looked sincerely and directly into my eyes. A man with nothing to hide."

"That'd be a miracle," Dana said sarcastically.

"Our tastes in music are similar, too. He sat at my piano and played Billy Joel's song, Piano Man."

Dana sang, *"Sing us a song. You're the Piano Man."*

I chimed in: *"Sing us a song tonight. Well we're all in the mood for a melody, and you've got us feeling all right."*

"Wow — I just realized we're both dating pianists!" Dana said.

"Oh, I'm not dating Marten. Really, I'm not. But we did enjoy the evening and we had a nightcap of cappuccino out on the balcony, under the stars. It was rather romantic, I must say."

Dana held both palms up. "Well? Did he kiss you good night, at least?"

"Only a quick brush on the cheek. And remember, he *is* a client, first and foremost. I'm not sure if he'll call me again on a social basis, but I think there's a good chance of it!"

Dana headed for the window and proclaimed to the world outside, "Julia Tyler *has* started dating again, whether she wants to admit it or not!"

I couldn't help but giggle. "Oh . . . and when we were out on the roof, he asked me if I had a telescope."

Dana raised one eyebrow. She no doubt imagined him a voyeur.

I hated to pop her balloon. "Odd . . . he seemed relieved when I told him I didn't."

"Well, shit!" Dana said.

Emilio burst into the office. A crisis in the kitchen.

"Shit, double shit," Dana hissed. "I gotta run. Why don't you go on in and help yourself to some lunch? On the house!"

Chapter Twenty-Three

More Than a Client

The Monday morning sky was unusually dark. Flashes of lightning bolted from clustered nebulous clouds. With a humidity rate of 95 percent, the air held nothing but water. I slept better in a thunderstorm than any other time. When I opened my eyes, I was stunned to see how late it was, and I hurried out of bed to check on Boone. It appeared that Andie had already taken him to school. Thunderstorms frighten the child — he'd probably trotted into his mother's room and awakened her. *Good for him.*

The elevator bell rang and I summoned the lift — a soaking wet delivery boy from the florist shop carrying a long, white box. I handed him a tip but he would hear nothing of it, claiming the sender had already taken care of it. I hoped the sender was Marten. I read the personally scripted note:

> *When I awoke I thought it merely a dream. Then . . . I smiled. Thank you, Julia, for making my Saturday a special one.*
> *~ Marten*

The box contained a dozen pink long-stemmed roses which I promptly arranged in a Waterford vase, added water and placed on the kitchen island. The flowers were sure to brighten up what had promised to be an otherwise gloomy workday.

The racket in the heavens prevented me from concentrating effectively on my work duties, so I took an early lunch break and paid my personal end-of-month bills, reducing my checking account balance to $100 even. That was cutting it way too close for my comfort. I frowned as I sealed and stamped the envelopes. My condo maintenance fee wasn't due until the fifth of next month. I'd pay it online, whereas I mailed checks for most of my other expenses. I could've paid them online, but I had personal reasons why I didn't. For one thing, the health and life insurance companies charged me fifty cents for each online payment. Wasn't that extortion to charge *me* for paying *them*? So, I used their enclosed envelopes and I provided the stamps. Truth be told, the real reason I posted checks was so I could send them down the mail chute. I'd listen to them shuffle all the way down and think of the people who had done the same thing in the past, as this building had always housed businesses and residences alike. I wanted the history of The Clifford's past to remain, plus I liked contributing to our USPS.

I tossed my checkbook into its home in a kitchen drawer, then ground a large scoop of coffee beans and inhaled the welcoming fragrant mixture — chocolate almond beans mixed with the heady scent of roses. Each petal was wrapped tightly around another, virgin-like. One was beginning to open up, ever so slightly. I took it as a sign.

Tuesday and Wednesday were nearly as dark and stormy as Monday. I'd transferred the crystal vase back and forth from the kitchen into my office but had forced myself to keep my mind off Marten for the most part. Fortunately, I was swamped with new business generated from the Open House. There were phone calls and e-mails to answer and reports to run.

But at night . . . ah, the nights, When I finally collapsed into bed, my head was full of dancing and stargazing. I thought about our first encounter at the Little Rhein Steak House. Even then, I'd felt a peculiar connection with him . . . familiar, somehow. He hadn't telephoned since our time together on Saturday, but I thought nothing of it. I had no plan to fall in love — I was in love with the feeling of being entirely alive.

Day by day, each rose opened gracefully. The sun came out in full force on Thursday and the first petal fell. That's when I saw him again.

Marten stopped by to deliver his clinic's lease agreement for the company file. He arrived at two o'clock, asking me to edit some basic data in the accounting system using the new, official address on Navarro Street.

I browsed the documents as we walked down the hallway to my office. "I don't see your signature on here."

"No. I'm a representative, a *consultant,* you might say — not an actual owner of the business."

I located Marten's folder, removed it from my filing cabinet and seated myself at the computer. He pulled up a chair alongside and reached into his portfolio, handing me a slip of paper. I took it and looked at him expectantly for clarification.

"We like to pay in advance."

"But . . . this is made out to me personally, and it's *your* check, not that of the business I'm to handle for you. It could be a problem for me tax-wise."

"Do with it as you please, then." He waved dismissively, as though he had no worries as to how I applied the funds.

What was that supposed to mean? I said no more as I edited the company's address data, while Marten talked non-stop about the weeks of remodeling ahead before his clinic would open to the public.

"I remember the day I signed on the dotted line," I said. "I was just as excited as you are with plans for the design of my new office and home. It's all so hectic and exhilarating at the same time, isn't it?"

Marten, wound-up and fidgety, stood behind me while I made the last couple of entries into the computer. "I love to watch you work," he whispered.

I swiveled my chair and smiled up at him. "I like for you to watch." Now, I hadn't actually *meant* for that comment to carry a sexual suggestion, but I realized it had sounded that way. *Oh well, we are in a massage room.* After a long pause, I continued keying data and prepared to close the file.

"Oh, wait." He rested his hand loosely on my shoulder. "Would you mind leaving the file open tonight? My London associates need to access our financial information on their end. They have data to add and the time-zone thing makes it hard to do. I might have a few entries to make tonight, too."

"We're using a shared software program, so you or your associates can log in whenever you need to enter necessary data, probably your Payables and Receivables, right? You just have to use your own respective passwords." I thought it strange that he didn't know this already. Why would he need me to leave my entire accounting program wide open? I would never do anything that foolish.

Marten shuffled around in the tiny office space, exploring my book shelves. He selected *Accounting Techniques for Dummies* and flipped through its pages. "I wonder if they make one of these books for an ignoramus like me opening a health clinic. I never expected the red tape — the hoops we'd have to jump through."

"If there's anything I can help you with, just call."

"Thanks. I'll keep you in mind." He tucked the book back into its slot. "So . . . this was a massage room years ago. Where does that little door lead?"

I described the exit hallway and how each massage room had its own entrance for privacy purposes. "There's a secured door at the end of the hall that opens into the common stairwell, the one all tenants can use. We've had to use it a few times when our private lift was finicky. Usually we just have to go down one flight of stairs and get the public elevator from there, or we can take the stairs, if we're in need of exercise."

"Plenty of escape routes from your condo, I see."

"I've never thought of wanting to escape from here. This place *is* my escape!"

"I mean, in an emergency," Marten said. "Of course, you have the old metal fire stairs on the exterior, too."

"And, here's something else not many people know about the building," I said. "This room we're in was exceptional during the days of the old club, not only because it was the largest, but because the dumbwaiter from The Stock Market opened in here as well as in my kitchen. I like to think that the most pretentious of men got their massages in this very room, and they probably ordered delicacies at their whim." I chuckled. "Can you imagine people indulging themselves so?"

Marten nodded emphatically, as though he didn't need imagination. He gazed into the distance, as if recalling the grandeur and opulence of even the simplest of meals wealthy people were served in England. His eyes returned to the present. "Do you ever use it? The dumbwaiter?"

"Not this one — not anymore. Dana frequently sends up our lunch, but I access it from the kitchen side. I've covered over this one with shelving, as you can see. I needed the wall space more than the luxury of private food delivery. Boone loved to ride in it at one time, and Andie let him! It drove me crazy because I didn't think it was safe. I wouldn't mind losing a meal in there, but not my grandson. He hasn't asked to ride in it lately. I guess the newness has worn off, thank goodness."

"I'd imagine he's much too large to fit in there now, anyway."

"Probably." I'd remained seated and Marten stood closer, tracing the top edge of my computer monitor with his finger. "I wonder . . . did American presidents visit the club?"

"It's rumored they did. Hundreds of dignitaries have been massaged in this very room, don't you imagine?" I let out a long sigh and leaned back slightly in my chair. "Sometimes I feel an overpowering tranquility while I work, like I'm getting vibes from those old days."

"More than just simple massages took place here?"

I looked up at him again. "Oh. Well, I should think." I paused. "Actually, Doc says hookers snuck in through this little back door."

"No! You don't say."

"For real! Way back in the early 60's when Doc was a new club member, an older lawyer friend of his paid for his very first massage in this same room to celebrate his passing of the medical exams. This was a two-person massage room, and they discussed business during their massages. Anyway, at the end, a hooker walked in that door right over there. Doc was shocked!"

"Why did he tell you this?"

I laughed at Marten's mortified expression. "Oh, because he 'politely' turned it down and walked away. Left the girl right here in this room with the lawyer who had stuck around merely to *introduce* the girl. Apparently, she was one of his favorites, I don't know. Anyway, I try not to think about what happened in here!"

"That's quite a story."

"It's a true story, too. Doc says he went to the check-out desk and tipped the masseur who seemed confused that Doc had left his lawyer friend in the room with the girl. Doc just smiled and told him he wasn't into that sort of thing."

"Hmm," Marten says. "I wonder what the masseur thought."

"Oh, you'll love this. He was so impressed with Doc's moral ethics that he arranged for his sister to meet him. That's how Doc and Nina met. It's definitely a wonderful and colorful true story."

Marten stood, staring at the little door. "Hmm. Hookers, eh? Perhaps we should try it out. Maybe one is waiting right outside that door."

I shrugged one shoulder and handed Marten my cell phone. "Here you go. Call and see if they come in. Their number is on my speed dial," I said sarcastically. My armpits had that prickly feeling I always got when I was nervous, and I held my breath.

Marten locked eyes with mine, took my hand, removed the cell phone and returned it decisively to my desk. He brought me to my feet and pulled me close, tipping my chin upward.

One always remembers the first kiss, if it is memorable, and I knew I would never forget that one. His lips were like silky-soft cushions. I sank into them, surrounded with comfort, hoping the moment would never end.

Finally, I pulled away, gazing into his eyes, just like in a romance novel. Ugh.

"I feel like I should ask you what you're doing the rest of your life," he said, and we both laughed like giddy teenagers. "But seriously, what are you doing Sunday? I assume from our previous conversations you won't be spending it in a church. I'd like take a walk with you downtown, if the weather is nice."

My second date with a client, only now he wasn't just a client, was he? One kiss changed all that. Yeah, I don't make a practice of kissing my clients. Now I could worry about the juggling part for real, as if I needed something else to worry about.

After he left, I returned to my office. The check was there — *Pay to the order of Julia Tyler, $2,000.* That could definitely solve my money crunch; some of my regulars had been slow to pay lately. I'd decreased my personal salary by half this month. But this confused me. No one else ever paid in advance . . . and without an invoice.

Opening my personal accounting program, I clicked on the "Send Statements" tab and prepared monthly reminders to my overdue clientele. While the printer did its job, I puzzled over my cash-strapped predicament. I wondered about the high-class prostitutes who'd entered through the little door. They'd been paid plenty to do a lot more than kiss their clients. Would it be immoral for me to accept money from Marten? I placed Marten's lease documents into his file, dropped the check in with them, closed and locked the filing cabinet. *This is getting me nowhere*, I thought. I cut my work day short.

Grabbing a bottle of Frederick's favorite Chardonnay from the wine cooler, I made a phone call to see if he was in his apartment, one floor below mine. I selected two medium-sized water glasses from the cabinet and ran down the stairs.

"Welcome!" Frederick proclaimed upon my arrival. He eyed the glasses suspiciously. "We're doing some serious drinking, I see. No offense, but I believe I'll enjoy mine from a stemmed crystal, thank you." He went for the bar and chose a more appropriate wine glass.

After fluffing a silk throw pillow meticulously on one end of his couch, he said, "Sit down right here, Sweetie. Now, what's up with you? Tell me everything!"

Slowly, the wine had the desired effect and I loosened up. I shared the story of my romantic experiences, bringing Frederick up-to-date about the Saturday in Gruene and New Braunfels, the roses, the mysterious check and the kiss.

"Julia's been a busy lady," Frederick said.

"But, who *is* this man?" I said. "The thought *too good to be true* comes to my mind."

Frederick frowned. "Explain," he said.

"How could I be lucky enough to have such a good looking man with interests the same as mine just simply walk into my life?"

"How could he *not*, Jules? It was bound to happen sooner or later. You're worth it, don't you see?"

"I don't know about that. Dana likes to say you have to kiss a lot of frogs. I haven't kissed any since Richard."

"Marten Wells is your Prince Charming, straight from the palace. He's no frog at all!"

"What if he's a chameleon, telling me just what I want to hear?"

Frederick tsk-tsked and shook his head. "Why would he do that?"

"No real reason. But I can hardly think of anything else but him."

"You worry too much, Jules. You're not getting married — you just met the man, which, by the way, would make a *marvelous* romance novel. I can see the book cover now ... the two of you dining at adjacent tables — the Arneson Theater in the background."

"Well ... *you* write the story. I'll take half the profits. Which brings me to another question. I wonder how much money he has?"

"Julia! Honestly!"

"Oh come on. He's not generating an income yet, as far as I can tell. Oh, of course, his personal finances are none of my business, but when you get kissed the way he kissed me, it can't help but come to mind."

"Do you think he's interested in you for your money?"

"I'm not wealthy, by any means."

"You do have some hefty assets and a profitable business. But, no, it wouldn't be the money. He obviously has funds of his own, living at the Hilton the way he is."

"A girl does have to think of these things, you know."

"Not just a girl. I do too, whenever I meet someone. It's called self-protection."

"Richard left me well protected, and I'm very careful not to squander what's left of it."

"What's *left* of it? Did you invest it all in the condo?"

"No. When Boone came early, the neo-natal expenses were sizable, and, since Andie was on *my* health policy, Boone wasn't covered."

"I did not know that!" Frederick said. He thoughtfully shook his head.

"There was no need for me to tell anyone. Well, of course, Doc knew. But I worked out a repayment plan and finally got rid of the debt last year."

"Didn't Richard leave a trust fund for Andie?"

"Well ... yes."

"Seems to me she should have been able to use it to pay her son's expenses."

"Technically, she doesn't get her inheritance until she's 21, in three more weeks. There was a provision for emergency expenses, but I didn't want to use her money if I didn't have to."

Frederick raised his voice. "*For her own son?*" He shook his head again and studied me with alarm. I suppose he thought it wasn't a good financial move on my part. I'd begun to think that, myself. Anyway, I hoped he was beginning to take my current dilemma seriously.

"I wonder what it would be like to be married to him?" I smiled, realizing I was getting way ahead of myself. "I'm thinking too much again, aren't I?"

"That's easy to do. But, look, you're only going for a walk on Sunday, right? And what possible hidden motives could Marten have, anyway?"

"Whatever they are, I can handle them. And I'll make it my business to find out if there are any."

"Try not to put a label on your relationship this early in the game. Maybe he just wants a lover, nothing more."

I wiggled my eyebrows. "That would work for me."

Chapter Twenty-Four

A Walk Through the City

Sunday morning, still in my pink chenille robe, I ventured out onto my rooftop garden with a thermos of coffee and my favorite mug to watch the sunrise. The purple and orange horizon promised a beautiful day for a walk downtown with a forecasted high of 76 degrees. February in Texas — it would only get warmer from here.

I added seed to the birdfeeder; BB pellets were scattered underneath. If only I could get rid of pesky squirrels. Until I found a way, I'd continue aiming at the bushy-tailed thieves. The BB gun chased them off only momentarily, but I was satisfied to make my point. They always got the last word, perching on the feeder, poking their heads this way and that, chattering and staring through my office window, daring me to use something more effective. I would never intentionally hurt a squirrel, of course. So I bought extra birdseed instead. It was like the old video games Boone played at the ice cream store next door; he had to insert a quarter to play, but it was worth it.

Before long, my thermos was empty and the sun had made a brilliant debut. I quietly slipped back inside. Andie and Boone were still asleep, but they'd get up soon for a trip to Houston with Britt to spend the day with his parents.

I stepped into a white sweat suit and pink running shoes, applied a touch of blush and ran a comb through my hair. I fastened tiny, pink pearl earrings. Then, I jogged down Commerce Street to meet Marten at the Hilton.

He was waiting for me in the lobby, wearing khaki shorts and a black long-sleeved linen shirt, brown leather loafers — no socks. He sported a smart-looking Mexican silver chain around his neck and appeared deep in thought, possibly a little annoyed. He brightened when he saw me walk toward him, offered a peck on my cheek and led me down the stairs to the Hilton's sidewalk café. We filled our plates at the brunch buffet and carried them out to a waterside table.

Across the river, sightseeing barges waited in preparation for the tourists who had already formed a line at the ticket booth. Marten placed his napkin on his lap and glanced across the river. "Tourists!" he said with disgust. "They all look the same, and most of them are fat!"

I scowled at him. "Did we get up on the wrong side of the bed?"

"Well . . . just look. Okay, half of them, anyway," Marten argued.

I assumed he'd be in a better mood once he had breakfast.

Marten cast his eyes toward an over-sized teen-aged boy walking by. Tilting his head sideways, Marten said dryly, "That just about says it all."

I turned in my chair. The boy was wearing an extra-large tee-shirt with a bold message on the front: *I'm Not Fat, I'm American!*

"Sad, but true, I suppose," I said with a sigh.

Marten held his fork, topped with a portion of western omelet, in mid-air. "That's what I'm saying."

"You won't get an argument from me, Mr. Wells, but it's no skin off your nose. You're British."

"Thank God."

I released a boisterous sigh. "If you don't like it here, you know where the airport is."

Marten groaned. "I'm sorry. I don't try to be rude."

"You don't? It comes naturally, then?"

"I apologize, seriously."

I tilted my head slightly and cast a thoughtful look upward, as though I had a decision to make. "Apology accepted."

I cut into a Belgian waffle with whipped cream and blueberries on top. "Oh man. Delicious. You can't blame people for wanting to eat this kind of stuff! Here, try a bite," I said as I sent a large piece on a fork across the table.

"Umm. No wonder everyone is fat if this is the kind of food they eat. It *is* delicious."

"Shame on you, Marten! Anyway, personally, I find it thrilling to live vicariously through vacationers. Many are here for the first time and you can put yourself into that moment if you try."

"At least they're looking downward, at the river. In New York, they walk on the sidewalks looking up, like they've never seen a tall building in their entire life."

I was still determined to brighten the mood. "Why do you Brits have no sense of humor? Tourists in Gotham City merely want to spot Batman. Or Superman — you know he can leap tall buildings in a single bound." I took another bite of my waffle.

Marten chuckled. "One of them slammed right into me, face-first, not watching where he was going."

"Which one was it? Batman or Superman?"

Marten made a face at me.

"A tourist, I'll bet." I said. "Well then, one must be not only a defensive driver in New York, but a defensive walker as well." A server topped off my coffee, and I added cream to the cup. I took a sip, and even that was perfection on this beautiful morning. "Oh, but I do so love New York. When were you there?"

"Hmm? Oh . . . last summer," he said.

Marten had directed his gaze down river toward the Arneson Theater, and I wondered if he was thinking of the night we first made eye contact.

After a few moments, he glanced back at me and continued, "I met with some bankers."

I looked at him blankly.

"When I was in New York, I mean."

"Oh . . . sure." Hoping to add even more to the lighter atmosphere, I said, "I think the tallest building along the Riverwalk is your hotel, here. I've seen old photographs of it, back in the day when it was built, and people were in line all along this very sidewalk, gawking, just like in New York, watching those rooms be put in by crane."

"Now, *that,* I'd like to see. Do you have the photos?"

"I'll show you next time you're at my place. They're in a book called *A Dream Come True*. It's the story of the architect's plan and development of this entire area."

After breakfast, we ascended concrete steps to Market Street, crossed it and cut through a parking garage.

Pointing to my Jeep, covered with dust from my last trip to Evergreen Cemetery, I said, "This is where I park. It's the only disadvantage to living downtown. Bringing in groceries can be a chore. Sometimes I splurge and have them delivered."

Marten used his forefinger to print "WASH ME" on the Jeep's rear window. I was glad to see his improved mood. We continued through the garage and strolled the length of Presa to Houston Street. We passed River Protocol, Inc., and suddenly the Alamo appeared, as if out of nowhere.

"Look! The Alamo," Marten said. "I was surprised when I first saw it — to find it located right in the heart of downtown."

"Lots of people are shocked that way."

"I overheard a boy ask his mum, 'Why did they build the Alamo downtown?' Of course she explained to him that it had been the other way around."

Marten handed his camera to a passerby and then he slipped his arm around my waist to pose for a photograph with the mission in the background.

"Are you familiar with its history?" I asked.

"Absolutely. American history is one of my favorite subjects. I even went to see the IMAX presentation. Good . . . but a little pricey."

I stood with my hands on my hips, considering the old mission. "With IMAX's location right across the street, maybe not too overpriced. The theater's always full, anyway. I went just last month with Boone's class to see it for probably my 10th time! Whenever friends visit from out of town, that's where they want to go, so I always oblige. And, the film does wrap up the meaning of *Remember the Alamo!* into a neat little bundle. You know, over 200 men lost their lives in that battle." I wondered if I sounded like a tour guide.

"Here's the engraved monument," Marten said.

We observed the granite structure, taking turns reading names. "Their fate was death — they bravely died for freedom."

"I knew that much," Marten said. "Ironic, I thought, too, how Santa Anna went about bragging all over Texas of his victory here, and a bunch of Texans who heard about it joined up with Houston's army to get revenge. Texans are a proud bunch."

"*Remember the Alamo!*" I shouted.

"Revenge is sweet, so they say."

"Amen to that," I added. "I wasn't born in Texas, but I got here as fast as I could!"

Marten laughed. "You could pass for a pure-bred Texan, if you ask me." He took my hand and gazed into my eyes. "We make a good team, don't we? Come along. There's something I want to show you."

We sauntered along Crockett Street to Presa. Marten pulled a shiny key from his pocket and unlocked the iron gates leading into Charles Court. During business hours, the gates stood wide open, but it was a little too early for the shops on a Sunday. We followed the brick walkway past a koi pond where the path curved toward an amusing water fountain, achieved by three-foot tall concrete walls spaced 20 inches apart, painted inside and out with vibrant aqua and purple. Lights on the inner sides of the walls illuminated vertical jets of clear water as they shot out from the center, cascading in vertical waves. We stopped momentarily to admire the splendor of it, mesmerized by the rhythm of the water columns.

"Noisy art," I said. "This is my favorite composition on the court."

"Not me. I like that upside-down sculpture of a nude woman over there."

"Pervert."

He laughed and buzzed my cheek with a kiss. I recalled our first kiss in my office and I longed for a repeat of its intensity. I'd replayed the emotions in my mind countless times already. Surveying the entire perimeter of the court, I assured myself we were alone. I reached for Marten's hands and wrapped his arms around my waist. He eagerly leaned into me and our lips meet briefly, but voices drifted in from the front of the court. Marten released me and smiled his signature crooked grin. He led me further down the walkway to a vacant building at the opposite end. I could see its potential for a children's health clinic; with huge windows front and back, I saw right through it to Navarro Street.

He opened the door and guided me inside where our passion could be quenched without interruption. His kiss was even more delicious than before and I savored it with my eyes closed.

Eventually, I opened my eyes and looked around. Sunlight streaming in from the street side created a bright and cheerful effect, highlighting tiny dust particles bouncing off the old brick walls. A set of narrow stairs on the front end led up to a landing where a small, rectangular barred transom window allowed more light into the vast space. Marten playfully chased me as I ran up the steps, stopping momentarily to view the courtyard from the transom.

Upstairs was a sizable loft. "How quaint! I love this space." Graffiti gang-type designs jumbled all together were spray-painted on the outer wall. One in particular caught my attention. It resembled a lizard inside a triangle. I pointed to it. "What's that?"

Marten shrugged. "I don't know. It's nothing that matters, I'm sure. Anyway, we'll paint over all of it. Look, here are the plans," he said, as he unfolded a set of blueprints onto a dusty work table, laying out the grid and motioning all around. He pointed downward to the first floor. "The examining rooms are there, reception room to the right by the front door, and up here we'll have our executive offices."

My imagination took over as I visualized primary colors: reds, blues and yellows; dancing bears in striped jumpers; monkeys in polka-dot pants; maybe an Old World nursery rhyme design, seeing as the idea for the clinic came from Europe. I pictured Humpty Dumpty having a discussion with Alice in Wonderland on the first floor wall facing the loft. Wouldn't kids love it?

Without a second thought, I said, "Let me do the decorating for you!"

Marten appeared taken aback. "Oh, we'll leave that up to the professionals."

I realized I must have gotten it from my mother, the self-confidence that I could be an interior designer without the training. My impulsiveness sometimes reared its ugly head. But, his response hurt my feelings.

He seemed to pick up on my disappointment. "Actually, it's out of my hands, anyway. I believe it was already put into motion last week with a local design firm."

"I see. Who is it?"

"I don't know. Like I said, it's not in my area of expertise."

"Oh well," I sighed. Just because we'd kissed didn't give me the authority to be his decorator. He was probably afraid I'd go pink crazy.

Eventually, Marten showed me out and locked his empty building. We walked back into the court, stopping briefly at each European-style statuette and modern art sculpture. At the front of the court stood Zinc, a champagne bar and restaurant facing Presa Street. Housed in a typically narrow, downtown building with the customary polished old wood floors, Zinc boasted handsome glass doors on both ends — yet another fashionable structure on the court one could see straight through. Along one side, above the bar, wine and champagne bottles hung in overhead racks. Bar stools and tables hugged the opposite wall.

"I believe they're open," Marten said. "Would you care for a glass of wine and a light snack?"

"Sounds delightful. I'll wait out here. Whatever sounds good to you will be fine with me."

I commandeered a table beside one of the fountains. Marten soon joined me, followed by a waiter carrying a tray and a bottle of 2005 Treana Red.

We nibbled on almond-stuffed olives, brie and flatbreads. "This courtyard . . . the fountain, even the koi pond. It all causes me to reminisce," Marten said. "Working here will be just what I need. I feel I'm a young boy again." He held one hand firmly onto the top of a jet of water at the adjacent fountain, causing spurts to arise through his fingers. His shirt sleeve got wet but he didn't seem to care.

"Tell me about your childhood," I said. "What was it like where you grew up?"

"Truthfully? Just like this courtyard, here. We lived in a tiny village in Wales where Mum had a pastry shop. Our flat was over the shop, so my alarm clock was always the aroma of hot croissants. Outside the doorway was a cozy walled courtyard with an arched stucco entrance from the narrow, bricked street. In the center of it all was a fountain, and at one end Mum tended her herb garden. Our customers sat at round picnic tables and enjoyed their pastries and coffee in the mornings."

I could picture it as though I were there at that very moment. "I'd love to visit Europe someday — I adore old architecture."

"Brick on the ground evokes treasured memories for me — brings me back, every time."

"What did your father do?"

Marten's face took on a thoughtful look and I settled in for a long story.

"He was with the government and traveled a lot," Marten said. "His visits home were infrequent. So he sent money instead, and plenty of it. My mother always had the utmost regard for him but they were never married. One thing I remember about him was his love of soup. Mum would make his favorite — comfort food, you Americans call it. I've eaten delicacies from around the world, Julia, but you put a bowl of soup in front of me, and I'm in heaven."

"You must get that from your father."

Marten nodded. "That's why I was eager to try Dana's Stock Market. I'm anxious to get my own flat so I can get back into cooking. As a teenager, I worked with Mum every day in the shop. I'm a pretty good cook, you'll see. I have all of her recipes: bouillabaisse, bisque, chowders, even gumbo."

"I wonder if Dana would be interested in those."

"I'd be happy to share with her. She could name one after Mum: *Adelina's Olde English Chowder*. That would make me very happy, indeed."

Marten poured more wine. "Here's to soup," he said as he raised his glass to mine.

I thought of something Boone had said when he was two years old: "Boone calls toasting 'cup fights'."

"Hah! The things we adults take for granted, like a simple toast, must look quite peculiar to a small child. Then, here's to soup and cup fights." We touched our glasses together.

"You know what? Dana makes a fantastic cheddar cheese beer mixture, almost a fondue, that would be great with this wine," I said. "And maybe some French bread. I wonder if this restaurant would want to carry it on their menu."

"You might mention it to her. She could expand her business even further that way," Marten said. "Have you ever thought about going into marketing? You have good ideas. Perhaps you could increase *your* business, as well."

"Thank you. You're developing yours, mine is growing and Dana's is, too. That's accomplishing much in today's economy for all three of us."

Marten inhaled deeply. "My business is a dream come true for me, but there is something I need to ask of you. While I'm very proud of what we're doing here, and construction will begin either tomorrow or Tuesday, some of my business associates are . . . oh, what would I say? More conservative and private than I. They may feel my having a social relationship with you is inappropriate. Bah! It's an old-fashioned attitude, in my opinion."

"I've had qualms about dating a client, I'll admit."

"I see. Then let's do it this way: my request to you is that you not return until the place is completely remodeled and ready to open for business. I'd like to take you in and surprise you. I want to savor the look on your beautiful face when you see it."

I shrugged. "Okay. I like surprises."

"Good. It's settled."

We jogged across Presa Street, through the parking garage, and across Commerce, back to my place. It was two o'clock. I moved behind the kitchen bar to make coffee.

Marten stretched his arms and he yawned. "I could sure use a steam bath right about now."

Above the roar of the coffee grinder, I said, "Help yourself. I'll give you the client discount."

He entered the kitchen, came up behind me and wrapped his arms around my shoulders, both hands dangling enticingly between my breasts. "Why don't you join me?"

His cologne aroused me. "Wouldn't that require the removal of some clothing?" Granted, I had been naked with Dana in her tree house, which had seemed natural at the time, although not sexual. Unclothed with Marten, however, would be sexual. But then, I rationalized, sex is natural, too.

"Definitely naked," he replied, "unless you'd feel more comfortable in our skivvies."

I laughed at the thought of us running through the steam room in our underwear. His warm breath on the back of my neck sent familiar tingles all throughout my body. The next move was up to me — of that I was confident. I turned to face him, his arms still around me.

"We enjoyed our first kiss in a massage room," he said, as he brushed a lock of hair away from my ear. Then, he whispered, "How about we enjoy something a little more serious in the steam room? What do you say we add a little spice to the history of the bathing lounge?"

I leaned in closer, our lips nearly touching. "A little spice, you say?"

"I want to make love to you, Julia. I've wanted it since that first night I saw you."

I'd wanted him, too. From that first night — I couldn't deny it. He was the man who jump started my battery. Why not open the passenger door and let him in for a ride?

Chapter Twenty-Five

No Privacy At All

Monday morning brought a bright sunny day, but with unusually strong winds. The giant trees lining the river swayed precariously, dispatching flocks of annoying scrub jays and song sparrows to seek shelter elsewhere. Mine was the only office with a window, due to its location at the beginning of the long hallway. I moved away from the window and noticed Andie leaning against the door frame with a smirk on her face.

"What's with you?"

"So! You and Marten did the dirty?"

"What are you talking about?"

Andie held up a packet of two condoms. "Don't these usually come in threes?"

My underarms prickled and my face was on fire. "Did you snoop around in my room?"

"Wasn't me. Boone brought them to me and asked me what they were. He found them on your nightstand."

On my nightstand — what an idiot I am. My dead husband's voice is yelling in my brain: "*Julia, you see what I mean about not allowing a child to enter an adult's room. Now, look what you've done!*"

"Boone!" I swallowed hard. "Uh . . . what did you tell him?"

"I told him they were condoms," Andie said, much too casually for my liking.

"You told him they were condoms? Just like that? What did he say?" I was nearly panicked to the point of hysteria.

"He said 'Oh'."

"He said 'Oh', that's it?" I swallowed again, but the lump in my throat felt permanent.

"Mom, it's okay. He knows what condoms are."

Unbelievable. "He knows what condoms are? At the age of five? Isn't that a little young?"

"Mom! You're repeating everything I say! Calm down and listen to me. With your history, and mine, of being pregnant in our teens, don't you think it's a good idea to educate him early?"

"Yes, but *five*?"

"Sex is a perfectly natural bodily function. Mother, look at me! You're stuck in that religious upbringing of yours. Remember, you're supposed to be in religion recovery from your childhood."

"Yes, but . . . but . . . ."

"Don't worry — I've got a handle on it. I'm his mother." Still leaning against the doorway, waiting for details, she inquired, "So . . . was it good?"

I shook my head slowly because I wasn't sure whether I should share tidbits of my sex life with my daughter.

"It wasn't good?" Andie stomped her foot as though she was astonished.

"I didn't mean the sex wasn't good," I hissed as I gestured Andie away. "Hit the road."

Andie didn't budge. "Mom, we're not just family. We're friends, too. Friends share stuff. So, come on, out with it!"

I took a slow, deep breath and gradually let it out. "It was okay, I guess, but not great. Anyway, only in the movies is sex for the first time fabulous. Surely you know that, right?" Andie's face went blank and I realized that my daughter's experiences hadn't been as unfulfilling as mine. "Actually, he rather rushed through it." I couldn't believe I said that.

"You can fix that," Andie said. "Slow him down and show him what you like. I had to do that with Britt."

I plugged both ears with my index fingers. I was in no way ready to discuss my daughter's sex life, although, since we'd dissected mine, it was rather rude of me not to let Andie talk about hers. Andie would probably never want to use the hot tub again if she knew what had gone on in it. Now that I thought of it, maybe she and Britt had used it, too. I shuddered.

Andie patted my shoulder, snickered and headed for her own workstation. Her hair was fixed differently in back, in a twist of sorts.

"What did you do to your hair?"

"It's a chignon," Andie replied as she twirled around in a circle. "Britt's mother showed me how to fix it. Do you like it?"

"Love it!" I said. *So that's what a chignon is. I'd thought of it as a twist, held by one hairpin. The pin is pulled out, the hair flows past the woman's shoulders, halfway down her back. Then, she shakes it a bit, rather like a foreplay move. Too bad I didn't know that when my hair was all one length. I might have tried it.*

Chapter Twenty-Six

Fredrick's New Love

Frederick swept up and disposed of the last of the hairs sacrificed in the name of design. He opened on Mondays mostly just for walk-ins. The only appointments he made were with tourists who'd stumbled on his *Before and After* photos over the weekend and scheduled time, usually early on a Monday, and at a premium price depending on Frederick's mood. The salon was closed on Sunday, but Frederick's mobile number was posted outside for clients' convenience. Since business was slow, he relaxed on his sofa, wondering what to do that evening.

A dark-skinned man with the most remarkable blue eyes Frederick had ever seen walked in from Presa Street. He ran his fingers through an abundance of black wavy hair. "Could you possibly work in a haircut?" The man's custom designed Armani suit enhanced his strong physique.

"Sure, sit yourself down." Frederick discerned the guy was frazzled, definitely in need of a special BTS treatment, so he went right to work with his scalp massage technique.

The man sighed. "Oh my, that is amazing. I can't even begin to tell you how much I need that."

"I thought you might like it. And let me tell you, not just everyone gets my special treatment." Frederick allowed his customer a full five minutes to unwind, then said, "Stressful day?"

"More than usual," the man said, "though they've all been hectic here lately."

"You're here on business, then?"

"Yes, real estate."

"I've often thought that would have been my second career choice." (Frederick used this line frequently, and it worked for the most part. But once he said as much to a mortician who quickly sensed Frederick's insincerity. He didn't tip, and he left right away. Frederick had confessed to Julia what happened, although not taking any blame for his indiscretion. "I swear, Julia, those people must have no sense of humor.")

The Armani guy seemed to take Frederick's comment seriously. "You could have put your massage technique to good use! Buyers are dreadfully uptight. But, I admit, I do meet a variety of interesting people. Some can be rather difficult, though, like today."

Frederick set his gaze on the man's light blue eyes in the mirror. "It's the same here. Everyone wants to be first. It's just 'me, me, me,' isn't it?"

"Yes, and it's tough making each client feel special. You have a big deal going with huge earning potential and the little guy wants to be treated the same. It's a challenge of the game. Thank God my work day is over."

"Mine, too," Frederick added, not skipping a beat. "How long have you been here? I would remember if I'd seen you before."

"A few weeks. I transferred from a commercial realty firm in Miami. I don't know how long they'll need me here; a few months at the most."

"Miami, South Beach," Frederick said. "I know it well. I hop down there three or four times a year."

"Really? You do look somewhat familiar. Perhaps I've seen you at one of the clubs."

"*Jazz Infusion!* I'll bet. It's the beach all day, then slow dancing under dazzling lights for me — whenever I'm lucky enough to get away to Miami, that is."

"Then *that's* where I've seen you. Allow me to introduce myself — Leonardo Newman."

Before the night was over, they were sharing secrets over a five-course meal and a 2003 oak-aged Sonoma Valley Chardonnay — Leonardo Newman's treat.

Chapter Twenty-Seven

The Loft

Leonardo Newman and Perry Roberts moved their operation into the old building on Navarro Street at Charles Court. The lower area remained empty, but would be transformed to resemble the beginnings of a health clinic within the week. Roberts commandeered the loft for himself.

Amigo had painted the loft walls Sienna Mustard, with the exception of one small area where gang members had vandalized the empty building and left a piece of graffiti, a lizard, presumably some gang's signature mark. Roberts hung an empty picture frame over it; he admired the sly lizard symbol, had no idea what it stood for, but he found it amusing that a gang artfully marked its territory and now *he* was taking over. He photographed it — perhaps a logo for a new business venture? No. No more of that. But, it would forever remind him of the success he was soon to achieve in America, his victory — he would have the last word with the Vanderhawk family.

Throughout the morning, delivery men brought boxes of personal belongings previously used at the Hilton; an antique partners' desk Marten had spied in New Braunfels while on his first date with Julia; faded and tattered red and yellow oriental rugs from a local thrift store.

Roberts strategically scattered the rugs underneath chocolate brown worn leather couches and chairs. One sofa opened into a queen-sized bed where he would sleep. No more maid service — no matter — he would be entirely too busy to think about anything but getting the job done and blowing out of town. He arranged the furniture in a semi-circle surrounding a corner gas fireplace. He was pleased to find it still in working order; nights in San Antonio got a little frosty in February. Plus, it would save on heating bills; the Hilton was pricier than their budget had allowed — a detail Marten had repeatedly warned him about. Nevertheless, Roberts had been hell-bent on reliving the days when he'd worked for the Vanderhawk family. They'd spared no expense to keep him happy. Besides, in the end, those people would ultimately pay the Hilton bill and even the lease on this very warehouse. *Fuck you, Sophia Vanderhawk.*

Roberts' computer station, printer/fax machine, and filing cabinet fit perfectly along the ledge, a half-wall facing the open area of the warehouse. From downstairs, the half-wall prevented anyone from seeing into the loft, but it gave Roberts the advantage of easily supervising activities below.

Roberts stood with Leonardo at the computer display as they calculated Lady Sophia's tour schedule via the Tyler woman's connection to River Protocol, Inc.

"According to this," Roberts said, "our little Sophia will recap her entire world tour here at the Arneson with a 14-minute speech — the only time in history her long-windedness will serve me well."

Leonardo laughed. "She does like the sound of her own voice."

"Thank God I won't have to listen to most of it," Roberts said. "Fourteen minutes to complete the snatch — what a stroke of luck. It'll be a walkover, mate."

Leonardo beamed; they could easily do the job in half the time. "We'll be back at base before anyone detects a problem."

Roberts shuffled through a stack of photographs, stopping at one of the Arneson Theater. "We've got to follow her schedule religiously. If any changes are made, it's imperative we know immediately."

"I can eyeball it 24/7 as long as Marten keeps the link functional," Leonardo said.

"Marten might be a problem."

"How do you figure?"

"I don't know . . . he's distracted, somehow. Did you notice him helping us move in here?"

Leonardo shook his head.

"No, of course you didn't, because he was nowhere to be found. The bastard! He acts like a man in love."

"Umm . . . I've a little action going, myself," Leonardo said, blushing.

"Big fucking surprise, you twit. Don't we all?"

"But love?" Leonardo countered quickly. "No way — not in the plan. Are you sure you're not paranoid about your nephew?"

"Maybe. I don't know. Perchance he's staying in character, the way some actors do when they're on a movie set, but I have a gut feeling. I've known him since he was a kid, and he's not himself lately."

Roberts' intuition had kicked in, and, while he had been suspicious in the past over *trivial* details, his hunches were usually justified in the end. He knew they could maneuver this project without much more help from Marten, but that would require two large *ifs*. *If* Marten kept his damn mouth shut, and *if* Marten maintained the link from Julia's end. Any other connection they might attempt would arouse questions for which they had no logical answers.

Roberts ran downstairs to use the loo. The tiny room was an eyesore with its concrete floor, filthy commode and old brass hinges hanging on the doorway, but missing its door. Because it was on the lower level, he rarely would have to look at it and it accomplished its purpose. They weren't going to be there long enough to put money into aesthetics. Amigo and his Mexican carpenter buddies wouldn't care.

On his way back up, Roberts paused on the landing to inspect a tiny barred window overlooking Charles Court. He'd never dreamed they would find a spot as perfect as this one; Leonardo's real estate prowess came through for him. Roberts had his favorite view — looking down on people. He observed the eclectic collection of tables and chairs out in the court. Soon, people would watch breaking news on their tellys and brag: *Oh, yes, Charles Court. I know right where that is! I had the most wonderful time there — nibbling on fancy cheeses, sipping pricey red wine, relaxing beside the dancing water fountains, blah, blah, blah. And I sat not 10 feet away from the very spot where that poor little boy was held for ransom!*

Roberts grunted and said, "Come back in seven weeks, you indulgent Boomers. I'll give you something exciting to tell your spoiled rotten grandchildren!" In the background, Leonardo snickered loudly enough for Roberts to hear. *What a brown-noser, kissing my ass all the damn time.* Roberts headed back up to the office area.

Leonardo had printed Lady Sophia's full schedule and the two men analyzed it together. "Seriously," Leonardo said, "there is no opportunity as golden as this one at the theater. We have to make it work, whether Marten is of much more help or not. But, damn it, if something goes wrong and we make a quick change, if he thinks we're sharing the profits equally he's got another think coming." He noticed Roberts' hardened face. "Then again," Leonardo said, "he's gotten us this far — I give him credit for that."

"He can have all the credit he deserves," Roberts said. "He banked us 100 percent. Probably took every penny he had. But we're nearly finished with our need for funds. Soon, we'll have plenty of cash. And yes, I second the motion: if Marten thinks he can walk away from us without so much as a stain, he's wrong — dead wrong."

"Now's no time for guessing. Why don't you talk to him, find out where his head is?"

"I'm not sure even *he* knows the answer to that question, which is precisely what worries me. But, of course, I'll feel him out . . . *when* he decides to show up again!"

Chapter Twenty-Eight

Anniversary

I'd drawn a large red X on my day planner, just as I'd done on the sixth of February for the past five years. Not necessarily a vacation day. A mental health day — wasn't I entitled to one? I fastened the brass snap, snug at the waist of my jeans, pulled on a black tee shirt and my black leather jacket — no pink on this day. I finger-brushed my hair, not bothering with make-up.

I tiptoed through my office and out the secret door, down the hall to the stairway exit because I didn't want the noisy elevator to awaken my family; what would my daughter think if she knew what I was up to?

The Paseo del Rio reflected a full moon on the river as I marched beside it. I followed its bend past the Little Rhein Steak House. I climbed up the grass-covered terraced bleachers across from the Arneson River Theater to the edge of the miniature community of La Villita, where the quaint shops and galleries were currently dark inside. At the arched concrete entrance to the little town, I selected a brochure from a plastic box and sat on the top grassy mound to read the pamphlet while I waited. It didn't tell me anything new, but it helped pass the time until the bank would open. "La Villita, now on the National Register of Historic Districts, was San Antonio's first neighborhood, originally a settlement of primitive huts for Spanish soldiers back in the days of the Alamo. It had been the site of General Santa Ana's cannon line. In the early 1900's, the area deteriorated, but with the Riverwalk development, preservation began, making La Villita a thriving art community now, as well as a monument to San Antonio's past."

My attention was usually drawn to three shops in La Villita: Bonsai Arbor, a store whose windows displayed lush Asian-inspired plants;

Village Weavers, where I'd purchased colorful tablecloths, rugs and furniture throws; and Chamade, where most of my custom-designed jewelry had been purchased through the years.

Next to Chamade stood The Little Church of La Villita, a tiny chapel where Doc and Nina had been married. The chapel was still a favorite wedding site, and just last month Nina and I lunched together on a Saturday at the Guadalajara Grill and watched a smiling bride burst through the front door of the chapel. She tossed her bouquet, took her groom's arm, and he escorted her down the narrow cobblestone walk to a waiting limousine.

Nina had said, " Look! That was me in the 70's. Oh, how I wish we could go back and do it again."

"Why don't you?"

Nina stared thoughtfully at me, slowly nodded and smiled. "Yes! Next year is our 45th anniversary. What a great idea. Will you help me plan it?"

I brought myself back to the present moment and pulled my knees close to my bosom and wrapped my arms around my legs. The shallow river was now a dance partner with the sunrise, contrasted with the bare Arneson Theater stage, but I visualized a future scene. Children singing. Children dancing. Less than seven weeks away. According to Lady Sophia's appearance schedule, Chesley and 20 other boys and girls, clothed in costumes representative of their ethnicity, would be right over there. I could almost reach out and touch the stage. I planned to arrive early to secure a front row seat when that day came.

Immediately behind the Arneson, construction had recently begun at the Water Works Company. Why did they tear up the site right before such important visitors? I recalled my teen-aged years living in Louisville, where the Derby City planners scurried to finish clean-up projects in time for the legendary horse race. Many celebrities had their one and only view of Kentucky during that week in early May, and Louisville made sure their impressions were good ones. Maybe the Water Works would finish by the time the British guests arrived.

I reminded myself that the exciting news here in San Antonio was still top secret, the press release being one week away. I'd forgotten that I was privy to the confidential information and I laughed inwardly. *I always assume everybody knows what I know.* How I was worthy to have access to such information was beyond me, but I appreciated that my clients trusted me. I wouldn't betray their faith in me.

As I glanced over at the Little Rhein, I thought about the night I saw Marten there, and I wondered. *How much in life is coincidence, and how much is planned? And if it's planned, then who in the world is designing my life?*

Always the questions in my mind — I figured this might be the way some people pray — asking God silent questions. It was as close to prayer as I'd come since my parents died. I analyzed everything, compared it to what I knew and tried to make sense of it all. I was content to think of the times I received answers to questions I hadn't even thought to ask. I often wondered about my mother; did she ever question events in her life? Or had her religious beliefs satisfied her curiosity?

If I was meant to meet Marten, that restaurant was the perfect pre-meeting scenario, like something right out of a romance novel, which I don't read anymore, although here of late I've had the urge to buy one. Must be the sex. Five straight days of it so far and sometimes twice a day. It's coming back to me, like Dana said it would. Marten is improving, and, since I discovered what a chignon was, so am I. Why, I could fit right into a paperback romance with a hair style like that.

Still, red flags sometimes popped up, and, while I didn't consider myself psychic, I paid attention to them. Something troubled me, but I couldn't sort it out. Maybe I needed more data to input into my machine of a brain before I came up with an answer. Could it be sex outside of marriage? After all, I *had* been raised with strict morals. *The first time I tried it, I ended up pregnant. Is that what's bugging me? I hope not, because I'm NOT gonna give it up.*

~*~

At nine o'clock, I was waiting at the bank's entrance for a security guard to unlock the door. From my safe deposit box I retrieved an envelope, inside of which was a yellowed piece of paper folded into thirds. Richard's suicide note — his perfectly logical explanation of why he chose not to stick around those extra two years — the doctors had given him that much

— and help me get through our daughter's illegitimate pregnancy and our grandson's birth. I'd read it many times but never took it to the graveyard, or even out of the bank, for that matter. Today would be different. Richard had a lot of listening to do.

~*~

I pulled into Evergreen Cemetery, got out of my Jeep and headed straight for his monument. I settled myself cross-legged on the ground on a thick layer of soft pine needles.

"Richard, you wrote it, now you have to hear it. It still cuts deep, right through me, but the knife gets shorter each year."

> *Julia:*
>
> *I am sorry, my precious wife, but I am simply not strong enough to see this through. I've been emasculated, and you deserve much more. I am too weak to bear the thought any longer that I have let my little girl down. Yes, and you, too, Julia, I know I have.*
> *Was Andie seeking a father figure just as you were when we met? She must have been . . . .*
> *I was attracted to you back then because you needed me. That was selfish, I realize.*
> *Mother blames Andie's promiscuity on your liberal attitude, but I know it is my fault. I cannot bear the guilt. I let her down as a father in so many ways, ways you cannot imagine, you, the perfect mother.*
> *I know you will be strong. You always have been. You did not really need me, you merely thought you did, and I reveled in being needed.*
> *Please forgive me.*
> *With Eternal Love, Richard*

"You remember that?" I screamed at the stone. "Do you? Leaving me that note to find underneath my pillow when I got home from the hospital the day you took your last breath. Oh, that was rich! Can you imagine my despair? I was alone . . . all alone." I vigorously shook my head. "How could you have done that to me if you truly loved me?"

Rising up, I rested on my haunches. Leaning in close, looking the monument right in its imaginary eye, I said, "I've been fucking someone, Richard. That's right . . . I used the F-word. What? You don't want me to use that word for making love? But it's not love, Richard. It's sex, that's all it is. And I like it."

I methodically refolded the letter, dropped it into my purse and forced myself to breathe in deeply through my nose, exhaling through taut lips.

I laughed out loud. "Guess what! He's a *bastard*. Isn't that ironic? I'm sleeping with a bastard! And your grandson is a bastard! But, guess what again. People don't think any less of Marten — or of Boone. People don't even care; this is the 21st century, after all." I reflected on the speech I'd prepared; I didn't want to leave out something important. "Oh, and he isn't thinking of investments when we do it, like you always seemed to do. He's thinking about *me*! That is to say, if he *is* thinking of anyone or anything but me, he's a damn good actor."

I came to a full stand, towering over the monument, telling myself that it was truly Richard I was looking down upon. I raised my voice to continue. "You were in *remission* for Christ's sake! Cancer hadn't even come close to your liver, but you found a way to ruin it just the same. You and your heavy-duty pain pills and God knows what else."

Softly now, but with a definite edge to my voice, I added, "I used to wonder how long you planned your exit, but now I honestly don't care. You're just as dead. It worked — your strategy. You win," I sighed.

I wiped debris from the bench and sat down, looking upward for a sign of some kind, but the day was clear — not a cloud in the sky. I considered that Richard might not actually be listening to me. It would be just like him, to be off somewhere, busying himself with mundane details in his head.

"Has your mother been to visit you? Silly question — of course — she's your mother. Has she told you about your grandson and how he's endeared himself to her? Why, the woman has melted like a chocolate bar on a downtown sidewalk. She'll do anything to spend time with Boone. Andie drives him up there to see her at least once a month. Madelynne's even treating Andie differently nowadays. Don't you see, Richard? She's mellowed. I think she realizes it's wrong to judge people so harshly.

"So what? Your daughter was pregnant at fifteen. Big deal. You scrutinized it to death . . . took it as a personal failure. Was that because you couldn't fix it like you did *our* own pregnancy by marrying me? Surely you didn't think you were supposed to be in control of the entire universe — of *everything!* For you to cop out on me like that, to abandon your daughter and your grandson, was despicable." I wagged my finger at the tombstone. "Shame on you! I doubt I'll ever let you off the hook."

I got up and walked around the quiet graveyard, weaving between headstones, careful not to step on the graves. *I wonder if anyone else ever comes here and talks to their dead, or if it's just me.*

After a few minutes, I took my seat back on the concrete bench. "Look. What I mean to say is that I don't get it. You asked for forgiveness, but you wrote your note when there was still time to stop it, before you chugged all that garbage. So what kind of apology is that, I ask you? Here, allow me to answer that for you: It's diabolical — that's what it is! Furthermore, it's taken me a long time to figure out something else: When a person tells me something, and it doesn't make sense, it's because they're lying. You weren't really sorry, Richard. Did you lie to make me feel better? No, you lied to make yourself feel better."

If a man is dying a sure death, was it suicide to hurry it along? I hadn't decided the answer, or if there even was one. I stood up. "Oh yeah, that pine cone thing you did was a nice touch. Thanks. I hope, in time, I won't need to understand your death to forgive you. We'll see."

On the way home, Josh Groban's song, *To Where You Are*, played. It wasn't a coincidence. I'd inserted the CD in advance to accomplish my purpose.

> *As my heart holds you, just one beat away, I cherish all you gave me every day.*
> *'Cause you are my forever love, watching me from up above. And I believe that angels bleed, and that love will live on and never leave.*

The song played in a loop three times as I screamed, beating my fist on the steering wheel. The Jeep maneuvered on autopilot along the straight Texas highway.

Chapter Twenty-Nine

Gazpacho

Dana's Gazpacho Recipe
1 pound vine-ripened tomatoes
1-1/2 cups peeled, seeded cucumber chunks
½ cups chopped bell pepper
½ cup parsley leaves, or to taste
1 clove garlic
¼ rounded tsp. cumin
½ rounded tsp. salt
1 tsp. red wine vinegar or cider vinegar
1 tsp. light honey
2 tsp. fresh lemon juice
1 T extra-virgin olive oil
Cayenne to taste.

Core the tomatoes and cut them into large chunks. Peeling and seeding are unnecessary. In a blender or food processor combine the tomatoes with all the remaining ingredients except the cayenne. Puree until as smooth as you like. Transfer to a container and add cayenne to taste. Cover and chill. Serve cold. Makes 3 cups.

The sweet aroma of tobacco wafted into the elevator even before it opened, and I knew why. Doc was lounging on the J Sofa, smoking his pipe. He was the only person I allowed to do that, out of respect for the old health club days, and because the scent reminded me of my father. Doc always remembered the anniversary of Richard's death and showed his support one way or another. He never said a word, just showed up with an empathetic smile.

Doc met me at the elevator. Removing a clean, white handkerchief from his pocket, he gently wiped the residue of tears from my cheek. He took my elbow gently with one hand and said, "How about Dana's Special of the Day?" Down we went into The Stock Market's kitchen.

"I set a small table for our privacy in my office," Dana said.

"Oh, you expected us?"

"Well, sort of. I mean, you do have a tendency to become depressed about a week ahead of time. You've been breaking out in tears when it's least expected."

"True, that." I usually appreciated the kindness they show me, but that day was different. I was on fire with anger quickening through my veins.

Emilio brought three bowls of gazpacho and a hot loaf of French bread to the table. Dana poured Chianti and went right into her annual ritual about how brave Richard had been. Oh, she proclaimed, how he would have hung on longer if there had been any possible way!

I watched Dana's lips move, but heard only a buzzing sound, like high-frequency power lines transmitting dangerous signals. I couldn't take it anymore. I slapped the tabletop with my flattened palm, rattling the silverware. "Bullshit!" I said it right out loud in front of Doc, which ordinarily I would never do. Doc didn't flinch, although he hated foul language as much as Richard used to, but I had more respect for Doc's wishes than I'd had for my husband's.

Dana blinked. "What'd I say?"

Doc saw what was coming and placed his hand over mine. "Are you sure you want to go into this?"

I jerked my hand away and retrieved the letter from my purse. "I couldn't be more certain. Enough of this secrecy! It's time Dana knows the truth. I'm sick and tired of hearing Richard's praises every year." Passing the letter to Dana, I said, "Read this! I found it under my pillow the night that son of a bitch died."

Doc's eyes widened — he was obviously shocked that I was carrying the note around with me. Doc knew the truth about Richard's death; he and Nina had come over and stayed with me after I'd found the note. He reached for my arm but I threw him a look.

He settled back into his chair, arms folded. Then, his gaze traveled across the table to Dana; he'd resigned himself for whatever would happen next.

Dana read every line. Her brow furrowed and her eyes appeared unfocused as she stared into the distance, like she might find some explanation off in space. "I don't get it. I wasn't living here then, but I knew he had cancer; isn't that what he died from?"

I coolly shrugged both shoulders. "Actually, not. Richard died from embarrassment over having a pregnant 15-year-old daughter. He'd been squirreling away drugs, painkillers and other pills. His blood tests showed high levels of all kinds of lethal stuff. The doctors knew, but didn't tell me."

"I asked them not to," Doc said. "At least, not right away. As a matter of fact, I'd hoped she would never have to know the truth."

Dana squinted. "The truth? Like, uh . . . Richard committed suicide?"

"Yes, he did," Doc said. "Apparently, he took his stash to the office and swallowed everything at once, fully aware that it would do immediate and irreversible damage to his liver. His death would logically be attributed to cancer."

"To the medically inexperienced, of course, like his daughter and his wife," I said. "He'd locked his office door, and told his assistant to hold his calls, so his slick little maneuver wasn't discovered for several hours. From the time he lost consciousness, it took him less than a day to slip into a coma. I stayed at the hospital, by his side the entire time, nearly a week, not fully comprehending what had gone wrong. I had believed he was in remission."

Dana held her arms up, as if to say STOP! "Let me get this straight," she said. "Your husband died, you went home, and when you went to bed, you found a note he'd placed under your pillow over a week before?"

"You got it, babe," I said. "I hadn't slept in my own bed for a week, since I'd stayed with Richard in the hospital. He'd probably stuck it there prior to leaving for the office, *before* he even took the pills! I nearly fainted when I found it. I called Doc, and he and Nina came right over. We were up all night."

"Like I said," Doc continued, "it had been my hope she would never have to know the truth, and if it hadn't been for the suicide note she wouldn't have. I was shocked that he'd left a letter. If I'd known there was such a thing hidden under Julia's pillow, I think I would've removed it."

"Apologizing for killing oneself ahead of time is such an insult," I snorted, "a *cowardly insult*."

"It's not like a person can pull the trigger first and take care of personal business later, Julia." Doc said. "When *would* you have had him apologize?"

I wrinkled my nose as if I smelled something repugnant. "No, I suppose not. Fair enough, I'll give him that."

Dana turned pale and ran her fingers through her hair. "All this time I've been feeling sorry for him. But, wait. If he wanted it to look like cancer, why the memo? What the actual fuck?"

I glanced quickly at Doc.

"You have to understand the difference between men and women to even begin to absorb the complexity of the situation," Doc said. "Women are much stronger than men. Without his woman, a man is nothing."

Dana had tears in her eyes, and I wasn't sure if it was from Richard's farewell letter or Doc's admission of how weak men are. Dana has reminded me on occasion that women are the stronger sex, but this was probably the first time she'd ever heard a man admit it with such humility.

Dana said, "Then, why didn't Richard rely on Julia?"

"I've already figured that one out," I interjected. "He was too proud. He would have considered that the ultimate weakness, to lean on a woman, especially the mother of his daughter — the mother who had allowed his little girl to get pregnant."

"Killing himself wasn't the ultimate weakness?" Dana's voice squeaked. "My God, all these years, you've kept this secret." She folded the letter and gave it to me. "You're braver than I will ever be, Jules," Dana said. "I would have made sure everyone knew what that man put me through. You're more honorable than most."

"It's not honor, Dana. It's fear. For Andie. She would be crushed, undoubtedly blame herself, and our pretty little drama queen might carry the guilt forever. I keep quiet for Andie, is all." I stuck my spoon into the gazpacho and stirred, then put the spoon down and glanced up at Dana.

"And maybe for Madelynne, too," I said. "Plus, he's dead just the same and nothing will bring him back. Anyway, do you notice how people believe what they want to believe? Take his mother, for example; she knew he was in remission, yet Madelynne never questioned his sudden death. She automatically blamed the cancer, the perfect answer to a question she was afraid to ask. She never inquired of details, and I offered her none. Why, she may have been resentful enough to blame Andie, too, had she known that her son offed himself."

Dana nodded. "It's best that everyone had the cancer to blame, I suppose."

"That's the way I saw it at the time," I said.

"Julia, may I see the letter again?" Doc asked. "I read it only that once, and you promptly whisked it away."

Doc scanned the note and waved it gently at me. "I always assumed you had destroyed this, young lady. Frankly, I'm stunned you didn't. That night, I was concerned for your despair only and no one else's. But, now I can sense the anguish in Richard as I read this again.

"Remember this: whatever a person does, they justify in some convoluted way, if only to themselves. The degree of guilt Richard felt over having a pregnant teenager is excessive in my opinion, but, as you will recall . . . he was dealing with layers of emotional pain, his own mortality, and he was weakened considerably from fighting the disease for so long. Yes, the doctors had said he was in remission. But, he knew sooner or later he would go under. He confided in me one time that he didn't believe he could face more treatment. He felt guilt, too, for being a burden to you, no longer an asset."

"I never thought of him that way! Naturally, he was always weighing assets with liabilities. It's all he knew — financial balance sheets!"

Doc leaned closely toward me. "The only road to inner peace, Julia my dear, is through compassion."

"Compassion for Richard?" I wailed.

"Humph!" said Dana, briskly refilling my wine glass . . . then her own.

Doc momentarily covered my drink with his hand. "Yes, empathy and concern for Richard — a man who did his best, even though you don't agree with his decision. But, his action says nothing about you; it speaks only for him. It was not about you, Julia. You are doing yourself no favors by taking responsibility for another person's choices. True, Richard didn't behave in such a way as you would have chosen, but, once again, it was his choice, and, if you can let the anger go, you'll find peace. It's the only way."

The three of us sat quietly as Doc's words reverberated. The gazpacho remained untouched. The bread was cold. The wine bottle, empty.

After a few minutes, Doc added, "Consider this. Here might be the last piece of the puzzle: Richard wrote the note under the assumption that you would immediately learn the cause of his sudden demise. He felt he owed you an explanation — clear and simple. He probably thought he would die immediately that day."

"Hmm." I bowed my head and thought about the likelihood. Richard may not have considered that the doctors might hide the truth, wouldn't tell me what was actually happening. I faced Doc and nodded. "Yes, it could very well have been true."

"We've never spoken of this," Doc said, "because, whenever I attempted it, you brushed me off. And, one more piece of advice while I have your ear — I think you need to destroy this deadly piece of paper or Andie will surely find it someday, just as you did. Do you want that to happen?"

I quickly shook my head. "Of course I don't." I sighed deeply. "I haven't been thinking clearly, have I? Okay, I'll get rid of it." I took it from Doc, wadded it up into a ball and stuck it into the pocket of my jacket. Although I felt relief by confiding in Dana, I realized that one more person knew something I never wanted Andie to find out. "Dana, you must promise me that you will never say a word to my daughter about this."

"Promise? That's a given. I can't imagine a scenario where I would ever want to hurt Andie."

Doc said, "Fact of the matter, Richard would have most certainly died of cancer. The type he had was incurable and he probably had less than two years. His eventual end could have been even more painful than the actual death."

"But he would have had his grandson for two years. That is, his grandson would have had him," I said, sadly.

"The reality is this," Doc said. "He made his choice to leave early. I don't know why. He wasn't strong enough . . . that's what he said in his note to you. You would be wise to believe him. He did say that you were strong, and you still are. I venture to say you always will be, no matter what adversity comes your way."

Chapter Thirty

Olga

Olga Gonzalez was dreaming. She ran through a field of grass after a heavy downpour. When she saw a rainbow, she ran faster, farther, to a pot of gold where her grandfather waited for her. He seemed troubled, agitated, saying things she didn't understand. Then, she woke up. Olga was a superstitious woman. She believed strongly in ghosts and knew for sure her dead grandfather had spoken to her many times. But he was from German heritage, as were many in the San Antonio area of Texas. Olga had barely understood him when he was alive. Still, the dream was unsettling.

She was finishing the third mural for Mr. Perry Roberts, and there were several more to go. He had paid her handsomely already, and promised connections in high places, told her to expect contracts beyond her wildest imagination. At least that's how her husband Eduardo interpreted it. But something about Mr. Roberts' eyes held a sinister element, *menacing*. She doubted she could trust anything he said, but she was smart, *worldly-wise,* confident she could handle this little guy. What's more, the hostility he tried to hide actually excited her.

She barely grasped his style of English; he wasn't from around here — that much she understood. She read *gringo* body language loud and clear, and this *Roberto* was all man even though small in stature. Olga figured her *grande* breasts did a lot for landing this gig — he rarely took his eyes off them. Of course, he stood nearly four inches shorter than Olga, which put her bosom right at his eye level. The first time she caught him ogling her, he winked and said, "*Mamá.* Everything's big in Texas, eh?" He was about the height of her husband, which made her wonder if all of Roberto's body parts were similar. Eduardo was more than adequate —

one of the main reasons she'd kept him around so many years. Her nipples hardened at the thought.

Mr. Roberts paid more money than these murals were worth, painted on sheets of plywood as they were, but who cared? If he was dumb enough to pay, she'd paint anything he wanted. The artistic exposure would be invaluable. Her murals were to be displayed in large storefront windows of a health clinic on Navarro, a busy downtown street. Everyone walking or driving past would notice. Her signature on the bottom, *not* in small letters, would be seen. At the clinic's Grand Opening, she was to hand out postcard-sized replicas with her name and contact information printed on the back. Mr. Roberts said he would help her design the cards on his computer, if she so desired. She figured she might have to do more than paint for him; at least, she hoped so. One thing for sure, Eduardo wasn't going to get her anywhere. This was Eduardo's last stop on the Olga bus route, whether he knew it or not.

I told that worthless sumbitch I'd be rich and famous someday. Maybe this Roberto fella is just what I need. She considered seducing him, but decided to wait and see what moves he might make first. In her sexual fantasies, she was always helplessly taken advantage of. *If only I could speak Inglés better.* Who needs words, though, when the chemistry is this strong? *Química!*

Chapter Thirty-One

Valentine's Day

As I sat in my usual, early-morning perch with my hot coffee, I browsed the news release about Lady Sophia's upcoming stopover. I'd read it online the day before in Forrester's blog, but wanted to see the newspaper's account, too. I was so relieved that the visit would not be a secret any longer. After today, everyone would know.

We Love Lady Sophia

Love is sprinkled abundantly along the Riverwalk today, and before long it will be here to stay. Lady Sophia Louise Vanderhawk will make San Antonio the last stop on her eight-month tour agenda, *Our Children — Our World*. She will arrive with her son, Chesley Regan Vanderhawk, on March 22. During their six-day stay here, she will visit at least 10 of our local schools and tour the historic missions San Antonio is proud to call its own.

Chesley Regan Vanderhawk will participate with a hand-selected and diverse group of children in a farewell program on The Arneson Theater stage on Saturday, March 28. Prior to that presentation, Lady Sophia and Chesley will make several stops, visiting all of San Antonio's public schools and missions in Lady Sophia's quest to encourage world peace. "Adults are set in their ways," Sophia has said, "but the minds of children are innocent and open." Her tour will grace San Antonio for six days of school visits, luncheons, perhaps a few surprise appearances and plenty of hand-shaking.

To accomplish her goal of a more peaceful world, Lady Sophia has selected children from all over the globe. She has provided many youngsters with computers and teaching software, and has set up a communication agenda so they can stay in touch. She encourages them to correspond with one another and plans to reunite them frequently. What a remarkable scenario it will be to watch as it unfolds. Our city is pleased and proud that she has chosen San Antonio for her last stop on the circuit before she returns to London.

~*~

Dana stomped off the elevator and headed into the kitchen with a folded newspaper in one hand. "No rush hour traffic on Saturdays — I got to the restaurant early today." She whacked the newspaper on the countertop, filled my copper teakettle with water and set it on the stove. She clamored about in a cabinet, removed a canister of ginger green tea and fingered the loose leaves into an Oriental pot. Then, she slammed the cabinet door shut.

"What's wrong?" I said.

"Nothing. Not a single, solitary thing."

"So. . . lots of things, then?" I'd seen her act this way before, usually when she was without a boyfriend. But she had one now. Maybe he wasn't meeting her needs. I knew I'd find out if I waited long enough for her to start a rant.

She held the newspaper article in front of my face. "Isn't this fantastic news? Lady Sophia is coming right here to the Riverwalk!"

"Hmm? Oh, yes. It's wonderful."

"You've known all along haven't you?"

"Umm . . . yeah, I've known for a few weeks." I pointed to the article, "In fact, I contributed to that."

"*Contributed*? I suspected you wrote the entire thing!"

"Well, I did, but Forrester didn't put my name on it."

"Why not?"

"He prefers not to broadcast where he keeps his business data. It's fine with me, considering how much he paid me to write it."

"Aw, that guy's just paranoid. What's he afraid of? Somebody hacking into your computer system and grabbing River Protocol's secrets?" Dana laughed as she poured boiling water into the pot. "Impressive Valentine theme you went with. So, do you have any plans for tonight with Marten?"

"Not yet. I think we've both skirted around the term 'Valentine's Day,' to be honest."

"Why? Don't they have it over in England?"

"I'm sure they do. Isn't that where it originated? No, that was in Italy, but Europe anyway." I shrugged. "Personally, I think it's much too soon for us. And maybe he doesn't think it's a big deal."

"Or . . . he feels it should be reserved for sexual couples, *lovers*," Dana said, drawing out the word "lovers" with a conspicuous question mark on her face.

She was obviously fishing so I tugged gently on her lure; I smiled knowingly and raised one eyebrow.

"Oh. You're having sex with Marten *already*?"

"Well . . . you, of all people, ask me that?" I said in mock offense.

"What's *that* supposed to mean? Are you calling me a slut?" Dana's voice had a definite edge to it.

This game was risky but fun. Maybe she was on her period.

"It means this: you have gotten involved sexually with men within the first few days of a relationship. Of all people, you should understand why I would want to do it too."

"Oh, I suppose I should. I do . . . really. It's just not like you, is all. Be careful, you don't want to turn into me."

"Why, what's wrong with you?"

Dana heaved a sigh, and by the look on her face I could tell I was about to be honored with a story — the real reason why Dana was banging around in my kitchen.

"I'm not sure if it's me . . . or Nathan," Dana lamented. "It's just that he hasn't wanted to do it yet, and we've been dating nearly four weeks. I'm about to explode. I think he's hiding something."

"Hiding what?"

"How would I know? That's why they call it *hiding.*"

Touché. "Well . . . let's think. He *is* a pianist and a dancer, doesn't that just say *gay* to you, or am I stereotyping here?"

"Geez, Julia! How unsophisticated of you to even *think* that. He most definitely is not gay. That, I know for sure. I mean, we've messed around and I know I turn him on. He claims he wants it to be special and just at the right moment. So, I wait. Maybe tonight. After all, it *is* Valentine's Day." She reached for a banana on the counter. "The banana has a nice shape to it, don't you think?" Dana giggled just like the little girl I remembered.

"Richard was one of those guys who wanted to wait," I said. "You don't find them on every street corner, but when you do, I think you've found something good. He put me off for weeks. I was a virgin and he didn't want to be the first unless he knew for sure he was Mr. Right. He was like my father, always wanting to do the *right* thing. In other words, I married my father."

"A lot of girls do that and they don't even realize," Dana said.

"Now that I think of it, Richard was awfully considerate as a young man."

"Considerate . . . then, of course, there was his religion," Dana said.

"It was more his mother's religion, but, yes, he was afraid of going to Hell if he did the *wrong* thing. He'd make comments like, "Here is the way it's done," as if there were no other. Life's experiences were filed in one of two categories: right or wrong — black or white. No color for Richard, not even gray areas."

Dana slowly peeled her banana. "So how *did* you nail Richard, anyway? I never asked you about that." She nibbled on the fruit.

"He had just received his Bachelor's Degree from the University of Kentucky and I was about to graduate from high school. We celebrated at a bash on a houseboat on the Ohio River, stocked with beer kegs. Richard overdid it, went overboard, so to speak; he never could hold his liquor very well. I hadn't acquired a taste for alcohol and I was underage, anyway; Richard never offered me any booze — aiding and abetting — that ethical and legal lingo.

"After the party, we went for a moonlight drive through Cherokee Park, with me at the wheel, of course. The next thing he knew he was in the backseat of his Chevy."

"Nice move."

"Yeah, I'd made up my mind if I couldn't get more intimate

with him soon I'd go after somebody else." I blinked, thinking how cold that sounded.

"You got him drunk," Dana declared, "and took advantage of him, you hussy." She slid the banana in and out, between her lips.

"All I wanted was to be loved. But, yes, you're right. And you know what? All these years I've used the excuse that I was only 17 to keep from feeling guilty about what I did, but I know it wasn't right. He kept saying over and over, 'We shouldn't be doing this, Julia,' but I paid no attention to him. He had a woody that wouldn't quit. I took him out of his misery, that's all. It was only one night and we got married pretty quickly after that, and you know the rest. Stop it, already, with the banana!"

Suddenly, Dana swallowed one large gulp of fruit and screamed, "I just *now* realized what you've told me!"

"What?"

"You and Marten are actually having sex? Omigod! Tell me everything. Is he as good as he looks? Tell me all about his big, hard, throbbing . . . ."

Now, *that* was the reaction I'd expected in the first place. Of course Dana wanted details, so I gave her what she wanted because, after all, we were blood.

"At first Marten didn't have a clue how to please me. I was disappointed . . . and frustrated. I'd assumed he would be the perfect lover. I thought he would've had lots of experience with women."

"Romance novels . . . they stereotype good-looking men that way," Dana said.

"And soap operas . . . talk about promoting unrealistic expectations! Anyway, each time we're together I show Marten something I like. He's become quite satisfactory, I must say."

"*Each time*? Like how many?"

"Oh, I've lost count by now. Plenty." I knew the exact number; I'd made squiggle marks on my day-planner, sometimes two per day.

Dana groaned, probably because she was currently celibate and I wasn't. "Yeah," she said, "I would have figured him to be a ladies' man from the get-go. Well, goes to show you never know. I wonder what Andie will say?"

"She already knows."

"Humph."

"Even Boone knows, it seems," I mused.

"Eww."

"Well, I'm sure he isn't aware of all the details of sex at his age. But he knows what a condom is."

Dana sat there, staring at me. "I'm the last one to know — go figure. So, how big is he? You didn't answer me."

"Oh. Well. Okay . . . you know those cucumbers you used for the lassi at my Open House?"

"Shut up!"

We waved our goodbyes through the elevator gate, and I watched Dana's melancholy face descend.

It was the same pout she wore at the age of fifteen. An old amusement park on the banks of the Ohio River had an impressive wooden roller coaster with a killer first hill that neither of us could get enough of. But, standing in line on a hot July day was not our scene. Dana flirted with the greasy ride operator; we rode seven times in a row until other customers complained and he made us get back in line — something about losing his job. Dana ignored the *No Loitering* sign and she hung around and promised to go out with him that night. He let us ride that coaster for one solid hour after that. To hell with the other customers!

After we girls had gone to bed, I'd heard someone outside making a lame attempt at birdcalls. The slimy coaster guy, one and the same, so I pretended to be asleep. Dana slipped out of the house and spent several hours with him up in that tree house — naked, no doubt. The next morning I didn't ask and Dana didn't tell, but the rest of the summer we rode the coaster every day of the week as many times as we wanted without stopping until the coaster guy got fired. I felt bad about it, but Dana just shrugged and said, "Hey, we all make our choices. He made his." What wild and crazy teenagers we were back then.

I listened as the elevator reached its destination at The Stock Market. I hoped Nathan would come through for Dana. She wasn't used to not getting her way, and it wouldn't be a pretty sight if she didn't get laid soon.

Chapter Thirty-Two

Dinner With the Emmetts

Doc had talked with Marten about plans for the health clinic last week, and he'd invited us both for dinner on Sunday evening. Marten had surprised me with a drive to Gruene on Valentine's Day, where we dined at the same German restaurant as on our first date. Helga, the jealous waitress, wasn't there and the butter pats were cold. We spent the night in a bed and breakfast in New Braunfels, a Victorian-style house with a white cast-iron fence around the front. Doc and Nina's house was located in an upscale community north of San Antonio, conveniently on the way back home.

The aroma of Nina's pork tenderloin roasting in the oven with small red potatoes, green peppers, leeks and cilantro filled the house. The scents had even wafted to the front porch. I'd brought a German chocolate cake from a Gruene bakery, and I placed it on the dining room table. Doc was there, reading his Sunday paper next to a toddler in a high chair.

"Oh, look, a baby!" I said. "Does he belong to anyone I know?"

"He belongs to us! This is Samuel, our grandson," Doc said proudly.

I swooped up Samuel into my arms and he beamed a toothless grin.

"Rebecca and Michael arrived unexpectedly, late Friday night," Doc explained, "and we're babysitting for a while today while they look at a house."

"A house?"

"Can you believe it?" Nina said as she entered the room. "I'm so excited I can hardly sit still. They want to relocate here to be closer to us!"

I coddled and fussed over Samuel while Doc told Marten about their daughter, Rebecca, an ER doctor in Seattle. She and her husband were tired of the cold and rain in the Northwest and had wanted to move back to Texas for some time now.

"Doc will love being close to the grandchildren. Of course, I will too," Nina said. "We usually see them only twice each year. They always come home for Christmas, which we do up big in our family. This year we're going to take them on the Disney Magic Ship, a cruise during Christmas week . . . the Caribbean: Grand Cayman, Cozumel, Key West and the Bahamas."

"Whew! That's going to be one boatload of kids. Are you sure you can stand it for seven days?" Marten asked.

"Of course," Nina said. "We love young people. That's why Doc is a pediatrician. He's always had a special relationship with his patients and their parents. We've even socialized with many of them, and we have photographs of thousands of children in photo albums we've kept through the years. Every once in a while, we look after one of Doc's patients. We even keep a baby crib in our spare bedroom, which is probably why Julia asked if Samuel belonged to anyone she knew. You never know who you'll find crawling around our house."

Doc sat up a little straighter in his chair. "I've followed my patients into adulthood," he said, "and I've doctored their children as well. I even have a few great-grandchildren coming in."

"You don't look old enough for that," Marten replied.

"My age has nothing to do with it. It's the age of the mother that causes early grandchildren. Take Julia here, for example. Who would ever suspect her of being a grandmother?"

"Amen to that," Marten said, and he smiled at me, the way he does sometimes that melts my heart.

I knew it was a compliment, although, if I could turn back time, I would not have had a baby in my teens, nor would I have wanted Andie to follow my reckless example. I caressed Samuel's sweet-smelling scalp as he rested contentedly on my lap. "Oh, this brings back delicious memories." I chuckled. "I thought I was perfectly capable of having a baby at 18, but, looking back, it's amazing I came through it like I did. I mean, I was so young and didn't know a thing, but I sure *thought* I knew it all."

"Was Andie born here in San Antonio?" Marten asked.

"Yes, but just barely. We moved six weeks before she was born. Richard worked in investments and insurance and was offered a spectacular job shortly after his graduation, so we ended up here. I didn't know anyone but his mother, and she lived five hours away. Nina adopted me, you might say."

"When she arrived in town," Doc added, "she came to see me in search of a pediatrician. She obviously needed a female adviser, and Nina, who is also my office manager, took a liking to her immediately."

"I asked Nina every question imaginable, and she always patiently answered every one. I read how-to books on every subject from breastfeeding to name selection. When Andie came along, I realized I wasn't as baby-smart as I had thought."

"You were the perfect mother, Julia," Nina said. "And you still are."

"You're too sweet. The credit goes to you and Doc. You took me in just like one of your own children." I held Samuel up and kissed his exposed belly. "Does Rebecca breastfeed?"

"Well, of course," said Nina.

"That's good to hear."

"It's not like the old days," Nina added, "when nursing wasn't considered smart, thanks to the formula companies' propaganda, when women weren't always supported by their husbands."

"Was your husband a comfort when Andie was born, Julia?" Marten asked.

Nina scoffed. "A *comfort*? Now that's one word you wouldn't use to describe Richard."

"No," I said. "Actually, Richard's mother had him convinced that breastfeeding wasn't healthy, and he worried himself sick that Andie was either malnourished or eating too often, so he wasn't much support at all."

"He didn't understand that mother's milk gets digested much faster and easier than formula," Doc said. "It's the food God designed for baby."

"You must have missed a lot of sleep, since he didn't participate in nighttime feedings," Marten said.

"At first I did, but then I figured out I could bring her into our bed and nurse her whenever she wanted." As I thought back to those days, I felt a cramp in the pit of my stomach. "Richard hated that. He insisted it wasn't healthy for babies to sleep in the same bed with their parents. But I'd learned by then not to pay much attention to him. His only real participation, honestly, was to criticize the way I did things." I snickered. "Except diaper changes; he wouldn't change a soiled diaper — said I was the pro, that he couldn't do it as good as I did. Yeah, right. Anyway, at the time he was preoccupied with being successful in his new career."

"Not a multi-tasking sort of fellow?" Marten summarized.

I visualized Richard, his finger pointing right at my face: 'Julia, you could *live* on a merry-go-round, I'm sure of it.' I took it as a compliment when he tried to insult me with sarcasm, asking if I'd been born and raised in an amusement park. What better life than on a carousel: fanciful prancing horses, vibrant music, and a 360 view of the world. That's what I wanted back in the day . . . color . . . music . . . to see *everything.*

Merely the thoughts, memories of Richard's inattentiveness to me after our baby arrived caused my neck muscles to tighten. My heart rate quickened. I felt a panic attack coming on and I knew I should change the subject, but I blindly pushed onward.

"Richard busied himself with all sorts of life's little problems. He could *not* just take a seat, relax, and do nothing, and he usually managed to do two things at once, so yes, he *could* multi-task, but those tasks had to be the things he enjoyed doing before he'd attempt it. Even when I phoned him at the office, I heard him shuffling papers in the background."

I searched for a way to change the subject, but I couldn't stop the rampage I felt coming. "And didn't *that* piss me off? You'd think a wife could have her husband's undivided attention when she needed it!" My voice level raised an octave, and I became conscious that I was raving like a lunatic. With a baby on my lap!

Samuel whimpered and reached for his grandmother. Doc, Nina and Marten stared at me with pity, but I hadn't said it to get sympathy. Anger — wasn't that one stage of grieving? And here I'd believed I was beyond that stage. Or maybe I skipped it and was going backward for a while to catch up.

Nina lifted Samuel off my lap. "Come here to Granny, Sam-Sam." She caressed his back and walked over to the bay window so he could look outside.

"It all caught up with him, anyhow," I said in a calmer voice. "He fussed, fumed, and fretted the entire 16 years of our marriage. He worried enough for both of us, so on my carousel I stayed. I raised our daughter the best way I knew how. Andie and I had fun, usually just the two of us together, while her dad planned for the future. He spent more time in the future than the present. Sadly, he didn't make it to the future."

"He passed away at what age?" Marten inquired.

"Thirty-nine, five years ago.

"Now here I've gone and painted such a bad picture of Richard," I said, "but he wasn't *that* dreadful. Our relationship was definitely of the parent/child variety, though. He was afraid I'd grow up and become independent; I struggled to do exactly that. Turns out, his methodical indulgence in the fussing and fuming he was known for became the breeding ground for his cancer. Most people thought that's what killed him, the cancer."

Marten immediately asked, "Wasn't it?"

Doc and I exchanged looks and he took control of the conversation. "Yes, of course. Richard's medications were complicit, but ultimately cancer was the culprit."

Good ole Doc. Always truthful, but spoken with words to cover it up.

"I know one thing," I said, "all the worry and stress he brought upon himself by fretting over every little thing surely brought on the cancer. In fact, he'd worried for years that he would get the disease someday."

"Well, there you go," said Doc.

"It's such a shame he couldn't have lived to see his grandson," Marten said. "Those blue eyes and blond curls."

Nina spoke up. "If he'd appreciated what he had in the first place, he could have been around much longer."

"How is that?" Marten asked.

I flashed Doc a look of concern, or more likely one that asked for help. *I'd thought we were in the clear.*

"Pay no mind," Doc said, shaking his head. "The issues are old ones, Nina, and none of our business. Let's talk about something else. Anything."

I was all for that. I wondered how much longer I could trust anyone with the secret. In three more days, Andie would be 21 — old enough to hear the truth. It would be better if she heard it from her mother than from anyone else. But just the thought of telling my daughter made me dizzy.

Samuel giggled and pointed out the window. His family had pulled into the driveway and were making their way to the front door. Rebecca and Michael and their son Christopher, age 10, came in and seated themselves with the rest of us at the dining room table.

After all introductions were made, Christopher excitedly described a house they found. "My room has a loft where I can hide from Samuel."

"Oh, I can't imagine wanting to get away from Samuel," I said with an engaging smile, baiting the boy.

Christopher wrinkled his nose. "Sam-Sam bugs me sometimes. Anyway, our new neighbors have a kid my age and he has a tree house!"

"Excellent! There's nothing more exciting than a tree house," I said. "It's like being in another world, and it makes a good hiding place, too. You'll love it!"

I thought about Dana's tree house and wished I had one. I'd go and hide in it — hide away from all of the secrets of the world.

Chapter Thirty-Three

Olga Cashes In

Olga worked early mornings to take advantage of the sunlight pouring into the empty building through large windows on both exterior sides. But, with each mural she painted, the room darkened when *Roberto* placed the 4x8 plywood sheet in a window no sooner than the paint had dried. The Navarro Street side was complete, already blocking out a large amount of daylight. Late into the afternoon, Olga used the glow from overhead interior fixtures, but it wasn't as effective. *What is wrong with that gringo? A true artiste needs flawless light as an element, much the same as superior paints and brushes to achieve excellence.* Perry Roberts didn't seem to be as interested in her fine work as he was in a speedy product. However, mediocrity did not appeal to Olga Gonzales.

Even as a maid, she'd been meticulous to a fault. When she completed a room, everything was in its place. She would stand back and survey it like a photographer would frame a scene. Sometimes she would photograph it for her scrapbook.

Eduardo had told Olga that Perry Roberts didn't want anyone on the outside looking in while they were working on the clinic. That wasn't such a bad idea, Olga thought, but just when were they going to start framing up the walls? And the electrician — the only thing he did was hang those hideous florescent lights from the ceiling. At her insistence, Eduardo hung an old wooden door up at the restroom. He did a crude job — it didn't fit and wouldn't close tightly, but at least she had a tiny bit of privacy.

Olga painted from photographic images. She had taken several shots of the Alamo with a digital camera *Roberto* had given her. Then, last week while Eduardo was out, *Roberto* had brought her up into his loft and taught her how to transfer her photos onto his computer. He had stood close behind her, placed one hand on her left shoulder and his right hand on hers, maneuvering the mouse, showing her techniques to use: zooming in and out, cropping photos, and adjusting light and contrast. He whispered detailed instructions she didn't understand and she'd shivered when she felt his feather-soft breath and the prickle of his mustache on her neck.

She'd painted two replicas of the Alamo, making one background as it might have appeared in days of old. The second one was a modern version; its exterior was crowded with tourists. She went so far as to paint a Japanese family — a mother, father, and a toddler with a little camera, but just yesterday Eduardo had scolded her. He'd said she, *of all people*, should be sensitive and careful not to offend. *Roberto* had watched them from his loft and Olga knew for certain he was smiling as he overheard their conversation. She'd smiled, too, but only on the inside, when she recalled the way his hand had slowly inched its way from her shoulder down into the top edge of her low-cut sweater that day last week when he stood behind her at the computer.

Eventually, she changed the mixture on the scene in question — some African-American, Orientals, and Hispanic, but each with a camera. They were tourists, after all. When *Roberto* viewed the finished mural, he'd lightly swatted her butt, told her he liked her sense of humor. Then, he allowed his hand to rest on her backside, right where he'd smacked it. Olga quickly looked around to make sure Eduardo didn't see. *Roberto* whispered, "Don't worry, he's not here. I already looked out for him."

Olga was a quick learner and had transferred with ease nearly one-hundred photographs she'd taken all over San Antonio, mostly the Riverwalk area. Every time she uploaded a photo, she thought about how it felt when *Roberto* showed her how. And each time she thought about it, she was eager for it to happen again. As he'd stood close behind her one day, with his left hand where it shouldn't have been, he'd suddenly lifted his right hand from the mouse, slipped it down her sweater over her other breast.

Immediately excited, she'd swiveled the office chair around and said, "Come to Mamma." He'd hurriedly sat right down in her lap, facing her, pulled off her sweater and ripped the buttons off her blouse as he yanked it open. Yes, *Roberto* was a nasty, nasty man and Olga hungered for him.

She placed her plywood canvas facing Charles Court where the dancing water fountains stimulated her muse. She had a hankering for *Roberto* and was anxious for him to come downstairs. They were the only two people in the building, so she made more noise than usual in an effort to awaken him.

Chapter Thirty-Four

A Royal Gift

"Tomorrow is your birthday," I said while walking home from school with Boone. "Here you are, five years old, but you seem much older, sometimes. You're a great deal smarter than other kids your age."

Boone burst out laughing. "Grandmas always say that!"

"Well . . . I say it only because it's true."

He considered that statement. He squinted and angled his head. "Did you get me a bike?"

"There's no place to ride one where we live."

"A scooter, then."

"Same problem — no place to ride it."

"I could drive it around the condo."

"I'll think about it." No way was that going to happen, but the lad definitely had wheels on his mind.

We'd reached Navarro Street. "Let's look at something else for now," I said. "We'll cut through here and check out the pet shop."

The little bell atop the doorway chimed when we entered. Boone took off running to the aquatic display at the rear of the store. I found him peering into a large glass tank stuffed with bamboo and greenery. A lizard of some variety, lazily perched on a branch, chomped on a large leaf and engaged in a staring competition with Boone. The lizard blinked and Boone laughed. "I win! I want *this* guy, Gran."

Boone and Andie must have been coming here regularly. He'd already made up his mind long before we heard those door chimes. It would be just like Andie to invite a cold-blooded reptile into the house. She'd probably set him up — hinted to Boone to ask Gran to buy it for him. *Gran will, you know; she can't say no to you.*

"Chameleons are cold-blooded," I said. "They change colors whenever they feel like it and you never know what they're up to. Anyway, I was thinking of something warm and fuzzy. Would you consider that?"

Boone made a face and trudged on to the next glass display. "How about this? It's fuzzy."

I shuddered. "Come here, young man." I gently grasped the back of his little neck and guided him toward the front of the store. "How about we consider one of these? Kittens can love you back. Tarantulas can't. Look at that cute white one with the black paws."

Boone stuck his finger through the wire and wiggled it. Three adorable fuzz balls tumbled over one another to check it out.

The shopkeeper approached. "Have you found one you like?"

His shoulders slumped. "They're all right, I guess." A look of resignation spread across his face. "It's for my birthday . . . but I really wanted a bike."

"Boone is somewhat interested in your exotic creatures there in the back," I explained, "but I'm not sure I'd feel comfortable with a chameleon *or* a tarantula in my home."

"Ah, quite a predicament, I'd say. The lizard is actually an iguana, and they can be quite fascinating, but I'm in complete agreement with you regarding arachnids. Well, now, let's see." She paused, giving her shop a topical all-over search. "I know! We have *exotic* kittens."

Boone asked in a skeptical tone-of-voice, "What's *exotic*?"

"Oh, you know . . . somewhat foreign, could even be *alien*! Not your ordinary kind of pet — rather *mysterious*." She whispered the last word and looked around as though it was a secret between her and the boy.

Boone's eyes widened. "Show me!"

She took him by the hand and said, "Come with me." As I followed, I wondered if animals in the wild have a similar sense of foreboding just before they stumble into a trap.

We came upon a medium-sized glass enclosure with an attached sign that read *Abyssinian*. Inside, the feline gazed at us regally, head tilted upward, like a king awaiting the arrival of his court. His muscles flexed handsomely through a sleek, opulent golden coat while his jewel-like green-gold oval eyes studied me with curiosity. I judged him to be about four months old.

The cat fixed his eyes directly on Boone but did not blink. After a minute, Boone looked at me as if to say "what about this?" Without hesitation, the sales clerk selected a small key from her collection. She unlocked the cage and removed the cat, then escorted us into a private "bonding" booth. She motioned Boone to sit on the bench and she placed the animal carefully into his waiting arms. The Abyssinian nuzzled Boone's neck and chest, simulating a diesel engine purr.

The shopkeeper explained what she described as *royal attributes* of Abyssinians. Boone massaged the cat's belly and listened intently as she went on about pharaohs, pyramids and tombs. Again, a wild animal thought crossed my mind. I figured whenever they picked up the scent of something delicious, their immediate instinct told them to be extremely careful and outsmart the hunter. I estimated this breed of animal must be gold in more than just its color, but I didn't ask the price; the salesclerk would wait till the end of her sales pitch to mention it, I was sure, seasoned with fine points of authenticity and indisputable reasons we should own it.

She went into her office and soon returned to present a linen document with gilded edges. What did I tell you? She read off the otherwise unpronounceable names of this cat's parentage — undoubtedly, he was from a noble line of felines!

Boone said, "This cat is a *real* prince, Gran, like Prince Tuesday!" He hugged the golden beauty in a manner indicating he would never be able to put it down.

"How much is it?" I said. Stupid question; the ball was in her court — why did I even ask?

"Six hundred dollars," the clerk said, casually.

Six hundred freaking dollars? Whack! Heavy metal jaws clamped shut tightly on my leg. There was no way I *couldn't* buy it. *And here I took Andie for a fool when she bought that overpriced juicer on eBay.*

When I eventually dug into my purse for a credit card, I had also selected a carrier, tree perch and cat toys. Oh, and let's not forget the special food, not your standard, affordable grocery store variety, I might add. This breed apparently was known for its sensitive digestive tract. Why no, I did not know that. The bill came to just under $1000, including sales tax. I felt ridiculous because it was such a flamboyant purchase. Truth be told, I'd been taken by the cat, myself, but would've never considered buying a purebred just for me. The cat that was a prince — I would never tell anyone what I paid for it.

"I can't wait to get him home and play," Boone said.

"What will you name him?"

"I dunno. I think I'll get to know him first. It's gotta be something special."

"How about Grover Cleveland?"

"You're silly, Gran."

But it was no joke; Cleveland's face is on the $1000 bill.

Chapter Thirty-Five

Birthday For Two

Twenty-one years ago, I was in St. Mary's delivering my tiny baby girl. And exactly five years ago, that same child-woman delivered a son. Boone was born prematurely on Andie's 16th birthday. When she went into labor, Andie wasn't concerned about the early delivery, or the pain — only that the infant would have *her* birthday. She was never good with sharing, even as a child. That was probably my fault.

Last night, I reminisced with her about what a cute newborn she'd been, how perfectly round her face, her tiny head covered with a tassel of straight, light brown hair. "It fell right into your eyes . . . it was that long in front."

"Mother! That was then and this is *now*. I'm 21 — a grown up!"

"Oh? Well, that *is* good news."

~*~

I started decorating after Andie and Boone left for school. Yellow and blue helium balloons, strings attached, drifted aimlessly; vases of fresh yellow carnations adorned the end tables. Miles of yellow and blue twisted crepe paper hung from door knobs, cabinet handles, chandeliers and anywhere else I could find to attach ribbons of it. The party's theme was Sponge Bob — thus the color choice. Crabby Patty plates, napkins, cups, and party hats sat in place on the dining table. What's a party without a theme?

While stringing blue twinkling lights along the palm trees beside the grand piano, with a blow-up pineapple hut on top, my mind traveled back to my last party — the Open House. Only one month ago, and how things had changed. I'd acquired several new clients, one boyfriend and an expensive Abyssinian feline.

Grandmother Tyler arrived two hours early, bearing a mouth-watering flourless chocolate cake. She placed it in the center of the dining table. I'd extended an invitation for her to stay with us after Boone's birthday party, but she planned to visit a friend in Corpus Christi. "Thank you just the same, my dear," she'd said.

Madelynne settled herself on the pink leather sofa. "Can I do anything else to help?"

"Not really," I told her. "All that's left is to sit and wait for the little guest of honor to arrive." It was awkward to be alone in the room with Madelynne, and I searched for something to say. Her face pointed stiffly forward, her eyes moved from side to side, as though she'd never seen the room before. In a way, she hadn't. Andie had brought her to see the condo right after we'd moved in, but there were layers of sheet rock and paint buckets scattered throughout, sawdust an inch deep in places. Madelynne claimed to be highly allergic to any number of things and had gone into a sneezing fit within 30 minutes and had to be taken all the way home to Tyler, Texas, a 5-1/2 hour drive. I'd offered to book a hotel room on the Riverwalk, but she'd refused.

"Oh, goodness," I said. "Where are my manners? Come, let me give you a tour of the place, now that it's all finished."

Madelynne followed along and complimented me on the master bedroom. "It's striking, just as Boone told me it was. But I fear he spends too much time in here watching television," she added, with sharp-edged disapproval. I gritted my teeth. I'd presumed she would find something to complain about; she always did. This was the woman who raised Richard. His negativity made more sense as I got to know her better.

We eventually retreated to the sofa and I attempted to make my former mother-in-law feel at home by offering a cup of hot tea. Madelynne eagerly requested "Earl Grey with a drop of honey and a spot of cream," reminding me of Marten's favorite blend. Lucky for me, he wasn't nearly as *high maintenance* as Madelynne.

The cat awakened, slithered from his hiding place and promenaded into the living room. He jumped up onto the couch as though he owned it. The older woman was noticeably put off. I assured her Abyssinians were hypo-allergenic.

"Oh. Well." Madelynne plucked a small package of Benadryl from her purse to keep handy, just in case. She accepted the cup and saucer and sipped her tea. "Now, isn't this Andie's birthday, too? Let me think . . . how old is she?"

Well, now, Madelynne. You were more appalled than Richard when the girl got pregnant at 15 — do the math! I had never understood why the woman had purposely ignored the pleasures of grand-parenthood with Andie. It's not like she had others to dote over. She had her reasons, I supposed, however misguided. I asked Richard about it on several occasions, but never got any satisfying answers, only excuses. At least now, with a great-grandson, Madelynne finally seemed to be a little more relaxed and enjoying her family.

"Andie is 21 today," I said. "She and Britt are going out later this evening to celebrate like normal young adults. *This* bash will be tame compared to that one! Thank goodness we're not invited; I'm the official babysitter tonight."

Madelynne nodded and perceptively smiled, and it occurred to me that she never once asked if she could look after Andie while Richard and I went out to celebrate our anniversary. She'd always sent a card, so it's not like she didn't know when it was. While I attempted casual conversation with her, I felt a twinge of guilt because I was actually *glad* Madelynne was leaving for Corpus after the party. I wanted time alone with Boone; I had a special surprise for him.

~*~

The party started immediately after Boone's arrival from school. The royal cat was going berserk with the crepe paper and helium balloons. He had discovered the blinking palm tree lights and was chasing them up and down as they alternated. He'd knocked one tree over within the first three minutes. Only one of Boone's school friends was invited — it was more of a friend and family affair — not a little kids' party. Doc and Nina journeyed up from the second floor after office hours; Britt wandered out of his cubicle to join in the merriment. Frederick had attached himself to Dana downstairs at The Stock Market and they rode the elevator up for an on-time arrival. Dana opened a white cake box to reveal her rendition of a Sponge Bob confection with an abundance of yellow and blue fondant icing. Sponge Bob was smiling wide — holding a banana — the flavor of the cake.

Dana arranged it next to Madelynne's chocolate cake. "Now we'll have our choice of desserts, although I suspect only the children will want to sample this one. I just thought it would be cute to match the party theme, but I've got to warn you — this fondant is fattening!"

Boone was accompanied by his bestie, Simone Michaelson, who loved to smother Boone with advice. Boone ran his finger along the outer edge of the icing and licked it before Simone could stop him. She gasped and said, "Did you wash your hands?" Boone took on a stricken look and ran down the hall to the bathroom.

"Well, that makes it official," I said. "The adults won't want to get close to *this* cake. Boone has made his mark!"

When Boone returned, I gave him his choice: cake and ice cream first — or gifts. He chose gifts; Simone swiftly nudged his elbow. Boone said, "I mean cake." They enjoyed it with banana ice cream. I had a gallon of vanilla in case the banana didn't fly, but everyone seemed to like it. Dana chatted happily with Madelynne about her specialty cake recipe, and I thought of the banana Dana had been playing with only four days ago. Her dry spell had apparently ended. No, Dana may have her freaky side, but she wouldn't use Boone's birthday cake to send me a private message. That was just *my* freaky imagination.

In the middle of the party, the elevator bell rang and Marten's voice came over the speaker. *What is he doing here?* I hadn't invited him because his name wasn't on Boone's list. I hadn't thought anything of it — after all, Marten was my friend, not Boone's. I called the elevator up. When it opened, Marten, whose face was hidden by a large yellow box with blue ribbon, exclaimed, "Happy birthday, Boone!"

Oddly enough, and my first clue that something was definitely amiss, Andie literally jumped out of her chair. "I'm so glad you could make it!"

Boone's mouth was full of cake, but he managed a finger wave.

Marten carefully placed the package on the floor beside the gift table. I sized up the box. Was it large enough to be a bicycle? If so, Marten was in deep doo-doo. But, no, it didn't look the right size for that, unless it had to be assembled.

Marten said hello to everyone and introduced himself to Madelynne. "I'm a newcomer to San Antonio, one of Julia's clients."

Madelynne raised one eyebrow and said, "Oh, I see."

Great. Just great.

I placed a big slab of cake and ice cream on a plate and handed it to Marten. I didn't exactly know why I was mad at him, but I gave Marten the slice that had Boone's "unwashed" finger print on it. He offered me one of those special looks with a wink, the kind you get when you're sleeping with someone. I hoped Madelynne didn't see it.

Boone made quick work of opening his presents. He tore bows off and merrily ripped the wrapping paper, tossing it hither and yon. He seemed delighted with each gift: a Lego set from Britt, Lincoln Logs from Doc, a Sponge Bob puzzle from Frederick and a wood castle with plastic knights, swords and horses from Dana. He offered a polite "thank you" to everyone.

Andie whispered something to Boone. He had saved Marten's gift for last. When he opened it, he did so very carefully, as though he knew something about its precious contents. Andie was recording a video and I suspected I'd be on a YouTube clip tomorrow titled "What this daughter did to her mother will blow you away!"

I took deep breaths to stave off an anxiety attack when the unwrapping revealed the prize. *That cold-blooded lizard! How did he know about it?* Boone screamed for joy and jumped up and down. Simone's lips were O-shaped. Madelynne hurriedly popped a Benadryl into her mouth and reached for her cup of tea to wash it down. The cat, frantically batting a half-full helium balloon around the room, hunkered down on all fours and stalked its way toward the reptile's cage.

Andie glowed as though she'd just won the lottery. I attempted to make eye contact, but surprise! — my daughter wouldn't cooperate. Marten had been hoodwinked — and so had I, for that matter. Where, exactly, did Andie plan to keep this cold-blooded reptile, and precisely who would maintain the creature? I presumed it would be Andie, now that she was a grown woman, never again to be childish. What a joke. Boone would want to keep it in my jungle bedroom, I just knew it. Well! I'd be saying NO very soon. Let Andie figure this one out.

A streak of gold flashed through the air and landed on top of the iguana's cage, which tilted dangerously. The cat howled, jumped off, tucked his tail between hind legs and took refuge under the dining table.

Marten yelled, "What the — ?" He adjusted the cage upright and the iguana hurried to hide beneath copious foliage. Marten glanced at me. "Since when do you have a cat? I hope he doesn't try to eat this little guy." He stooped to retrieve the meowing creature, rubbed behind its ears, which was all it took to set off the diesel engine. "A purebred! And look, his coat is two-toned, like a *faux* finish. He's stunning. Does he have a name?"

Boone said he hadn't thought up a name fancy enough, and he went on to tell Marten all about the royal newcomer.

"We're looking for a noble, stately name. *Regal*," I said. "Do you have any suggestions?" I wiped off a glob of blue icing that had landed on the floor as a result of the pandemonium.

"I was reading a Gideon Bible in the hotel last night. There's a portion that describes the lineage of Jesus. Those names would be majestic, to say the least," Marten said.

I cut my eyes quickly toward Marten, trying to picture him reading the Bible alone in his room. He certainly added unexpected aspects to my parties.

Boone ran into his bedroom and returned with a tiny white leather book, *Holy Bible* inscribed in gold letters on the front. "Show me," Boone said and handed the Bible to Marten.

Madelynne Tyler beamed; it had been a Christmas gift from her. My heart pounded and I tried to remember how to breathe, since it didn't seem to come naturally.

Marten flipped through the pages and read aloud the passage where the High Priest, Zadok, carried the Ark of the Covenant.

"Oh boy! He was in charge of that?" Boone said.

"Yes, he had a very responsible position, this Zadok chap," Marten said.

"There is a song written about him . . . Bach, I believe," Doc added. "Zadok the Priest!"

"Can you play it, Marten?" Boone asked.

"Maybe. If I can find a copy of the sheet music, I might be able to."

"Then that's what he shall be named, Zadok the Priest," Boone pronounced with authority.

"Zadok is his first name, and Priest will be his surname," Simone said.

"Sir Zadok the Priest?" Boone said.

Simone laughed. "No, silly. Your surname is your last name, your family name . . . like Tyler."

Boone pursed his lips, tilted his head and nodded slowly, as though he had known but had temporarily forgotten.

"Zadok, Zadok," I said. "I think I could get used to that. I like it!"

"Ding! Ding! Ding!" Andie chimed in loudly. "Julia Tyler proclaims we have a winner!" I wanted to put a muzzle on her.

Zadok didn't seem to care what anyone called him; he'd retreated to a quiet corner of the living room, his head held high, tail all bushy and flickering, elliptical eyes focused directly on the reptile 15 feet away. Boone and Simone positioned themselves on the floor next to the cage, playing with the castle and the figures that came with it. They pretended the iguana was a medieval dragon, captured and kept in the tower of the castle, occasionally blowing fire from its nostrils. The lizard, as yet unnamed, flicked his tongue and blinked once.

Andie moved around the room with her camera. Dana worked in the kitchen, making a fresh pot of coffee and various blends of hot tea. Doc and Nina were deep in conversation with Madelynne about how wonderful grandchildren are. I was relieved to see her enjoy herself.

When the children tired of the new toys, they wandered over to the kitchen counter and Simone pulled her electronic tablet out of her backpack.

I took the opportunity to put Zadok away, carrying him down the hallway into the laundry room. I refreshed his water and dispensed a handful of high-priced nuggets into his bowl. As I was about to close the door, I noticed him gratefully watching me. "Oh, thank you," he purred. I reached down to pet him. I smiled, and sang, *"Welcome to the Hotel California. You can check out any time you like, but you can never leave."*

Simone was showing Boone how to play Hearts online, then she navigated to DisneyChannel.com and they played games on the website.

Simone had given Boone a subscription to the games so their players could meet and follow one another from one location to another. Simone had a tendency to touch her forehead, making sure her new bangs were straight. She told Boone she hadn't decided if she actually liked them or not. When Boone said they made her look smarter, a slight smile crossed her face and she nodded.

Andie plopped down on the sofa next to her grandmother. "I wish Daddy could be here."

"Yes, dear," Madelynne said. "He would so enjoy Boone."

"Well, yes . . . that, and to see how well *I've* turned out on *my* twenty-first birthday. Daddy thought there for a while I was headed straight for hell!" She giggled.

Madelynne nodded as though she understood perfectly her son's feelings; she'd probably shared Richard's opinion.

Boone cut short his video game and directed his gaze at me. "Why would he think that?"

The room suddenly took on the air of a tomb. As Dana poured Madelynne a cup of tea, she turned to me and raised both eyebrows with a look that said *what are you going to do about this one?* Thankfully, Dana said nothing.

Doc took charge. "Oh, it's just something people say. They don't mean anything by it."

"But . . . why?" Boone asked. His eyes betrayed a fear he tried not to show.

"You'll learn it at your church," Simone said as she condescendingly patted Boone on the shoulder. "Hell is this awful place God sends you when you're bad."

Madelynne was nodding again. I pictured her as a bobble-head toy, attached to the front pew of a fancy downtown Tyler, Texas cathedral.

Boone waved Simone off dismissively and said, "I know all about hell. But God wouldn't do that to Mommy!"

"Yes, he would, too. If she was bad, that's where she'd go!" Simone insisted. She reached for Boone's little Bible. Boone snatched the Bible before Simone could get it. "Mommy sends me to Time Out. That's what God should do."

Doc cleared his throat, stood up and told Nina they should probably think about getting home. They headed for the elevator, promising Madelynne they would drive up to Tyler for a visit soon.

Britt announced he had just a tad more work to do and walked quickly down the hallway to his cubicle. Andie stood defiantly, with her hands on her hips. She huffed and her eyes narrowed just like Zadok the cat's as she watched Britt disappear.

Frederick asked Boone if he could take some cake home.

"Who's gonna eat it?" asked Boone.

"Well you just never know, little one," Fredrick answered with a wink.

Dana went into the kitchen and wrapped take-out for everyone. Even Madelynne had pulled her keys from her purse and jingled them nervously. A mass exit was in progress and I was helpless to stop it.

Marten walked over to the iguana's cage and tried to communicate with it by shaking a green branch. The creature looked the other way.

"Guess what, Marten!" Boone said.

"Uh, let's see . . . it's your birthday?"

"Well . . . yeah . . . and I got email from Chesley!"

"You got —" Marten grasped the nearest chair.

"Are you all right?" I said.

He said he was fine but demanded a drink. Something . . . strong. Did he mean tea or alcohol? I was not about to serve booze at a child's party . . . especially with Madelynne in attendance!

"Oh! Can I meet the prince, too?" Simone said.

"He's not a prince, silly." Boone said.

"He's not?"

"Prince is just a title, but he's not a prince. Where did you get that idea, anyway? You know Chesley's surname is Vanderhawk, right?"

"Of course I knew that," Simone said indignantly.

If anyone was keeping score, Boone was winning. *Little kids and their games — just like adults.*

Boone said. "I don't know if *I'll* even get to meet him in person. But I might."

"When are they coming, Mom?" Andie asked.

"March 22 — in four weeks," I said, keeping one eye on Marten.

"Julia! That drink?" Marten shouted, even though I was standing not three feet away from him.

"I'm here in the kitchen," Dana called out. "*I'll* fix it." I watched her gather Bloody Mary mix from the refrigerator and vodka from the liquor cabinet. She made it a double, extremely heavy on the Tabasco, added a celery stalk and a tiny red straw. Marten would hate the heavy Tabasco! She had mixed it in a silver-plated Mint Julep glass I'd bought at Churchill Downs and she carried it to him on a silver platter, no less. The message was lost on Marten, but I'd had to stifle my sheer delight when Dana winked at me.

Grandmother Tyler said her goodbyes and air-kissed everyone but Boone. She ruffled his blond curls and left a bright red lipstick mark on his cheek. Marten sucked down his beverage, claimed to be ill and took his exit. As Frederick joined him in the elevator, he said he hoped Marten hadn't caught the flu that was going around. Andie stomped down the hallway with the children into the play room to find a place for the new toys. Dana and I were left alone to clean up. We just stood there for a few moments, looking at one another.

"Peculiar," I said. "*Quite* peculiar."

"Agreed," Dana said. "Goes to show you shouldn't discuss religion or politics at a kid's party."

Chapter Thirty-Six

A Close Encounter

The next morning, I thought about Boone's party the instant I woke up. It actually had been a lot of fun, in spite of the menagerie, and Boone had thanked me repeatedly. Andie and Britt had helped Boone set up the iguana's cage in the toy room. I overheard Andie instruct Boone as to the chores he'd have to do regularly. *Oh that's going to last, all right*, I thought. *She expects a five year old to be responsible for that cold-blooded creature? I'll be the one who'll end up doing it.*

I gave Boone a laptop after everyone else had gone. One of my customers had replaced a few older models and asked me if I'd care for a freebie. I jumped at the chance to get Boone his own computer. Maybe he was too young, but Simone had one and she was only six. Besides, I didn't want him using my office equipment anymore.

I lay in bed longer than usual, thinking about how lucky I was. Every year, I'm predictably melancholy the day after Andie and Boone's birthday, wishing somehow Richard could have been there with me. I thought I'd sneak in a quick trip to the cemetery today.

~*~

I went to Boudro's and ordered a Prickly Pear Margarita which arrived right about the time Marten did.

He sat across from me and appeared on edge. "Is something wrong? Your text seemed urgent."

I studied his face, squinted my eyes and stirred my drink. "Why did you buy that stupid lizard for Boone?" I demanded.

"Oh, that." Marten relaxed a bit. "Andie called me early yesterday morning. She inquired if I was coming to the party. When I told her I hadn't been invited, she apologized all over herself — said it must have been an oversight."

"That brat — she wasn't even in charge of the invitations. Boone did it himself . . . with my help, of course. So then, what happened?"

"I asked her what I should bring, and she told me about the iguana . . . said Boone would *absolutely die* if he didn't get it."

I took a deep breath and let it out slowly, emitting a thin whistle from between my clenched teeth. I shook my head and sipped through my straw. "I don't know what I did wrong with that child, but she's not turned out the way I'd planned at all!"

Marten laughed out loud.

"It's not funny."

"Yes, it is, Julia. Chill. You did everything right. She is her own self, a 21-year-old woman. But, that's all she is — 21. She's young. You can't control her any more than you can control the weather."

I wondered why he hadn't phoned me just to make sure I actually would approve of a cold-blooded reptile in my home. Wouldn't that have been a sensible question to ask? And wasn't he the one who just last month had insisted Doc call and make sure he could come to my Open House? Wouldn't that indicate he was a man sensitive to the desires of others?

"I tried to ring you up, but your mobile wasn't on," Marten said, as though he'd read my thoughts.

"You could have left a message."

"There was no time for that. Look, do you want me to return the gift?"

"Of course I do."

Marten looked at me with disbelief. "Okay. I'll do it tomorrow."

"But you can't, and you won't. I know it — you know it. So why on earth do you even ask?" Disgusted, I turned away from him. Was this another one of those *red flags* I'd warned myself about? *Don't think about it*. I watched a family of ducks paddle upriver and listened to the usual comforting Riverwalk sounds: the birds singing, the trickle of the current, the chatter of passersby. Even the familiar, shrill whine of a police car siren right above us on Commerce was a welcome remembrance that this is home. My safe place.

Taking a deep breath, I lightened up. Everything was all right, after all. "Boone named him Greenie. The stupid lizard," I said.

"Greenie his first name — Stupid the surname?"

I snickered. "That's right . . . or maybe it's the other way around."

We finished our guacamole without further conversation.

"Chill, you say?"

Marten smiled. "It's an American saying. I borrowed it."

I smiled back at him. "I shouldn't be mad at you. Andie is the one who's got me pissed. But I'm so angry with her that I can't even talk to her about it right now. It's *my* house — she should have asked me first. She went behind my back every way she could; she always does. When her original ploy didn't work, and I brought Zadok the royal cat home, she figured she'd use you and get what *she* wanted. She probably thinks she's blameless, though. She's always gotten what she wanted, one way or another. And, no, I didn't do everything right — I spoiled her as a child — this is just a consequence."

Marten reached for my hand across the table and squeezed it. "Richard was her parent, too. Surely he must share the responsibility if you're so intent on blaming someone."

I offered one last smirk and dipped a chip into what was left of the avocado mixture. "Trust me. I've already held him liable for lots of stuff. I can do that, now that he's dead."

The waiter arrived. Marten ordered the Niemen Ranch Pastrami Sandwich, and I settled on the Blackened Yellowfin Tuna Salad, even though I didn't have much of an appetite.

"We had a huge conflict about religion, Richard and I. He thought I was surely going to hell for not going to church, and for lots of other reasons. Like the cussing I did just to spite him. I figured that if there was a hell, and I never believed there was for a minute, he'd go there for being so critical of his wife, because I knew exactly what the Bible says about that."

"What's it say?"

"You should know. You're the one who reads it in your hotel room."

"I didn't get that far. I fell asleep."

I stared at him for a moment. "The Bible absolutely commands a husband to honor and cherish his wife. He is *not* to criticize the hell out of her." I chuckled at the pun.

"I'll keep that in mind, in case I ever decide to become a husband."

"Glad I could be of help!" I ordered another drink. I'd already ruined my kid; I might as well "chill" now. Besides, everything really was okay. So I had a stupid green iguana in the house — so what?

"I know this is a cliché," Marten said, "but I just have to say that you are truly beautiful when you're angry. Your eyes sparkle and your complexion flushes. It's heart-warming."

I laughed. "Andie's behavior is probably the only thing that causes me the frustration that makes me this mad. Sometimes memories of Richard cause it, too."

"I'm sorry about that, but I quite enjoy the feisty Julia when she comes out!" He smiled that crooked smile that always got to me. "Does anyone ever mention that you look like that actress—."

"Jessica Chastain! I get it a lot. Even complete strangers have approached me, inquiring."

"I can see why," Marten said.

"A few years ago I was with Dana on a weekend trip to New York City and we lunched at a crowded ethnic restaurant in SoHo. Suddenly, Dana noticed a woman walking right toward me with a napkin in her hand, so she jumped out of her chair and claimed to be my agent, saying 'Yes, she will give you an autograph, but please don't engage her in conversation while she's eating.' Afterward, the woman walked out the door with a friend, excitedly waving the napkin with *my* signature on it. We've chuckled about it ever since."

The musical notes of Marten's voice had calmed me down and I'd forgotten why I'd been angry in the first place.

~*~

I made myself as comfortable as possible on the concrete bench. "I gave Boone a laptop last night for his birthday, Richard. I've installed a separate phone line for him that allows only a slow dial-up because I don't want him connected to my business service. I haven't mentioned this to another living soul; well, actually you're not technically a living soul, which is probably why I'm telling you."

I'd felt guilty for giving Boone such an expensive gift at first, even though it had been free to me. Of course, with Zadok in the picture, the laptop didn't seem nearly as extravagant. Add the appearance of Stupid Greenie, and the expense issue was null.

I was in the middle of our conversation, going on about the party and what fun it had been, ". . . until the end, which was somewhat weird, to tell you the truth." Before I could go any further, I heard the crunch of rubber on gravel, glanced up, and saw a beige land yacht in the form of an aging Lincoln Continental pull into the cemetery. "I may have to tell you the rest of the story later, because you know I'm not comfortable talking to you while the living are close by." I stood and brushed off the back of my jeans.

"Oh no! Please don't leave." Madelynne rushed toward me, her arms flailing about.

"Hello, Madelynne. I didn't recognize your car. Come. Have a seat."

We sat together on the bench, awkwardly at first, both unsure of what to say at Richard's grave. Madelynne was the first to speak. "I didn't expect to see you. I mean . . . I didn't realize you would still come here after five years."

"I visit Richard a lot," I said. Silence ensued.

Eventually, I said, "Did you have a nice visit with your lady friend in Corpus?"

"Lady friend? Oh, uh . . . yes." She kneaded her hands. "We played cards and this morning we went to Cracker Barrel for breakfast. I was going to stop by your place to give Boone a box of salt-water taffy I bought for him. I'll give it to you before we leave here."

I knew Andie wouldn't allow Boone to eat it — bad for his teeth, but it was a nice gesture. "This was a mistake," Madelynne said.

Surely she didn't mean the box of taffy. I waited for her to continue.

Madelynne pointed to the monument with my name on it. "I don't know what I was thinking. I suppose this is what they mean when they say one shouldn't make major decisions during the first year after the death of someone close."

"Uh huh," I nodded my head in agreement. "And I'll admit, at first I was shocked to see my name here. I wrestled with it for months. But I finally realized why it affected me so. After I lost Richard, I felt so alone that sometimes I'd pinch myself to make sure *I* was still alive. But now when I see it, I smile. You see? There's no date of death under my name — I'm very much alive, although I admit, the grieving process was long and rocky for me."

"I can have it redone if you'd like." Tears ran down her cheeks.

I wrapped my arms around my mother-in-law. "Leave it. We'll see what the future brings."

"Julia," Madelynne sobbed, "honestly, what caused Richard's death? I'm sorry to bring this up, but I never understood, really not."

I removed a tissue from my pocket and wiped Madelynne's tears. I smiled lovingly at the older woman and lied straight-faced. "Madelynne . . . dear Madelynne. I'm unsure of the medical terminology, but he had some sort of a reaction to the medications they had used to treat him. It put him into a coma and he was too weak to recover."

Richard's mother sighed with relief. "So, he's in heaven, then." Her tears of sorrow changed to those of joy.

Why, of course. That's what religion often does — persuades a person to worry so much about the illusive afterlife that they don't enjoy the life they have. I recognized the anguish of a loving mother who had struggled for five long years with the notion that her dear son might have actually gone to a place of fire and brimstone for taking his own life. Madelynne will never get those five years back, but one little white lie from me and the next five will be much better for her. I'm not afraid of the consequences, either. Anyway, evidently, she wasn't as oblivious as I had thought — she *had* considered the possibility of suicide. "He's right up there," I said, pointing upward. "And sometimes he visits me right here." I waited for a response.

Madelynne bit her lower lip. "You need to get on with your life, dear," she said. "That Mr. Wells seems like such a fine young man. I think he's sweet on you."

"I think you're right. What should I do about it?"

"Fuck him, dear." No, of course Madelynne didn't actually say it. She merely raised her eyebrows and cast a knowing smile my way. Then, to my dismay, she broke down in tears again.

I tightened my arms around the woman and stroked her shoulder. I handed her another tissue.

"Thank you," Madelynne sobbed. "Oh, Julia . . . my friend in Corpus is not a lady."

I blinked. I always enjoyed a story with a twist or two. "She's not?"

"No — *he's* not.

"Oh. You have a gentleman caller?"

Madelynne nodded. "Oh, my goodness in heaven. What will the family think of me?"

"Are you serious? I'm happy for you. Everyone needs a mate; it's only natural. Mr. Tyler's been gone an awfully long time."

"That's why I came here today . . . to tell Richard about Edward," Madelynne confessed.

Well, now, Richard's getting a whole lot of news, here lately. "Your son will be delighted! Have no doubt of that. When can we meet him?"

"He wanted to come to Boone's party, but I was too embarrassed." She chuckled. "I'm just an old fiddle-fart, a worn out fuddy-duddy."

"Oh no, you're not. You've only just begun. Tell you what. Let's make it a double date. How about next weekend? I'll bring Mr. Wells and you bring your fellow, Edward. Just a foursome at first."

"Yes, all right. Then, we can introduce him to the rest of the family gradually." She placed her hand over her bosom. "I don't think my heart can take anything more sudden. I've already met his daughter and grandchildren. They're delightful, and they seem to have taken a liking to me, as well!"

Imagine that. "This is fantastic news, truly it is! But, now I've got work to do. I'll leave you here to visit with Richard. Pour your heart out, Madelynne. It always works for me. This place is exceptionally alive with energy, like the vortex sites in the rock formations in Sedona."

Madelynne squirmed, probably puzzled by the word vortex. Too *New Age* for her.

"It is for me, anyway — to each his own." I touched the granite monument and ran my fingers lightly over my own engraved name. "Or *her* own," I added. I headed toward my Jeep, then turned back. "Call me when you decide where you'd like to meet for our double date."

I'd never felt so happy after spending time with Madelynne.

Chapter Thirty-Seven

Night Paint

Olga had gone out at three o'clock Sunday morning for one particular photo shoot when the full moon illuminated silhouettes of shops and restaurant fronts while the river reflected lights from ornate lampposts and building windows. She'd taken the Hilton's elevator all the way to the top, since it was the tallest building on the Riverwalk and afforded the best advantage for a grand view of the city below. Later, when she enlarged the photo on the computer to study it, she'd had to catch her breath when she clearly recognized both Eduardo and Perry Roberts in the background. There they were on the roof of the Arneson Theater! But why? She'd planned to follow Eduardo Sunday night to see for herself, but he hadn't gone out.

Olga was determined to find another way. Today's painting project depicted the Riverwalk at night. Olga came in earlier than usual for a reason. She needed to be there when Roberts trotted down the steps with a magazine, headed for his daily constitutional. That would give her a good 15 minutes for sleuthing. She gave the canvas an all-over black coat of acrylic. She'd cropped the two men out of the photograph before she fastened it above the easel for reference; she didn't want Roberts to know she'd caught them. She had the original unedited image on her flash drive. Just in case.

Roberts was never human until he'd taken his morning dump. Today was no exception. He hurried past Olga, stopping long enough to check out her work, tapping his finger on the photo. "You captured it," he mumbled. She glanced to make sure he'd shut the door of the john.

She quietly sneaked up the stairs and opened Roberts' files on his monitor. There were so many pictures — aerial shots — or maybe they had been taken from a tall building. Could've been the Hilton, Olga thought. Roberts certainly hadn't gone out of his way to keep the file private. She'd expected him to have it protected with some type of code, but she'd already found his list of passwords in a separate desk drawer when she'd been snooping around the week before. Had he wanted her to find them? She shook her head. Who could read the mind of her *Roberto*?

There it was — the frame she wanted to see! Yes, it was the roof of the Arneson Theatre, but the view he'd given her to paint had been cropped to such an extent she'd been unaware at the time what she was duplicating. Why had he wanted a mural of it? The painting had been done to scale, and Roberts had ordered it in twelve equal parts. Two days after she produced the first one, it was gone. She asked about it, but he ignored her. The same thing happened with her second rendition. She'd put her breasts within three inches of him, with her hands on her hips, and insisted he tell her where her paintings had walked off to.

"We're putting all twelve of them in a clinic we've just opened in Florida. When we're finished here, I'll fly you down and show you. Maybe the four of us could sneak in some beach time while we're there," he'd said to her breasts. "Remember, I predicted you'd be famous all over the world."

"I'd love to go to Florida with you, *señor*," Olga had said.

"Keep those paint brushes swirling, *chica*." Roberts stood close to her as he spoke. He'd done that more often as time moved along — whether Eduardo was in the room or not. Eduardo always looked the other way.

Perry Roberts had given her a Spanish-to-English Dictionary CD, and she'd been practicing whenever she could use his computer. She no longer needed Eduardo to translate, but sometimes she pretended to, so her husband wouldn't get suspicious. She longed for the day when Eduardo would no longer come between her and her new lover.

She prepared to close the file when she noticed a shadow across the room. Startled, she looked up to see *Roberto* less than two feet away. He looked at the monitor, then at Olga. He looked at the monitor again. There was no point in closing the file now.

"Like what you see, do you?" Perry Roberts growled.

Olga had been holding her breath and she let it out all at once. "I no comprehend. Are my paintings in Florida? Or not."

"Not."

Olga put her hand over her mouth and closed her eyes tightly. What did this mean? Was she in trouble?

"You've been a bad, bad little *chica*, haven't you?"

Olga shook her head. "Why bad?" She continued shaking her head. She flinched as *Roberto* slid one hand into her blouse. He quickly lowered his zipper with the other hand.

"I've got something here for you *chica,* and I think you're going to like it."

Sí, I like it, *señor."* Eduardo usually came into work around noon, so Olga relaxed. She figured as long as she let *Roberto* have his way with her, she could get by with being a snoop this once. She tilted her head back, flashed him a reassuring smile and spread her legs. Afterward, he appeared deep in thought, as though he was making a momentous decision.

"You wanna earn a half-million dollars?"

Sí . . . yes."

Perry Roberts nodded. "Those murals aren't in Florida — they're right here on the Riverwalk." He directed her attention to the computer. The twelve sections had been installed by Roberts and Amigo, one at a time, on top of the Arneson Theater's flat surface under the cover of darkness. They had fashioned a partial fake roof fourteen inches above the real one. Roberts planned to use the 14-inch space to wait until the time was right, and then he would drop down into the Arneson Theater through a weakened portion of the roof and kidnap a child. Olga voiced her concern, not about the legalities, but that children might be hurt. Roberts assured her the boy would not be harmed. It was illegal, certainly, but not dangerous. If she wanted in, he had the perfect role for her to play. "Amigo is in for only $50,000 — why not say yes to a half mil?"

"*Sí* . . . yes," she shouted.

"When we're done, you come with me and we forget all about amigo, *sí*?"

"*Sí, señor!*"

Chapter Thirty-Eight

Ribs With Fredrick

I walked Boone to school on Friday and discovered that the private elevator had stopped working when I returned. It happened sporadically, as the elevator was old and required lots of TLC. I slipped into the building's maintenance office and made a report of it, and then I took the public elevator up to the fifth floor, where I heard loud music coming from Frederick's apartment. I knocked on his door and he slightly cracked it open.

"I'm craving barbecue ribs," I said, "and, since they're your downfall as well, I thought I'd ask you for a lunch date."

"Oh, Sweetie, I don't know. I'll check my schedule when I get to the salon. We'll text, okay?"

I saw the shadow of someone in the apartment, but I didn't stare. Frederick was discreet about his love life and didn't talk much about it. He'd wanted someone to grow old with, but so far it hadn't worked out. He shared his home only one time with a man he loved but, after five years together, the guy started finding fault with San Antonio. He complained of being sick and tired of living in a city that he felt wasn't gay friendly and he wanted to move to New Orleans. Frederick was entirely satisfied with his location and couldn't visualize moving his business to a new place and starting over. His partner pouted for a few days and took off by himself. Frederick hadn't heard from him since, not even a *having a wonderful time wish you were here* postcard. Frederick, though heartbroken, had never given up his search for a lifetime partner.

~*~

Frederick was able to get away for lunch, so we met at The County Line Grill. We both favored their thick and juicy ribs with a crispy slice of bacon on each rib. The outside seating allowed a perfect view of the grand La Mansion Del Rio Hotel. A young couple had stepped out on their balcony. We were always amused by watching happy vacationers, and I realized I had yet to arrange that four-day weekend trip I'd decided on just before the Open House. My life had changed dramatically since then. In fact, I barely recognized my old life anymore. I hadn't even felt the need to go to Richard's grave as often.

"Look at them," Frederick said. "You can tell this is their first time on the Riverwalk."

The lady on the balcony took a few photos with what appeared to be a disposable camera. The couple sorted through their hotel information packets, probably planning which attractions to visit. The bellhop arrived with their luggage and escorted them back inside and closed the balcony door. In a matter of minutes they would descend into the magical Riverwalk world.

"When they get home they'll take their film to be developed," Frederick said, "and they will gaze at the photographs — the Alamo, the missions, maybe the chapel at La Villita. But it will be the Riverwalk images that will remind them of their weekend romance." He sighed.

"I'll always remember the first time I saw it. Richard and I had just moved here and he was eager to show me the Riverwalk more than any other place in San Antonio. Of course he'd grown up in Texas, but I hadn't been crazy about moving out west after he received the job offer. I was seven months pregnant and didn't know anyone here. His mother wouldn't accept me — the barefoot and pregnant girl he'd hooked up with from Kentucky. Besides, she lived miles away. He knew the Riverwalk would change my mind about what Texas had to offer, and he was right. That's the day I fell in love with Texas."

"First time on the Riverwalk is like the first time making love. There are no words to describe it." Frederick sighed again.

I considered his body language. "Anything you want to tell me?"

He smiled, but with sadness in his eyes. "Nothing yet."

I held my arms out, wide open. "Right *here* is the most romantic place on Earth, at least from what I've seen of the world so far. I wish I could've known the Riverwalk's architect. He had a dream and made it come true. You have to admire his vision and commitment."

"Speaking of architects, how's Marten's new clinic project coming along?"

"Okay, I guess. He showed me the empty building a few weeks ago. I assume it's on schedule."

~*~

After lunch, I walked with Frederick to his salon, and proceeded farther down the street to deliver a written proposal to a new client. I headed home along Navarro, and on the spur of the moment decided to stop by Marten's new office to see for myself how the remodeling work was going. Frederick had awakened my curiosity.

As I neared the site, colorful painted murals in the store-front windows caught my eye. Signed by Olga Gonzales — a local artist, perhaps. The murals made it impossible to see inside, so I entered quietly and looked all around. The place was thick with cigarette smoke and odors of body sweat. With insufficient ventilation and no air-conditioning, it felt stuffy enough to be a sauna. Four Mexican men with hammers and noisy saws didn't notice my entrance. But what kind of carpenters were these, anyway? I couldn't imagine how their machinations would create examining rooms. No framing of walls had been done. Nothing was attached to anything permanent. The entire space was all still wide open. I made a mental note to ask Marten what was going on here. I'd learned a thing or two about remodeling strategies, but this didn't fit into any work plan I knew about.

"Hello there!" My voice echoed throughout the cavernous room.

All heads turned, and the men in the construction crew looked as though they'd seen a ghost.

"Ah ha! I caught you!" I joked, but the men only glared, stopping me cold. I stood still at first, and then shifted my weight from one foot to the other. "Uh . . . would you guys like something to drink? I'd be happy to pick up some refreshments next door for you." I thought maybe a beer would cure their doldrums. They put me in the mind of zombies, or droids, as they stood shaking their heads in unison.

"*Gracias*. No ma'am, we must finish our job," a short Hispanic man replied. He glanced apprehensively upstairs.

I followed his gaze and saw the familiar graffiti on the wall. Why had they painted all around the lizard design and hung an empty picture frame over it? The half-wall prevented me from seeing anything else, but I guessed the upstairs was the last area scheduled for renovation. Someone was up there at a computer, but his back was to me and I couldn't see his face. *How odd . . . especially on a hot day like this.* A number of ceiling fans were running at high speed. Maybe they had a cooler iced down with Coronas or Dos Equis upstairs. Was this what Marten meant when he said his employees thought he was a slave driver?

The short Mexican man swatted through the stifling air with his hands, motioning me out. I nearly tripped as I backed out onto the sidewalk, and it was then that I remembered Marten's request that I not return until the clinic was ready to open. Another red flag — brushed off with a fleeting thought — guilt for going against his wishes. I wouldn't say a word to Marten about this incident and hoped the construction workers wouldn't, either.

Chapter Thirty-Nine

The Proposal
"Leap and the net will appear." ~ Julia Cameron

I was not in love with Marten, which is why I was shocked when he asked me to marry him. Our relationship was so very young, and, while it was monogamous (for me, at least), I considered it more as an affair than a courtship. I assumed he would return to Wales after setting up his clinic in Texas — a marriage proposal was the farthest thing from my mind.

Still a virgin when I met Richard, there had been only three sex partners in my life. No one knew about the second one. I'd presumed there would be a handful more before I settled down again.

~*~

The express elevator opened into The Stock Market's kitchen. Dana and Emilio were reviewing the day's menu, and Alexander was filling the sink with soap suds.

I took Dana by the arm, pulled her aside and whispered, "Marten is supposed to be the first in a whole string of suitors, isn't he?"

"Damn straight!"

"That's the way I'd envisioned it," I said. "I'd thought I would take all the time I needed to grieve the loss of my first husband, time would pass, then there would be a take-a-number, take-a-seat kind of thing."

"Sure," Dana agreed. "Like a mid-life crisis."

In an attempt to relieve emotional tension, I pressed two fingers to the middle of my forehead. "Or . . . like something *you* would do."

"*Touché* . . . that, too." Dana scribbled a note on the menu and handed it over to Emilio, and then she turned her full attention to me. Apparently, this promised to be a conversation worth sinking her teeth into. "So . . . go on."

"Well . . . maybe I'm going to skip that phase of my life."

Dana threw both hands up into the air. "Good God! I give up. What on earth are you talking about?"

I leaned toward Dana's ear and whispered as quietly as possible in the noisy kitchen, "Marten proposed last night."

"Holy shit!" Dana screamed.

Emilio dropped the large lid from a stainless stockpot. The dishwasher went for it and tossed it into the suds. Then they both stopped what they'd been doing and stared at us.

"Sorry boys — girls only," Dana said as she dragged me into her office and closed the door. She sweetly embraced me, then held me at arm's length, fixing her eyes on mine. "Proposed . . . as in marriage?"

I nodded. "I told him I'd have to think about it. It's all happening so fast . . . too fast."

"Tell me everything!"

"It was totally out of the blue. We'd eaten take-out Chinese at my place. I thought he was leaving, when he turned around and asked me. It was surreal, like he was asking if I wanted to see a movie or something. I've always figured I'd get married again, but never imagined such a casual proposal."

"I'll say, like one of those *oh by the way* things. Weird! I remember my second marriage. It kinda went down that way, too. And it didn't last long, but it was some of the most fun I'd had in a long time."

"I'm not looking for fun," I said. "I'm looking for forever love."

"Yeah. So go for it. What's eating you?"

"Am I to grow old and die having had sex with only *two or three* men? I thought maybe I'd have a couple of years of chocolate sampling. You know, take a bite, and put it back in the red heart-shaped box. Try another. It's worked for you, anyway. How else will I know which one to keep?"

Dana threw her head back and laughed. "Yeah, it's worked for me, but . . . oh, how do I say this?" She scratched her head, pulled a chair from across the room adjacent to her desk and pointed. "Sit down here." She settled into her own oversized swivel chair. "Listen and learn from the Great Teacher." Dana's violet eyes took on their familiar sparkle, assuring me I was in for a treat.

"Sex with many partners is overrated," Dana explained. "It's all the same. Like sampling chocolates, after a few bites they all taste alike." Dana frowned. "No, I take that back. You seriously can't compare men to fine chocolate, Julia. It's not at all similar."

"But isn't there the ultimate sex partner somewhere down the line waiting for me?"

"Sure he is, and when you find him, he'll be in-between jobs, or his work requires *frequent travel*, so he says. But, hey, he's fabulous in bed, right? And then, one day you've got an emergency, and you track him down. Voila! — his damn *wife* answers the phone. I always loved it when that happened," Dana mused.

"Gee, I never thought about Marten being married."

"He's not — he doesn't have the indentation on his finger, nor does he display the symptoms." Dana fixed her eyes on mine again. "I've had your back, you know. Anyway, back to sex — some guys don't care whether you get anything out of it, while others roll you over all the frickin' night long until their erection drug wears off. Some go to sleep right after — even nod off during — as I recall." Dana laughed at a memory. "Some want it three times a day while others maybe . . . oh . . . every month or two. Dicks come in all shapes and sizes. This one guy I knew had one so small I couldn't even tell if it was actually *in*! But, hey, you pretend it's all good. You fake it, you groan, you smile and sometimes you fall asleep wondering what in the hell is wrong with you.

"Your perfect sex partner will probably be a pain in the ass to live with. He'll leave his socks on the floor, a ring in the bathtub that makes you want to puke, and, oh yeah, get this: he can never tell whether the dishes in the dishwasher are clean or dirty. I remember Ramone, the drummer. I knew if he asked me one more time if the dishes were clean I'd kick his ass out."

"What happened?"

Dana quickly shrugged her shoulders and cocked her head to one side. "He asked me one more time." She giggled.

I watched my cousin with delight. "You're the bomb, you know that?"

"That's what I've heard. Look here, Julia . . . if you've found a good man, one who's *trainable,* well, hell — take him to the altar, if that's where he wants to go!"

I felt a frown coming on. "The *altar* . . . sounds so permanent."

"Doesn't have to be. Divorce is easy to come by — trust me." Dana tilted her chair back, swinging her legs freely back and forth, like a little girl with not a care in the world.

"Easy for *you* — you don't have to be the perfect role model for your offspring."

Dana sat upright again, took a deep breath and sighed. "It's not that I didn't want any. I would've loved to have had kids. I've waited too long, now."

"I'm sorry; I didn't mean to be insensitive. I always assumed you didn't want children."

"Well . . . I did. Still do. Only with the *perfect* father." Dana shook her head "Like I said, I've waited too long." She gazed out the window.

"What about your piano player? He seems like he'd make a good dad."

Dana snickered. "I'm not looking for a sperm donor at this stage of my life. Even if I had one, I'd probably have to use an obstetrical specialist for high risk pregnancy at my age."

"I don't believe that for one minute. Women over 40 are successfully having babies nowadays."

"Hmm. Maybe. I'll give it some thought. But let's get back to you and *your* piano man."

"If you insist," I said.

"When I was younger," Dana continued, "I wanted to experience it all. Always being told No — No — No — because of our religion, you understand. So, I repeatedly told myself *Oh, yes, I can!* But I have a few regrets, I'll confess. And, Julia, you don't *need* a lot of partners. It's not *you*. If you're comfortable with Marten, and God knows he is certainly good-looking enough, then go for it. He's got money, he's classy as hell and he wants to marry you. Hire a maid to pick up his socks and clean his bathtub ring! What's the worst that could happen, anyway?"

"I just don't know if I'm ready to settle down. Sexually, I mean. Richard was such a prude in bed. I always had to fantasize about someone else."

"So what?" Dana shook her head. "You're no different than any other woman."

"But I had plenty of fantasies, and not just when we were making love."

Dana said nothing. I picked cat hairs off my black dress slacks. "Richard always said I lived in a castle in the sky."

Dana took a moment to think about my confession. "Maybe you *had* to live in a daydream to be married to him?"

"Maybe." I giggled. "When we traveled, for instance, he'd naturally talk about the office, investments, you know the drill. So, I'd scoot over and snuggle up next to him and position his arm around me. He hated it when I did that — didn't want to drive single-handed, but I insisted. I'd close my eyes, tune him out, pretend I was traveling with a new lover. We'd even walk the beach holding hands, me and my invisible boyfriend! Good God! I even had conversations with him — out loud — when no one else was around!"

"Oh, I love this!" Dana said. "Let me tell you about my favorite — it's on a party yacht, and this guy — tall, dark and handsome, of course. . . ."

We spent the next hour comparing notes about how creative we were. We finally agreed that the more ingenious the fantasies, the more innovative the actual sex life was.

"Mature people aren't embarrassed to admit it," Dana said, "and imaginative partners like to share their ideas, even dress in character sometimes."

"I don't think I could get into that, but you never know."

"You wanna know what I really think?"

"Enlighten me," I smiled sweetly at her.

"I think Richard kept you tame for so long, you're not sure how to get yourself on the wild side. Why *did* you marry him, anyway?"

I thought back to the woman in Frederick's chair that day of the Open House. Why had her daughter married that moron? Not that Richard was a moron. No, far from it. But why do we settle for less and make these long-term commitments? I knew my own answers.

"Dana, I married Richard because I was alone, pregnant and afraid. But what I don't understand is why I purposefully got pregnant in the first place. I guess I was a clueless teenager who thought she knew what she wanted. After a few years of marriage, I spent so much time wishing for my freedom that when he died I was horrified. Had I caused it to happen? I mean, I *had* imagined how liberated I would feel if he weren't breathing down my neck. But I'd never wanted him dead; I only wanted to feel more alive. It's been five years and I've not felt alive until now. I don't know if it's love, but I've never felt as full of life as I do with Marten."

"You've had enough drama," Dana said, "losing your parents, pregnant at 17, married young, becoming a widow and a grandmother — all in under three decades. Marten could be just the thing for you now. You told me your sex life has improved, did you not?"

"Yes. Sex is good. And Marten 'gets' me. It took effort and time to train him; I can't see breaking in another one."

"Then, don't put that scrumptious chocolate back in the box. It might get old and dry while you're sampling the rest of them. Or, someone else might come along, see how yummy it is and gobble it up. Boone likes Marten . . . Andie likes him . . . what more could you ask for? Marry him and give yourself permission to feel alive forever."

I couldn't argue with Dana. Her advice made sense. And if it wasn't love, surely it would grow into it.

~*~

I knocked on Frederick's door and saw his peep hole darken. He opened the door and said, "Enter, darling."

"I have only a few minutes," I said as I seated myself on his art deco sofa.

He perched on the other end and looked at me, waiting.

I smiled and said, "Marten wants to get married."

Frederick's brow furrowed. "Hmm . . . to anyone in particular?"

"Well, he asked me, so I'd say it's safe to assume it's *moi*."

Frederick sighed, still frowning. "This is fast."

"Fast . . . yes."

Frederick took a breath and held it; I waited to see what he would do or say next. "I've heard it said, 'Marry in haste, repent at leisure.' Sounds like you're considering that strategy."

"Yes. I am."

Always the professional stylist, Frederick grinned and said, "I'll do your hair!"

And that . . . was that.

Chapter Forty

Marten Quits

Roberts stopped abruptly while jogging down the steps. He'd casually glanced out the transom into the courtyard and caught a glimpse of none other than Marten! He grabbed a pair of binoculars hanging from a nail beside the window. There he was. Yes, it *was* definitely Marten, standing at Zinc's bar. He hadn't answered his texts or phone messages for two days. It was as though he'd vanished. Should Roberts go down and confront him? No, he couldn't afford to be spotted in the city right now. The time was too close. He'd wait and watch.

Marten set his empty glass on the bar, tossed a few bills on the counter and walked through the doorway into the courtyard.

Roberts re-hung the binoculars and alerted Leonardo. "Marten's heading this way."

Amigo and one of his carpenter buddies, framing a wall in what could pass as a receptionist area on the first floor, looked up at him.

"What are you lookin' at?" Roberts barked.

They went back to work. *Bang, bang, bang.*

Marten fumbled at the door with his set of keys. When he entered, Roberts and Leonardo were both on the landing, arms folded across their chests. Marten lifted the canvas on Olga's latest work in progress. "You call this crap art?" he said. He looked at his partners and slowly climbed the stairs.

Roberts read guilt on his nephew's face. He sharply turned his head, stared pointedly at the Mexicans. Amigo was attempting to sneak a quick look out of the corner of his eye. Roberts glared at him and he returned to his hammering.

When Marten reached the landing, he was smiling. Roberts and Leonardo were not. Without a word, the three of them continued on to the top floor.

"Two nights in a row we've been unable to access Sophia's schedule because the proper channels aren't open online," Roberts claimed. "You're not answering your phone, not returning messages. What the hell are you trying to pull here, Marten?"

Marten faced them resignedly. "I'm having second thoughts. I'm no longer convinced you plan to pull this off without anyone getting hurt. I blocked the link until we had a chance to fully discuss it." Marten had a remote access to the link from his laptop, but he'd not mentioned that fact.

"You sure as hell aren't helping the situation by keeping information from us," Leonardo said.

"Don't lay that one on me. We've plenty of time yet. Anyway, if changes are made it will be at the last minute — thus the term 'last minute' changes. It's not as easy as you think to access those computers at Julia's place without rousing her suspicions. It's nearly impossible to get into her office when she's there and she changes the password so often I can't get in when she's not there."

"That's why you installed a password override, right?"

"Yes, of course. But even when she's not there, the place teems with employees during the day. The lift is ancient and makes way too much noise to try getting in at night. Julia is already curious and is asking questions."

"What kind of questions?" Perry Roberts asked.

"Nothing to worry yourself about. She's a professional, and she collects data from clients occasionally to keep their finances in order. Our finances are a joke as far as the clinic is concerned. They don't exist. It's going to be harder to hide that fact from her. She has asked for bank statements so she can reconcile our accounts. Hell, we don't even have a bank account."

"Then open one, you Muppet. You should have thought of that in the first place," Roberts said. "Wasn't that your job? Covering all the angles?"

"It's too late to open a phony account. She'd see the date — that would be the first thing she'd look for."

"You didn't think of it because you weren't thinking at all!"

Marten took a breath and sighed. He splayed his fingers. "Here's the deal: I refuse to lie to her any longer."

Roberts clinched his hands into fists behind his back. "What are you saying?"

"I've proposed marriage and I think she will accept. Bottom line — I want out."

Roberts could hardly believe his ears. Was Marten in love with her? *Son. Of. A. Bitch.* He'd seen this coming and buried his head in the sand, refused to trust his "premature paranoia" as Leonardo had described it. This was outrageous from every angle. But if Marten wanted out, how far *out* did he plan to go? Would he go to the police?

"You know we can't have you going to the authorities," Roberts said.

Marten scowled. "Of course I'm aware of that. I have no interest in doing so."

"What about my sister, your mother? The way they treated her when you pushed your brother down the stairs and she got blamed and fired? Have you forgotten our objective?"

"Stop! Please . . . don't." Marten took a step backwards, as though that would remove him from his memories. "I'm the one who has to live with that. As far as what they did to her, I've shrugged off the cloak of resentment which you obviously still wear. I comprehend completely your issues with the Duke and Duchess, but your issues aren't mine. And besides, nothing from the past matters to me any longer."

"This sudden change of a lifetime all because of a woman? I don't believe it," Roberts said, violently shaking his head. He went for his lower desk drawer and grabbed a bottle of scotch and a glass he'd swiped from the Hilton.

"Let me put it in plain words," Marten said. "I've never met a woman like her. My one and only opportunity to change my life — I'm taking it. I never saw it coming, never considered it would happen to me. I've provided all you need in the way of funding for this project and have no interest in standing in your way. All I ask is that you let me out."

"Simply let you out — that's *all* you want?" Leonardo said.

"I will keep silent; you have my word. I've gotten you this far, and no one will ever connect us if you follow the plan we designed. The only thing to be changed is where to hide Chesley while you wait for the ransom — you can't keep him here, you know?

"I wouldn't be that careless, Marten."

"And above all, I don't want you to tell me where that will be. I'm sure Leonardo can find another safe place. That's what we've used him for, and I will hear nothing more of it — I'm out."

Perry Roberts thought about their plan — he'd thought of it as Plan A, which stood for *astounding*. Roberts' idea — he'd designed it — was perfect and they'd agreed to invent an alternative one only when or if they felt the need, precisely because circumstances might change, preventing their original scheme from being effective. Perry Roberts had considered what those circumstances might be, done the what-ifs over and over, but never dreamed of *this* twist. And now, the *only* strategy he'd devised had just gone down the crapper. While he was furious with his nephew, he could understand the dilemma Marten faced. After all, he had grown quite fond of Olga, the woman he thought fondly of as Chunky Funky, and he'd lain awake at night conjuring up ways he could have her on his little tropical retirement island all to himself.

Roberts said. "Let's say you back out. How will you cover yourself?"

"I *have* backed out."

"Go on, then. But how, exactly, are you going to do it?"

"I'll tell Julia the clinic didn't work out, the funding didn't come through, or some other such nonsense. You needn't worry about me — I'll find other means of suitable employment. I've never had a problem with money before and I won't now. We'll go along just as we always have — you and I. I won't let you down; I'll keep the network connection open right down to the end, I promise you that. Living with her in the condo will make it that much easier. I won't do anything to jeopardize your mission, but I don't want the responsibility of it on my conscience. In the final few minutes before the event, you and I will no longer be in contact, and I will not have any further participation. As soon as it's over, and you've received the ransom, I'll restore Julia's connections and there will be no trace that she was hacked. No one will ever be able to see it — I'll have it cleaned up so well. And when you divvy up the booty, I want no part of it."

"What? Your investment! You mean to say you don't want your money back?" Leonardo asked skeptically.

"That's an inappropriate question, Leo," Roberts, highly irritated, said, "and frankly none of your business. I'm handling the funds here. You'll get your share, the amount we agreed upon. Perhaps a little more *if* this requires more time from you."

Leonardo wadded up a piece of paper, threw it into a cardboard box they used for trash, turned and ran down the steps.

"You've gone and made the little queer sick!" Roberts let out a shrill laugh.

"Give my share to him. I don't care. Consider my funding a contribution to your cause," Marten said to his uncle. "It's the least I can do. The Duke did more damage to you than to me anyway."

"*My* cause? It was always *our* cause . . . until now."

"People change, you know. My vision is clearer. I don't want to be responsible for causing harm to a child ever again, or to anyone. Boone is a little boy not much smaller than Chesley. And Julia, well, when I look at life through her eyes, the world doesn't seem nearly as evil as I've always thought. It was an accident, back when I was a lad, and nothing more. I didn't mean to hurt Basil and my mother knew that. Those people did what they had to do at the time, and unfortunately she got in the middle. While I used to be convinced there had been malice, now I know it not to be true. In your case, however, I believe there was, and I understand your hatred. I had it too, but it's gone, now. I won't stand in your way; I just don't want to be a part of the resulting outcome."

"Does anyone care for my opinion?" said Leonardo, who had returned and was sitting silently at Roberts' desk.

Roberts and Marten looked over at him.

"I say we let him out. He's lost the stomach, or heart — whatever — for the job. No balls . . . well, they're in another place." He snickered at his joke, but the other two men didn't respond. Leonardo coughed superficially. "We can handle this without him. He's done his part, or most of it. There's simply more money for the rest of us. That doesn't hurt my feelings at all."

"Well, there you go," said Marten. He'd suspected Leonardo had been eavesdropping all along at the bottom of the stairs. "More money for you and freedom for me to begin a new life. That's what you two will do, after all is said and done, isn't it? New lives somewhere? I'll just be doing it here on the Riverwalk, and I won't know where you are. You, on the other hand, will always know how to reach me."

Roberts said, "How can I be assured you *will* do your part down to the end?"

"Do I need to repeat myself? You have my word. I can't give you much more. But you know it's good. It has always been good."

Perry Roberts smiled for the first time. "Okay, we'll give you what you want. Which I suppose is a future with a woman you love. And when you think about it, this lark brought you to her. Maybe she's a gift from my dear sister to you, her son."

"Don't get sentimental on me," Marten quipped.

"No, not sentimental. Maybe I've changed my mind about certain things, just as you have," Roberts said.

Leonardo stood from his chair and walked over to Marten, reaching out to shake his hand. "Good luck."

Roberts, standing behind Marten, placed a firm grip on his nephew's shoulder. "Don't forget your commitment to me until the end. If blood is spilled, it will be on your hands."

Marten removed his uncle's grasp. "No blood — that's always been the rule. It needn't change because of my absence. I know you won't do it, but my advice to you is to quit. Stop this now, before it's too late."

"I can't. I'm in too deep, and you know it."

"That's what you always told me, that *I* was in too deep. But look how easily I just ended it! You can, too, if you want to."

"This is all I've thought about for decades! I can't even begin to *want* to stop."

Marten shook his head and turned to run down the steps. He walked out the door into the court.

Roberts followed him down the stairs, turned the dead lock from the inside, and peeked through closed blinds. Marten glanced back, puzzled. He had undoubtedly expected much more of an argument and speculated why they had simply let him go.

Roberts feared he would never see his nephew again. Sure, he had those last few commitments to fulfill, but after that? He felt like his sister died all over again. Marten was all he had left of her, after all. He'd thought often of how the Vanderhawks had treated Adelina after Basil died, shaming her, making *her* look guilty. He hadn't known where they'd sent her, at first. And now Marten was no longer interested in revenge? *How can he just walk away like this?*

~*~

After Roberts watched Marten walk through Charles Court and out the main gates at Presa Street, he ran back up to the loft. "There goes a man in serious denial. If Marten thinks he's getting out with no trouble, he's sorely mistaken." He cut his eyes to Leonardo who was studying the ceiling with his feet up on the desk, devising their next move. "What are you thinking, Leo?"

"Our project will need some adjusting, that's a given. It will work smoothly only if everyone involved is 100 percent committed. He would be a hindrance, possibly ruin the whole thing. Letting him out is all we *can* do. But can he be trusted? You tell me."

"I don't trust anyone. If I did, it would be Marten. But I don't. I need to find a way to watch him when it all comes down."

"I'm sure if we put our heads together we can construct a strategy. I have an idea already, as a matter of fact. As it turns out, I have developed a relationship with a man who lives in the condo beneath Ms. Tyler's."

Perry Roberts perked up. "What do you have in mind?" After he heard Leonardo Newman's proposal, he knew it was even more perfect than the original plan had been, and up until then he hadn't thought that possible. "Leo, my man, you are pure mastermind . . . unadulterated genius."

Chapter Forty-One

Commitment Tattoos

Leonardo stood at the massive window overlooking the Riverwalk in Frederick's living room. He thought about the apartment directly above and wondered what progress Marten had made with Ms. Tyler. Would she actually accept his proposal? It made no difference to him, personally, but it would definitely facilitate his plan if Marten moved in up there before the big event.

He studied the ceiling; return air vents had been placed up high. He would need a tall ladder to reach them. He hoped Frederick had one in storage. He wondered if fragments of conversations traveled easily from one unit to another. He would have to be very careful.

Frederick came up beside him and offered a glass of chilled white wine. "Don't you just adore high ceilings?"

"These old buildings are grand." Leonardo swirled the glass and tested the wine's bouquet. He raised an eyebrow — a signal of approval. "Your crown molding is lovely. This condo is truly unique; you do know that?"

Frederick nodded. "I've worked my bum off to afford this place."

"How's your electrical? I hope it's been brought up to code."

"Oh yes. I had it all redone when I bought it."

Leonardo had hoped the wiring would be outdated, making his job a little easier. "I'd love to find a place to rent like this one. Everything on the Riverwalk is so pricey, though."

"You can stay here while you're in town, if you'd like," Frederick offered cautiously.

"Seriously? Why, that's quite generous of you. I'll think it over." This was Leonardo's first time in Frederick's condo. He'd been careful not to be spotted coming in late last night; he couldn't risk being seen *living* here.

Yet he'd anticipated the invitation, easily goaded Frederick into it. He was ready with something even better, if Frederick wanted assurance.

"I truly enjoy your company," Frederick continued. "The guest room is all yours."

"Actually, I've been thinking quite a lot about our relationship."

"Oh?"

"Haven't you?"

Frederick blushed. "Yes, I confess I have. You go first!"

"I know it's only been a short while since we met, but I feel such a strong connection to you."

"I feel the same way!"

"I don't want to jinx it by moving in together too quickly, though."

"I see." Fredrick's voice dripped with disappointment.

"Cheer up, Freddie! After a great deal of consideration, I've gone and done something out of the ordinary. I hope you don't think me too pushy. I'm having the letter F, for Frederick, of course, tattooed on my inner thigh to signify my strong feelings for you; a commitment, you might say."

"Oh my lord," Frederick said as he gave Leonardo a fierce hug. "How perfect! I might do the same . . . with the letter L."

Leonardo frowned. "Let's get mine finished and we'll see how you like it. It's being done in stages, and I'm keeping the first part of it bandaged for now because it requires antibacterial ointment. I'll be able to show you the finished product very soon." He held his robe open so Frederick could see the gauze patch. The patch, like Leonardo's professions of commitment, was only a deception with nothing beneath it. "It's still quite sensitive," he warned.

Frederick giggled. "Commitment tattoos. I'm so excited I've got goose bumps."

"It's quite the extraordinary design," Leonardo said with a suggestive wink. "I know you'll simply drop dead when I show you!"

Chapter Forty-Two

Wedding Plans

The day before our wedding, the phone would not stop ringing and I was totally fried before noon. I'd delegated most of the routine work to my employees and retreated to my bedroom with a pot of calming herbal tea. I lowered myself into a cushy zebra-striped chair and took one more look at my to-do list. I'd never planned a wedding before. Flowers — check. Linen chair covers — check. Wedding favors — check. I shook my head and wondered what goofball had ever come up with the idea for wedding favors in the first place. *What a waste of money. I have to reward people for coming to my wedding?*

Marten knocked lightly on the bedroom door and peeked in. I had given him the elevator password, so it wasn't a surprise when he showed up unannounced with his laptop, two leather suitcases and one canvas toiletry bag — the entire extent of his belongings in the USA.

I had emptied a closet already, so I sat on the bed watching as he whistled *The Yellow Rose of Texas,* sliding hangers onto the upper rod — two business suits, three casual sport jackets and crisply starched and pressed white shirts. He placed four pair of shoes on the floor and filled three small drawers with khakis, black tees and skivvies.

"You travel lighter than anyone I've ever known," I said.

"Everything else I own is in my cottage in Wales."

"When can we go?"

"I promise — someday very soon. We can select any furnishings you'd like to have shipped here. I'm eager to show you Mum's quilt collection, too. Plus, I'll give you a complete tour of Europe. Once the clinic is opened and we're not so rushed — as soon as we can take the time for a real vacation."

He walked to the edge of the bed and cradled my hands. "I love you so much. We're about to create the perfect marriage."

After locking the bedroom door, he sat next to me and held my face lovingly in his hands. One touch from Marten was all it took to release my stress and worries. We slid under the covers and quietly had ourselves some afternoon delight.

Afterward, he re-packed for Sedona — ready for our four-day honeymoon.

~*~

I pretended to be asleep. I hadn't enjoyed sex but I'd faked it. What on earth was I thinking? I dug my toes deep into the mattress and thought about applying the brakes on this circus-train of a marriage. The raw fact was that I didn't really know one true thing about love. And I knew very little about Marten, definitely not enough to marry him. But I'd given my word and everyone knew. How embarrassing it would be to postpone it now! Marten's reservation at the Hilton ended and he'd wanted to live together while we planned an elaborate wedding, inviting his friends from all over Europe and holding the ceremony in an ornate church somewhere. The whole thing made me sick when I thought about it. If we'd had a guest room, I might have agreed, but there was no way I wanted Boone to see me sharing my bed with someone who wasn't my husband. I thought of what Madelynne had said about herself: "I'm just an old fiddle-fart, a worn out fuddy-duddy." I felt exactly like that. A small and quiet ceremony on the river bank would solve my dilemma, and then we'd throw an extravagant party here in the condo later, tropical plants and all.

The next morning Boone ran into my bedroom, already dressed in a tuxedo. "Get up, Gran! It's your wedding day!" I pasted a smile on my face, got out of bed, and told myself everything would work out.

Chapter Forty-Three

Honeymoon Brunch at L'Auberge

The steep, red rock hills on either side of the road entering Sedona were adorned with Mother Nature's art — a diverse variety of cacti, flowers and greenery. I'd instructed Marten to drive slowly so we could soak in all of the beauty, but he ignored me, maintaining his normal speed — nine miles over the legal limit.

We had flown into Phoenix on Saturday and stayed at the Marriott Courtyard Airport that night, due to our late arrival. Sunday morning, we picked up a rental car and headed north for the two-hour drive to Sedona. The tone of the remaining three-day honeymoon was set on that day. I wouldn't actually label our conversations as arguments, or even disagreements in actual fact, but merely conflicting opinions interspersed with occasional sighs of irritation and awkward silences.

"Why are you going so fast?" I said. "Are you sure it's wise, since you aren't used to driving on the right side of the highway?"

"I've already adjusted to American road rules — don't worry so much. Anyway, we're on a mission — the Sunday Champagne Brunch on the terrace of L'Auberge that you love so much," Marten said.

"I love it, yes, but we'll be too early to be seated."

"You want a creek side table. Better early than late."

I turned my head toward the passenger window and rolled my eyes. Marten glanced over just in time to catch my reflection in the side-view mirror.

~*~

Marten had been taken aback when Julia accepted his marriage proposal so quickly and had been in a fog ever since. Not in a good way, such as walking on air, but having the inability to think or see clearly. He'd expected events to fall into place slowly, but Julia had jumped into planning their small wedding and honeymoon without discussing the details with him. Oh, she'd offered, but what did he know about those things? He told her to take care of it, but he secretly thought she was moving too fast. She had said *he* was moving too fast, but he'd had less than two weeks to vacate the Hilton and had figured he would move in with Julia. He didn't see the point in renting an apartment, and, while she wholeheartedly agreed, she'd insisted the wedding should come before he moved in, not after. Something about Boone and setting a good example.

Well, that, he understood. He admired her morality, in fact. He knew from past experience that what a woman chose to do for her offspring could change her life overnight. His mum, for example, had moved quickly because of him, but she'd had no choice. The Vanderhawks carted her out less than one week after little Basil's funeral. Marten had determined at the age of four that nothing good comes from any major event which happens unexpectedly.

He glanced at Julia again; the sun's reflection off the red canyon walls cast even more color through her hair. She was a beautiful bride, and he vowed to do whatever it took to make her happy, to be a good husband. She deserved nothing less.

He pulled onto a bricked driveway and maneuvered around the narrow winding slope, down to the bottom of the hill where Oak Creek was particularly shallow and noisy. When they neared the terrace, Julia squealed with delight to see their reserved table *was* creek side. The heavens offered its blessing on that remarkable day as the sun shone through the tree canopy. The dining tables were randomly placed and swathed with linen, full china and crystal settings, and protected by large market umbrellas. After they were seated, graceful white ducks strutted toward them, stretching their long necks looking for handouts. "You'll have to wait," Marten said. "We haven't a crumb for you yet." The never-ending quacks, the rush of creek water, and the frequent pops of champagne corks were all pleasant accompaniments.

~*~

We couldn't seem to find a topic of conversation, so we eavesdropped on others. One couple discussed their 10-year anniversary party at that location next year. They would reenact their vows there at L'Auberge on the terrace. They casually tossed a price of $40,000 around. Marten threw me a surprised look with a raised eyebrow. We hadn't spent much for our wedding, maybe a grand total of $2,000, counting the tux rentals, flowers and wedding favors. Of course, we hadn't had a reception yet.

"Did I tell you Nina wants me to help her arrange an anniversary party for them next year?" I said. "A vow reenactment!"

"Oh? That will keep you busy!"

"It'll be fun," I said. "They're the happiest couple I know."

~*~

Marten nodded agreement. He hoped he and Julia could become a happy couple, but the immediate future nagged him to a point where he found it hard to feel anything but dread. He had done the right thing, backing out of the kidnapping, and he'd thought that would resolve his angst. It did not. Now, he worried about how his newly acquired family would experience the upcoming horrible event. Boone and Chesley had become online friends and it would be devastating to Boone if Marten's uncle caused anything vile to happen to Chesley. His mind searched for a plan to get Julia and Boone out of San Antonio that day. He would have to take a bold stand, though, because he knew Julia had every intention of attending the program at The Arneson. That, he could not allow.

He worried, too, about finding a job, *anything* to make it appear he was being productive. His family estate was healthy and he could withdraw funds whenever he needed. But he kept that a secret; another secret — what was the harm? He knew the answer. His entire life was built around them — a house of cards — he was fatigued from it. Happy couples were not fashioned from secret lives. Marten would eventually tell her the truth, everything, *after* the dust had settled and Chesley was safe. He'd even found himself worrying about Chesley's safety. He couldn't imagine Roberts doing anything to jeopardize the child, and especially the ransom. Chesley would have to be alive and unharmed before Roberts would get the money. Marten shook his head and hoped his uncle would keep his promise to him and finalize the caper without a hitch.

~*~

"What's bothering you?" I said.

"Nothing, why?"

"You're frowning."

"Oh. Well, my stomach is quite upset. Excuse me while I locate the restroom."

"It's up the hill in the restaurant where the brunch is laid out." I watched Marten walk away. I hoped he would feel better and could enjoy the scrumptious offerings. I was eager for champagne after the cork-popping started, even though it wasn't quite yet 11:00 a.m. Eventually, servers began pouring, asking each customer ahead of time if they cared for any. When they came to our table, they poured without asking. "Was I that obvious?" I said, laughing. The server smiled and said, "How are you this fine morning? Shall I pour for the gentleman?"

"Oh yes, please do. He'll be right back." I suspected that driving too fast on the curvy roads into Sedona had caused motion sickness. I lifted my flute and drank half of the liquid in a very unladylike manner. I didn't care if anyone noticed, either. Our first meal together as husband and wife, yet I felt no desire to share the moment with Marten. He'd been acting weird ever since he said "I do."

The man at an adjacent table was going away for a while and his wife said she missed him already. They were calculating what their schedules would be until they saw one another again. It sounded like he would be gone for a month. I wondered if I would ever feel that close to my new husband.

~*~

Marten returned to the table and said, "Did you miss me?" He noticed she hadn't waited, so he drank his champagne while she finished hers. He found it curious that she hadn't initiated a "cup fight" with their champagne glasses to celebrate their marriage. (Maybe the groom was supposed to do that. He wondered about the protocol.)

"Ah, much better now," Marten said. The server appeared, refilled both flutes, and directed them to the buffet.

This was the brunch of all brunches due to the creek-side location with its canopy of grand trees, and an unmatched French buffet up the hill. They would walk up creek stone steps to the restaurant's sunroom with its glassed walls and high domed leaded-glass ceiling. After filling a plate or two, they would bring them back to the table. It was a hike, but worth it just for the overall adventure.

They discovered a magnificent spread: Smoked Norwegian salmon, rare beef tenderloin with horseradish glaze, custom omelets and strawberry crêpes. Chilled shrimp was accompanied by celery with dill and crème sauce. Baked Brie oozed out of pastry shells. Exotic French cheeses mingled with wafers and chicken liver *pâté*. Desserts, too many to try at one sitting: dark chocolate chip scones and Grand Marnier liqueur-soaked orange butter cake for example.

~*~

I filled a dessert plate to the brim. I eyed the flan, but decided not to appear gluttonous by piling it on the heap. I took photos of miniature chocolate cups filled with Chambord black raspberry liqueur topped with a fresh raspberry, and little crescent-shaped pies with crème filling and chocolate linings. Marten seemed embarrassed, but other people were taking pictures, too. I tried to ignore him, but his attitude reminded me of Richard's.

We ate slowly, and I hoped we appeared to enjoy the morning as any newly married couple would, rather than both of us wondering what on earth we'd just done. I felt like Dorothy from The Wizard of Oz, as if I'd survived a vicious tornado and hoped to simply click my sparkly red shoes to put everything together again. I glanced at my wedding ring. Marten had shopped at an estate jewelry shop located in the Menger Hotel, next to The Alamo. They'd helped him select the perfect symbol, and, although it wasn't a wedding ring *per se*, it was exactly what I had wanted. The filigreed white gold, in an oval shape, was set with five opals among a bed of small diamonds.

A woman, several tables over, caught my attention. Her hair was bleached platinum blonde, and she wore entirely too much makeup, expensive linen cropped pants and a loose-fitting peach blouse (so no one would notice the extra 20 pounds in her midsection). She sat abnormally rigid and slid pastries underneath a cloth napkin on her lap. I wasn't sure I'd actually seen it, but sure enough, there another tidbit slipped under the napkin and into a purse on her lap!

"Don't look now," I whispered. Marten immediately turned sideways to look.

"I *told* you not to look!" I hissed.

"Well, then, what is it I'm not looking at?"

"There's a lady stealing pastries!"

"Hmm . . . not much of a lady, then," Marten said, while staring at his cell phone.

"Now she's holding up an ugly blue suede purse with fringe on it, and showing it to her husband as though it's new or something. I wish I could hear what she's saying. . . and why doesn't she carry a purse to match her outfit? Oh my god, she is so busted — her handbag is full of croissants! I don't think her husband was even paying attention."

I took a sip of champagne. "Are you listening to me?"

"Sorry, I've got to answer these texts."

"On our honeymoon? For crying out loud." I closed my eyes and sighed. I took a deep breath and wondered if I should possibly risk one more trip up the hill for that flan I'd lusted after. I knew I could walk up the hill, but could I fit the dessert into my already full digestive system? Probably not.

"Okay — done," Marten said as he turned around and looked again. "Now, what were you saying about a woman stealing food?"

"Never mind."

Marten returned to his cell phone.

Shortly, we overheard a fellow with a New York accent say, "This is a nice little brunch." He was with a group of eight, and they all expressed agreement. He then asked, "How much is this costing?"

Marten glanced at me and whispered, "How much is it?"

"I don't know!" I shrugged my shoulders. "Considering the flavor of the food, its presentation, and the ambiance of the location, I'd say it's much more than just a '*nice little brunch*' and it's worth whatever they charge. What difference does it make?"

I stood and made one last trip up for flan which was just as sublime as it looked, and, as it melted in my mouth, I knew it would be the last bite I took that day. I'd told myself not to overdo, but had done it anyway.

As we walked up the hill to the car, I confessed, "I've sufficiently stuffed myself to the point of throwing up."

"I know. I feel exactly the same," Marten said. He opened the passenger door for me.

"You didn't seem to eat enough to cause that." I said. "Maybe you're allergic to marriage."

Marten laughed. "Now you're joking. I'm the happiest groom in the world!"

Chapter Forty-Four

Home at Last

The flight home from Phoenix had been uneventful, but our luggage was delayed and it was past eleven o'clock at night when we finally got to the condo. Andie had taped a note to our bedroom door saying she and Boone were with Britt and would be home later. I wondered how late "later" would be.

After a quick shower, we unpacked our bags and Marten carried his soiled clothes down the hall into the utility room. I had thought he would continue to use a laundry service, but apparently not. I doubted he knew I didn't even own an iron! This wasn't the Hilton, but he'd figure that out in due time.

Suddenly, he rushed out of the laundry room, holding his nose. "This place stinks to high heaven!"

"What is it? The iguana's cage needs cleaning, I'll bet." Marten probably knew what I was thinking, that it served him right for buying Stupid Greenie in the first place.

"It's not the iguana — it's the litter box. Andie gave us her word that she and Boone would do their chores while we were gone. Looks like we were duped."

"Fooled again," I said flatly. "Welcome home to family life, dear."

Marten stomped his foot on the floor. "Dammit! There are going to be some changes made around here, I can assure you!"

"Oh . . . really?"

"Of course! I can't tolerate that odor, nor can I abide people not holding up their end of an agreement."

"Okay, well, good luck with that." I finished unpacking, and, when I carried a basket into the laundry room, I had to agree with Marten. "Oh, boy. What a piece of work," I called out. "This place stinks!" I was about to transfer Marten's clothes from the washer into the dryer, but I didn't know what setting he'd want, and I didn't have any intention of starting a pattern for our future — Julia Tyler, laundry clerk. I cleaned up the cat's mess, freshened the litter box and told Zadok how much I'd missed him. He missed me too, he purred. He slithered aggressively in and out between my ankles and purred so loud Marten could hear him all the way into the kitchen.

"Hey, boy," Marten said as he entered the utility room. "Did they take good care of you while we were gone? Huh? What's that you say? You made a feast of Greenie?"

"Oh, God." I laughed. "I can only hope!"

Marten chuckled along with me and playfully tapped me on the bottom. "I see you made the place livable again."

"Somebody had to do it. I couldn't let Zadok spend another night in this mess, and I could not imagine waking up to it myself. Nasty! So . . . I went ahead and got it over with. I'm not about to check the toy room, though. Greenie can rot, as far as I'm concerned." Marten knew I didn't mean it and he threw me a skeptical look.

He tossed his clothes into the dryer and figured out how to turn it on. He followed me back into the master bedroom, where I slipped into a pair of fresh cotton pajamas. "You coming to bed?"

"Not yet," he said. "I've got work to do."

"It's late. Aren't you exhausted?"

"No, plus I want to grab my clothes out of the dryer as soon as it's finished. You go ahead and I'll follow shortly." He kissed me goodnight and I fell asleep within minutes.

About an hour later I was awakened by loud voices coming from the kitchen. Andie and Marten were into a spirited conversation about who, exactly, was responsible for what. It seemed that Marten was getting the worst end of the deal. No surprise, there. Andie was a handful, a *manipulator.* Poor Marten, I thought. He'd undoubtedly never before encountered a hard-headed, strong-willed woman like my daughter. I plunked a pillow over my head and drifted back off to dream of Sedona's red rock canyons.

Chapter Forty-Five

The Honeymoon Is Over

Frederick handed me the mirror and twirled my chair around.

"I love it, as usual."

"You are the landscape and I am the architect."

"We're quite a team, aren't we?"

"That we are. Now, show me your wedding album!"

"Let's go sit on your sofa," I suggested, "and look at them together."

"Sit? Um, well . . . I'll just stand here by your side, if you don't mind."

"You got a problem with your rear end? Seems to me you'd want to relax after being on your feet all day long."

"Well, yes, I do have a problem with my bum, as Leo would say."

"Leo?"

Frederick blushed.

"Well, out with it. Who is he? Is he British? I've never heard *you* refer to your bottom as your *bum.*"

"Leonardo Newman — he's an amazing man, and, yes, he does seem to use quite a lot of British slang. I think he picked it up from some clients he worked with."

I couldn't help but snicker. I wondered exactly what his bum problem was.

"And it's not what you think it is," Frederick snapped, as though he'd read my mind.

I shrugged and took my thoughts to another place. "Here, look at this photo. Wasn't it the most perfect wedding setting? The Wedding Island, right in the heart of downtown San Antonio. I was pleased to be able to use it on such short notice, and grateful for the lovely weather that day."

"Yes, it was beautiful. Maybe I'll get married there, someday."

"You will? That would be perfect. May I presume you're making a commitment to Leonardo?"

"Tattoo commitments." Frederick grinned and took this Leo fellow's business card from his wallet. On the back was sketched an "L" in Edwardian Script. "It's tattooed on my left cheek. He's getting his with my initial," Frederick excitedly reported, as he slid the business card back into place.

"So, when's the wedding?"

"All in due time, child," Frederick said with a grin on his handsome face. "You will be the first to know."

Frederick returned to the picture album. "Oh, and little Boone looked spectacular in a tux. Of course, Marten did, too."

"I hadn't planned on putting Marten in one, but Boone was dead set on wearing a tux, so of course the groom had to wear one, as well!"

"But, look at this one." Frederick scowled. "Why is Andie wearing such a dreadful look?"

I sighed and slowly shook my head. "That girl. Come to find out, she'd always planned on having *her* wedding there, or so she claimed. She was pouting because for once she wasn't the center of attention, I suppose."

"That vile child. Someday she'll regret showing her dreadful self off like this."

"Yeah, when I'm dead, probably."

"Let's hope it doesn't take her *that* long to grow up," Frederick said. "Oh, and look at your handsome linen suit. Where'd you get it?"

"The Vintage Trunk on the north side. A 1950's designer piece. Don't you love the color?"

"I do, but I was surprised to see you wearing a pale aqua. I'd expected pink."

"The cooler shade looked better with my hair."

"You did look beautiful, Julia. I was so happy to be included!" Frederick turned the page. "Hmm . . . now who was this gentleman here?"

"Oh, that's Reed Michelson, Simone's father. He's a Special Services Agent for the Riverwalk."

"He's attractive," Frederick said.

I shuddered. "He is not!"

"Is to me," Frederick said.

"Poor Simone. You remember I told you about her father. He's the one whose wife left him for another woman."

"Yes, I remember now. Is that why he's wearing such a ghastly expression?" Frederick chuckled. "Or maybe he wants to use the Wedding Island for *his* next marriage, too?"

I took a closer look at the picture. "Oh, man! Looks like he's giving me the stink-eye, doesn't it? I just remembered . . . Reed asked me out right after his divorce, about a year ago. I told him I wasn't ready to date, and he made me promise to call him when the mood finally struck. I guess he felt wounded that I went and got hitched without giving him a chance. See there? It just all happened so fast. I forgot about him, really. Besides, I wouldn't have gone out with him — he always wears that uniform of his. I doubt he ever wears anything else!"

Frederick raised one eyebrow. "Umm . . . I wonder if he sleeps in it." He winked.

I raised an eyebrow, too.

"It would be odd, though," Frederick said, "being married to Simone's father."

"Yes, well, if you will recall, marriage wasn't even on my mind until a few weeks ago. I still can't believe I went through with it."

"Why did you invite him?"

"To escort his daughter. Boone insisted Simone be in attendance."

Frederick nodded. "Probably wanted her to see how cute he was in a tux!" He continued shuffling through the pages while I answered my cell phone.

"I'm anxious to see the video," Frederick said. He handed the book of pictures to me. "When's the big party?"

I disconnected and forcefully threw my phone into my purse. "The reception is the farthest thing from my mind right now!"

"Why? What's wrong?"

"Marten. He's locked himself out of the condo, it seems. I gave him the new password but he doesn't remember. I'm not about to give it to him over a cell phone. Christ! He's a lot of trouble, that man."

Frederick gasped. "Can't he just take the public elevator up to the fifth floor and climb the stairs one flight to use his *real-life key*?"

"Apparently he doesn't think with the brain in his head."

"Oh my God! Are you not happy?"

"Happy? Don't make me laugh. No . . . happy hasn't hit me yet. You know what? It's the same as it was with Richard — I can't seem to do anything to please the man. Funny, I was perfect just the way I was *before* he married me, or so he said."

"You're perfect, now change," Frederick moaned, and he rubbed the back of his neck as though the stress of my confession was more than he could handle.

"Don't worry." I squeezed his arm. "It's just a period of adjustment, I'm sure. Everyone goes through it."

I hurried from the salon, postponing other errands I'd planned. Out of breath, I entered The Clifford's lobby only to realize I hadn't needed to rush after all. I'd trusted Britt with the password while we were gone. Now he'd shown up early for work and Marten was profusely expressing his gratitude. He failed to notice I had dropped everything just for him. We rode in silence as the elevator delivered us to our happy home.

Chapter Forty-Six

The Water Bill

Marten and I sat at the small ceramic-topped bistro table by the kitchen window with our hot beverages. He read the newspaper aloud.

"Soap will be arriving in two weeks," he said.

"Soap?"

"You know . . . Lady Sophia." Marten blinked and looked out the window. "That's what we Brits call her sometimes. I suppose you've never heard of it."

I thought of the days not so long ago when I enjoyed the morning ritual entirely by myself. I'd cherished my alone time. Marten was a chatterbox when he woke, but I needed distance between my awakening and the audio of a new day.

I liked to quietly sneak out of bed on Sundays and go out on the roof, but in no time Marten would show up with his cup of Earl Grey. The rooftop garden was my private breathing space, and I was surprised to find myself irritated when I had to share it. The first Sunday after our honeymoon, I'd playfully aimed the unloaded BB gun at him. "If you're not a cardinal you'd best retreat." His face took on the look of utter revulsion, and he brusquely grabbed the pistol from my hand and huffed back inside. Later that afternoon, he literally swept me off my feet and into our bedroom. Afterward, I gave it an 11 on the scale of one to 10. The following Sunday, he tagged along onto the rooftop like a forgiving puppy dog.

He trailed me everywhere I went, even on days when I made afternoon deliveries. I asked him why he didn't spend more time at his own office. He got offended, countering that if I didn't want his company why didn't I just say so. Of course I wanted to be with him, I replied, but inwardly I realized what "too much of a good thing" meant. He loitered, hanging around outside the doorway of my office when my business clients began their routine morning phone calls. It seemed to me that Marten had nowhere to go, nothing to do. He'd brushed off my inquiries, saying there was bloody little for him to do until the clinic opened. I'd almost questioned him about the mess I'd seen at his "clinic" but zipped my lips just in time.

He checked the mail religiously, but always handed the household bills over to me without comment. I wished we'd taken the time to discuss financial aspects of our union before we got married. But he'd rushed it — said he needed to vacate the Hilton and didn't want to sign a one-year lease on another apartment. I hadn't wanted him to move in with me if we weren't married because it was important for me to set a good example for my grandson. So, here we were, husband and wife.

He continued reading the article aloud about the aristocratic visitors, then lowered the paper. "Does Boone know, yet, if he'll be allowed to actually meet Chesley in person?"

"What?" I realized I'd been only halfway listening to him.

"Never mind." He headed for the elevator. "I'm going to the lobby for the mail," he mumbled.

I watched him descend as I poured a half cup of coffee. *What a strangely mercurial man. Surely, we can make this work, somehow. We have to make it last, if for no other reason than the sex.*

Marten had developed the habit of entering my office when I was on the phone with a client. He would reach into the back of my blouse and unfasten my bra. I'd attempt to push him away, but it excited me so that I often cut the phone call short and gave in. We'd had sex on the floor of my office so often that I actually stored a blanket and pillow in the tiny closet for the occasion. After, while sitting at my desk, as hard as I tried I couldn't think of one good reason to worry about our marriage. My perfect sex partner was a pain in the ass to live with, just as Dana had warned he might be, but who cared?

Marten returned from his mail run, slammed the elevator gate open, stormed over to the kitchen counter and threw the parcels onto the bistro table. One of the larger packages slid across, knocking against my cup, spilling its contents. I quickly grabbed a roll of paper towels and soaked up the mess before it reached the envelopes. My tranquility was ruined but I was more concerned with my business correspondence.

"I'm sorry," Marten said. "That was an accident."

"What's wrong with you?"

"These damned utility costs. I didn't realize it took so much to keep this place comfortable. Look at this water bill! How on earth do we use so much water?"

"Oh, here, give that to me. That's Andie. She's been selling Luxury Baths like crazy."

"Luxury Baths?"

"You remember, I told you about them a long time ago. She sells gift certificates at $200 each for people to come in and bathe in the famous lounge. She sold a lot of them around Valentine's Day. That bill is from last month's usage."

"So where did she put the money? There should be a fund somewhere for this expense."

"It's our arrangement that she would take the profit and I'd cover the expense."

Marten's eyes widened in horror, and I held up my hand, palm toward him as if to stave off his anger. "I know . . . I know. I've spoiled her."

"She will never learn anything this way. You're doing her no favors."

"I'm perfectly aware of my inadequacies as a parent. And you haven't offered to chip in on expenses here yet, you know."

Suddenly I recalled the downside of marriage, the part where I had to take into consideration my mate's wishes. A sickening feeling nose-dived through my soul. I remembered the disadvantage of having to answer to a man whenever I spent money. Like on our honeymoon in Sedona when I'd wanted to purchase a pricey souvenir. He'd insisted it was just a piece of junk, so I put it back on the shelf. *I should have given this marriage thing more thought before I jumped into it.*

"That's not the point, Julia. And I'm not accusing you of being a bad parent. But you can't continue protecting her from the realities of this world. It's not healthy."

"Oh, Marten, it's just a water bill. And it's my way of helping her get on her feet financially. She's putting it in a savings account. Anyway, I don't expect you to understand — you're a guy. You have no idea what extent we mothers will go to for our children."

Marten's contorted face frightened me as he rushed toward me and shoved the café table over. My favorite earthenware cup crashed to the floor, breaking into so many pieces I knew it could never be repaired. Sobbing, I covered my mouth with my hand.

"*You* have no idea what I know about mothers," Marten hissed, his lips trembling. "Mine did more for me than you've done for Andie. She gave up her entire future for me, and the difference is that I appreciated it until the day she died, and even still. So don't expect me to appreciate your indulgence of your spoiled brat of a daughter."

"How dare you!" I screamed. "Who in the hell do you think you are?"

Marten opened his mouth to reply, but I interrupted. "Don't answer that. If you're going to treat me like this, you can just stay out of my way. A friend of mine once said that if someone treats you like a dog, just pee on their shoe. So you might want to take your shoes when you leave."

Marten turned and stormed toward the elevator. As the door was closing, I added, "If you have a problem with how this household is run, maybe you should have looked into it a little more before you made yourself a part of the family."

Marten yelled back, "Tell me how much money you want. I'll write you a check!" He descended just in time to have the last word.

I heard a door down the hallway closing, probably Andie's bedroom. Had Andie overheard the argument? Of course, she must have. I allowed myself 10 minutes for a good cry. Then, I went to work, busying myself all day to keep my mind off my new husband's bizarre behavior. I took a sleeping pill and went to bed earlier than usual. When he came home, he quietly slipped into his pajamas, shut our bedroom door and shuffled down the hallway into the living room where a leather chair opened into a twin mattress. I was only half awake, but glad he hadn't tried to slink under the covers and make amends. I might not have been able to resist.

Chapter Forty-Seven

Is There a Doctor In the House?

I hung up the phone. "I'll be up in five minutes," Doc had said. I'd told him his transcription was ready for pick-up. I could just as easily have emailed or faxed it, but old-fashioned Doc wanted hand-to-hand delivery. He always appreciated a little "father-daughter" time with me at the end of the day, and I liked it, too. I'd asked him to come up to my office because I wanted privacy.

"I've got the best news!" Doc said the moment the elevator opened.

"Great! I could use some of that. What's happening?"

"My daughter Rebecca is moving here immediately. The house deal went through, and, on top of that, she was offered a position in a local medical practice that rotates ER doctors from one hospital to the next, whenever the need arises. It's exactly what she was hoping for!"

"Perfect," I said. "So Christopher will have his loft!"

"That's right. Rebecca says they're all so excited. They've already started packing."

"Well, this is wonderful, Doc. Here, let me run into my office for your paperwork." I headed down the hallway. Doc followed right behind me. "Anything wrong?" Doc said. "You commented that you could use some good news."

"Well, yeah. Have a seat," I said.

"Okay. I take it this visit was for more than just the purpose of my collecting my dictation?"

"Right. Originally, it was, but I don't want to float a dark cloud over *your* good news. I just don't know who else to turn to."

He pulled up a chair next to my desk. "It's okay, my dear. I've got all evening. Take your time."

"It's Marten. Everything is wrong. We haven't spoken for three days. At night when he thinks I'm asleep he comes in here and uses the computer. I've checked his browsing history, or tried to, but he's deleted it. I don't know what he's up to."

Doc sighed, staring at the floor for a few moments. "Now I'm in a tight spot. I must make a decision to break a confidence or to not bring comfort to my Julia."

"What do you know about him? Has Marten has spoken to you about us?"

"Not about the marriage, no. But it's no surprise that your relationship is severely affected. You see . . . ." He pulled his chair closer to mine and leaned toward me. "Where do I begin?" he whispered.

"There's no one here but the temp down the hall. You needn't worry about being overheard. She keeps her iPod buds in her ears the livelong day!"

Doc laughed. "iPod . . . I was only recently introduced to that newfangled contraption by my grandson. Old people and technology don't mix well."

"Perhaps not, but you don't have to worry about it, because you're not old. Now spill the beans!"

"What I am about to tell you has to be held in strict confidence."

I nodded agreement. "Understood."

"Marten came to me a few days ago . . . when was it? Last Friday? Or was it Thursday? No, it was Friday, I'm sure of it. I remember now, because I had just seen little John Michael and he comes on Fridays for his allergy shots."

I heaved a sigh.

"I'm sorry to exasperate you so. I don't know why I always get carried off the subject. So, on Friday Marten came to me at the end of office hours. He was distraught about the demise of the health clinic."

"What? It's not happening after all?"

"Apparently not."

I frowned. "He must be devastated."

"He's troubled, definitely. He heard talk of liquidation and he fears they may be forced to consider bankruptcy. He asked me not to say a word to anyone, though."

I sat quietly for a moment. "I hope you haven't lost an investment."

Doc shook his head. "It never happened. He didn't pursue it, and it had seemed fishy to me, anyway, so I wasn't interested."

I grasped my chin in the palm of my hand. "Hmm . . . that explains what I saw the day I stopped in over there. It didn't appear any progress had been made to remodel the warehouse. I never said anything to Marten, because he'd told me specifically not to go back until the place was ready for business. I didn't want him to know I'd gone over there against his wishes. I'd almost forgotten all about it."

"Well . . . that coincides with his explanation. He discovered that his partners were unethical, men he could no longer deal with in good conscience. He's severed all ties with them and advised me to forget about volunteering over there if or when it opens. They apparently are unscrupulous businessmen whose main objective is making money, not the health and welfare of children, as he'd originally thought."

"Sounds like the health care system here in America, huh?"

"It's much better than it was before."

"Yeah, but far from perfect," I said.

"Oh, Julia. It will never be all done. Don't you see? We live in an imperfect world, but there's always room for improvement."

"Okay. So go on about Marten. What does he plan to do?"

"He's terribly worried about finances, but he doesn't want you to know. He asked me to help him find employment. I'd imagine he's in your office at night searching for jobs. That would explain why he erases his browsing history."

"Why wouldn't he share this huge piece of information with me, his wife?"

"He wants you to feel safe. Secure."

"Well, I don't."

"Of course not."

"I thought he had a fortune. Not that I married him for money, but I never dreamed I'd have any concerns. No wonder he hasn't pitched in on the household expenses. It also explains his irritation over the huge water bill we had last month . . . and his peculiar behavior of late."

"I hope it helps you understand his moods. I shouldn't tell you this, but he asked me to prescribe an anti-depressant."

"Did you?"

"No. I don't know his health history. I gave him the name of a good psychiatrist. I suspect he may have a mental health issue with mood swings."

I laughed. "You think so, do you? He definitely needs a mood stabilizer of some kind. You know, Doc, I want him to feel that I understand what he's going through, but I'm not sure how I can without telling him you told me."

"How about a little white lie? Say you discovered that an employment search site was used on your computer and see what he says."

"He'll probably blame it on one of the employees. But, sure — I'll try it. Why not?"

Chapter Forty-Eight

Another Proposal

The next morning, Britt whistled a tune as he got off the elevator and bopped into the kitchen. He sat down at the bar and smiled. I glanced at the clock; he was early. I figured he probably wanted something, perhaps a schedule change, or maybe a raise. Britt usually worked afternoons but today was his full day at the office. He always went straight to his cubicle once he arrived, although occasionally he would arrive an hour ahead of his afternoon shift, and he and Andie would visit in her room. I didn't approve of this behavior, but, as long as Boone was in school, I ignored it.

I offered him a cup of coffee and he stirred in a spoonful of sugar.

"It's going to be a hot one today," Britt said as he stirred.

"Yep."

Britt poured another sugar. I watched when he absentmindedly spooned in the third one. Surely he wasn't going to drink that concoction. He obviously had something serious on his mind.

"What's up?" I asked.

"Oh, well, um. I'm pretty excited. I've made an offer on a house. I'm supposed to hear within 24 hours if they accept. I'm trying to get pre-qualified, so I wanted to give you a heads up in case the mortgage company calls for employment verification."

"Sure thing. So . . . tell me all about the house."

"It's an adobe-style stucco, three bedrooms, on a cul-de-sac in Northern Woods, a new gated community. I've clocked it — 25 minutes in rush hour — not bad. It's exactly halfway between here and the university. My realtor says it's a buyer's market right now, and the resale value will do nothing but go up."

"Practical thinking, there," I said, although Britt had never impressed me as a *subdivision* kind of guy. Concrete and steel, maybe, but a cul-de-sac? I added, "Also encouraging. It sounds as though you plan to stay with us here at Tyler Professional Services."

Britt smiled slyly. "Of course I plan to stay. I hope *you* don't have other plans for me."

I smiled back at him. "Your plans are my plans, Britt. Your work is excellent. I couldn't ask for a more reliable employee."

"Yes, well." He cleared his throat and took a drink of what was now mocha syrup. "I'd like to be more than just an employee."

"More? Part owner, perhaps?" I kept a straight face, but I knew what was coming next.

"What I'm trying to say . . . I'd like to ask Andie to marry me."

"Oh, I see. Thus, the family-style home purchase?"

"Yeah." He chuckled. "Andie tells me she wants a white picket fence. Maybe I'm trying to bribe her this way. Do you think I'm crazy?"

"This may be just me, Britt, but Andie has had a picket fence style of life for years; she just doesn't recognize it. She's always thought the grass was greener on the other side. Although, come to think of it, maybe green grass *is* what she wants. There isn't much of it here — just brick and concrete, mostly."

"She wants a yard for Boone, and sidewalks without tourists in his way, so he can skateboard and ride a bike."

"Oh, I know it." I nodded thoughtfully. "So a yard she shall have. And neighborhood sidewalks, too."

Andie had talked occasionally about having a place of her own, and I agreed it would be a healthy thing for everyone concerned. They couldn't stay here forever, and, with the addition of maniacal Marten, I supposed it seemed only natural that Andie would be anxious to move out. She'd probably hinted the same to Britt, signaling him in her calculating way to *do something*!

But, I've been Andie's personal maid and built-in babysitting service for years, and, once Andie leaves the family compound, she will get a true taste of what life is all about. Responsibility with a capital R. If she says yes to marriage, she'll have even more responsibilities. *Someday she might look back to find the grass was pretty darn green where she came from, but by then she'll be a wife and she will be stuck. There will be no turning back.* I realized I'd been thinking about *my past*, not Andie's future.

Britt stared at me, waiting for an old-fashioned answer, a yes or no. I felt my mean streak taking over but I tried to control myself. While I wished for my daughter's happiness, I resented this pipsqueak trying to horn his way in. I was losing control of my universe.

"If you're asking my permission, *of course* you have it. I wish you the best, Britt. Certainly, you have my blessing. When will you ask her, or have you already?"

"She's seen the house and she loves it. But, no, I haven't actually got down on one knee and proposed."

"Well, good luck with getting her out of bed on time to come into work."

The mean streak was coming out. I felt an incredible urge to escape the condo. I rinsed my cup and jammed my bare feet into my loafers. "She's still asleep this morning, as a matter of fact," I added. "You'd better go tell her the good news about the offer, if she doesn't already know. I'm going downstairs, so tell her to get Boone up and ready for school. She may as well start getting used to the task right away."

Britt blushed and went for Andie's bedroom.

I entered the elevator and went straight down to The Stock Market and marched into the soup kitchen.

"Well look at Mrs. Grump!" Dana said.

"I need to vent in the worst way!"

We went into Dana's office where I explained Britt's marriage plans.

"Julia, don't you see this is the best thing that could happen? You act like he's a green ogre coming to whisk your fair-haired princess out of her ivory tower, never to return."

"I feel so shriveled up, so *useless*. No one needs me anymore," I cried.

"Oh, please. First you complain because you have to do everything for her, and now you whine because she won't be there for you to wait on hand and foot."

"Pretty ironic, isn't it?"

"And," Dana said, "to top it all off, to live in a small community will be the greatest thing for Boone. He'll make all sorts of friends his own age. You can even buy him that bicycle he's been wanting."

"It would be fun to take him shopping for a bike," I said. But at precisely that moment I realized I was about to lose my grandson on a daily basis. I went from happy back to sad.

Dana put her arm around me. "With training wheels at first, Julia. And remember those scooters we used to have, and how we played hopscotch and jacks on the sidewalks? Think of all the awesome designs we wrote on city sidewalks with colored chalk. He'll have the kind of childhood we had, not this hot, concrete world with tourists all over the place. The only wheels here are strollers or wheelchairs."

"You're right." I sniffed. I unwrapped a set of silverware from a table adjacent to Dana's desk and wiped my tears with the cloth napkin. "We raced our roller skates and wore those homemade stilts my dad made all over the neighborhood, remember? Those memories we made have kept me going, and I've worried that Boone wouldn't have a memorable childhood. Oh," I sobbed, "but how am I going to go all day without seeing him?"

"I imagine you'll see him more than you think. It will be a good thing for you and Marten, too, to get your marriage on more firm ground . . . to have more time alone to work out these differences between you."

I squinted through my tears. "I'm sacrificing my grandson for my marriage; is that what you're saying?"

"No. I'm saying everything happens for a reason, and I know you believe that. It's all in the timing. Just roll with it, honey. Don't fight against reality — life goes on."

I considered my cousin's advice. Marten was no longer sleeping in the chair hide-a-bed, but he stayed way over on his side of the mattress. "The marriage has reached an impasse, that's for sure. It definitely needs work and I guess I'm gonna be the one who has to make the next move."

"That's what I'm saying."

I handed the napkin to Dana. "Sorry about the mascara stain."

"Don't worry about it," Dana said as she threw it into a heap of other soiled linens. "What about the cat? I guess you're going to lose him, too."

My eyes opened wide. "Over my dead body," I growled.

"But, he was a birthday gift from you to Boone, right?"

I nodded and broke into tears again. Dana unwrapped another set of silverware and handed me the napkin.

Chapter Forty-Nine

Changes

By the end of the week, Britt had an accepted offer — two of them, in fact. Andie was sporting a one-carat princess-cut solitaire set in platinum on the fourth finger of her left hand. (A starter diamond, she'd whispered to me.) They hadn't set a wedding date and, just as I figured, they'd live together for a while first. Andie had assured me that Boone would remain in the same school, come to the office every afternoon and would also be here on weekdays during summer break while she worked in the office.

"I'm sure he'll want to sleep over a lot, Mom. We can keep his bedroom and playroom just as it is, can't we?"

"I suppose," I mumbled. "Except for Greenie. You'll have to make room for him at your new house."

"It's not healthy to move iguanas around, I've heard."

"Oh, honestly? He seemed to do just fine when he was transferred from the pet shop in a cardboard box. I'm sure he'll adjust."

Andie bit the inside of her cheek. "I'm not sure if Britt will allow it."

I laughed. "*Allow?* Britt will have to deal — it's not up for negotiation. I never wanted a lizard in my home in the first place. I would have told you that if you'd asked. Mr. Iguana goes with you and Boone."

"What about Zadok?" Boone asked. "I can take him, can't I, Gran?"

"Of course you can, sweetheart."

"Britt is allergic to cats," Andie offered meekly.

I threw my head back and snorted. "Nice try. Abyssinians are hypoallergenic. Britt will be just fine."

Boone grinned. "I couldn't go anywhere without Zadok and Greenie."

Andie put on her pouting look. I didn't expect I'd miss her all that much. The most difficult part would be the loss of a daily interaction with my grandson. Weekends would probably be the worst. No grandchild, no cat — only one newly unemployed husband with mood swings. *Whoopee! Remember that adventure I craved? My life is careening at light-speed. And Lady Sophia will arrive in three more days!*

Chapter Fifty

Kiss and Make Up

I slid under the crisp, clean sheets and positioned my fluffy pillows all around just the way I liked them. Marten appeared to be asleep. I lay quietly for a while, thinking of how life would be changed once Andie and Boone were gone. No Zadok. No Greenie . . . well *that* would be a blessing wouldn't it? I thought of the look on Andie's face when she realized she would have to cart the entire zoo into the suburbs with her. I giggled out loud.

Marten turned toward me. "Are you still awake?"

"Umm. Just wondering how it'll feel with everyone else gone. Maybe we should get a dog."

Marten sat up and propped his pillows against the rattan headboard. "Do you honestly need a new diversion?"

"I'm joking. I don't want another living creature to take care of for a long, long time — if ever."

"Maybe Andie and Britt will give you a second grandchild someday."

I sat up and reached for Marten's hand. "I hope they do . . . if they want to, that is. I'm sure Boone would be thrilled."

"Julia, I need to talk to you. Is now a good time?"

"I think we *are* talking now, Marten."

Marten smiled. "I hate to bring this up if you're wanting to get some sleep . . . but, well the health clinic has fallen through and I've been searching for another opportunity. I think I've found one."

"Oh, no! What on earth has happened?"

"I'd rather not go into it right now because that's the bad news, as they say. But the good news is this latest opportunity. I've been doing online research in your office at night and I'm terribly excited about it, but

I don't have all the details yet. I know it will require some travel and lots of hard work, but I'm positive I can make a go of it."

"Travel out of the country?"

"No, thankfully not. I can't leave the United States for some time now."

"Why not?"

"When I entered the States, it was with a tourist visa because I wasn't sure if I would actually be working here. And at first I did spend a few weeks as a tourist. Once we got married, and I filed for adjustment of status, they informed me that I cannot leave the country until I've received my documentation or else I won't be allowed to return."

"That seems rather harsh."

"It has a lot to do with visa fraud — people coming to this country to get married for only one purpose: to be allowed to stay here legally and not because they fell in love with a vibrant, sexy redhead like you."

We made love and Marten fell asleep shortly afterward. I realized I hadn't asked him about his new business venture. I was curious as to how much traveling would be involved. *Won't it be divine if he's gone on Sundays so I can have the rooftop garden to myself once in a while?* The devil inside me smiled deviously and I drifted off to sleep.

Chapter Fifty-One

Lady Sophia's Surprise

I heard the news from my cell phone on Sunday morning while out in my rooftop garden. Lady Sophia's plane would land in less than two hours, and there had been a slight emergency at the hotel where she was to stay. Something about a plumbing leak — more like a flood — in the Presidential Suite. It would take a minimum of four hours to prepare her room. Their entourage needed a place to relax and hide out, away from the public eye. Noah Forrester from River Protocol, Inc. had contacted Reed Michelson for suggestions regarding security. They agreed my place was perfect, with a private elevator and lobby downstairs. Could I entertain them until later that evening? Chesley wanted to meet Boone, the boy he'd been communicating with via e-mail, and Sophia needed to kick off her shoes — someplace with a secure Wi-Fi connection, she'd requested. I had so much to do to get ready. I hurried into the condo toward the kitchen.

"You won't believe it!"

"What is it?" Marten asked.

I opened the refrigerator to check on what we had on hand. Not much. "You can't leave America, so England is coming to you!"

Marten poured a cup of tea and stirred a little milk into the brew. He placed the milk container into the refrigerator and kissed my cheek. "How's that?"

"It's your Soap. She's coming here!"

Marten laughed. "That's old news, Jules."

"No, you don't get it. I mean right *here*. To our condo. In about three hours, they'll be stepping off *that* elevator over there," I pointed emphatically, "and walking into our home!"

Marten frowned. "How can this be happening?"

I filled him in on the hotel calamity as he sipped his tea. His only response was "Hmm." He stood and walked into my office and shut the door. *How odd.*

I pressed the speed dial for The Stock Market. When Dana answered, I said, "Thank God you're working today. I need help in the worst way!" Dana quickly put together a menu of chilled soups and tapas. She arranged for a portable salad bar to be delivered within the hour.

"I'll serve everything myself," Dana said. "Gives me an excuse to rub shoulders with nobility."

By the time Dana got everything set up, Boone had his shower and was all dressed, every little curly hair in place, and he bounced joyfully on the pink sofa, waiting for his new friend, Chesley. Andie had called Britt and he came right over. I couldn't help but roll my eyes; they were both dressed to the nines.

"Where's Marten?" Britt asked.

"Um, I think he's working in my office," I said as I headed down the hall. But, when I opened the door, no one was inside. I checked every other room in the place, but Marten had vanished without one word of explanation. *I've been preoccupied; maybe he told me he was leaving and I didn't hear him.*

Vanderhawk Security's team came up first and gave the go-ahead for the rest of them. When the elevator opened, Lady Sophia took my breath away. She was even more beautiful in person than in photographs and on television. Boone spent an hour or so with Chesley in the toy room, with Zadok and Greenie, of course. Sophia mentioned my recent marriage, so I went to retrieve our photo album, but it wasn't where I usually kept it. I'd wanted to show her a picture of Marten.

Noah Forrester engaged Lady Sophia in conversation, and, when I returned to the living room, he suggested I lead the way on a condo tour. I happily obliged, and, upon our return down the hallway past the old massage rooms, Sophia inquired about using my internet. I showed her into my office and invited her to make herself at home at my work station. The framed picture of Marten and me that I normally kept on my desk was gone. I knew I hadn't moved it. It had to be Marten, but why had he hidden all visible evidence of his presence in San Antonio?

~*~

The next three days were a flurry of activity. Sophia sent me a lovely English tea set with a note of thanks for allowing her to kick back at my place on the date of her arrival. She had apparently taken a liking to me and invited me to attend her visits to school functions where she and Chesley would appear. I felt obligated to go, and Noah Forrester couldn't have been more pleased, since he thought of me as River Protocol's ambassador. Boone wanted to go, of course, and so did Andie, of course. Andie allowed Boone to miss school on Monday but, once they realized how boring those events were, they opted out for the next two days. Andie would rather work and Boone didn't want to miss school, even though Montessori encourages cultural activities outside of the classroom.

On Thursday, Lady Sophia accepted my invitation to breakfast. Dana catered a brunch as only Dana can, and the boys headed for the playroom after they ate. Lady Sophia sent her bodyguard with the boys and suggested Dana join us, which left the three of us relaxing on my J Sofa with the gifted tea set on my coffee table.

"This is so thoughtful of you, Julia: serving with this." Lady Sophia said. "It's rare for me to have the opportunity to actually *see* a gift I've sent, let alone use it! I suspect many believe a gift from royalty or nobility is a trophy which must be proudly displayed but never touched."

I nodded my agreement. "This is a special occasion, worthy of English china, and I appreciate your accepting my invitation this morning."

Sophia sighed. "It's quite the refreshing change from my ordinary routine these past few months."

"Are you satisfied with what your tour has accomplished so far?" I asked.

She took a deep breath and appeared to think about the entire eight or nine months they'd been traveling. "It's a daunting task, world peace. Evidently I've been unable to achieve it." She grinned and laughed, which triggered the same response in Dana and me.

"Peace on Earth will probably take much more than what you're doing here, but I'd like to think it's possible," Dana said.

Lady Sophia shrugged. "Who knows? I'm going to confide in you: I'm not as idealistic about it as I used to be."

"Maybe you're weary from travel and public appearances," I said. "Once you have time to rest and re-group, you'll realize that your idea of working with children is the best way."

"It's all about the children, isn't it?" Lady Sophia said.

Lady Sophia called for her son. "Chesley Regan Vanderhawk." The boys ran into the living room, and Sophia said, "We must go now to rehearse with the children who'll perform at the Arneson Theater on Saturday." As they headed for the elevator, Sophia said, "You must visit us in London! My Chesley has insisted that Boone come to play someday soon. So bring your son, and your invisible husband, of course."

I snorted, right in front of nobility. I was so embarrassed. But it happened. I quickly regained my composure and said, "Marten owns an estate in Wales, and we plan to journey over within the next few months. I'll let you know when that's scheduled and perhaps we can plan a visit."

~*~

Dana and I sat alone on the sofa for a few moments, absorbing the events of the morning. "What on earth just happened?" Dana asked.

"Oh, that." I sighed. "I'm sure Marten would never agree to go to see her. He seems to want to remain invisible. He left quite early for work this morning, and he even hid our wedding album before she showed up here last Sunday. Then, *he* disappeared for the entire afternoon."

"Why did he do that?"

"I didn't ask him."

"Why not?"

I didn't answer.

"You don't want to know, do you?" Dana said.

"No, I don't. And what's more, I don't even care. I've grown tired of trying to understand him. He had his reasons." I drained my cup and set it on the coffee table. "I'm sure I'll find out all about it someday."

As it turned out, *someday* was closer than I realized.

Chapter Fifty-Two

Leaving the Country

Hand-in-hand, Marten and I walked to Boudro's at five o'clock that evening, early enough to snag a water-side table and guacamole for two, a Prickly Pear margarita for me and a Mojito for Marten. I wondered if he should be mixing alcohol with his medications. I briefly thought of Richard's death and brushed the memory away. I couldn't ask Marten about the combination, for he'd not told me he was taking anything, but I'd seen a prescription bottle in his shaving bag. I'd also noticed his stabilized mood, which I greatly appreciated. I wasn't about to rock the boat.

"Julia, I must ask you a very large favor, my darling. I got a call this morning from my barrister, the attorney in Wales who handled Mum's estate. I've received an offer I dare not refuse. It seems someone's gone bonkers — they're in love with the cottage and have offered nearly double what I thought the old stone structure was worth."

I had been lost in thought, mesmerized by our server's elegant preparation of guacamole. "What? The cottage was up for sale? Why would you even consider that?"

Marten nibbled absentmindedly on the end of a sugar cane stick. He dipped it back into his Mojito and used his napkin to wipe sweat beads from the glass. "I put it on the market after our wedding. I thought you knew."

I leaned toward him and growled, "How could I have known? You didn't tell me." People were staring at us. "You told me we could use it as a vacation cottage!"

"My new business venture needs more capital! Now please lower your voice. This is very difficult for me as it is."

"Oh. Well then—." I signaled the waiter for another margarita. The first one was only halfway finished; obviously I would need another sooner rather than later. "So, what's the favor?"

"I haven't left behind much of value there . . . except for the quilts. They're stored in a cherry trunk in the attic, and I'd like you to retrieve them and whatever else you may desire as keepsakes. I've already sold most of the furniture, and my barrister boxed up the rest. He says it's all ready to go."

"Oh . . . I don't know about this, Marten. You promised me we would ship the furnishings here to the States."

"Julia! You *know* my financial situation. I had no choice!"

"You should have told me before now!"

"Yes, I realize that. I'm truly sorry. I've handled everything poorly, haven't I?"

"You certainly have." I sucked on the straw down to the bottom of my margarita glass. Our waiter headed my way with another. Not one moment too soon.

"Mum's jewelry is in a London depository box. You must go and empty it. The jewels are yours to keep."

I looked away and watched a boatload of tourists paying rapt attention to the chatter of their guide. I took a sip of my fresh drink and licked salt off the edge of the glass. I was being bribed with estate jewelry! I took a deep breath, and let it out slowly. "Marten . . . uh . . . the thought of traveling alone to Europe isn't the least bit appealing to me."

"I'll arrange for a private driver to meet you at the airport," Marten urged. "You can use him all week — go anywhere you want."

"Let's both go!"

"I wish we could, but you know I can't leave this country until I have all my documents. In addition, I have urgent meetings to attend for days on end with regard to the new business, papers to sign and the like. I'll fax the closing forms over on Friday, and the attorney will turn the keys over to the new owners on Monday. That leaves only three days to vacate the property. I can't possibly be two places at once, so that's why I need you."

His prattle made no sense at all. "Why can't the lawyer just ship everything to us?"

"Primarily because there are documents to be signed for which facsimiles are not legally accepted in London. You'll find them in the side drawer of the roll-top desk in the cottage. I'll arrange for you to sign my name with a Power of Attorney, since you are my wife."

There was that word again — *wife*. The rock that had made a home in my stomach did a 90-degree flip.

"And, Julia, in case you don't know already, it would mean the world to me for you to catch a glimpse of where I grew up. Maybe you'll understand me better when you observe the village where I spent most of my childhood. And, yes, I hope we can go together someday soon, but I seriously doubt we could ever gain access to the house, and, even if we did, it wouldn't be the same."

I empathized with Marten. At one time, I had attempted to go back to my childhood home, but when I pulled up in front of the house I couldn't make myself get out of the car for at least half an hour. When I did, I stood on the sidewalk and gaped at the house, remembering each and every nook and cranny inside. I imagined conversations between my parents, saw my pets, and so forth. I knew the people who had bought the house, and I felt sure they would let me come inside, but I didn't want to, given that it was no longer occupied by my own family.

I'd been observing Marten's body language. He was anxious, but that was nothing new. He seemed frightened, and more apprehensive than normal, though. "You didn't realize when you left that you'd never be able to go home again, did you?"

Marten toed the bricks and mortar in the sidewalk. "No," he said. Then, he brightened. "Would you take photographs? Unfortunately, I didn't think of that before I left. I thought it would all be there when I got back." He reached across the table for my hand. "You've changed my life more than you will ever realize."

He'd changed mine even more. I imagined walking through the cottage, climbing the narrow stone steps to the attic, and opening that magical cherry trunk to discover those primitive quilts and linens Marten loved. I envisioned clusters of antique silver frames displayed on a dusty fireplace mantle — family pictures — perhaps one or two of Marten's father.

Another barge tour floated by and brought me back to the Riverwalk. Marten had obviously thought this whole thing through. He'd made up his mind, and it appeared to me I had no more choice in the matter than Marten did. "Well," I said, "it is what it is, I guess." I found myself warming up to the idea.

"I know how much you'd wanted to attend Lady Sophia's program on Saturday, and, with this change of plans, you won't be here for that." Marten said. "I truly apologize for messing up your schedule, but I see no other way."

"Boone will be disappointed, I'm sure. But honestly, it doesn't matter to me. I've seen enough all week to last a lifetime. It's been exhausting, frankly." I was curious what his answer would be to my next question. "Speaking of Boone, what about him? Britt won a trip to Dallas for the weekend for a Cowboys game. That is, a friend of his who's a Riverwalk tour boat guide won it, but can't use it. So he gave it to Britt. He and Andie won't be home until Monday."

"I'll collect Boone from school tomorrow, and Saturday morning I'll take him to Schlitterbahn. Some rowdy romping in the water park will do us both good. He'll have a fun weekend and you'll be home by Sunday, unless you want to stay a couple of extra days to do some sightseeing. I'll arrange your flights." He picked up his phone to call the airline.

"Okay. Arrange a couple extra days for me to be a tourist . . . but I wish you could go with me."

"Next time, I promise. And Boone is always in good hands with me, you know that."

Chapter Fifty-Three

SAT to LGA

Traffic was going nowhere. I glanced at the digital read-out on the dashboard; I had plenty of time before my flight. I closed my eyes and pinched the bridge of my nose — re-thinking my packing frenzy from early that morning. Had I forgotten anything? Not that I could do anything about it now. Cosmetics, three white cotton blouses, two black skirts, one red sweater, two pair of khaki cargo pants, one pair of black, flat-soled dress shoes and one pair of white sneakers. Airline ticket, passport, picture I.D. and an assortment of jewelry in a velvet pouch in my laptop case on wheels, which doubled as my carry-on. Good — nothing had been overlooked.

I massaged the back of my neck as my mind wandered. What might I see in my short time in London? Definitely the typical first-time tourist attractions: Changing of the Guards, Trafalgar Square, and Big Ben. I wished Marten could have gone with me. Next time, he had said, but when would *next time* be? The trip up to Wales would be nice, to see where he had grown up, and to retrieve his mother's quilt collection, but I'd much rather he be there with me.

Pink Floyd's song, *Hey You*, drifted softly from the radio, and I hummed along while Zadok purred in the backseat. *Zadok in the backseat?* I looked abruptly sideways and noticed a black diesel Mercedes idling alongside. I raised the window to eliminate the nauseating smell of diesel fuel. I chuckled because I'd always likened our Abyssinian's purr to the hum of a diesel engine. I checked the clock again. Traffic hadn't moved for five minutes. According to the radio announcer, an accident a mile up the road was in the clean-up stage. I glanced over at the Mercedes again. The windows were tinted so dark I couldn't see the driver. I recalled having spotted it last week, or one just like it — almost felt it was following me at one point on my way to the cemetery, but I'd chalked it up to too much late night television and my imagination.

By the time I reached the airport and found a space in long-term parking, I wheeled my luggage up to the Delta ticket counter with only 30 minutes to check in and make it through security. I was glad Marten had urged me to leave early. It was nice, after all, to have someone looking after me again. I guessed that's what marriage was all about, the give and take. The moments of exasperation had to be traded for the moments when you knew you could fall backwards into the arms of someone waiting behind to catch you, someone you could trust entirely with your life.

The cold, damp smell of jet fuel and moldy carpeting in the ramped jet way made me wish I could turn around and go back home. Once aboard, I found Row 4 and excused myself to the passenger in 4C, a large balding man with headphones hanging around his neck. He heaved a sigh as he got up to allow me into 4B. The window seat, 4A, was occupied by a pre-teen boy with short brown hair, flat on the top, and an extremely runny nose. He had stowed his green and brown camouflage backpack under the seat in front of him. I politely smiled at him as I sat down. He abruptly turned his head toward the window. I slid my laptop case under the seat in front of me and settled in for take-off with a Lawrence Block paperback.

"Here, Brendan, take this," said a woman sitting across the aisle, in Row 5. I looked over and saw what I guessed to be the boy's mother and two more boys, smaller than Brendan. The mother handed a CD player across the aisle to the man with headphones (which were now placed firmly on his ears) but he seemed oblivious to anything but his music.

". . . and Bobby wants the video game," the mother added.

Brendan dragged his backpack out from under the seat and passed the video game over to me. Headphone Man refused to acknowledge any participation in the family trade-offs, so I was in the middle, handing mother and son their desired objects without as much as a thank you from either. The mother added, "What about the games?" Brendan dug deeper into his bag, retrieved two plastic cases and handed them to me, now the official go-between. I watched the boy out of the corner of my eye. He had coughed, sneezed and snorted continuously since the plane took flight. I hoped it was an allergy and not something contagious. He wiped his nose on his shirt, then he raised his knees and rubbed his nose on his pants. How many germs had I picked up from passing electronic gadgets back and forth?

What kind of a mother would put her snot-nosed kid on an airplane without tissues? And seat him next to a stranger, at that. I had a package of them in my purse. "Would you care for a tissue?" I asked. He ignored me. Either the kid was embarrassed, or he was a brat. Boone would never behave in such an ungrateful manner.

A half hour into the flight, Brendan discovered the plastic window blind: open — shut, open — shut, open — shut. The flight attendant came through with the beverage cart and asked me what the boy would like to drink. Apparently she thought I was his mother. I shrugged my shoulders and looked over at the kid, but he had vanished into thin air. The last I'd noticed, he had let his tray table down in preparation for a beverage. I peeked under the table and sure enough, there he was, hiding.

"Hey, Batman," I whispered. "What do you want to drink?"

"Wadda they got?"

"Everything."

"Pepsi," the boy demanded. *Caffeine,* I thought.

"May I move to another seat?" I inquired of the attendant.

"Sorry, but this flight is entirely full."

"Then he'll have something clear, bubbly and non-caffeinated, whatever you have, and I'll have a Bloody Mary, triple vodka."

The flight attendant frowned and craned her neck to look under the boy's tray table, as if to think: *Poor boy, his mother drinking triple shots on the flight, no wonder he's hiding.*

It was going to be a long journey. When Brendan's crew-cut slowly emerged from under the tray, I stifled the urge to put my hand on top of his head and push him back down. Like a snake coming out of a basket, charmed by a flute, he slithered out of his hole and sat upright, swinging his legs, waiting for his cola. I smiled; well now, won't he be surprised? When the flight attendant handed the boy's Sprite to me, I placed the drink decisively on his tray and looked him squarely in the eye. *I dare you to complain*, the look said.

He blinked, and he worked the window cover again, up — down, up — down. The plastic cup sat, sweating.

I was determined not to let a pre-pubescent boy get the best of me. I knew what Boone would say. Last year he and I had gone with Andie to Boudro's to celebrate their birthdays, and a couple at an adjacent table were bickering loudly. Andie turned around constantly, gawking at them. She whined, "Those people are ruining the atmosphere here, not to mention my birthday." "Turn your *listening ears* off, Mommy." Boone said. "My *what*?" Andie exclaimed. Boone's teacher had taught his class to do it when they were bothered by distracting or unpleasant sounds. "I love it," I'd said, to which Andie replied, "Humph."

I booted up my laptop. I hadn't used it for quite some time, but had charged the battery for the trip. I would turn off my *listening ears* and develop a spreadsheet for one of my new clients. A bubble popped up on the monitor — did I want to clean up unused icons? While checking to see what those icons might be, I noticed a document by a name I didn't recognize. *Clifford 12*. I right-clicked on the properties tab to see what it was, only to find that it was a very large file named *Archival Resources*, and had been downloaded on Friday, January 23, over four months ago. That was the day I'd set up Marten's files and he had left that one orange disk behind, wasn't it? *Clifford 12* must be the one I'd copied and intended to delete, but had never gotten around to. I opened the folder. The file contained extensive historical information on The Clifford Building, including the layout of all six floors, and extensive commentary on the private elevator. Marten had told me he was interested in the past and current development of the Riverwalk. Maybe this was part of his research.

I had an indescribable urge to get back home, yet I couldn't explain exactly why. "Always trust your gut," my mother had told me repeatedly, and right now my gut felt like I had swallowed sour milk that was curdling inside, begging for a way out. I looked back at the lavatory. There was no line, but I couldn't bring myself to excuse my way past Headphone Man. I looked at Brendan's untouched drink. (He was on the floor, again.) I went for it and chugged it all. The carbonation helped and would have to suffice until I got off the plane.

Chapter Fifty-Four

Tattoo Fiasco

While Frederick was in the kitchen preparing Italian spinach lasagna, Leonardo locked himself in the bathroom. He couldn't risk Frederick barging in now, of all times. With his pocket screwdriver he removed the switch plate cover on the outlet above the bathroom sink. He detached the ground fault receptacle and clipped the ground fault wire.

"Soup's on," Frederick called out, and he jiggled the doorknob. "Are you okay in there?"

"Be out in a moment." Leonardo quickly replaced the cover and slipped the screwdriver behind the tank. He flushed the toilet for effect, washed his hands, and joined Frederick at the dining table.

"You make me so happy," Leonardo said. He took Frederick's hand and went on to say how he knew they would be together for a very long time. "You do feel it, don't you?"

"Nothing would make me happier than to spend the rest of my life like this."

"Then we will make it so," Leonardo said, fully satisfied — mission accomplished. "Let's celebrate our commitment with a fine bottle of bubbly in the hot tub. What do you say?"

After dinner, Frederick prepared the bath and set a silver bucket beside the tub with ice and wine.

Leonardo began clearing the table.

"Our tub is ready, Leo," Frederick said, invitingly.

"You go on in. I'll just quickly finish up in here."

"Let me help you and we'll go in together."

"Actually, I would prefer you go first." Leonardo smiled seductively. "I have a little something I want to surprise you with."

Frederick smiled in return. "Then . . . I'll be waiting . . . anticipating," Frederick sang. He knew what Leo's surprise was. He had a surprise of his own: a fancy "L" on the upper left cheek of his derriere. He had thought, *What the hell. Why not? If he dumps me, I'll turn the other cheek, have a fancy R put on the right, find another lover, and tell him the letters are directional signals.*

Leonardo watched Frederick go into the bath and lower himself into the deep water.

Frederick called out. "Ahh . . . it's perfect. Don't take too long. The temperature is *just right,* to quote little Miss Goldilocks."

Leonardo carried the dinner dishes from the table to the kitchen sink. He turned on the faucet and used the spray attachment to spritz water through his hair. Then he filled two wine goblets and carried them into the bathroom, handing both to Frederick.

"You opened a bottle?" Frederick said. "I already brought this one in here."

"Oh, dear," Leonardo apologized. "I didn't realize. I should've paid more attention."

"It's okay, now we have twice as much liquid to celebrate with!"

"Good for us, right?" Leonardo said. "Here, hold these two while I prepare myself for your royal highness." Leonardo turned on the whirlpool and set it for forty-five minutes. He pretended to study his reflection in the mirror for a moment, and then he removed Frederick's red blow dryer from its wall holder.

Frederick held both glasses high above the bubbles. "How on earth did you manage to get your hair wet?"

"You don't even want to know," Leonardo spoke at full volume over the noise of the bath jets and the blow dryer. "Besides, you wouldn't believe me if I told you."

"It's only going to get wet again silly, so put that harebrained blow dryer away and show me that sexy 'F' on your muscular thigh."

"Hold your horses, mister." Leonardo looked at Frederick in the mirror. "I want to look *just right* when I show you. I know what a stickler you are for a good hairdo."

Leonardo moved leisurely toward the tub, holding the dryer in his right hand and untying the belt of his robe with his left, allowing it to fall open. He watched Frederick's expression carefully. *Now* is the time, he thought. Turning again slightly, as if to insert the blow dryer into place, he released his hold on it.

Frederick had expected to catch sight of a sexy tattoo on Leo's thigh and didn't notice as the appliance fell into the water. He grimaced in shock, his eyes glazed over and the wine glasses slipped from his fingers. Leonardo smiled kindly at his lover as he watched him slowly disappear into the swirling bubbles.

Chapter Fifty-Five

USA to London

The flight from San Antonio arrived late at LaGuardia. I had forty-five minutes, barely enough time to use a restroom and run to catch the next flight to Heathrow. Once I boarded, I found an empty row, and, as soon as the pilot gave the go-ahead speech, I removed my seatbelt, flipped up the arm rests, stretched out and drifted off.

When I awakened, I opened my computer, but a pop-up indicated a low battery. I had only 90 seconds to shut it down, so I pulled up *Clifford-12* and quickly scrolled down to the end where a list of my clientele was noted — contact names and numbers, addresses and websites. I shook my head in disbelief. Why would anyone want that information, and what would they do with it? I snapped the laptop shut and tried to get back to sleep. I dreamed of children dancing on the Arneson Theater stage. One by one they danced to the edge and fell into the river. I was sitting in the front row and I jumped into the water to save them.

At Heathrow, I retrieved my luggage, but none of the black-suited chauffeurs held up a card with the name 'Tyler' on it. *Dammit — Marten promised!* I wheeled my bag over to an escalator and up to the Skye Lounge, where I ordered a Cobb salad and a glass of Pinot from a waitress who looked to be around Andie's age.

I sat at the bar with my head in my hands. Something was very wrong, but exactly what was it? I saw myself as the nun, Miss Clavel, in the fictional Madeline series. The nun was in charge of 12 girls in a private Catholic school in Paris, with Madeline being the only orphan. Once, in the dark of the night, Miss Clavel shot up in bed, pointed her index finger toward the ceiling and declared, "Something is not right!" Clavel rushed into the girls' bedroom and found Madeline suffering from acute appendicitis.

"Here you go, Mum," the young waitress said. The salad was accompanied by a hot croissant, and I tied into it. I'd had only peanuts and booze since breakfast, many long hours ago. My thoughts went back to Miss Clavel. Madeline had emergency surgery and recovered. But what if that feisty nun hadn't paid attention to *her* gut? Madeline's appendix would have ruptured and she would've died right then and there, with all of her schoolmates watching, horrified. And since the appendix story was the first of the series, there would have been no Madeline books, no dolls, no paper cuts-outs, no Madeline. I could only imagine Andie having been raised with Barbie dolls rather than Madeline. Barbie: the sexy clothes, high heels, fancy hair and make-up. Townhouses, beach homes, swimming pools, convertibles. Why, Andie would be even more of a drama queen, if that was even possible. I laughed out loud at the thought.

I dug into my purse for a Xanax, but thought twice about mixing it with the wine and that triple Bloody Mary from the infamous Brendan flight. Was there a moral to the Madeline story? She followed her gut and saved not only Madeline's life, but the entire literary series! But what did *my* gut say? Considering I hadn't fed it properly, it was rather hard to read.

Finally, I approached a ticket counter to inquire of a return flight to San Antonio. In three hours, the same plane I'd been on would be returning to La Guardia. Should I fly back home right away, or should I stay and finish the task Marten had assigned to me?

Back at the lounge's bar, I called for another glass of wine and thought about my predicament. I needed to find an unoccupied table where I could plug in and boot up my computer to send Marten an e-mail. Surely this whole issue with the Clifford files had a simple explanation. I tried to calm down, but I kept remembering my Texas bumper sticker of years past: "I got here as fast as I could." Something told me to get back to Texas as fast as I could.

I went for a dark corner in the rear where I saw a small round table with an adjacent outlet. When I opened my laptop, sure enough, the low battery signal flashed. I plugged a cord into the device and attempted to insert the other end into the double wall outlet, but it wouldn't fit. I felt like an alien on an unknown planet. I dropped backwards into a chair as tears flowed down both cheeks.

"Will this help?" The American voice came from a man with rather long sandy-blond hair. He reminded me of Val Kilmer, the actor, in his younger days. He wore black jeans and a turtleneck and his computer was plugged in next to the outlet I'd attempted to use. He handed me a dark, square-shaped piece of plastic, and it was then that I realized electric current was different here in Europe. How could I have been so brainless?

"I'm sorry. I don't know how I could've forgotten such a thing," I explained. "Well, I *did* pack in a hurry."

"No worries. Lots of people don't think about it till they arrive. Use this for as long as you want. I'm waiting for my ride to Istanbul — I'll be here for hours." He smiled as I plugged my laptop cord into the adapter.

Thank you." I held out my hand. "Julia Tyler."

He responded with a firm grasp and said, "Josh Katzen. Don't mention it." He reached into his pocket and handed me a white handkerchief.

"Thanks, again" was all I could say. He smiled and went back to the elaborate work station he'd set up in a neighboring booth.

I stared at the wall. A mural covered most of it — a field of lavender with a surreal castle in the background. The lavender field represented the ocean I'd just crossed and the castle was The Clifford Building, my home, safe in San Antonio. I analyzed my overwhelming desire to go straight home. *Why go home now? I have a job to do here, and surely this issue, whatever it is, can wait a few days.*

I'd gone off "half-cocked" once years ago and felt so entirely foolish afterward. Was I doing it again? I'd taken desperate action without all the facts, so my question to myself now was, "Is this going to be another one of those times that I'll live to regret forever?" I'd tried to forget my days of bad judgment, thinking I was beyond it, but that old saying "better safe than sorry" kept floating through my mind.

"Isn't it working for you?" Josh Katzen had pulled up a chair next to mine and was pointing at the blank laptop screen. I hadn't even thought to power it up.

I snorted. "Nothing is working for me today."

"Maybe I can help." He leaned over and pushed the ON button. "There you go. It's working now."

"It's not my computer," I explained. "It's me! You see, I don't know whether to do the job I came here to do, or turn tail and run back home. I've had so many red flags popping up lately, red is the only color I can see right now!"

With a knowing look, Katzen nodded. "With all due respect, ma'am, red wine won't help you reach an intelligent decision."

Before I could think of a way to tell him to mind his own business without losing the adapter he had loaned me, he said, "Single malt scotch works best for me." He laughed. "Seriously, you're in a tight spot, I can tell. You want to talk about it — or not? It's up to you. I keep secrets for a living, so spout it out if you want. If not, I'll take no offense and disappear."

I studied the man's face. His deep blue eyes seemed honest enough. But how could I consider myself a good judge of character anymore? Maybe I *should* get a second opinion, though. Besides, I'd never see him again, so what was the harm?

Josh Katzen, the man who claimed to keep secrets for a living, studied *Clifford-12* thoroughly while I explained my situation. I watched as a sense of alarm developed in his demeanor. Katzen leaned back, balancing the chair between its rear legs and the heels of his leather boots. With his chin in his hand, he stared at me for what seemed an eternity. Finally, he let out a sigh. "Your concerns are well founded. You say he left a file in your office when you signed him on as your client, a few days after you'd met?"

I nodded and blinked, feeling really stupid by now.

"He has no idea you've a copy of this file? Are you absolutely sure?"

I nodded again. "I never mentioned it. I'd forgotten about it, actually."

"For him to have the blueprints of the building you live and work in coupled with a list of your clients, can mean one of two things: He may have been searching for a very secure place to keep his financial information. A business he could trust completely."

I sat up straight and mentally prepared myself for his next suggestion. "Or?"

"Or . . . he's using your business to watch one or more of your clients by logging into your system when you're not aware of it."

"Why?"

Katzen grunted and shrugged. "Any number of reasons. If you think about it, you might come up with one."

"You are one suspicious secret-keeper, Mr. Katzen,"

"Paranoid to the highest degree. But it's kept me alive. You want more advice?"

"Yes I do."

"Do what he sent you here to do and hurry up with it. Forget the sightseeing — that goes without saying. Then get the hell out of this country back to your own. Don't tell him you know anything. Don't ask questions. Act normal. Can you do that?"

I nodded.

Katzen reached into his wallet. "Here's my card and phone number. Contact me on a secure line, preferably a burner phone, when you get back and I'll walk you through the process to find a Trojan on your computer and possibly get rid of it — if there is one. And, Ms. Tyler, if there is one, you must realize he may be dangerous. We'll have to decide what to do at that time." Katzen scratched the stubble on his chin. "The fact that he married you so quickly worries me. Whatever he may have up his sleeve, you've got to be able to outsmart him. We'll work on that plan once you've found a Trojan or similar spyware, okay?"

Katzen stood up to leave.

I brought myself to my feet and angled my head, squinting at him. "Who are you, really?"

He laughed. "I told you. I'm just Josh. I can't say much else, but I can tell you this: if you can trust me more than this new husband of yours, I'm afraid for you." He took on a serious expression. "I hope I'm wrong."

"I hope you are, too," I said as I handed Josh Katzen my business card.

He put it in his wallet and packed up his gear. "I've got to head over to the International Terminal now. Keep the adapter and the hankie. I've got millions of 'em." He zipped up the front of his jacket to within a few inches of his black turtleneck shirt. "Keep in touch."

"I don't know what to say."

He patted my shoulder. "You'll be okay. Godspeed."

I watched the back of Katzen's leather jacket until it mingled into a collage of hoodies, business suits and London Fog overcoats.

Chapter Fifty-Six

Decision Time

When I sat down again, I could think with a clear head, at last. So I was right; Katzen's gut feeling matched mine. I hadn't imagined a problem at all. Maybe I did have one; maybe I didn't. The only decision I had to make was whether to return home right away or head to Wales to clean out the cottage.

My thoughts went back to that bad decision I made once, the one that still haunted me — a mistake based on my lack of critical information. For reasons of his own, Richard had kept his cancer diagnosis from me for nearly three months, during which time his behavior changed drastically. He was more distant than ever and often not in the office when I called. Most nights he claimed to be working even later than usual.

I was convinced my husband was having an affair. I watched General Hospital religiously, after all, and Richard showed all the signs. Andie was 14 at the time and busy every evening with her friends or with homework or whatever. I was 32, lonely and feeling unloved. I didn't like the way life was treating me at all.

I'd show him; I'd have my own affair. I chose a man named Luke from my weekly book club, picked him out like he was a Godiva truffle in a gold foil box, and in no time I was faking orgasms on Monday and Wednesday evenings at The Budget Motel. It didn't take long for me to realize this wasn't the answer. I stopped the affair as abruptly as it had begun and apologized to Luke for using him, but he assured me I could use him anytime I wanted. That made me sick, and I never showed my face at the book club again.

In the end, I'd demanded an explanation from Richard. When he gave it to me, I hated myself for distrusting him. He said he was trying to protect me, but he should have had enough faith in me to be truthful. That fact, however, did not erase my guilt. I vowed never to speak of the affair to anyone.

Would I be able to trust Marten once he vindicated himself regarding this *Clifford-12* business? *Who cares if I'm acting on emotion alone? So what if I go straight home and it's a big mistake? It'll only cost me a day or two of travel time.* Oh, of course Marten would be upset that I didn't follow his plan, that I spent more money than necessary to reschedule the trip. But so what? He'd been upset about money before and he got over it. He could get over it again.

Yet, if I went directly to Wales and took care of business, threw out my intent to sightsee, like Katzen said, I could be home by tomorrow morning or early afternoon at the latest. That would be soon enough, wouldn't it? I was in no mood to act like a tourist, anyway, not with this craziness running rampant in my head. And as far as Marten's estate jewelry, it would stay in the bank lockbox, safe and sound, for now. Jewelry was the last thing on my mind. I transferred a few items from my roller bag into my carry-on, and stashed the larger bag in a locker and headed for the Hertz counter for a rental with GPS.

Chapter Fifty-Seven

Set to Go

Leonardo quietly removed the ladder from Frederick's hall closet and concentrated on the job at hand. Afterward, he stowed the ladder and called Roberts. "We're a go here. I've got visuals with audio inserted through two vents — her living room and her kitchen."

"What about the offices or bedrooms up there?" Roberts inquired. "We'll need those too."

"I can't get to them. This apartment is only about one-third the size of the one above it. I have no way to snake the wiring around. I think we're good with this."

"You're sure? You got recording capability?"

"Yes, I'm sure, and no, I can't record, but I'll be watching. I'll keep you informed of his every move."

Roberts laughed. "I'd give my right nut to have a picture of the look on Marten's face when I show up on the elevator with Chesley Regan Vanderhawk in a box. Puts me in the mind of Prince Albert in a Can." He laughed so loudly that Leonardo held the phone away from his ear.

"I'd like to see it, too." Leonardo said. "Use your smart phone if you can. What about the computer connection? Is it still good?"

"Hold on — I'll check on it now," Roberts said. When he returned to the phone, he said, "Yes, it's good. We're at eleven hours and counting. Stay put."

"Will do."

Leonardo filled the sink with hot suds and washed the dinner dishes he'd personally used. He dried them carefully with paper towels to remove fingerprints and put them in the cabinet, sliding his plate underneath a stack of others. He rinsed Frederick's dinner plate, glass and silverware and dropped them into the dishwasher. He thought it best not to leave evidence that Frederick had had company for his last supper. Frederick's silver tub-side bucket and wine bottle went back to where they had been kept. If all went as planned, there would be no indication that anyone had been in the apartment other than Frederick. At any rate, by the time any investigation might get underway, he'd be long gone to a place with no extradition treaty with the U.S. or Great Britain.

He went into the half bath to relieve himself, thankful that his dead lover had more than one lavatory so he wouldn't have to use the other one. Frederick was an innocent bystander — it happened sometimes. The one who got in the way, Leonardo thought. *If Marten hadn't backed out, none of this would have been necessary. Dead Fred isn't my fault.*

He packed his briefcase and swept up tidbits of dust that had fallen from the vents onto the hardwood floor as he'd worked. He adjusted the tiny cameras on the other end and watched for a while to see what was going on upstairs. It was dark up there. He assumed the boy to be in bed asleep and Marten would be in Julia's office where he belonged, keeping the Trojan link functional. In any case, Marten's new wife was far away and out of the picture. Leonardo said a silent *thank you* to Marten for making that happen — doing what he'd promised.

With nothing left on his agenda until early tomorrow morning, Leonardo wanted to find some action to soothe his nervous energy, but he couldn't risk being seen going in or out of Frederick's apartment now. He'd have to content himself with the knowledge that all of his efforts were about to pay off. He selected a book from Frederick's library wall and he settled into a cozy recliner for the night.

Chapter Fifty-Eight

The Day

Today Perry Roberts' silks are blue and gold and his ride is the favorite for this race. He weighs in, mounts up, and prances toward the track, head held high. He feels not only the warmth of the sun on his back, but the adoration of the cheering crowd as they focus on him through their binoculars.

At the starting gate, the bells ring and the gates swing open in unison. His horse bolts onto the track with purpose. The pounding hooves thunder on the arid dirt track, intoxicating the jockey. He closes in easily on the lead. Finish line in sight, Roberts knows victory is his.

The horse stumbles, throwing Roberts forward, and he watches helplessly as his steed crashes on top of him. Frenzied is the pack coming from behind. Some go around while others fall on the heap of human and horse flesh. Perry Roberts cannot feel his legs.

At 4:00 a.m., Perry Roberts woke up in a sweat. He'd had similar dreams, but this one was so vivid, he thought it was the real thing. He had positioned himself in the tight ceiling space just before midnight. There was barely enough room to turn over. Only a very small man or child could fit in here. He had been dozing fitfully and his legs had gone to sleep.

He had given himself an enema last night, reminding him of his jockey days. But this time he hadn't done it for weight loss; there was no provision here on the roof of the Arneson Theater for bowel activity. He felt around for the small, plastic flask in his backpack, removed the lid and pissed in it. He put it back into his pack; he wanted no obvious DNA left behind. Of course the investigators would probably find a hair or a fleck of skin, but he didn't want to make it easy for them.

Undoubtedly they would be the FBI, since a kidnapping would have taken place, as well as Interpol. No worries. He planned to be far away from Texas by the time they figured out his identity. Six more hours until curtain time.

Chapter Fifty-Nine

Coming Home

I hoped to board as stand-by on a redeye flight home; while I waited, I noticed the date on my ticket. I inquired at the counter, where the agent explained it was the purchase date of the flight. I'd had very little sleep, so I counted on my fingers for accuracy. Marten had purchased my ticket two weeks ago! And yet, I'd heard him on the telephone less than two days ago making the reservation. To whom had he been speaking — a time and weather recording? Was it possible he wanted me out of the country on this *specific* day? He must have, and I couldn't help but think it had something to do with Sophia Vanderhawk. I'd been suspicious ever since he disappeared the same day she arrived in our condo. I'd told Dana that I didn't ask Marten about it, but I did. In fact, I'd been aggressive about it to the point where we argued for an hour. He finally admitted he'd known her when they were young, that she wouldn't recognize him now, and that the memories were extremely painful for him. That's all he would say about it, except that it would be best for me to "leave it alone". Afterwards, we walked to Boudro's and he gave me his speech about the importance of my coming here. So here I am.

It made no sense, nor did the fact that the cottage in Wales had been full of furniture, wooden shutters and linen drapes at the windows, and not a cardboard box to be found, packed or empty. It did not appear to me that anyone had prepared the cottage to be sold, no "For Sale" sign in the window — none in the yard. There were no papers to be signed in the top desk drawer. I'd tried repeatedly to call Marten but couldn't get a signal. The only thing he had described with any accuracy at all was the ornate cherry trunk.

I'd emptied the chest, one quilt at a time. The trunk was unlike any I'd ever seen in antique shops in America, and its construction suggested a custom, one-of-a-kind piece. I carefully turned it upside down looking for a maker's mark. That's how I discovered a small hidden drawer underneath. In it was a leather packet containing several pages from an old journal or diary, likely Adelina's, four old photographs, and three letters addressed to "Dearest Adelina" that were held together with a faded yellow ribbon. I sat on the floor cross-legged to study the pictures. Three of them were of Marten as a child with his mother and, in the other, a man was holding up a toddler, presumably Marten. I thought the man looked vaguely familiar; yes, in fact, he resembled Duke Vanderhawk. But why would he be holding baby Marten up in the air? Had Marten's mother known the Vanderhawk family? That would explain how Marten and Sophia had known each other. But who was *Marshall Edmond Wellman?* It was written on the back of the photo, but had Marten's birth date written next to it.

Marten had lied to me; there was no other way to look at it. He owed me an explanation, and I wasn't about to wait another day for it, nor was I going to ask for it over the phone. I wanted clarification now, and now was when I was going to get it. I refolded the quilts and placed them all back into the trunk, with the exception of one small blue and white nursery coverlet. Marten had said it was his favorite. I would give it to Boone, or maybe Nina would like it for Sammy. One thing I was certain of, Marten would never get his precious little baby quilt from me. He didn't deserve it. He'd sent me across the ocean on this ridiculous escapade for his own secretive reasons. I would never trust him again.

I tucked the leather packet into the zippered compartment of my laptop case, wheeled it out to the rental, fastened my seat belt, and took off like a Nascar driver out of Pit Road.

Chapter Sixty

The Day Continued

Leonardo had obtained and set up tiny disguised cameras in strategic locations in and outside of the theater that relayed real-time images wirelessly to Roberts' cell phone. He had worked with Eduardo to check the efficiency of the installation.

At 7:00 a.m., through an antennae device Perry Roberts had inserted into a small hole he'd drilled into the false roof, he saw the sun shining brilliantly. *What a great day for a tragedy*. Directly below, inside the small theater, a crew mopped the concrete floor and set up for the presentation. Three hours until show time. He watched the monitor and felt relief when the workers brought in several small chairs for the children to use while they waited to go out on stage. He had hoped they wouldn't be standing for two reasons. It would make too much noise when 20 kids and two bodyguards fell to the floor. Of even more importance, he wanted to avoid injuring Chesley. Not that he cared about his welfare. As a matter of fact, he would like nothing better than to end the life of Sophia's little heir apparent. It was crucial, however, that he nab him alive and keep him well. Leonardo Newman's positioning would ensure that. In fact, Newman had become much more valuable than Marten would've been. Roberts smiled inwardly with satisfaction, knowing that Marten believed himself to be entirely in the clear. *No, nephew. You have a large part yet to play.*

He fingered the monitor to display the outside stage area. Several big shots were there already, rehearsing their speeches. Across the river on the grass-covered steps, a few tourists were gathered. Little did they know they were about to get more than their money's worth. The price of admission to this performance had been $100, or so he'd heard. *Small price to pay for a show like this one.* Perry Roberts smiled to himself. Did he feel cocky? Just a tad. But he reassured himself it was well deserved. People would be bidding hundreds of dollars in online auctions for those used ticket stubs tomorrow.

He opened up another flask, and tipped it up all the way. *Scotch in the morning to you, Perry Roberts, ole boy!* Like one of Pavlov's dogs, he expected to hear Marten berating him for mixing alcohol with such an important project. Evidently Marten didn't get it. Roberts couldn't make it through one day if it didn't begin with booze. Although he preferred it on the rocks, this would have to do. And Marten was *almost* out of the picture, anyway.

~*~

9:00 a.m. Security wasn't nearly as tight as Roberts had expected. If the American President were here, the sky would be full of helicopters, the ground covered with uniformed officers, and dogs with better sniffing abilities than any human would be on patrol. Maybe Sophia had called them off; he should have expected that of her. The Riverwalk hadn't even been closed to sightseers, but the only barge floats on the river were now loaded with blue uniforms.

Arneson Theater buzzed. The waiting room was full now, just as planned. *Thank you, Julia Tyler, for your connections.* Roberts spied a little Asian boy tugging on a guard's coat. The kid was grasping the crotch of his pants. One guard looked at his watch and leaned over and said something to the other. He took the boy by the hand and led him toward the bathroom. Roberts thought of offering the boy his little bottle, but he saw that he had virtually filled it up already, what with all that Scotch whiskey he was consuming. He figured he could piss in the now-empty flask if he had to. *Do kids pee their pants when they're unconscious?* He doubted it, and figured it was probably like being asleep. Then, he chuckled. *Kids wet the bed, don't they?*

Roberts came back around to his mission of the day. He studied the face of Chesley Regan Vanderhawk. Lady Sophia was leaning over him, straightening his vest. Roberts had not been this close to a Vanderhawk for nearly 30 years — only a ceiling away, now. *A ceiling that will soon crumble.*

The boy seemed like a nice enough kid. Even on local television interviews he had come across as intelligent and caring. He'd grow up to be a snob eventually, though, just like the rest of 'em. Plus, if he had any of his mother in him, God help him. There was one hell of a sneaky bitch under the cool facade of that woman. He eyed her momentarily, pleased that her world of comfort was about to come to an end, just as his had done so many years ago.

In just over one hour, when Sophia had gone out onto the stage, he would infuse a sleeping gas into the room, quickly rendering the occupants unconscious. He patted his sidearm which he would use if the gas didn't work fast enough on the adults. *This is going to happen today, one way or the other.*

Chapter Sixty-One

London to USA

On the flight to San Antonio, the couple in front of me occupied themselves with prolonged tongue kisses. I saw them through the space between their seats, and I would have appreciated it if I hadn't been so mad at my so-called "husband." I noticed a solitary diamond on the woman's left hand. *They must be newly engaged. They sure as hell aren't married.* I pulled out the leather portfolio and studied the four pictures again, plus the old diary pages which were dated over three decades ago. I shuffled through them and I wondered if someone had been in the process of writing a crime novel about a child being pushed down the stairs.

When the plane landed, the couple in front of me was still going at it.

In the main terminal, the colorful red, yellow and blue ceramic tiles on the floors and walls, and the waft of refried beans and warming tortillas offered me welcome relief. It seemed like ages since I had been there, not just a mere 30 hours or so.

An older woman, presumably the male passenger's mother, met the kissers at baggage claim; she hugged the guy and then stood back and extended her hand toward the woman. She quickly looked her up and down and said, "It's so nice to meet you. Did you have a good flight?" I knew good and well what the mother was thinking: "How many children do you want and is there any history of mental illness in your family?" At least that's what had crossed my mind, albeit briefly, about Britt Waterman. But Britt and Andie's future was no longer my concern. I should've asked more questions of my new husband's family history — *before* I married him. But, I suspected now he wouldn't have told me the truth.

Chapter Sixty-Two

The Day, Concluded

10:00 a.m. The program began right on schedule with music from the Scottish Pipe and Drum Band. At 10:30, Sophia made her way out onto the balcony, and Roberts watched her waving enthusiastically to the roaring crowd. In all probability, she likened herself to the Pope.

"Good morning, everyone," Sophia purred into the microphone. The crowd cheered and clapped. "It's such an honor for me, and for Chesley, too, to be here with you good folks in San Antonio, Texas." The southwestern audience roared ever louder.

Roberts snickered. *Honor?* He'd never known *honor* to be a part of Sophia's personality back in the old days. And he didn't believe for a minute that she'd changed.

Fourteen minutes to go. He donned his gas mask, pulled a small cylinder from his back pack, stuck it through a tiny hole in the roof's floor and turned the knob wide open.

Sophia's speech continued. "As you know, we've traveled the whole world over, uniting children of all races, from all walks of life — for the purpose of bringing peace to our planet."

Roberts snorted. *Peace on Earth, my ass.* He watched everyone in the room below close their eyes and slump in their chairs. One guard had been standing, and he fell onto a group of children, a silent, slow-motion descent.

Roberts used a small hand drill to make six strategically located holes. Working undercover of moonless nights, he'd worked with Eduardo to compromise the old roof to a large extent during the past two weeks, leaving only a small area of adobe brick. He now used his strength to push until a two-foot square of the aging plaster roof fell to the floor. He lowered himself into the room through the opening along with two large flattened packing boxes and a roll of shipping tape he'd hidden in the small area. He opened his backpack and removed a tan shirt and shorts with an embroidered patch reading *All Brand Computer Repair,* Olga's handiwork. He put the boxes together, one on top of the other, with the top box open into the bottom one. After Roberts had assured himself they appeared to be two separate boxes, he placed Chesley into them. He tossed his backpack in with the boy, sealing the contraption with tape. He strode to the rear door.

~*~

Olga pulled a white delivery van up to the curb in front of the former Water Company building. The sides wore removable *All Brand Computer Repair* logos. She slid off the driver's seat and opened the side door, grasping a metal dolly. She pushed the two-wheel cart up onto the sidewalk and around the back of the old Water Company, down the little pathway toward the Arneson Theater. Checking her timepiece, she smiled smugly to herself.

Perry Roberts, my hero, Olga thought, as he stepped into the narrow passageway between the two stucco theater buildings. He nodded in a businesslike manner. Oh, how sexy he looked in a delivery uniform. Roberts lifted what appeared to be two boxes, stacked vertically, onto Olga's cart, handing her a wad of bogus paperwork, just in case someone happened to be watching. She signed and ripped off the top copy and handed it back to him. He shoved it into the front pocket of his shirt and winked at Olga. Even that aroused her. *Soon*, she thought. She turned around and carefully wheeled the cart, confident that Roberts was ogling her back side. She gave it an extra wiggle, traveling back down the pathway. She slid the boxes into the van's cargo hold at the side door, collapsed and replaced the dolly, then hopped into the driver's seat.

Roberts had taken the opposite route, circled the Water Company, and ended up on the other side of the van at the same time as she. He pulled their precious cargo across the back and removed it from the truck, sliding it once again onto the two-wheel cart, now on the street-side of the vehicle. Anyone who might chance to notice would see what appeared to be a normal delivery at the driver's side of the truck. And the passenger side would provide another, yet completely different, view of something innocent-looking, nothing to remember in fact, if anyone was watching. Olga moved toward the passenger side, and out the door, while Roberts jumped up into the driver's seat. Olga pushed the dolly across the street and into the parking garage.

She glanced sideways, watching Roberts pull into traffic. He would park the van a few blocks away and remove his uniform to reveal cargo shorts and a yellow San Antonio tee shirt. So far, so good, thought Olga. Roberts would then take a leisurely walk up Commerce Street and punch in a code at the entrance to The Clifford Building. He would appear to be no one special, merely a resident of one of the luxurious apartments within.

Olga wheeled the dolly up the parking garage ramp to the second level to where Eduardo had parked a black SUV with dark tinted windows the night before. He'd disabled a security camera pointed in the direction of the vehicle. Olga removed her long-haired wig and a taut, tan shirt, under which she wore a green-striped peasant top. She lifted the box directly into the hatchback of the SUV and drove down the ramp. She pulled the elastic edge of her peasant top down low on her shoulders, exposing considerable cleavage, and paid her parking fare. She wanted the man to remember her tits, not her face, and she could see by watching his eyes that he would. She turned left on Presa, left on Alamo and left again on Commerce, landing right in front of The Clifford Building. Olga switched on her flashers, pulled into the delivery space and wheeled her valuable container through the front door.

In the lobby, Roberts stood beside the elevator. He entered the security code on the password bypass device planted by Marten on the night of the Open House. "I've waited a long, long time to see for myself the actual interior of Ms. Tyler's place . . . or, *excuse* me, Julia and Marten's condo." He laughed like a madman, loud and long. Olga had heard him laugh that way a few times and it always reminded her of the Phantom of the Opera. She liked listening to the soundtrack of the Broadway play, but Roberts's laugh gave her shivers.

However, just as with the Phantom's story, there was no turning back. They arrived with their delivery right in the middle of their targeted destination.

Chapter Sixty-Three

The Exchange

Marten had a full day of fun planned with Boone, but the boy had begged to sleep in, "just a little longer," so Marten headed to the kitchen, clattering around making breakfast. Soon, Boone caught the aroma of chocolate chip pancakes and he bounced out of bed. They had packed a bag with swimming gear, towels, and dry clothes the night before. After breakfast, they remained seated, perusing Schlitterbahn brochures.

Marten heard a sinister and way-too-familiar sound, the shrill laugh of his uncle somewhere in the distance. He checked the clock in the kitchen, and his heart rate quickened. He'd meant to be gone long before now.

The elevator launched and Boone said, "Is it Gran? Back from London?"

"No, son. Going from Texas to Europe is more than a day trip." Marten was thankful Julia was out of the country. "Maybe it's the tour van I called to take us to the water park in New Braunfels." *But, they didn't use the call button*, Marten thought. *The password bypass!* He had to act fast. But do what, exactly? He'd stored a handgun in his locked suitcase, but was there enough time to run and get it? Marten was halfway out of his chair when the elevator opened to reveal a short, heavy-set Hispanic woman with a push-cart containing two Dell Computer boxes, one on top of the other. She grunted as she pushed the cart into the condo. Behind her stood Roberts — a gun in his hand — pointed directly at Boone. Marten jumped up, knocking his chair over, and stepped toward Boone in an effort to shield him. Boone cried out, went quiet and looked up at Marten with a trusting face — as though he fully expected Marten to do something about this invasion.

Roberts kept his weapon aimed at Boone. "Don't even think about doing anything foolish, Marten."

Marten stared at the gun. "Foolish seems to be your department, from what I can see. What are you doing here?"

Roberts tilted his head toward the woman, and she reached into her pocket, pulled out a plastic bag with a damp cloth, and placed the cloth securely over Boone's nose.

"What in bloody hell?" Marten rushed Roberts, who turned the gun on him, now.

"Now, now. Surely you didn't think it would be that easy, did you? You walked away like a cold virgin from her lover, already aroused by her flirtations with no turning back possible. You, my nephew, deserve much worse than this, in my opinion."

"*This?* What *is* this? I haven't done anything to ask for trouble."

"Ah, but I have to assure myself that you'll keep quiet throughout this ordeal. Your new little grandson here will be my insurance policy until this day is over."

"Why are you doing this? And how did you know he was here?" Marten's thoughts spun out of control.

"I have ways of knowing things; you know that . . . and I just told you why — insurance. The kid won't get hurt as long as you keep your bloody mouth shut."

Marten watched in horror as the woman pulled a box cutter from the rear pocket of her shorts. With a sadistic look in her eyes, she winked, then turned to the box and swiftly slid the razor-sharp edge at the top where it was taped shut, opened it and removed a limp Chesley. She laid him on the floor. Marten grabbed the back of a chair and collapsed into the seat. *They've gone and done it! And this is the safe place they chose? Oh my God!* He told himself to think — think of something — but what? The woman folded Boone's body, as limp as the English boy's, and lowered him into the box.

Marten shouted, "No! You can't do this! Why don't you leave them both here until this is over?" But, now, the container was back on the two-wheel cart and the woman went straight for the elevator. Chesley lay lifeless on the floor as the lift disappeared from view.

Roberts held out a plastic grocery bag. "Open it."

Marten found a handwritten note, but he was shaking too hard to read it. A syringe was also in the bag.

"Remain calm," Roberts said. "Our subject, here, is heavily sedated, but in no danger, same as your new grandson," Roberts advised. "Make sure you keep this boy just like he is. Your instructions are in there. Read 'em." He stepped slowly backward toward the elevator. "I'll keep in touch."

"Wait! What do you want from me? I don't understand," Marten pleaded.

"Read your instructions. I'll call you within 15 minutes. This will all be over soon. No funny business, you hear me?"

"*You're* pulling the funny business. I gave you my word I wouldn't interfere with your plans!"

"Yeah, well your word is all but worthless, as I know well. Listen, mate, this is what it looks like. Our caper had you in it all the way. You were committed. Hell! You even paid for it all. But then you changed your mind like some silly schoolgirl — you walked out on me, last minute. I refuse to take chances. Things are going to get real intense around here, you know, house-to-house searches and all that rot. You'd fold in a heartbeat, Marten. I know you'd turn me in."

"What am I supposed to do with this kid if there *is* a house-to-house search?"

"Use your imagination. If he gets discovered before the ransom is transferred, the little Boone-boy gets it. Sorry, mate. Like I said the day you walked out of this caper, if blood is to be spilled, it will be on your hands."

Olga had sent the elevator up; Roberts backed into it and he was gone.

~*~

In the lobby, Roberts made final adjustments to the elevator. *If anyone wants to get up to the sixth floor, they'll have to hoof it all the way.* He checked his timepiece and peered out the glass through the front door. Olga's SUV was gone with Boone in it. No frenzied police, no screaming tourists — a good sign — the kidnapping hadn't been discovered. *Thank*

God for our long-winded Sophia. Perry Roberts stepped casually out onto the sidewalk, hands in his pockets, whistling like an everyday person on Commerce Street. He checked his watch again. Ten minutes had passed since she'd gone onto the stage. Four minutes to spare. Perfect. This was one of the moments he'd anticipated when he'd checked to make sure the wireless signal reached from the theater to Commerce Street. He pulled his cell phone from his pocket and watched Sophia at the theater.

He walked down Commerce toward Presa. When he arrived at the entrance to the soon-to-be ill-famed clinic, he stood perfectly still, one ear cocked. In the distance, Lady Sophia's voice carried on the breeze, winding down her 14-minute speech.

"Allow me to introduce my son, Chesley Regan Vanderhawk."

Quiet.

She repeated the introduction.

Nothing.

By God, we've done it! Roberts zeroed in and took a screen shot of Sophia's alarmed face. He slid the phone into his pocket, closed the door behind him and turned the deadbolt. "Olga!" He shouted, up toward the loft. "Here I come. Get your sexy self ready!"

Eduardo Gonzales stood at the bathroom doorway, staring furiously at Roberts with piercing, cold eyes. "$50,000 is not enough."

"I owe you an apology, Amigo. I thought you'd already taken off."

"I am here, waiting for my money," Eduardo said, "like you told me to."

"Of course you are, as am I. As far as what work you've done for me, and what I owe you for this, I comprehend." Roberts nodded. "You're right. You've worked hard and you deserve more. How about we raise it up to one million?"

Eduardo considered the offer, and said, "Two million and you keep the whore."

Roberts pasted a condescending smile on his face. "You've got it, my amigo." *Small price to pay for Olga, considering Eduardo might never see a penny of it.*

Chapter Sixty-Four

Home Sweet Misery

My suitcase was among the first off the plane. I grabbed it and hailed a cab, which would get me home faster than my Jeep. There would be no way to get my car into the parking garage, anyway, since this was the morning of Lady Sophia's appearance at the Arneson Theatre. The car-parks had probably filled up by seven o'clock that morning, if not the night before. Plus, this way my Jeep could simply remain at the airport for later in the day, in case I found it necessary to return, tail between my legs, for the next flight out to London. That would only be if I was wrong about Marten. But I didn't believe for a second I was wrong. He was up to no good.

The police had closed off several streets; the taxi driver cursed and complained, said he couldn't get any closer than two blocks from my building. I didn't argue with him. I walked the remainder of the way. Once in the lobby, I found the elevator door wide open. *Odd.* I pushed the button . . . and waited. I tried the public elevator, and it was out of order too. *Not again.* Of course there would be no point using my cell phone to call Andie to order the elevator up from the condo because she was in Dallas. And Marten would already be gone with Boone to the water park. *As usual, I have to do everything myself around here.*

I climbed the stairs to the second floor with my luggage trailing behind, and used my key to let myself into Doc's office. I was thankful I'd had the foresight to take my keys along, rather than depending on the elevator to be operational. I slid my suitcase out of the way behind a large elephant ear palm in the waiting room.

I cradled my laptop case as I climbed to the sixth floor and unlocked the door to my laundry room. Laundry baskets of clean clothes (obviously abandoned by Andie) were pushed up against the rear door, but it eventually slid open just enough for me to slip in.

I leaned on the folding counter in the laundry room, stood quietly, and took some time to catch my breath. I thought about calling the elevator company — maybe they could make an emergency run — but, no, they couldn't possibly get access to the building today. I was so tired, but relieved to be in my own home — my nest. I picked up a towel — soft, white, Egyptian cotton, oversized — and held it to my face. Inhaling the scent, I tried to figure out how I would approach Marten on my issues with him when he arrived home. Maybe I'd have time to contact Josh Katzen to help me find anything suspicious in my computer.

From the adjacent room, I heard a hinge squeak, although that wasn't possible. Or was it? Everyone had the day off. I snuck a peek into the hallway. Marten was backing out of Boone's room, closing the door behind him. In his hand, he held a syringe!

Boone! What was Marten doing to him? I took one step back and held my breath. Should I run to Marten for an explanation? No, I would think this out. I glanced out again. Marten was headed down the hall toward the living area.

I crept into Boone's room and pulled back the covers from his still, little body, but it wasn't Boone at all; it was Chesley Regan Vanderhawk!

Chapter Sixty-Five

Marten's Dilemma

After Marten heard the elevator stop, he'd placed one ear against its brass housing. Sounds of Roberts, dismantling the mechanism, echoed up from the lobby. *How naïve I am,* he thought. He'd never suspected his uncle would resort to a switch. Even so, he should have made sure Boone was out of danger, as well as Julia. Perry Roberts had covered all the bases — what an achievement. And, Marten had to admit, he was probably right. Marten *would* have found it difficult to keep quiet, or at least act natural, if the police were to pound on his door, asking questions of everyone along the Riverwalk. If they showed up anytime soon, he would appear complicit, exactly what his uncle was aiming for!

Just the fact that he had married Julia and moved into this condo put them in danger, hadn't it? Well . . . now what was he going to do? Hope and pray this would end soon, that's what. And thank God Julia was halfway across the globe by now. *Maybe it's possible she'll never have to know. I have to think of something!* However, the more he thought, the more he realized that, now that Boone was involved, his hopes to keep Julia in the dark were null and void.

Marten headed for Chesley, knelt down and placed his hand on the boy's chest. His breathing was slow, but regular. Marten scooped him up and carried him to Boone's room. Satisfied that the boy was resting comfortably, he let himself out of Boone's room, closing the door behind him. He walked slowly back up the hallway into Julia's office with the intention of removing all traces of the now unnecessary Trojan. However, his brain was too stunned to concentrate and his fingers shook so badly he couldn't accomplish the task. It would have to wait. He left the syringe on Julia's desk and headed for the living room, sat on the sofa, head in his hands. With his cell phone beside him, he watched it, willed it to ring. He had to hear Boone's voice, to know he was okay, alive.

From out of nowhere, Julia burst into the room. "Where's Boone? What have you done with my grandson? And why is Chesley in Boone's bed?"

Chapter Sixty-Six

The Truth - Finally

Marten gasped. He paled and grabbed his chest.

"Don't you even *think* about dying on me," I snarled.

"What . . . why are you here?"

"Here are the rules: *I* ask the questions — *you* answer. Now, exactly what situation is it, *Marshall Edmond Wellman,*" I demanded, "that *you've* gotten *us* into?"

"Chesley was kidnapped," Marten blurted out. He evidently could see no other way than to just go ahead and get right into it, and good for him because I'd traveled back five thousand miles to get to the truth. "They brought him here for safekeeping, but they snatched Boone as security — so I wouldn't, or couldn't, go to the authorities. In a nutshell, we're trapped until the ransom is paid."

"Boone was taken?" I felt the blood drain from my head. I swallowed hard and sat on the opposite end of the sofa.

Marten held up an index finger and placed it over his lips. He reached for a newspaper and scribbled in the top margin. He tore off the corner and handed it to me. *"Be aware! We might be monitored; it could be video or only audio. They may be watching our every move. Trust, me, I know how these people work."*

These people? Trust you? I made a fist, crumpling the pathetic note into a tiny ball. Just like Richard, I thought; he could only put his ideas on paper. Oh, no. Couldn't say it right out loud. Men . . . such cowards . . . all of them. I glared at him. I scarcely opened my mouth and words tumbled out. "I can honestly say I hate you."

"That's exactly why I wanted you on another continent today."

"Oh. I see. You sent me away because *you* were up to no good?"

"Not *me* — I got out of it weeks ago, you must believe me, Jules. I tried to tell you. But I was fearful of what they might do to you as a consequence of my exit. I never once expected this complication with Boone. He wasn't even supposed to be here, you know."

I vigorously shook my head, not because I knew where, exactly, Boone was supposed to have been, but because of my confusion over what was actually happening. *Complication* with Boone? All neat and compact, his label, *"complication"* and I resented that he'd made it seem so insignificant, so inconsequential. "Since you seem to know everything about what's going on, why don't you come clean and tell me all about it?"

Marten frowned and wet his lips. "It started so very long ago. I hardly know where to begin."

"Just spit it out!"

Marten sighed. "Frankly," he said, "I had hoped the day would never come when I would have to tell you the truth about myself."

"About yourself? So, you've been lying to me since the day we met." I nodded repeatedly, finally understanding what it meant to get your head wrapped around something. All of those red flags I'd ignored since January actually meant something. *If only I'd paid attention to my gut.*

Marten stared at his shoes for what seemed an eternity.

"Haven't you?" I demanded. "Answer me!"

Marten slowly met my gaze, his eyelids lowered somewhat, like a man formulating a plan — what to say next so he wouldn't look so bad — as bad as he really was. He said, "Listen . . . I'm sure Boone will be released unharmed. Once the ransom is paid, it shouldn't take long."

I was skeptical of his kidnapping explanation, although the wailing of multiple police sirens down on Commerce Street was hard to ignore. "If both boys have been abducted, then why isn't it on the news?" I walked to the window and looked down on the Riverwalk. People were running every which way, and a helicopter had just come into view above the tree line.

"You have impeccable timing, Julia. It all went down just moments ago." He reached for the remote control. CNN flashed up on the screen with a crawl running along the bottom. "You understand, don't you, that no one knows about Boone yet? It's Chesley they'll be searching for."

"Well . . . that's easy," I screamed. "He's right here under our noses!"

"Yes, but calm down. If we go public with that, Jules, Boone will be killed, don't you see?"

Reality finally bored into my brain. I slid down onto the hardwood floor like a rag doll. *Stop this ride; I want to get off.* My carousel was spinning way too fast. Have you ever felt a sensation in your brain where you close your eyes tight, tighter now, your brain spins around so fast and you finally open your eyes because you're afraid what will happen to you if you don't? Information overload, I called it.

Marten reached for me. I pushed him away.

"The old plan was that no one would be hurt." Marten offered in a soft, whiny voice, probably recognizing only after he said it that it was a moot point.

"How green are you, Marten? This thing is huge! How many people are dead already? We have no idea, do we? Start at the beginning and don't leave out one sordid detail. But before you do that, you've got to know — whatever they do to Boone, *you'll* pay for. Personally."

"I know you want revenge, Jules, and no one understands that better than I, believe me."

I closed my eyes and pushed a loud, hefty sigh from my lungs. "Oh, please, believe *you*? And stop calling me Jules. You've lost the privilege."

Marten splayed the fingers of both hands — conceding defeat. "Actually, this all started out of a need for revenge, a sick, dark, smoldering need. And it started long before you and I ever met."

I pinched the bridge of my nose, thought of my jungle bedroom with its leopard-print comforter and how nice it would be to take a nap — to escape. Jet lag was not a pretty thing. Maybe this would all go away if I slept a while.

The words from Marten's mouth came rapidly, sounding like the thin buzz of a mosquito. I held my hand up, palm facing him. "Time out. First, tell me this."

I ran to the laundry room and retrieved my laptop case. My hands shook uncontrollably, but I managed to hold the photo of Duke Vanderhawk and little Marten in front of his face.

"My father," Marten said.

"Your *father?*"

I turned the photo around where the name *Marshall Edmond Wellman* was written. "If Duke Vanderhawk is your father, why did you tell me both of your parents were dead?"

Marten shrugged one shoulder, like there was nothing to tell.

"What other lies have you told?"

He leaned his head back on the edge of the sofa for a moment, tilted it forward, resting his chin on his chest. He inhaled, and then exhaled, resolved. "Too many. Far too many lies." He looked into my eyes. "My mother was the nanny for Lady Sophia and then for her baby brother, Chesley Basil. When Basil died, my mother was let go because she wouldn't tell them everything she knew. And they were convinced she was withholding valuable information."

"Was she?"

"Well, yes . . . she was protecting her son."

"You? Who, or what, exactly, was she protecting you from?"

"It appears . . . that is, well, the fact is . . . I killed my half-brother, Basil. Apparently, I pushed him down a long flight of stairs. But, I don't have any tangible or solid memory of this — I was only four years old. I do have dreams, though, lots of them. I guess I remember it only in my dreams." He slowly shook his head, then added, "Mum had my name changed after that."

I tossed a sofa pillow onto the floor and sat on it, rocking back and forth. Still shaking, I held onto the photo and leaned against my laptop case. Even though it seemed crazy, I grasped the implication of it. First off, the Vanderhawk family had an unusual affection for the given name of Chesley, and secondly, I suspected that Sophia named her own son after her dead brother out of guilt — she'd caused his death and then lied about it.

"Marten," I said softly. "You didn't push the baby down the stairs."

Marten glared at me. "Sophia told mum I did."

"That was a lie, Marten. *She* was the one who was responsible." I handed him the diary pages that I'd read on the plane. "I skimmed over these on my flight home, and I assumed they belonged to your mother. But now I'm sure they were written by a teenaged Sophia."

After he'd carefully studied them twice, he appeared to have a real memory of that day. He returned to the journal and read aloud, "She wrote here: 'After we returned from our park outing, our nanny left me in charge of Marty and Basil so she could run to the loo. She wasn't gone long, but she'd left us on the top landing, waiting.'"

He looked to me for an answer to his mother's negligence, but I shook my head.

Marten excused her, "Well, I guess it was urgent, otherwise she wouldn't have left a six-year old girl in charge of two little boys."

I nodded my agreement. I'd already read it, of course, but it made sense to me now. I'd been too tired to pay attention to what little I'd read, but now I understood that what I'd determined to be someone's crude novel notes was essentially a true crime story told by Sophia, several years after the fact!

More animated now, Marten said, "I always held tight to my baby pillow because Basil thought it was his. He grabbed it away from me and I tried to get it back. That happened a lot. Sophia got mad and said, 'Oh, just let the whining little baby have it.' *She* snatched it from Basil and he lost his balance. I remember now! In my dreams, I capture my pillow from mid-air but I can't reach Basil. I hear a baby's cries for the longest time, and then I wake up. Yes, Basil screamed *forever* after he fell, it seemed to me. Sophia had gone to get Mum. When she soothed him, he stopped crying and Mum put him to bed. I didn't know Sophia had lied and said I pushed him. I think I must've blocked out the whole thing by morning when I found out he'd died during the night."

"I wonder when your mother realized the truth. And why she kept this valuable information hidden in a trunk with your photos."

"I doubt she knew it was there. We were moved from the mansion right after it happened. I'll never forget that day."

"But these pages were dated years after that. So how would they have reached your cottage in Wales?"

Marten rolled the facts over in his mind. "There is only one explanation: Mum's brother, my Uncle Perry." Marten clinched his fists and breathed heavily. "He's the one responsible for this kidnapping and he got me in on it because of my guilt. Damn him — he deceived me!"

"Hmm. So you, in turn, deceived me."

"Oh my God! Yes! All of this for nothing! I feel horrible for what I've done to you."

"Yeah, well," I snorted. "That doesn't change anything."

"I guess it doesn't, does it?"

Marten and I sat in contemplative silence, each with our own thoughts: Marten sifting through his past to reach the present, and me reeling from what I'd discovered so far. Not all of it made sense to me, and I recalled the conclusion I'd reached a long time ago after Richard died. *When a person tells me something that doesn't make sense, they are lying.*

"My uncle was a jockey for the Vanderhawk family," Marten said. "He was a sicko, a psychopath who hid in the stable loft to spy on people. He told me he'd seen Sophia in barn stalls writing in her diary *and* having a tryst or two with the handsome lads who worked in the yard. When he got canned, he came to live with us. Because of his notoriety, he had a nose job done to change his looks. He left the country after that, and we didn't hear from him for a long time. I'll bet he planted these pages there, but didn't tell his sister. He's sinister that way. It would've saved her so much misery."

"Or . . . maybe he did show her," I suggested. "She read them and tucked them away because she couldn't, or wouldn't, say anything to anyone because *she was liable* for leaving her charges alone, at the very least."

Marten's eyes narrowed, shooting daggers at me.

"It's just a theory, Marten."

"You're wrong. She would've told *me* the truth."

I thought about that; what would I have done? I'd kept Richard's suicide note hidden for years, so who was I to judge?

"Yes, she probably would have told you. This confession in writing from a young Sophia places you in the clear, Marten, and it will help you sort it all." I wondered if he would ever confront Sophia with it, or just let it go. That would be a decision he'd have to make, eventually.

The ashen look on Marten's face was replaced with red rage. "All of these years, the answer was there all along. My uncle owes me an explanation and when this is over I'm going to get one!"

I laughed. That had been my exact feeling yesterday in London.

"How can you laugh at a time like this?" Marten's disgust with my reaction caused me to laugh even louder. He had no idea what was coming next, but I explained it to him just the same.

I took a few deep breaths and I said, "It's the irony. I came directly home to demand an explanation from *you*. You left a computer file right here on this sofa you're sitting on, on the day we installed your business program. I copied it just in case we needed it, but I never thought about it again. During my layover at Heathrow, when I saw the details of my client list and The Clifford Building's design schematics, I knew something wasn't right. So here I am, demanding that explanation."

Marten retraced his steps from memory. I watched his eyes move quickly, from the sofa, to my office door, then to me, but he would not make eye contact. His face flushed again and tiny sweat beads popped up all over his forehead. He'd *known* he screwed up at the time, but up until this very moment he thought he'd gotten by with it.

"It's obvious, now," I said. "Your explanation is no longer necessary. The blueprints led you through the building and into my office. My client list — that's a huge clue. Riverwalk Protocol, Inc. allowed you to keep your finger on Sophia's movements while in San Antonio, right?"

Marten nodded, his head still bowed.

"But how did you get my client list?" I asked. "I thought my system was secure."

Marten would no longer hide behind his uncle; his resigned demeanor told me that. "My uncle used a guy named Leonardo Newman who has ways of finding stuff, information, to sell to other people."

"Other people — criminals like your uncle." Where had I heard that name, Leonardo Newman?

I stood and walked to the sofa. "Look," I said. "I'm glad you'll find resolution from your past, but nothing is solved in present time. My grandson is still missing, taken hostage by your uncle who you say is a psychopath, and Sophia's son is sleeping down the hall. If I hadn't found that disk, I'd be in London sightseeing right about now. What was *your* plan to save Boone?"

"I didn't need a plan to save him!" Marten yelled. "We were going to the water park for the day, but then he wanted pancakes, and . . . oh, God."

"Yeah, that's what I figured," I snarled. "It's a good thing I copied that file, then. Right?"

Marten cradled his head in his hands and sobbed.

Chapter Sixty-Seven

Rescue

My cell phone vibrated — Caller ID read SIMONE-HOME. "This waiting is driving me crazy," I said. "I'm going into my office to get my mind off it."

"They're monitoring your computer, you know." He cast me a pathetic look.

"Ya think?" I slammed my office door shut and locked it before answering the call in a whisper, "Simone?"

"Ms. Tyler? Gran? Boone's in a strange place."

Is this girl psychic? "What do you mean, Sweetie?" I methodically removed the files and books displayed above my workspace. Did Simone know what she was talking about? I detached two shelves from their hooks and I stacked them on my desk. Marten's syringe was there, and I slipped it into my cargo pants pocket.

"I was playing a computer game," Simone said, "and I got an instant message from him. He's been *kidnapped*, Gran. By a gang! He says he's in a big ole building with boards all over the windows and a weird painted design on the wall — the gang's *sign*!"

My heart literally skipped a beat. "Did he describe it?"

"A lizard in a triangle. He says they have a picture of it on the computer, so he sent it to his e-mail."

"Oh my God." I felt faint. If Boone had sneaked into their computer, what would happen to him if he got caught? Shivers ran down my spine. "Simone, why is he using their computer?"

"They're letting him play games to keep him quiet. They don't know he went online. There's three of them, and while the two men argue, the woman watches after Boone. She doesn't know much about computers, he said. And, uh . . . this doesn't make sense to me, Ms. Tyler. He says you would know what to do, but that you were in Europe, or something? He says for me to tell my dad, but he's at work."

Her father was Special Officer Reed Michaelson, and of course he'd be working today with this big event going on. I needed to find Reed immediately!

"Simone, I know exactly what to do. Give me your dad's cell phone number!"

She had to look it up, so I held on. I retrieved an unmarked key from my desk drawer and quietly opened the small doorway leading out into the outer hallway. I tiptoed over to the door that led to Boone's playroom and used the key to let myself in. We always kept the small hallway doors locked for safety. I pulled his birthday laptop from its case. While I waited for it to boot up, Simone returned with the number. I wrote it down twice, tore the paper in half, and stuck both pieces into another pocket of my cargo pants.

"Hold on Simone. I'm checking Boone's e-mail now." I crossed my fingers in hopes that Marten, or anyone else who might be listening, hadn't heard the sound of the dial-up connecting. No one knew about the additional phone line I had specifically installed for Boone's dial-up and very slow internet connection. Chalk one up for me!

When the message finally came through, sure enough, there was the design that I had seen in what was to have been Marten's clinic. I had the same satisfying feeling of victory whenever Boone and I finished one of his puzzles and the complete picture showed up. I now *knew* where my grandson was! *Oh my God! There never was a children's clinic, was there?*

"Simone, I'm going to call your father. Please stay right where you are in case I need to call you back, okay?"

I quietly opened the door from the play room into Boone's bedroom. I cradled little Chesley in my arms, wrapped in a blanket. He was sound asleep. I trusted that he was not dangerously sedated and hoped he would have no memory of this day. I knew Boone wouldn't be so lucky — he already knew he was in trouble. But if it was the last thing I ever did, I would make sure he lived through it — bad memories or not. I had to think fast, and, while I had always prided myself on being a problem solver, this was too much. *Think on your feet,* Richard used say to me. Funny that I'd remember what he'd said at a time like this.

I carried Chesley through the narrow back hallway and into my office. I laid him on the floor, and then I removed the remaining shelves and brackets on the wall above my workspace. I piled them on top of the books I'd already removed. I hoped the old dumbwaiter door would open without making a sound, but what were the odds? It hadn't been used for a long time. The dumbwaiter was the only way I could get that little child out of the condo and into a place where he could be rescued. I'd thought about my private lift which emptied directly into Dana's kitchen, but it wasn't working. And neither was the public elevator, so when I considered carrying him down the entire six floors of stairs, I knew the only way to get him into Dana's was to exit through the Clifford's front door, walk around the sidewalk, run down the outside stairs on the Riverwalk and go in through the restaurant. With Chesley's face all over the media, there was no way I could get by with it. People would think I was kidnapping, not rescuing him. I'd probably be arrested or shot, considering our Texan *open carry* law. Everyone had a gun but me. All I had was a BB gun. But I was a good shot, and I wondered if Dana kept a pistol in her kitchen. Then I remembered the small handgun in Marten's locked suitcase. He'd asked my permission to keep it in our closet when he moved in, which, at the time, I thought was respectful of him. *Thank you, Marten.*

I needed to know what part of the house Marten was in; I went to the kitchen and turned on the faucet, pretending to get a drink of water. I reached for the wooden block of kitchen knives, and slid my ultra sharp paring blade out. Marten hadn't moved from the sofa. His head was bowed, his shoulders shaking. *Good. Cry your eyes out.*

I increased the volume on the television. A house-to-house search was being conducted, the reporter said.

"I'm sorry, Julia," Marten said. Once again I thought of Richard, how he'd apologized only to make himself feel better.

"Don't talk to me." I went back into my office, again slammed the door and locked it. I thought, *here goes,* and I pried the dumbwaiter door open. It made an earsplitting squeal. Marten probably could've heard it.

Undaunted, I carried on. I gently folded little Chesley into the small space, shut the door, replaced the shelves and walked into the living area.

Marten squinted. He knew I was up to something. However, I wasn't into giving myself away at this point. How could I trust him anyway? He'd botched up everything already. I grabbed the newspaper and sat down next to Marten. I wrote in the margin: *I think I know where Boone is.* Marten's face turned the color of celery. "You *know*?" He whispered.

I have a good idea, I wrote on the paper.

"Where"?

"Where do *you* think?"

Marten lamely shook his head. "I honestly don't know. I've been blindsided by my uncle's actions, bringing Chesley in here and taking Boone. I never once dreamed he'd do this."

"You managed to get *me* out of the country. Now, tell me why you didn't do more to protect Boone!"

"I tried! We were eating and they came up the elevator out of the blue. They were between us and the bedroom. They had a gun on Boone — there was no way I could even run for it. A stocky Mexican woman grabbed him and put a wet cloth over his mouth. Then they put him in a box on a dolly and backed out as quickly as they came in." Marten was sobbing now.

"They? A stocky Mexican woman and who else? Your uncle, right?"

Marten's eyes told me the answer. He nodded.

"They'll sure as hell wish they'd never messed with me and my family, I promise you that."

~*~

I reached for Marten's hand and squeezed it. It was obvious that he'd thought he was protecting Boone by planning a trip to the water park. If they'd left on time, none of this would have happened to Boone. If his uncle had shown up here with Chesley, he wouldn't have had anyone to trade for him. That brought me to the thought that either Marten had given him the password, or had actually called the elevator up himself. I studied Marten's face. No. Why even ask him? I'd never get the truth from that man.

Marten said, "I need to check on Chesley."

I stood, "I'll do it; I have to use the bathroom, anyway." If anyone else was listening, I hoped they bought it. That would give me the two or three minutes more that I needed to get out, and keep Marten on the sofa, rather than checking on Chesley himself. The boy was currently safe in the dumbwaiter, but that was my secret for the moment.

I went into our bedroom and took care of the handgun issue, ran down the steps and beat on Frederick's door. When what I believed to be his shadow showed through the peephole, I said, "Frederick, it's Julia. I need help!" But he didn't open it. He probably had his lover in there and wanted privacy. At that moment, I remembered the business card Frederick had proudly showed me. *Leonardo Newman* was that tattoo guy! I wasn't the only one in trouble. Frederick was too — I just knew it.

I pulled my cell phone from my pocket and entered Reed Michaelson's number as I raced down the steps to The Stock Market. I'd tell him to get someone up here on the double to rescue Frederick.

Chapter Sixty-Eight

Plans Change

Leonardo Newman could hardly believe it when Julia appeared on the other side of Frederick's peephole. He'd been just as shocked as Marten when she had confronted him earlier. Leonardo watched the scene unfold as Julia listened to Marten's side of the story, and he'd kept Roberts informed throughout. The latest message he'd sent to Roberts was that she was finally resigned and compliant. They were confident she would play along to save her grandson. Perry Roberts had sung Leonardo's praises all morning long with the brilliance of his surveillance plan. However, Leonardo had no choice but to report *this* unexpected turn of events, and he was none too happy about having to do so.

Leonardo picked up his phone and told Roberts that Julia had knocked on Frederick's door. "She just now ran off, but she was on her cell. I couldn't see which way she went, but she looked determined."

"How the hell did that happen?"

"One minute they were together on the sofa, and then she went to check on the British boy. Wasn't two minutes till she was beating on this door down here!"

"Did she have the kid?"

"No, only her. The boy is still in the condo," Leonardo said, although he wasn't sure. She could've done something else with him when she was in her office. He recalled the peculiar floor plan of the sixth floor.

"Then she's going to cause this boy's death over here," Roberts said. "The bitch needs to be stopped — can you handle that from there? Wait! Hold on!"

Leonardo hadn't planned on this. They should've known the woman would be suspicious, but to think she would come back thousands of miles at a time like this was *never* considered. He'd watched her go through security at the airport on Friday, assuming she'd boarded. Now, he wasn't about to gun her down in plain sight. He wasn't a hired killer — Frederick was his first and last. Anyway, what could she do? Oh, hell. She could do a lot. For one, she could call the cops and tell them where Chesley was — to hell with her grandson. Was that who she'd called? No, she seemed smarter than that.

Roberts returned to the phone, "Listen, never mind about her. The transfer is coming through now. Is everything set from your end?"

"Yeah. I'm waiting."

"All right then. Leave everything — get out of there now. You've got to get to the SUV. I've begun the transfer into your account."

~*~

Perry Roberts had changed into a pair of casual slacks, a sports coat, and a casually knotted tie to disguise himself as a businessman during the escape. He would walk casually through Charles Court alone, but with Olga and Eduardo following close behind, looking like any other Mexican couple. They would cross the street into the parking garage to the SUV where Eduardo, after having changed the license plates, had parked it two spaces down from where it had been earlier that day, checking to verify the garage camera was still out of order. Leonardo was to be waiting and ready to go, inside the vehicle. After they left the downtown area, Roberts would give Leonardo the money transfer receipt and drop him off at the airport. (Roberts had insisted it was entirely too risky to fly today.) What they would do next would depend on Eduardo's attitude. However Eduardo chose to leave the picture, they would be rid of him, and Roberts would drive Olga two miles further to where he had a brand new luxury vehicle waiting for her. They would drive off into the sunset together. He'd bought a two-room rustic cabin in the heavily wooded mountains of Wyoming, and had stocked it with plenty of provisions, enough to last at least six months. After he was sure it was safe, they would leave the country for good. Their beach house awaited, where they would enjoy sunsets with tropical drinks on the deck and make love to the sound of the pounding surf.

Roberts looked down from his loft. Olga sat on the bottom step, ready to go, tightly holding Boone on her lap. Roberts directed a money transfer from one account into two others for Leonardo and himself. He'd set them up in preparation for this glorious day. Now, they'd actually pulled it off. The only thing he hadn't decided was how to get Eduardo Gonzales out of the picture without paying him *two million dollars*. He had transferred the money into a separate account, but he could recall it in an instant. He'd never had to pay for a woman before, and he wasn't about to do it now. However, Olga had made him promise not to hurt the man, so he decided to play it by ear for now. He printed a receipt for Eduardo and stuck it into his jacket pocket.

He sat briefly at the monitor and smiled as the transactions closed. *Success at last!* He unplugged his laptop and stashed it in his shoulder bag. He glanced slowly around for one last look at his loft. He took a mental picture of it, the mustard yellow walls with the painted "gang sign", the worn oriental rugs and the old leather couch. And the desk where he'd educated Olga about computers, and other things. All of that he would gladly leave behind. *Lofts and balconies — the story of my life.*

He called down to Olga and Eduardo. "We're out of here. Leave the kid, but make sure he can't get away." Olga grabbed her roll of packing tape and the box cutter.

As he descended the stairs, Roberts glanced out the transom window and nearly lost his balance. Was that Julia Tyler running through the gate of Charles Court heading straight for the clinic? He ran back up and crouched behind his desk while making an instant decision. He feared he might regret it later, but he had no choice; Marten must pay for his betrayal. *Damn you, Marten. How else would she know?*

Rather than take the time to alert Olga, Roberts made a phone call. The city police desk clerk took the message: a sighting of the kidnapped British boy in The Clifford Building! Roberts had pulled a fake accent from his collection and claimed to have spotted Chesley on the sixth floor while delivering a pizza to Tyler Professional Services.

~*~

Eduardo had taken one step outside, into the court, when he turned to watch Olga still trying to restrain a feisty, squirming Boone. "Hurry, woman, we gotta go!" He stopped suddenly when he turned to find a handgun pointed at his chest with Julia Tyler on the other end.

"Back into the building," she said.

He called out in Spanish to Olga as Julia pushed him forcefully back into the warehouse. The outer door slammed shut behind them.

From the loft, Perry Roberts watched Eduardo, Olga and Julia Tyler scramble for position around the boy. The Tyler woman held a handgun aimed steadily at Olga. *Marten even sent her over here with his gun!* Roberts nodded smugly — he had made the right call to strike back at his traitor nephew. Olga screamed and Boone struggled to get away, saying "Gran! You're here!" In one swift movement, Olga grabbed the back of Boone's shirt and held the box cutter to the side of his neck. She screamed in Spanish, "Put the gun down or I cut the kid."

Chapter Sixty-Nine

Speak English, Bitch

I shouted, "Speak English, bitch!"

The Mexican man translated: "She will cut his throat. She will do it!"

Adrenaline rushed through me and I reacted as any other grandmother would. Or so I thought later, as I tried to explain my actions. Without thinking, I took aim and shot that woman right between the eyes.

It felt surreal as I watched Boone crumple to the ground along with the woman. Her box cutter raked down the side of his leg just above the ankle and blood ran in every direction.

When the man ran toward me, I lowered the pistol and pulled the trigger again. The shot barely grazed his leg, although I'd aimed higher. His wound slowed him down long enough for my purpose.

I dropped the gun, scooped up Boone and clamped a hand around his leg. I don't know how I got the door open; I may have gone right through it. I had what I'd come for.

Screaming tourists formed a pathway as I ran through the court.

I reached Zinc's back door as police with their K-9s filed in through the front. I'd called Simone's father, Reed, on my run from the condo and instructed him to set a rescue in motion and here they were, just after the nick of time. The officers headed for me and Boone, followed by a TV reporter and cameraman.

A crowd formed at both entrances to the bar. Through the pandemonium, two cops pressed me into a chair.

The bartender snapped on a pair of latex gloves and pressed a bar towel against Boone's ankle, leaving my hands empty and covered with my grandson's blood. I kept screaming for an ambulance, but, when the reporters didn't recognize Boone, they just yelled, "Chesley! Chesley!"

The police dogs were in a sniffing frenzy, for Chesley, of course, not for Boone. Everyone was more interested in Chesley than in Boone, just as I'd suspected would be the case.

"Chesley is safe . . . he's okay. Call an ambulance!" I ordered.

The bartender, one hand keeping pressure on Boone's ankle and the other pressing a spot higher on Boone's calf, said, "Max, call 911." A muffled voice from his shirt pocket said, "Calling 911." Thank God for smart phones!

Only Dana and I knew where Chesley was. I had left Frederick's and gone into the Stock Market's kitchen. Dana summoned the dumbwaiter and got the boy out and into her office, but she was to tell no one until she got a phone call from me. I'd given her the slip of paper with Reed's phone number on it, in case there was any question later on. I'd watched anxiously for the arrival of the dumbwaiter to make sure Chesley was safe, but I was certain if anyone knew where he was, they would do nothing for Boone. Saving lives, one at a time, was my plan — my grandson first.

Chapter Seventy

Grand Finale

Reed Michaelson insisted I tell him everything, but I needed to be with my grandson in the ambulance and I wasn't about to waste precious time on sketchy details which would undoubtedly invite more questions. I told him two things: that I suspected Frederick was being held hostage in his apartment on the fifth floor of The Clifford Building, and that Chesley was safe with Dana in The Stock Market kitchen. I explained what little I knew about Leonardo Newman. If only I had taken two minutes more to explain *how* Chesley had ended up in my condo in the first place, it might have made a world of difference. Nonetheless, Reed instructed two officers to escort me to the hospital behind the ambulance, and he directed the others to follow him to the Clifford Building. He called for the media to join the parade. Reed loved attention, and this capture would afford him plenty of it.

If they had entered The Stock Market on the river level, the K-9s would've clearly gone straight for Chesley in Dana's office. But, for some reason unknown to me at the time, they came in through the front door at The Clifford's lobby on the Commerce Street level. The dogs clamored for the private elevator that probably held Chesley's scent, but it wouldn't move. So, the officers, with rescue on their minds, directed them up the stairway to my condo. The press was not far behind. They never are. The police blasted the lock on my back door and marched down the hallway into the living room and put twelve bullets in Marten. His arms were at his side — the BB gun in one hand and his cell phone in the other.

Chapter Seventy-One

The Word on the Street

I stayed with Doc and Nina for two nights but hadn't been able to sleep. On the third day, Doc gave me a mild sedative and assured me that Boone was fine, just fine. I turned my phone off and slept for a long time. When I woke up, I found the phone was blown up with voicemails from Reed. The next day, I drove to the Riverwalk and parked in my reserved space. Just after lunch time, I walked unannounced into the downtown police station.

"I'm Julia Tyler here to see Special Officer Reed Michaelson."

The receptionist shot me a quick look and immediately buzzed Reed's office. She escorted me in to see him. He instructed her to shut the door, and I couldn't help but see how fatigued he looked, and anxious. He motioned for me to sit in a chair next to his desk. Nice.

I hid the hostility I felt and offered my best smile. "What's the word on the street?"

He laughed and seemed to relax a little. "Well, since I saw you last, we surrounded the Charles Court crime scene and cordoned off the Navarro Street warehouse. Just inside the rear door, Olga Gonzales was found with a bullet hole in her forehead. Her husband, Eduardo Gonzalez, lay a few feet away with a fatal gunshot wound to the chest." He looked at me with raised eyebrows and waited, as if to ask what I knew about it.

I shrugged my shoulders. "I know nothing about him," I said. What I did know was that my single gunshot hadn't done much damage to him, plus I'd left the gun behind. But, Reed also said that a search of the entire building revealed no weapons other than a bloody box cutter. Someone must have grabbed Marten's gun and finished the man off. I wasn't obligated to say a thing, though, because, the way I saw it, Reed had more to tell me than what I planned to tell him. Plus, I wasn't under investigation. Yet.

"Go on," I said.

Reed shrugged. "Detectives found the Navarro Street door ajar; a white panel truck parked at the yellow curb was determined to have been stolen and a City of San Antonio parking violation notice had been slipped underneath the windshield wiper. It's been hauled in for evidence."

"Hmm."

"Yeah, and a tangle of computer cables was found in the loft. That's about it. That's everything I know to tell you."

I glared at Reed and waved my folded newspaper in front of his face. "I've good-naturedly sat here listening to you give me the newspaper version, the same one I'm holding right here in my hand."

Reed took a deep breath. "What more do you want?"

I stood and slammed the newspaper on the side of Reed's desk. He flinched.

"I want to know why my husband is dead! What more do I want? Jesus, Reed! I told you Chesley was in The Stock Market with Dana. He was not in my condo, but my husband was, alone and unarmed. You had no authority to do what you did to him. And to me! I want the truth!"

Reed sat quietly for a while. "The truth . . . all right, then. Right after I got to the scene at Charles Court that day, we got a tip from a pizza delivery guy who allegedly had spotted the British kid in your place of business. I had to follow up on it, Julia."

"That doesn't ring true for me" I said. "Marten didn't even like pizza. He'd never eat it."

"The boy could've been hungry," Reed said.

"Come on! Think of this: If you were keeping a kidnapped kid in your apartment, would you actually order food delivery — invite a stranger in? How illogical would that be? Anyway, we always used the dumbwaiter to get food from the Stock Market. Then again, Chesley was in the dumbwaiter."

Reed's eyes opened wide. "What the . . . ?"

"That's right. That's how I got him out of my condo down to Dana's, which is right where I *told* you he was." It gave me immense pleasure to see Reed so flustered. "So, tell me, did your brilliant detectives find any evidence of a pizza in my home?"

"I don't know. But I had to chase the lead. You understand."

"Understand?" My voice was strong and forceful by this time. "Even though I had already told you where Chesley was?"

"Look. I had two leads, one from you and another from the pizza guy. I had a decision to make as to which one to check out first. As I recall, you'd led me on a wild goose chase over to Charles Court. The British boy was not there, and apparently never was at that location, and *you* knew it, didn't you? How do you think that made me look? I wasn't sure if I could trust you, so it was my call — I decided to check out the other lead first. I sent men up to the fifth floor to Frederick's place, and the rest of us ran up to the sixth floor. I knew if the kid wasn't there he'd be down at The Stock Market, like you'd said. He was safe there, anyway, while we ruled out the pizza guy story."

"A 'wild goose chase'? You idiot! I never told you Chesley was there."

"Your phone call was urgent, and you indicated you knew all about him, so what was I supposed to think?"

"You heard what you wanted to hear. I guess it meant nothing to you that Simone's best buddy was being held hostage."

"You didn't tell me that."

"Uh, yes I did. I told you your daughter had called me. Don't lie to me to save face. Ask Simone. She'll tell you. If she hadn't called me I would've never known where Boone was being held."

"Why didn't she call me, then?"

"You should ask her. But what would *you* have done if I hadn't arrived first? Would Boone have been left alive, or would you have allowed that bitch to use my grandson as a bargaining chip?" I'd challenged Reed. He slumped in his chair and didn't answer. "Your true colors are showing, Reed, and they are very, very dark."

"You shot that woman, didn't you?"

"That's enough! If this is where you're taking it, I want a lawyer. The tip you got was fake — can't you see? Open your eyes — Marten was set up by the person who'd taken Chesley and exchanged him for Boone."

"Who was it? Are you certain? If so, we're going to have to question you further."

"I'm certain, all right, and I'll tell you everything I know, give you all the dots and you can connect them, but I want my lawyer with me."

Reed nodded. "I'll make the arrangement, Julia. And thank you." He reached for the phone on his desk. "And . . . I *am* sorry."

You certainly are. Just another man apologizing to make himself feel better.

~*~

Even though Reed was a total disappointment to me, I thanked him for taking quick action on Frederick's situation. Unfortunately, it was too late when the officers arrived, but they found eavesdropping equipment dangling from the cold air return down the living room wall as soon as they walked in. The door had been unlocked, he said, so they hadn't blasted Frederick's door like they did mine. It was all I could do not to make a snarky comment about my hallway door they'd shot all to hell. Nevertheless, they'd found Frederick in his tub with a set of *two* crystal wine glasses at the bottom. And thank God Frederick had the man's initial tattooed on his *bum,* I thought. Talk about leaving clues *behind.*

I was heartsick about Frederick. And when I thought about Newman eavesdropping on us from Frederick's apartment, while Frederick's body was cold and lifeless in bathwater, it made my stomach roll. What kind of a psycho does that? Marten was right when he said *"They may be watching our every move. Trust, me, I know how these people work."*

Because of what I'd told Reed about Leonardo Newman, Reed said he had been arrested before he could leave town. And the best part — Leonardo Newman was singing like a canary! That brought a smile once again to my otherwise sad-sack face.

Chapter Seventy-Two

Perry Roberts' Getaway

Roberts ran down the steps to where Olga lay, dead. Amigo looked up at him, groaning, holding his bloody leg while grasping for Marten's gun on the floor next to him. Roberts grabbed it and pressed it deep into Amigo's chest. Amigo closed his eyes and mumbled Spanish words of prayer.

Why couldn't at least one thing go the way we'd planned? Roberts pulled the trigger. Now both Eduardo and Olga were dead. And it was Julia Tyler's fault! He'd seen the whole thing, and he was on fire — it spewed from his nostrils like a dragon's flame as he fumed, thinking, naturally, of revenge. He retrieved his computer bag, hung it over one shoulder, and exited through the Navarro Street door. He turned left and walked, trying to appear like a businessman. Hell, he *was* a businessman with millions in the bank to show for it! Yet, he had lost everyone and everything he loved. Except for the money. He now had control of all of it. He called Leonardo's cell, told him to pull out of the garage and pick him up two blocks over on Alamo. While he waited and watched, the SUV was surrounded by police when it turned from Presa onto Alamo. *God dammit!* He wanted to scream. He assumed Marten had betrayed Leonardo, too.

Julia Tyler caused of all this. She lured Marten into her bed, rushed him into marriage. She killed my Olga, and prompted Marten to betray me. I've lost everyone I loved. I have money and time on my side. If it's the last thing I do, I will get my final revenge. Julia Tyler must pay.

Chapter Seventy-Three

Aftermath

Nowadays, being a hero means more than it used to. If one is brave enough to wear the *coat of heroism* in public, strangers brush past you on the sidewalk, closer than they ever did before. Admiring glances reach out to touch that garment, to transfer a piece of its magic. They know who you are — all about you. News reporters and cameramen everywhere I looked. I was uncertain how to handle the notoriety. I longed for the days of anonymity, but doubted their return.

An instant heroine — I had single-handedly saved both children and outwitted the bad guys, according to the tabloids. Oh, sure, one of the scoundrels got away with tons of Vanderhawk money, but the children were safe. And wasn't it all about the children, after all? According to Lady Sophia, it was. Yes, I had taken out the woman who had kidnapped my grandson with my only prior weapons experience being a BB gun! I was invited to appear on talk shows and news programs. The "Don't Mess With Texas Granny," they dubbed me. The general public respected and cheered for me, the brave woman who had taken matters into her own hands and foiled the enemy.

I was one tough cookie, all right, and still alive to talk about it. So were the two little boys, although Chesley and Lady Sophia remained in seclusion and Boone said very little to anyone, which worried me. I wondered what sort of emotional trauma he'd suffered. I'd tried to get him to talk about it, but he didn't want to. He'd spoken so softly, I'd had to strain my ears to hear him. I tried not to think about it. Lady Sophia and I spoke briefly and she offered to pay for anything Boone needed, anything at all. But Andie made it clear *she* was in charge of her son's medical care. When I suggested therapy, she snapped, "I'm on it, Julia," after which she'd stalked directly into her bedroom and slammed the door. It was if she blamed me for everything!

Boone had offered, at least, that he thought I was *totally awesome, really, Gran, totally.* Doc Emmett said he knew I had it in me all along — the strength to do the right thing. Dana claimed that she could never have been so utterly bold and brave.

At Marten's funeral I was surrounded by well-intentioned friends and a lot of people I'd never seen in my life. Poor Dana was exhausted from tourists and her regular customers talking about it day and night.

Frankly, I couldn't believe I'd pulled it off the way I did. However, somewhere down deep inside I knew I hadn't been strong because it was the "right" thing to do, nor was I bold or brave. I liked Boone's description of "totally awesome," but the feeling I remembered the most from that event was one of "entitlement." Like, I was *inherently deserving* of the anger welling up inside. How dare someone take my grandson from his home — *my* home? How dare they think they could get away with hiding Chesley in *my* home? How dare that bitch injure *my* grandson? I had every right to explode!

So, within the next weeks, cards, flowers, letters and e-mails filled every vacant space in my home. I tried to respond to each one, but soon gave up on such a daunting task. I'd crash landed and was in a perpetual haze.

Chapter Seventy-Four

Cruise to Clarity

In due time, I was offered a European cruise to get away from it all. Doc and Nina insisted that I take the royals up on it. So I did.

After I boarded, I was surprised to be at the center of attention, a celebrity, of sorts. I wasn't prepared for that on a cruise ship, of all places, but it all worked out. The passengers and the crew were polite and gave me my space. I put my feet up on the sun deck nearly every day, and I consumed so much of the Queen's Earl Grey that I lost my addition to coffee.

I'd brought Marten's cell phone with me, just a little something to hold onto, like a security blanket. When I remembered he'd recorded phone conversations, I couldn't wait to listen. But, during the first message, I cried. After regaining my composure, I retreated to my suite and listened to the remainder in private, only one or two each day. Good thing I spaced them out, because I cried every time I heard his voice.

Before the damage had been assessed and cleaned up in my condo, I'd noticed tiny spots on the bottom edge of my J Sofa. Marten's blood, I'd assumed. If the investigation team had been in any way efficient, they would have noted the stains and confiscated the sofa. They were equally inept for not discovering Marten's cell phone underneath. I'd found it while on my hands and knees, inspecting the blemishes. Apparently, they hadn't thought the sofa held any clues at all, but I could've told them a thing or two about Marten's phone. However, I'd wanted to listen to the messages on it first, and it's a good thing I did.

The first calls were innocent enough, like the one where Doc and Marten had discussed the *supposed* clinic and Doc recommended me as an accounting service. My reaction was one of disdain, that Doc had walked right into *that* con, but then I realized I'd done the exact same thing!

The call where we'd confirmed our appointment for him to install his business files at my office. The following Saturday, when he invited me to New Braunfels for a German meal. I thought of Helga, how she'd fawned all over him, and I smiled at the memory. He was a charmer, there was no doubt about that. How we'd danced the night away in Gruene to Lyle Lovett's music, and sipped cappuccino on the roof, star-gazing. I forgave myself for falling for him so quickly. It had been a romantic, whirlwind courtship with a near-perfect storybook ending, *except* for the end, of course.

Some of those conversations between Marten and his uncle detailed their plans to deceive me and hack into my business system. What a scandal that might have created if the investigators had found that phone under the sofa! I could have been judged as complicit, even though I was oblivious.

~*~

The ship docked for tour excursions in the port of Bordeaux, France on the Garonne River. I met with a writer who interviewed me for his current work-in-process — a book about the kidnapping. I found myself telling him more than I'd meant to, but he assured me he would publish only what I approved of. His literary agent had said the major Hollywood studios were in a bidding war for the movie rights. It wouldn't be the type of romantic movie I'd daydreamed about months before, but it's what I got. Furthermore, spending three days in Bordeaux, touring local vineyards and tasting their wine, discussing every little facet, put the overall event into perspective. One vintner said he wished to create a wine label with my initials on it. I told him I'd think it over, but it felt like I'd been turned into a cash cow enough already.

After my time in Bordeaux, back on the ship, I found comfort and tranquility on my private balcony, reclining on a chaise as I sorted through details of my crazy life. I'd ordered tea and éclairs so often that my cabin steward managed to obtain the recipe for me. I hoped Dana could insert the delicacy into The Stock Market's menu. Each day, I filled pages of my journal with sketches and with a narrative of the sequence of events. I plotted my emotions and memories of the little things that I'd tucked away, little things I'd considered insignificant.

~*~

The cruise had one day remaining and I finally felt like I could heal, given enough time. The kidnapper had got away, and now everyone knew who he was — Perry Roberts, the ill-famed horse jockey. He'd be caught sooner or later, of that I had been quite sure — until I listened to the last recording!

Roberts: "You disgusting double-crosser!"
Marten: "Me? I certainly did not!"
Roberts: "You gave up my location and your gun to Julia Tyler."
Marten: "My gun? That's impossible."
Roberts: "Tell that to Olga, my lady with the bullet through her brain. You will pay, Marten, and so will your wife!"
Call End: 3/28; 4:07PM

I visualized Marten running down the hall into our bedroom to retrieve his weapon. His suitcase lay on our bed, its fine leather ripped wide open with my paring knife. In place of his gun, I'd tucked my BB pistol inside, a rather passive-aggressive "fuck you" type of message. I presumed he carried the BB gun into the living room and tried to figure out what on earth had happened. When the police broke through the back door, they saw him holding it, and the end of the story wrote itself. But, what did his psychopath uncle mean that Marten and I would pay?

Chapter Seventy-Five

Wherever You Go, There You Are.

There is a quote, attributed to Confucius, which says, "Wherever you go, there you are." So, when I returned from the cruise, even though I'd greatly benefited from the rest and regained the ability to put the events in perspective, reality stared me in the face. My emotions about Marten changed as easily as a chameleon's colors. I thought about how Andie had walked over to stand beside me at Marten's closed casket. "I'm glad he's dead," she'd whispered. It was a cold and thoughtless comment, but I understood how she felt. I didn't know, at that time, how to feel anything at all, and I doubted I ever would. Suddenly becoming a widow again presented me with a prickly déjà vu mood — alone once more — more than ever, it seemed.

I'd rewritten the scenario in my mind a thousand times. *My* BB gun! The innocent little pistol that wouldn't hurt a squirrel caused Marten's death. The police killed a man they thought was armed. Or would they have shot him anyway?

Well.

Nothing would bring Marten back, and what would I have done with him if he'd lived? That was the main question rolling around in my head.

Frederick was gone, and I blamed myself, even though he wouldn't want me to. I knew what he would say. "Julia, I'm going to roll over in my grave if you don't stop this nonsense immediately. It was *me*! I should've never gotten involved with that dreadful character. Remember when you told me I'd best be more careful with my impulsivity? Well, Sweetie, you were right all along."

But why did he have to die? Why didn't that awful lover of his simply tie him up and slap some duct tape on his mouth? He didn't have to kill him.

At Richard's grave, I'd cried, "I'm a hero to everyone but Andie." Not one leaf rustled in the breeze, no squirrels danced overhead, and no pine cones fell. Richard had apparently vanished with the others.

~*~

I'd been in touch with Josh Katzen, the man I met in the airport who kept secrets for a living, and he walked me through the steps to remove the malware from my computer. "It's now wiped as clean as a baby's behind," Katzen had said. "No one will ever know your business files were compromised, unless you want to go to the authorities with that fact, but I doubt it would serve you well." He was right on point with that observation. I'd been deeply troubled, afraid that my business reputation would be ruined.

I spent several days eradicating records of the existence of Marten's fake clinic. I searched the folder in my filing cabinet where I'd kept copies of his contract, emails and notes. The first thing I found was that strange cashier's check. I burned it along with all of the phony reports he'd given me. I deleted any mention of him in emails, even though I feared an investigation and a possible charge of destroying evidence or something, like an accessory to the crime. I couldn't sleep at night; my brain was on overdrive as I imagined myself in a courtroom, testifying that I'd deleted files only because the clinic had never progressed into a genuine client. But I realized I'd worked myself up, acting like a paranoid crazy person, so I let it all go, found a place of peace and let whatever was destined to happen . . . happen.

Oddly enough, nothing happened. At least nothing that affected me in a negative way. There was speculation as to how Chesley landed in my condo. My husband was dead, so they couldn't ask him; I had been on an airplane and had professed ignorance. Boone was never questioned — Andie wouldn't allow it, bless her heart.

The media got it all wrong when, after getting wind of Lady Sophia and Chesley's visit to my condo, they concluded that Chesley, not realizing he'd been kidnapped, was taken there to visit with Boone. I laughed out loud the day I heard that *Breaking News* segment. Were these people daft? I guess the media didn't get the memo about everyone else in the little theater having been incapacitated.

I'd expected a huge scandal involving Duke Vanderhawk's affair with Adelina, but the press went sideways with the big news about Roberts' history of having been a famous jockey employed by the Vanderhawk family. At that point, the tabloids focused on a complicated revenge theory, which brought the story back and running into the news cycle for another few weeks, including pictures of Roberts before and after his nose job, the latter picture provided by a hotel housekeeper. A scandal diverted, possibly thanks to Duke Vanderhawk's fortune and influence.

A password bypass device was found in my elevator. It was surmised the kidnappers had installed it that same day. I hoped that was the case, and that Marten hadn't given the password out.

I'd thanked Josh Katzen for his advice and I offered some of my reward money, but he wouldn't hear of it. I suspected he didn't want it to be traced to him, as he seemed to be the kind of person who stayed in the shadows.

The money came from a variety of sources: the Vanderhawk family and hundreds of strangers who sent donations; the book was selling well, and I inherited Marten's impressive estate in Wales. What a surprise that had been, and maybe the only tangible bonus of my legal marriage to Marten. Dana and I planned to go next month. I didn't know if I'd sell it or not — it would make a great vacation retreat.

Andie eventually moved out of my condo and into Britt's new house, but the days of her moving out were tumultuous. As it turned out, she actually *did* blame me for everything. And I do mean *everything*!

Chapter Seventy-Six

New Floor – New Life

Dana and I were seated at the kitchen bar, staring down a full pitcher of margaritas I'd just made. We intended to empty the thing and quite possibly make another.

Andie juggled an armload of small boxes, moving remnants of her belongings out of the condo.

"Want some help?" Dana asked. Andie didn't answer. Flesh-colored streaks trailed through her make-up. Her hair was pulled back in a lopsided pony tail. She'd obviously slept in her clothes.

"So, Andie, where's Boone?" Dana asked.

"With Britt, at our house, riding the new red bike we bought him last night." She said this with a smart-ass edge to her voice, without looking at either of us. She stepped into the elevator and pushed the button, feigning interest in the floor as she disappeared from view.

Dana offered me a sympathetic look and patted me on the arm.

"I'm going to miss them," I said. "I wish she could've waited a little longer to relocate. This sudden move won't help Boone's situation one bit, will it?"

"Sudden? Time has stopped for you, Jules. It's been longer than it feels to you. But it's Andie's decision, and she wants out. That girl is a certified brat, no offense, but it's all about her — always has been. Someday, I'm going to twist a knot in that little girl's tail."

"Good. I'll watch."

We sat in silence, staring out the window for a while. I checked my watch. "It's time — straight up noon." I filled two margarita glasses up to their salted rims.

"Hey!" Dana said. "You're getting a new neighbor, by the way. Did

I tell you I'm going to buy Frederick's condo? His family asked me if I wanted it . . . said they didn't want to deal with the public or realtors. They offered me a super good deal."

My brain trudged along in slow motion while I considered the prospect. "But, can you be comfortable living there?"

"I think so. Sure, I can." She plucked the slice of lime off the edge of her glass and squeezed it into her beverage. She sucked the tart juice off her fingertips and squinted. "Hell, yes! It's what Frederick would want, don't you think?"

"Um . . . yeah. I guess he would, actually."

"And Julia, you know I've always wanted to be just like you. You're so practical, yet classy."

I laughed. "Wow, that's quite a statement considering you're sober!"

"Yeah, I guess, but not for long," Dana said with a smile. "So, the thing is, I'm awful tired of driving back and forth to work. Now that the restaurant has solid footing, it'll be a good move all the way around. Besides, I wouldn't want anyone else to own the place. Maybe they'd have ulterior motives, like they'd buy it for the sheer pleasure of possessing a piece of history — if the unit had the chance to go up on the market publicly."

"That's a disgusting thought. Yeah, some weirdo might even turn it into a tourist attraction or something." I reached for my cousin's hand. "It'll be good to have you living so close, too. We can definitely hang out more."

"Watch late-night movies in your jungle room."

"Or my collection of old Oprah recordings I haven't gone through yet."

"Yep. Andie's moving out and *I'm* moving in," Dana said.

I eyed the exact spot on the floor where Marten had died. The hardwood had been stripped, re-stained and sealed — no evidence anything vile had ever happened there. Sadly, the floor hadn't retained its charming old look. The rear door was also replaced with a shiny new one. The cops had blown it to smithereens when they shot the lock out. I'd requested the door be replaced with one from an architectural salvage company, but no. To make it worse, they'd painted the door with a shade of white that nearly glowed in the dark. It's not like I wasn't grateful for the fix, but *damn!*

New floor, new door — my new life.

Andie reappeared for another load of boxes and cast a hateful glance toward me on her way through the open area.

"Let's get out of here," Dana said. She took me by the wrist. "Come on . . . follow me." We toted our drinks through my office, out the little door into the hallway, and down one flight of stairs. The yellow crime scene tape at Frederick's door was gone. Dana produced her key and we entered the grand foyer. I halfway expected to see Frederick round the corner. None of his furniture had been removed and the art on the walls and table tops were exactly as before. It was as though he was at the salon and would be home later tonight. I shot a puzzled look toward Dana.

"I'm buying it fully furnished — as is, so to speak."

"Why?"

Dana shrugged. "That's the way it is, Jules. I'll redo it in time, bit by bit. For now it's staying like this." Dana headed for Frederick's sound system and inserted one of his favorite CDs.

I wandered off alone and toured the rooms, one by one, until I found myself in the master bath. I lowered myself down to the cool tile floor and ran my hand along the porcelain edge of the tub. How could I have allowed this to happen? It was all so heinous, so *wrong*.

Dana stood in the doorway. "You know he died in here?

I nodded. "So I heard. I don't see how you can live here, especially with his stuff closing in all around you. Or do you *like* ghosts?"

"I'm good with it, plus I'm *not* good with decorating. Can you help me?"

She reached for my hands and pulled me up. We walked back into the living room to Frederick's large turret window, just like mine one floor above. I opened his Plantation shutters, stained light gray and sealed with several coats of shiny, clear lacquer. I adjusted the louvers and sunlight filtered in, reaching the opposite walls and fluttering about the room.

Dana brightened with the effect. "What are you thinking? Pink?"

I snorted. "I'm over pink. Finished! I'm going to redecorate, myself."

"But your leather sofa cost you a fortune!"

I fiercely shook my head. "It's got stains on the bottom edge, and I'm sure it's Marten's blood — ruined, saturated already — nothing I can do about it now. I'll have it reupholstered."

On our way back upstairs, Dana said, "So, if not pink, then what?"

"Oh . . . I see a clean pallet. White walls, ceilings, cabinets. Stainless appliances. Keep the gray-stained hardwood floor and window shutters, and accessorize with a rich color."

"Red?"

"As if!" I threw her a look of scorn. "Sure, if you want it to look just like your restaurant — go for it."

"Not red, then. Something else?"

"Something else, indeed." I winked. "There's a new book of color chips on my kitchen counter. Nothing 'day-glow', mind you, like that asinine white they used on my hallway door…hey, what about a soft lime green?"

Dana made a horrible face. "I absolutely detest lime green!"

"Oh. Well good 'cause that's what color I've been thinking about for my J sofa."

Dana brightened. "Then *I'll* use pink!

"What? Pink just isn't your color!"

"But remember I told you I've always wanted to be like you, Jules!"

Chapter Seventy-Seven

You Can't Talk to Alcohol

Andie stormed into the room wearing a judgmental sneer. "You're drunk!"

"Oh yeah?" Dana countered. "Well at least I'm not a bitch."

"Who says? Your mommy?"

"Since you brought it up . . . I've never treated my mother the disgraceful way you treat yours. She saved your son's life, for Chrissakes."

I tightly closed my eyes, dreading an imminent clash. I was just as helpless to stop the impending argument as I'd been to stop the train barreling down on my parents' car. I moved to the pitcher and filled my margarita glass to the top, thankful I'd made a second batch. Dana had made quick work of the first one.

Andie pointed her finger straight at me. "If *she* hadn't been in such a hurry to get laid, my son wouldn't have been in danger in the first place!"

Dana winced. "Ouch! You sure that's where you want to go with this conversation?"

"Who says I want to talk to you, anyway?"

"You started it," Dana countered.

"Whatever."

"Why don't you just finish moving out in peace?" I said. "There's nothing more I can say to you, Andie."

"Well there's plenty I have to say to you . . . both of you!"

"Fine." I conceded. "Give it your best shot."

"Go for it, big girl," Dana said. "Let it all hang out." She poured herself another round.

Andie took an offensive stance, hands on her hips. "People died all because they wanted to get laid. Take Frederick, for example. He got what he deserved."

"What a cold-hearted thing to say," Dana said. "What's this all about, really?"

"I just told you. Sex. My mother over there — with her head in the sand? — just had to have herself a piece of that Mr. Tall Dark and Handsome. Didn't give a damn that he might not be for real."

"And?" Dana says.

"And — *Poof!* Like a slick magic stunt she moves him in here. I'll bet she didn't even Google him first! Next thing we know, all hell breaks loose." Andie sniffed. "She brought calamity on the entire family. Nothing will ever be the same. Not ever!"

NO! — I didn't say it, but I heard myself think it — *NO!* It was a freight train of a word, lights on, illuminating the tracks ahead, heading out of a long, dark tunnel in slow motion. *Noooooo*, I wanted to scream at the people standing on the tracks, outside in the light, to warn them of danger. Had the engineer seen my parents before he plowed into them? With my elbows on the countertop, I rested my face in my palms, pressing my fingertips on my forehead.

"Stop it!" I screamed into my hands.

"Shut up, Julia," Dana said. "Just stay out of this. You've created a damned monster with this child and it's time I had my say. I've got this."

I surrendered quietly and went for the living room where I stretched out on the pink leather sofa.

"Well, girlie, just who *doesn't* want to get laid?" Dana said.

Andie opened her mouth but Dana wasn't about to let her say a word.

"Get with the program. Your mother got screwed all right. She wanted a life partner, an adult to share her life, a man who'd look out for her best interests. Like what you've got with Britt. But turns out that's *all* she got — screwed. And, she lost a dear friend — we all did. Frederick."

"*I* never considered Frederick *my* dear friend, and anyway he died because he just had to get him some, too," Andie said. She held her head up, her nose in the air. "If he'd been responsible, it wouldn't have happened. If Mom had been more responsible, it wouldn't have happened."

"Who do you think you are — Almighty God? Maybe you see yourself in your mother. Or perhaps you're feeling better than her because you got caught but you're not dead? Feeling a little smug? Or maybe you feel guilty."

"Oh that's stupid Freudian psychology! And it's not fair," Andie cried.

"It's your game, your rules, and you're not playing fair, little girl. Blaming your mother's relationship with Marten for Boone's kidnapping? Let's go back a step. If you hadn't wanted to get laid back in your high school days, there would be no Boone — no kidnapping in the first place. And I'll venture to say you didn't do research on that Norwegian geek before you nailed him, now did you?"

Dana, right up in Andie's face, glared. "Just how far back do you want to take this? If your Mom hadn't laid your Dad in the back seat of a Chevy, there'd be no Andie standing here whining like a little brat."

Still on the couch, I risked a smile. There was no stopping Dana, now.

"It was a Mustang. A red convertible," Andie said, "and don't bring Daddy into this. If he were here none of this would have happened. He would take care of me and Boone. I could always count on him. Mom, on the other hand, just goes off on a whim. I never know anymore what she's capable of. I can't depend upon her for shit. She has no right to ever see Boone again!"

A ping went off in my brain, transformed into a buzzing sound and bored a hole from one ear to the other. I stood, tried to balance myself and slowly made my way back into the kitchen, close to the action.

"You're the one who doesn't know shit," Dana spat. "It was a red Mustang only in your dreams. Wake up! It was a plain old Chevy, and dear ole Daddy, coward that he was, made damn sure he *wasn't* here to stand beside you till the end."

Instantly alert, I held my hand up to Dana's face. "Stop right now!"

"Show her the note," Dana whispered loudly, as drunk people often do.

I glared at my cousin. "You're cute when you're drunk, but you're way out of line," I said, calmly, as I led Dana to the elevator. "Here's that color chart. Go on down to your new place and look at blues and greens, colors to help you cool off. I've got this now. Don't come back until you hear from me. Please."

Dana left without another word. I wondered how I could steer Andie away from the mention of a note.

"What's she talking about?" Andie cried.

"She's buying Frederick's condo."

"No. She definitely said 'show her the note.'"

I shook my head and waved my hand in the air. "The note? I don't know . . . maybe she meant her mortgage papers. It's the alcohol. She's out of it."

I wanted to get Andie off the subject. "Look. What's wrong? Are you sure you want to move in with Britt? Are you having second thoughts? You said after I rescued Boone that I was brave, but now it takes even more bravery to watch you move out on your own. I know it's a natural and healthy thing for you to do, but you don't look happy. I want you to be happy, Honey."

"*I* never said you were brave. What you did was stupid and reckless. We're lucky Boone is alive; he's going to need a lifetime of therapy after what you put him through. I can't stay here and be reminded of your stupidity. Good God! You thought all that practice with a BB gun made you a capable markswoman? Reed Michelson said you should have let the police handle it."

"The *police* handle it? They botched it up enough as it was." Bile rose up into my throat. I thought back to the day in question and offered a clear explanation to my daughter.

"There I stood, the Gonzales woman holding my grandson. She was an obstacle that looked insurmountable. I took it as a challenge — rolled up my sleeves and got to work solving the problem. Yes, I blew her brains out, and some of them got on Boone. So what? He's alive, and with a little soap and water he'll be fine. We'll all be okay. What would you have done? Let the bitch cut his throat? Or would you have surrendered the gun and helplessly watched as she took him out the door," I snorted, "as if you'd *ever* catch up with her again and stand a better chance of getting him back? Ha, right! You and Reed Michaelson can kiss my fine white ass, both cheeks at the same time."

I looked over toward the blood stains, dry by now, on my sectional. "The police — what a joke. They barged in and shot Marten because

Reed told them that Chesley was in *this* condo, when Dana was keeping him safely downstairs in her office, awaiting the arrival of authorities. Reed gave the order, and I'm pretty sure it's because he wanted to go down as a hero. He called for the media to follow him that day. I heard him, myself!"

"A BB pistol is nothing like a real gun," Andie said, "and you weren't aiming at squirrels. He was your grandson!"

"Did you not just hear a word I said? Can't you give me credit for blasting my target right between the eyes, or does that fact not stand for much?"

"She must've had a wide head. You could have shot Boone! Did you even stop to think that he might have wondered if you were aiming at him?"

I blinked. "That's ridiculous! He knew better. Doing what-ifs is futile. What is — IS. Present time, that's where we are. Boone is alive and safe. So are we. It's over."

Andie snarled. "It's so far from over, Mother. Wake up! I'll never get past this and neither will Boone." She produced a gurgling, dark laugh from deep inside. "Am I sure I want to move out, you ask?" She turned toward the elevator. "Trust me — I can't wait to get the fuck out of this house!"

As the accordion gate closed, Andie called out one last thing: "You don't fool me. I'm going down to find out what note about Daddy Dana thinks I should see!"

Chapter Seventy-Eight

For Richard - The Last Chapter

As often as I'd sat on the concrete bench at the cemetery, I wouldn't have been surprised to find my sitzmark on it when I arrived that day. "The End," I read aloud. "I don't know why I'm even speaking to you, Richard. I mean, you haven't been listening to me for the past few weeks, the past few chapters. So, why *did* I finish reading the book here? For myself, I suppose, plus for all of the corpses who deserved to hear the ending, considering what we've put them through." I let out a long sigh, and I smiled as I glanced around the familiar graveyard that had become my spiritual energy point of enlightenment. The scent of sagebrush was a comforting reminder of all the conversations we'd had there. "The author did a good job, don't you think? Considering I didn't tell him *everything.*

"So, I fell for a criminal turned softie, a man who loved me more than he ever knew he could love anyone other than his mother. And I *do* believe a man should love his mother more than anyone. I know you felt torn between me and Madelynne. We were nothing alike, were we?" My thoughts went back to the February day when Madelynne and I sat on that bench together and made peace. We had grown much closer since then.

"Let's do the 'what ifs'. What if Marten hadn't died? Would I have covered for him and been an accessory to his crime? It's funny how you always think you know yourself, know what you're capable of, and then all of a sudden circumstances arise and you act like someone you've never known before. Like killing the Gonzalez woman. I would've said 'No, I would never be able to do a thing like that.' But I would've been wrong.

"What I'm trying to say, Richard, is this: I've forgiven you for your suicide because I get it now — that's exactly what happened to you. You were met with bizarre circumstances and acted like someone I couldn't understand. Quite simply, you panicked. Since I've seen both sides, I can finally say goodbye to you. I remember the way you used to put your arm around me, around my shoulders, really. I'd nuzzle my head safely into your neck and the cares of the world ceased to exist. I sure could use your arm around me one more time . . . right now."

I glanced all around, waiting for a sign. Still no movement to make me think he was there. This kidnapping thing was old news by now anyway.

"Richard, did you watch as Andie and Britt got married on the Wedding Island? There was never a more beautiful bride than our daughter. She's mellowed in the past few months, you know. In fact, I'm starting to like the woman! Dana convinced her that she was too drunk that one day to remember what she'd said or why. I'd already burned your letter, anyway. And I was wrong about the timing of Andie's move. She was actually ready to be in charge of her own household, living under her *own* roof, not mine. Imagine that! I see Boone every afternoon after school, but my nights and weekends are mine alone. I haven't lived entirely alone until now and I've grown to like it a lot.

"Andie has settled nicely into married life, and they're talking about producing another grandchild, next year if possible. You'll probably know about it before I do. If you're in charge of selecting babies, send me a granddaughter next time. You know, a tea party and dress-up kind of girl for me to spoil."

To say goodbye to Richard wasn't difficult, now. But I wanted to voice my future plans, just in case he was listening. "My predictions for the future are simple: Boone will grow into a fine young man, get married, and have our first great-grandchild. I will be happy for the rest of my life, and I plan to live to 102. Then, I'll be buried next to you in this little graveyard which doesn't seem desolate at all anymore. Especially when I think of being visited by our grandchildren and great-grandchildren throughout the coming years."

I had no intention of returning for a long time; I searched for one last thing to say. "Oh! Lest I forget, I have reacquired Zadok! The Abyssinian had a habit of jumping up onto Greenie's cage, tilting it to the point of its falling over. The last time it happened, Greenie escaped and Zadok chased him underneath Boone's bed. Greenie was finally found hiding in a shoebox, so Andie ordered Boone to take that cat back to Gran's!" I got my $1,000 exotic cat back! He lounges on the kitchen window sill, fascinated with those brash blackbirds, the infamous Great-tailed Grackles, as they glide like knives from Cyprus trees down to riverside dining tables, snatching tortilla chips and taking to the sky. I've imagined that patrons who blinked probably wonder what just happened.

I gently patted the monument, took one more look at our engraved names, and stood to leave. When I reached my Jeep, I pulled the visor down and looked in the mirror. Grabbing a handful of tissues, I wiped damp mascara from underneath my eyes. I smiled at myself, then, and flipped up the visor. As I slowly drove away from the cemetery, I caught an unusual sight in my rearview mirror. I stopped to watch — every tree and bush swayed, soothingly, all in unison. I could've been wrong, and maybe the wind just picked up right at that moment, or it could've been caused by the tears in my eyes, but it appeared Richard was waving! He'd kept still, for once undistracted, listening to me. He had been here all along. And now he was letting go, telling me goodbye. Goodbye Richard, my forever love. I drove along the gravel road and pulled out onto the highway, into my future.

THE END

About the Author

Joanna Foreman discovered the value of all five senses as she created her storybook life. Taste, touch, smell, sight, and sound play essential roles in her stories. While writing Riverwalk Chameleon, she made numerous trips to San Antonio, memorizing the Riverwalk's unique sounds, scenery, and aromas to stimulate her muse for continued writing. The sixth sense figures into her short fiction collection, Ghostly Hauntings of Interstate-65. In her memoir, The Know-it-all Girl Joanna describes herself waltzing through the hoops of her mother's religion, which she recognized as a cult only after she'd escaped from it. A member of the Southern Indiana Writers' Group, she has benefited from their red ink filled critiques and has contributed stories to their annual Indian Creek Anthology Series since 2006.

She stood barefoot with her husband Craig on St. Augustine Beach as they married in 2001. They reside in a modest home in the middle of two wooded acres, having put down roots "back home again" in Indiana, where they will live happily ever after.